Erringby

GILL DARLING

Fairlight Books

First published by Fairlight Books 2021
Fairlight Books

Summertown Pavilion, 18–24 Middle Way, Oxford, OX2 7LG

A CIP catalogue record for this book is available from the British
Library.

1 2 3 4 5 6 7 8 9 10

ISBN 978-1-912054-35-0

www.fairlightbooks.com

Printed and bound in Great Britain by Clays Ltd.

Designed by Edward Bettison

'So!' she said, without being startled or surprised; 'the days have worn away, have they?'

—Charles Dickens, *Great Expectations*

Prologue

August 1986

There was someone else in the room. Dawn light trickled between heavy curtains that hadn't been fully closed. Kit, lying on top of the bedcovers, the dog's huge weight at his feet, was aware of movement in the corner of the bedroom. Col was scrabbling in a bureau drawer, his back to Kit. As he left the room he turned and their eyes met for an instant. Col's expression was unreadable.

Under the antique bedspread Col's wife slept on. Kit leaned across to look at her alarm clock. A fraction before 6am. His immediate thought was that he had to be on the film set for seven. Then he remembered it was his day off.

His shirt buttons were undone to the waist, his belt unbuckled, the zip of his jeans open. Perhaps he had begun to undress himself in the fugue state between sleeping and waking, then sunk back into unconsciousness. He slid his hand below the waistband of his underpants and felt the clagginess of drying semen. What had he taken last night? There was the unfortunate tab of acid, then he and Marianne had shared a joint on her bed, half watching that weird film. He remembered Marianne, the film on her black-and-white portable set, just not how he came to be in her bedroom. Even without touching her he had a sense of her warmth and the softness of her body beneath the bedspread.

Kit tried to recall his fleeting, turbulent dreams: the old one, the child at a birthday party with jam on his face and hands, had merged with another, less troubling, of Marianne; she had been at the party with him, had come into the room where he sat, alone with the enormous cake, had said *There there* and taken out a huge linen handkerchief, started to wipe jam from him, wiping him down...

He was oddly and utterly at peace. Sometime, and soon, he was going to have to deal with waking up on his aunt's bed half undressed, her asleep beside him, and the fact that her husband had come into the room and seen them together, but for now he felt tired and completely calm. He lay back and closed his eyes. He wanted the day never to begin.

PART I

I

July 1974

Though classed as a river, the Meaburn was just a couple of yards wide as it flowed by Erringby Hall and in times of drought shrank so that you could walk across it. Marianne had just paddled in it, water shucking her flip-flops. She had taken the flip-flops off and waded further in, liking the feel of toes sinking into mud. It had been months since she had allowed herself an afternoon off. She scrambled up the bank and wiped her feet dry on the grass before throwing herself onto the rug.

Stupid, to be hiding in one's own home, but they annoyed her, all of them and not just Graham. Once the staff had left Erringby – that was a euphemism, she had dismissed them all – butler, housekeeper, head gardener, a reserve army of casual workers – once they had gone, belongings packed into trunks and cardboard suitcases, chuntering darkly as they went; in fact she couldn't be sure some toothless scullery maid hadn't muttered some kind of curse at her as she'd passed her in the hall – once they had all gone she had invited some of her acting friends to stay. None was in regular work, and the offer of free accommodation in return for help with upkeep of the house and the estate had seemed to her a good solution. She had had vague ideas of an actors' and artists' colony, a kind of English Yaddo, and at first things had gone well. Some of the friends stayed on, and friends of friends appeared, then friends of the friends of friends. By the time she realised that the idea of a working artistic collective was preposterous, that she was not the communal type, it had become hard to keep tally of who lived here and who did not. She had had to tell a few of them, bluntly, to leave: men, usually, who had their own ideas about how Erringby should be run.

Every morning she rose at six, peeling away from her warm bed and from anyone who might have kept her company, leaving him to snore on, and padded down to the kitchen, where she put on the percolator for the first of many coffees and made lists, endless lists, of things that needed doing. Some of which might get done; windows might be fixed or dripping taps stopped, doors reattached to hinges, flowerbeds weeded, the van's fan belt replaced. A couple of the women got a kitchen garden going with mixed success, although thuggish weeds now threatened to choke it. But some days, too many, nothing was achieved. It was a struggle, marshalling this ragtag army into doing anything useful instead of drinking beer and smoking dope and finishing up the hot water and using all the bathrooms, which then had to be cleaned, and plundering Uncle Harold's cellar.

And the summer was making them act strangely; arguments flared up over nothing, sexual intrigues sparked and burned themselves out over a couple of days, leaving the participants surly and cranky, which was tiresome. She supposed her dalliance with Graham might have been the result of her own head being turned by the sun. Graham was her age, twenty-six, but had the look of a man who scarcely needed to shave. He kissed like a boy, too. One wanted to wipe slobber off one's mouth when he had finished. But he was persistent and good-looking enough and he flattered her constantly and she had offhandedly screwed him a couple of times. He seemed to think it gave him dominion over not only her bedroom, but her. This was particularly irksome.

She pulled a Granny Smith from her pocket and bit into it, its flesh sweet and warm from proximity to her thigh. Two of the dogs had come with her, the elderly Clumber spaniel, a childhood pet fetched from her mother's house when she had moved here, and the younger wolfhound. This dog coped better with the heat. He trotted up and down the riverbank, occasionally stopping to lap at its edge.

She opened her battered copy of *A Sport and a Pastime*. So sporadic had her reading become that it took her some time to find her place, and even then she could not be sure. It was hard to keep momentum, this second Erringby summer, each day rolling out much like the last. It was hard having sole responsibility for a country house and its estate. The first winter had been tough, the endless roster of things going wrong – leaking pipes, cracked windowpanes, recalcitrant boiler – exacerbated by the soaring price of oil and the power cuts. There had been one evening during the period between the staff leaving and the friends arriving she had spent wrapped in a blanket in the gun room with just the dogs for company, candles wavering in the draught, trying to ignore the noises in the house, the creaks and groans, and beyond the house, the eldritch shriek of foxes. It was the closest she came to being frightened.

Her mother had been on at her again about selling. Someone might buy Erringby and turn it into a school, or a residential home. She knew someone who… Marianne had put the phone down on her, only to feel badly about it after five minutes, but when she picked up the receiver to call her back to apologise, Susannah was still talking, oblivious to having been cut short. She was becoming rather deaf.

'I don't know what Ludo was thinking.' This was her usual sign-off.

Marianne thought she did know what Uncle Ludo had been thinking. The solicitor's letter *had* been a huge surprise – she hadn't set foot in Erringby since that summer party when she had been fifteen, had more or less forgotten about Mark Hardy in the gazebo – but standing in the damp, chilly hallway of the Kensington house she shared with three other out-of-work actors, letter in hand, she had quickly joined the dots: the brothers' original wills had named each other as sole beneficiary, with Cousin Ronald the ultimate heir. Harold had died, his dark heart succumbing to a routine operation at Hereford County Hospital, whereupon Ludo had amended his will, naming *her*. And just in time: the ink on Ludo's codicil was barely dry when his own mild heart gave in, a few weeks after Harold's.

Her first day here as an adult, the surprising new mistress of Erringby Hall and its estate, had been in the early spring of 1973. It had been sleeting and her little town car had lurched and swayed, barely a match for the rutted and potholed driveway. Manning was waiting for her at the door, unsmiling. He had never liked her. Not before the 1963 party, not on the night of the party – he had made his sufferance known, as he led the way across the walled garden, flashlight in hand, and bedding and Great-Aunt Elinor's borrowed nightdress tucked in a neat bundle in his arm, towards the gazebo – no, certainly not then, and even less so now. He had expected, as had everyone, an administration of Ronald Fentiman as absentee landlord – Ronald had a pile of his own near Bath to keep going. Not this cousin once removed – on the distaff side, moreover – who had been *persona non grata* for ten years.

Manning had led the way through the vestibule that was as she remembered it, oak-panelled, glooming, the mirror in its heavy gilt frame facing a portrait of a sullen Victorian in a similar frame, and into the main Hall – she could hear Harold's capitalisation – and begun a monologue on features he deemed noteworthy. In the hall, Erringby's draughty revivalist centrepiece, hung more portraits, including one of Harold himself.

Manning was chillingly polite. *Of course*, he kept saying as they moved from room to room, he pointing out the Anthony Salvin ceilings, the oak panelling, the original wall coverings from Maple & Co, but it was as if rather than including her in his circle of knowledge the reverse were true: he suspected in her a profound ignorance of

Victorian country houses and was subtly drawing her attention to it. In fact her mother had told her that Erringby was considered a minor building, representative of Salvin's late, charmless period. Pevsner, in his Herefordshire volume, had been dismissive.

And *You will remember...* Manning had kept saying, which was more pertinent, for she did remember the downstairs rooms: the drawing room where the guests had assembled, the gun room where she had made that discovery of Olga and Daphne in the act of – something? – the library, where Uncle Ludo had almost broken down, the dining room, where she'd endured that terrible breakfast the following morning.

'Of course Mother and I never came in here,' she had said as they entered the billiard room. This room had been built out from the main part of the house in order not to disturb the ladies with the noise of play (*of course*) and was an immense space, the huge and hulking billiard table, covered by a red baize cloth, resplendent in its middle.

'Indeed,' Manning replied.

She went over to the big east window, rested one knee on the window seat and pulled aside the filigree curtain. Beyond the window the grass banked steeply down to a large expanse of lawn, in the middle of which was a mass of daffodils, perhaps twenty feet across. There must have been a dozen different kinds, their trumpets pointing to the sun in defiance of the English weather. A sight so glorious would make anybody's spirits sing, and for the first time she had felt a straightforward optimism at her inheritance.

Manning wore the grey striped trousers and long black morning coat of an *Upstairs, Downstairs* character. She had on a canary-coloured skinny-rib jumper and a wool skirt in a bold yellow, green and brown check. The skirt ended several inches above the knee. She felt his gaze even with her back to him.

This room had been a male enclave for all of its 109-year history. Uncle Harold, who played billiards – Uncle Ludo had not – would have sat on this window seat making catty remarks about such-and-such a body as a game was in progress. Had definitely done so that night in 1963. Concerning her mother. He hated her mother, for reasons that were obscure. And Marianne? Certainly Harold had talked about her to Mark Hardy. Perhaps had signalled to Mark, corralled him into a corner of the room. Sotto voce, a manly squeeze of the arm. There was a prize awaiting Mark Hardy in the gazebo, if he cared to claim it.

On the riverbank Marianne sighed. She gave up on her book, lying back on the rug and putting a forearm over her eyes. A half-remembered fragment of O-level Tennyson came to her ...*a land in which it seemed always afternoon...* What had become of her schoolfriend Alicia, with whom she had had a sort of love affair? She had not thought of her in years. She was drowsy, lulled by the heat into feeling aroused. Her hand strayed under the waistband of her shorts. The older dog yawned, stretched and settled, his muscles tensing and then relaxing, his warmth pressing into her leg.

The wolfhound's barking brought her back and she raised her head, her hand shielding her eyes. Someone was walking towards her along the riverbank. It was a man, a man she did not recognise, in silhouette against the glare. This side of the river was not a right of way, but Erringby's boundaries were porous. There was purpose in the way he strode towards her. He put his hand out to the dog, patted his head. The wolfhound was easily won over and trotted back, delivering the stranger to her. She sat up and waited for them to reach her.

*

'...And the Goteik Viaduct,' the man was saying. 'The most incredible bit of engineering. Half a mile long. The train goes over it at walking pace so as not to cause any damage. Three hundred feet straight down to the jungle – I swear I held my breath the whole time. Of course we went there illegally. I had to bribe several railwaymen in Mandalay. I was disguised as a Buddhist monk at the time. Even shaved my head.' He passed a hand over his hair, which was thick and dark and came down to his shoulders. He seemed pleased with its lustre and ran his hand through it again.

'You've never made love until you've made love on a night train in the Far East.' This was addressed principally to Marianne, seated to his left. At the other end of the table someone muttered something to their neighbour. They were ten that night, seated round the kitchen table. Someone had made a bean stew that was almost entirely devoid of flavour. They were drinking vintage Bordeaux with it.

The man's name was Col Greenfield. He was extremely tanned, and he had very blue eyes, and he looked at you intently when he spoke to you so that you were, momentarily, the centre of his world.

'I'm looking for Marianne,' he had called as he strode towards her, the dog leading the way, and when she had said, 'This is she,' he had smiled, and his teeth were very white.

He was not anything to do with the others. He had grown up around here, he told her as he stood on the riverbank and pulled out a pack of Gitanes to offer her one. Had been travelling for a few years and was now back and staying at his sister's while he decided what to do next. He had known the Fentiman brothers – *everyone knew them* – had heard that they had died and that a mysterious relative had moved in. Curiosity had propelled him along the banks of the river to find out for himself. Marianne could tell he found her attractive. Naturally, she invited him to supper.

'What is this?' she asked now, reaching across her plate and taking hold of a charm that hung from a leather thong round his neck. It was a kind of barrel, made of silver, set in an enamel frame trimmed with more bits of silver.

'It's a Tibetan prayer wheel,' he said. 'Do you like it?'

'I like it.' She twiddled the barrel so that it spun. In doing so she pulled him an inch closer. He smelled of sweat and of some kind of cologne or fragrance that she couldn't place. Incense. He smelled of incense. From the other side of the table she was aware of Graham glowering at her. 'I like it very well.' Col smiled at her.

Supper finished, the table broke up and people began clearing away. Col showed no signs of wanting to leave. A flurry of anticipation set up in her stomach and travelled down, settling between her legs.

'Would you like a tour of the house?' He said that he would.

'Marianne.' Graham was at the door to the larder. 'We need to sterilise these Kilner jars, remember?'

'We can do that tomorrow,' she said without looking at him, and took the stranger by the hand. 'Follow me.'

He was a revelation. Graham, barely grown in comparison, had hips made of coat hangers that threatened to leave bruises on the inside of one's thighs. This one had a heft to him: his chest, her knees either side of it; the broadness of his back, where she rested her heels; his cock, stubby and thick. When he tunnelled into her she had gasped in spite of herself and he had smiled at her knowingly. His arrogance and his self-confidence turned her on. It had been a while since she had so thoroughly enjoyed herself. She came several times but he was up for more; he pulled out of her, turned her onto her hands and knees on the bed, stood on the floor behind her and fucked her vigorously that way. Somewhere in the house a David Bowie LP was playing. She couldn't remember what it was called but she would find out, so that even if she never saw this man again she could play the album and remember.

'You like your sex, don't you?' he asked her. She pushed her hair from her eyes and fumbled for her cigarettes.

'Doesn't everyone?' she said, while knowing this to be not quite true; some of the men at drama school had turned out not to be that interested in it, or if they were they couldn't always keep up.

'Here, have one of mine.' He took the cigarette from her lips, got out of bed and crossed the room to fetch his shirt. She took in the view of him from behind. He had not an ounce of fat on him, despite his size.

'Very nice,' she said, as he handed her one of his Gitanes.

He settled down next to her and lit her cigarette, then one for himself.

'This place is amazing.' His gesture took in not just the room but the entire house.

'Yes,' she said. 'I'm very lucky.' And in that moment the irritations and frustrations of being in charge of Erringby Hall fell away and she was able to feel immensely fortunate at having inherited the place; it would be fixed someday and she would make a success of... *something*. It was summer. She had just had some of the best sex of her life. Her body ached in a way that was deeply pleasurable. 'I'm lucky,' she repeated. The David Bowie had finished and whoever had that bedroom – Sasha? – had put Joni Mitchell on her record player. Marianne knew this one. She started to sing along with it. Col propped himself up on one elbow and looked at her. With a finger he traced a circle round her nipple, then cupped her breast and squeezed it. She stopped singing.

*

Col borrowed the Morris Traveller to drive the nine miles or so to his sister's house in Hereford. He had quickly sized up the crew assembled around Marianne: London types who talked a good game but were useless at the practical stuff. He managed to wangle it so he could work alongside her on tasks that he could tell were not to the taste of Graham and the rest, and together he and Marianne fixed a leaking downpipe joint at the back of the house, adjusted the hinges of a garage door so that it no longer snagged the ground, cleared a patch of brambles and nettles from a corner of the garden. He was hoping to make himself indispensable. They chatted as they worked, or rather he did, recounting his trip. London to Istanbul, then Tehran, Herat, Kandahar, Kabul, Peshawar and Lahore, on to India, Nepal and South East Asia, Australia and New Zealand. He spun anecdotes, exaggerating actual incidents – taking acid with a nephew of the Sultan of Brunei in Kuala Lumpur's swankiest hotel – and downplaying or omitting others – a dose of the clap in Varanasi. He made her laugh. She divulged little in exchange but he gathered she was fairly local herself; her childhood home was about twelve miles north-east of Hereford, though that was irrelevant really: she'd been at boarding school much of the time. Then she'd gone to London to study acting at the Webber Douglas Academy – Col pretended to have heard of it – and most of her experience had been in stage productions. Was Col a theatre-goer? She had looked at him with eyebrows raised and he admitted that no, he was not. She had nodded and he hoped that this was another plus point – she had tired of that life and of thespians and his unfamiliarity with that world would play to his advantage.

Did she like him? Col, in a sexual ferment, fervently hoped so. In fact – and this was a novel sensation for Col Greenfield – he needed her to. For he had decided, as he navigated the narrow lanes that led, in a circuitous way, to the A49, that he was finally, and properly, in love. More than with Sadie in Bristol. In fact, it occurred to Col as he drove, it wasn't Sadie he had missed after she booted him out (the outcome, in fairness to her, of his sleeping

with several other girls) so much as her kids. Col had babysat
Caroline and Michael while Sadie was at work and though, aged
eight and six, they were too old to have been his actual children,
he had loved the time he spent with them, reading boarding-school
stories to Caroline, building Meccano fire engines and cranes with
Michael. It was good practice for the children of his own that he
wanted one day.

He thought Marianne did like him but couldn't be sure, and
this intrigued Col, used as he was to women being charmed by
him, competing over him, lying back for him. He'd been aware,
these past three Erringby days, of Graham watching him with
Marianne, resentful, as if he had some prior claim, or thought he
did; Col had usurped him in the huge mahogany bed that sat like
a docked galleon in her room. The bed had a barley-twist post at
each corner but no canopy – French, she said, imported by Joseph
Fentiman, the ancestor who had built Erringby Hall in the 1860s
with the money from trading iron ore.

'So I'm still new money in the eyes of some,' she had said, and
Col, not really understanding, had gripped one of the barley posts
and said, grinning at her, 'You could have a lot of fun in this bed,'
and she had said, 'It was Uncle Harold's, so fun has been had,
yes,' and then Col was pulling her to him and they were making
love again. She was dazzling: she was a fertility goddess, her body
stupendous. He might lose himself in it. Col liked it when women
asserted themselves in bed. She made a lot of noise.

Crossing the River Wye, he reached a decision: Marianne was
the one. She was the fucking one. He'd come home.

He spent several hours at Flatley Close – more than enough time to
pack the few things he needed, but he wanted to stick around until
Bob came home from work to share his astounding news, also to
spend time with Christopher.

'That cousin no one's ever heard of?' Janet said when he told her his newly hatched plan of moving into Erringby, having fallen in love. 'Dear me.' Christopher was a more appreciative audience, though he was far more interested in Erringby Hall than in Marianne. Col told him about the bedrooms and the bathrooms, the two staircases, the cellars and the attics, the outhouses, kennels, stables and pigsties. And the land, of which the enormous garden was just the start: there was an orchard of apples, plums, pears, gooseberries and blackcurrants, a paddock and woodlands. And of course the riverbank. Janet tutted.

'When can I come?' Christopher, in his uncle's lap, twisted round to look up at him. He was less cherubic than he had been as a toddler, but his hair, growing straight from the crown into a fringe that was forever getting into his eyes, was still the colour of ripening corn and his eyes were still dark and full of mischief. He was, Col thought, extremely cute.

'Soon,' he promised.

'What day?' Christopher wanted certainty.

'This weekend,' said Col. 'Daddy can drive you over with Mummy and you can all come for tea. I'll make a cake.'

'Chocolate!' said Christopher, arms raised into the air. Col was going to miss living with him very much, but his mind ran on to the games they would have at Erringby: dens, tree houses, treasure hunts. And in a few years' time, perhaps, a tribe of cousins for Christopher to come and play *with*. Col had a vision of cooking breakfast for a horde of children on that antique range, the kitchen filled with noisy chatter. Of Marianne putting on plays in the library, all of them dressing up. He hadn't been listening to Janet and became aware that she was kneeling on the living-room carpet, scrubbing the wall.

'What are you doing, sis?'

'Toothpaste.' She went on scouring. 'It's the only thing that works on wax crayon. You've been driving me mad today, Christopher.'

Christopher ignored this.

'So can we?' he said. 'Go to Uncle Col's new house for tea?'

'Well. We'll have to see if we're free first.'

'You're always free,' Col said. 'What else would you have on?'

'What else would we have on?' echoed Christopher, before hitting on the obvious answer, 'Clothes!' and even Janet laughed.

Col wished Janet would ease up on Christopher, a little. His nephew was a kindred free spirit whereas Janet was for routine, for toys all put away and baths and teeth-brushing and a regular bedtime, and Christopher was a child who chafed at these restrictions rather than finding them comforting, exactly as Col had as a boy. He and Christopher had formed a secret communion of rule-bending in his time at Flatley Close. Bob had no views on childcare as far as Col could tell and besides, he was at work all day. Col would need to keep looking out for Christopher.

He arrived back at Erringby to find no other cars in the drive. The front door was open and the dogs tumbled out to greet him but otherwise the house was silent, had the air of having been hastily abandoned. There were odd items in the entrance hall: a sock, a pair of royal-blue running shorts, someone's copy of *Zen and the Art of Motorcycle Maintenance*.

'Hello?'

There was usually someone in the kitchen, cooking something awful and drinking tea, or wine from Harold's cellar, but it was deserted, as was the gun room.

'Marianne?' Col stood at the foot of the main staircase. It was unnerving, the house being so empty. He caught his own echo. Had they all gone on some impromptu outing? Unlikely.

He jumped at the sound of footsteps, spun round. She was carrying an enormous cardboard box from which spilled a jumble of clothes.

'Hello,' she said.

'Where is everybody?'

She shrugged. He was holding the rucksack that had accompanied him round the world and which now contained his entire wardrobe, and the LP case that held his favourite albums. He would go back for the rest of his records, which ran into the hundreds, some other day.

'Going somewhere?' she said.

'I've been to Hereford. To get my stuff. I told you.' Did he manage to keep from sounding reproachful?

'I don't remember asking you to move in.'

Col took a risk.

'No. But you want me to.'

'Oh do I!' This seemed to amuse her.

'Where is everyone?' he repeated.

'Oh – they had to go.'

'All of them?' To have had his fervent wish to have her all to himself granted, and so suddenly, was disconcerting. He had anticipated a winnowing out – starting with Graham – a gradual war of attrition.

'I believe so. I haven't done a thorough trawl.'

The next day it was Marianne who went off in the Morris Traveller. Col, not one of nature's early risers, found a note next to the range when he stumbled down. The note, short but provocative, had a single *x* appended. It was enough.

She wrote that she would be gone most of the day, buying paint and running errands in Hereford. Col purloined another vehicle – the Land Rover – and drove in the opposite direction to Ross-on-Wye, where the butcher greeted him by name. Then he drove back to Erringby, to get things ready, and to wait.

It wasn't easy to sneak into this house. The dogs – there were four of them – set up their welcome committee. She had come in via the back door and he heard her go into the kitchen.

'Col? Where might you be?'

'I'm in here.' He was in the dining room, setting the table. He'd found a damask tablecloth in a linen cupboard and an entire arsenal of crockery in the butler's pantry. He supposed it was valuable – it was certainly old – and he picked out a set he particularly liked – scalloped, with painted pink roses. *Limoges*, said the mark. He laid out two place settings with the bone-handled cutlery, also from the pantry. He was fashioning a linen serviette into the shape of a bishop's hat when she came into the room.

'Goodness!' It was the first time he had seen her taken aback, startled, even. A flash of something like annoyance passed over her face and for the first time Col thought he might have overplayed his hand. But he thought he knew how to rectify this.

'Marianne.' He took a step towards her. 'You look very beautiful.' And it was true, though she was sexy more than she was beautiful; there was something about the lack of attention she gave her appearance, the old, scruffy clothes, the absence of grooming, that was very alluring. He put his hand on the small of her back and pulled her towards him, saw her eyes widen momentarily but she capitulated, and they kissed for a long time, her tongue meeting his. As they drew apart she gave a tiny exhalation that held more than a hint of desire. *Keep that in the bank*, thought Col.

'I hope you don't mind,' he said. 'I thought we'd have a special dinner, since it's just the two of us.'

'I don't mind,' she said.

'I got some fillet steaks from the butcher's in Ross. We're having them with a red wine and mushroom sauce.'

'Heavens,' she said. 'Have I time for a bath?'

'So, how did you get rid of them all?' Col, emboldened by three quarters of a bottle of Château Lafite, leaned in conspiratorially.

'Oh, they left,' she said, and when he looked at her to go on added, 'It was for the best.' Somehow Col knew not to press it.

He suspected Marianne, once she had made her mind up about something, was not to be trifled with. Still, he needed to push home his advantage.

'But you spared me from this... from this...' He waved his spoon, searching for the word.

'*Cull*,' she suggested. 'Yes, so I did.' She must be serious about him, surely.

'Did you enjoy your meal?' They were finishing the pavlova he had made for dessert.

'It was wonderful,' she said. 'I haven't eaten such a meal since my London days. Where did you learn to cook like that?'

'I used to run a restaurant in Bristol,' said Col, which was near enough the truth; no need to mention Sadie, still less Michael and Caroline, though he had the impression Marianne would not be much bothered by Sadie or indeed by any of his back catalogue. 'High end.'

'You studied cordon bleu?'

'Well... Not exactly.'

'Autodidact,' she said. Col pretended to know what that meant.

'Why don't you play the piano for me?' he said.

There was a baby grand in the drawing room. She played tunes that Col, whose tastes ran more to *The Old Grey Whistle Test* than *Meet George Gershwin at the Keyboard,* was unfamiliar with, but she had a lovely voice.

'You sound like Marianne Faithfull.'

'Who?'

'Oh, come on!'

He stood behind her, kissing her neck, his hands on her breasts.

'You're putting me off,' she rebuked him, but she stopped playing and turned round and tugged off her dress. She wore no bra and her tits were perfectly round and very firm. He pulled her off the piano stool and onto the rug.

'I want to make love to you in every room in this house,' he said, unzipping his jeans.

'That could take a very long time.' She lay back on the rug.

'I know.'

2

July 1974

He woke the next morning naked on the bed with her asleep beside him, head turned from him, a jumble of blonde hair on the pillow. He kissed her hair and she mumbled something and shifted, but did not wake. He wanted to lie there and look at her but instead he pulled the coverlet up over her marvellous arse so that she wouldn't get cold. There would be time enough for looking at her.

His clothes were where he had left them, under the piano. He got up and went downstairs, still naked. Two of the dogs looked up from their baskets in the hall, sniffed and yawned, went back to sleep. Col thought again what an amazing house this would be with a bit of work. He went into the gun room, where there was a stereo, and put on his copy of *Tubular Bells*. He turned the volume up. The first thing he would do would be to wire up speakers so that they could hear the stereo in all of the downstairs rooms. He went into the kitchen, filled the kettle and put it on the range, lifted his arms above his head and stretched.

Col enjoyed inhabiting his body. He liked that it was tanned all over. It was good to be naked on this summer's morning. He wasn't looking forward to the English winter, to having to cover up with trousers, jumpers, coats, skin fading gradually to white. 'I'm in love with you, Marianne,' he had said to her on the drawing-room rug, and she had smiled at him and slid down his body to take his cock into her mouth. It stiffened now at the memory. He needed to mind himself on the cooker. He took two slices of bread and dropped them onto the range top, thinking about her, how wet and open she had been, how she had fucked him back, legs wrapped round him, hips pushing at him, matching him. 'I'm the best you've had, aren't I?' he had whispered, and she had only smiled at him, but in a way that meant he was right.

'Oh good heavens,' said a voice, and he spun round in surprise. A woman was standing at the door to the kitchen. She had a familiar look but she was old – at least sixty – and was dressed as if for church – twinset, court shoes, handbag. 'Goodness me,' she said. Her voice was clipped, patrician. One of the dogs had followed her. It stood behind her, sniffing.

Col's prick wilted at this intrusion. But he turned to face the woman without attempting to cover himself. He was aware of her eyes moving down his body and this emboldened him. She didn't look particularly horrified. Game old bird. From the gun room the music played on.

'Col Greenfield,' he said, stepping forward, hand outstretched.

'Susannah Lonsdale.' She ignored the hand.

'Marianne's mother. I might have guessed.'

There was the smell of burning. Smoke was coming from the top of the range.

'*Shit.*' He grabbed at the toast with his fingers. One of the slices fell to the floor. The dog got to it before he was able to pick it up. 'Shit.'

'How charming,' said the woman.

Yes, she had a look of Marianne, but while this woman might have been beautiful once she was old and cross, spidery lines round the mouth into which lipstick bled. Her voice, too, had a little of Marianne but she was loud, like a posh gym teacher.

'Are you another of Marianne's buccaneering types?'

'I don't know,' he said. 'Is there a type?' She ignored this.

'Are you intending to put clothes on?'

'Well, I don't know,' he said again. He was beginning to enjoy himself. 'I might.' He leaned against the dresser and folded his arms, assured in his possession of the kitchen.

'What?' she said irritably.

'I said I might,' he said, more loudly.

She glared at him. Give the old gal her due, she was standing her ground.

'Would you like a cup of tea?' he asked her. 'Or perhaps a small sherry?'

'Where is Marianne?'

'She's asleep.'

'Asleep! Marianne gets up with the lark. This is your doing, I suppose?' In response he bounced his eyebrows at her. She gave a *tsch* of irritation.

'What can we do for you, Susannah?' he asked.

'Mrs Lonsdale, I think, don't you? You could start by fetching my daughter.'

At this moment Marianne came into the kitchen, wearing a cotton dressing gown. She gave a shriek and turned away in shock, then turned back.

'Mother! For the love of God.'

'Marianne. I came to borrow your loppers. The apple trees have got themselves into a state. Who is this?' She waved a hand at Col. Marianne went over to him and took his hand.

'Mother, this is Col. My boyfriend.'

Col's prick started to stiffen again. He stood just behind Marianne to conceal it from the old gal. Marianne leaned towards his ear. 'But do at least put pants on, h'mmm?'

He passed Susannah with his back towards her, hands clasped in front of him, grinning at her over his shoulder.

'Lovely to meet you, Mrs Lonsdale.' She glared at him as he departed.

He found his clothes under the piano and pulled his jeans on quickly. The best place to hear what was going on in the kitchen was from the scullery. Side one of *Tubular Bells* had finished.

'...care what you do, but really. Even Harold would have drawn the line.' Mrs Lonsdale had one of those voices, hearty and adenoid-free, that rang out across lacrosse pitches, point-to-point grounds, restaurants, hotel lobbies. A voice used to being heeded. She was probably incapable of lowering it. Marianne's voice was softer.

'That's all you know,' Col thought she said.

'What has happened to the rest of them? The canaille?'

'It's just me and Col now, Mother.'

Col, hearing this, was very pleased. And she had referred to him as her boyfriend. But was she just winding her mother up?

'How long have you known this person?'

'Oh... about four days.'

'Marianne.'

She would be enjoying herself. Already he knew that she relished a spat.

'He acts as if he owns the place,' Mrs Lonsdale said.

'I suppose he does.'

'I know the type.'

'You do not. He's nothing like Father.'

There was a silence. Marianne would be making tea.

'I'm not sure where the loppers are, Mother. If you'd let me know you were coming...'

'They're in one of the outhouses, surely. If one can't call on one's own daughter...'

'As soon as I'm dressed I'll look for them.'

There was a pause, and Mrs Lonsdale said, 'The sex soon wears off, you know.' Col strained to hear, but couldn't catch Marianne's response. 'He's after your money and he's using sex to beguile you.'

'*Beguile me?*' Marianne laughed. He pictured her lovely face.

'I hope you're using protection.' Her mother's voice grew louder.

'Not that it's any of your business, but yes.' So she must be taking the pill. She was still laughing.

'Marianne, you can't go on like this.'

'Like what?'

'Playing at being the lady of the manor. Why don't you phone Carstairs, those land agents? They—' Marianne cut across her.

'We've been through this. I'm not selling. This is my home.'

'All these rooms, just for you and... Ludo can't have been in his right mind.'

'He had his reasons.'

'Because you were nice about his watercolours? Ridiculous!'

'Anyway,' said Marianne. 'I've got ideas for this place, all sorts of ideas.'

'What ideas?' Susannah's voice was cut glass dipped in prussic acid. Marianne's reply was drowned out by the whistling of the kettle.

*

They were in the gazebo. He had thought that she had shown him all Erringby had to offer but she kept on surprising him – outhouses and kennels and a dovecote and now this. The gazebo was a castellated folly, built into a corner of the walled garden that lay off the courtyard. It consisted of two square rooms, one above the other, the entrance quixotically located on the upper floor via a cast-iron stairway. She had let them in with a huge rusty key hidden under a brick. The lower chamber was filled with junk – a dressmaker's dummy, an old birdcage, dusty steamer trunks – but the upper room was laid out as a kind of study.

'Uncle Ludo's bolthole,' she had said. 'He came here to get away from Harold.'

A desk had been set up beneath one of the high windows, a shelf holding a few books sat against another wall and there was a small sofa, its upholstery threadbare. A folded army camp bed that might have seen service in the Crimea was propped up next to the bookshelf.

They had just had sex on the sofa, its frame creaking ominously beneath their exertions. Col sprawled on it now with her next to him, leaning on his bare chest and fiddling with the prayer wheel.

'You're the most amazing woman I've ever met.' Col kissed the top of her head.

'And you've met a very great many, I'm sure.'

He liked her mocking of him. It was good-natured, but there was an edge. It was sexy.

She sat up and combed her hair with her fingers, unsnagging some of its tangles.

'So,' she said. 'Col Greenfield.' She looked him up and down as if appraising him and again he saw Mrs Lonsdale in her.

'Yes,' he said, in mock obedience.

'You grew up in the village, where your parents still live. And you knew my Uncles.'

'They were the Fentiman brothers. You'd see them in the village shop. I never spoke to them, though, they weren't really part of our...'

'They weren't actual uncles. My grandmother was their mother's sister. You must know about the summer parties.' He nodded. 'Did you ever work at one?'

'My brother did, once. It would have been when he was in the sixth form, so... early fifties, maybe.'

'What did he say about it?'

'Apparently it got out of hand. He ended up getting very drunk with one of the other waiters in the kitchen. When he came home he was sick on the living-room carpet. My mum never let him go again.'

'Ha ha!' She looked amused.

'That was the only time any of us ever came to Erringby,' he said.

'Until now.'

'Yes.'

'And where is your brother now?'

'Glasgow. We don't see him very often.'

'And the sister – Janet, is it? In Hereford.'

'That's right. She's ten years older than me. Alan's one year older than her.'

'Are you like them?'

'Not at all,' he admitted. 'My mum had to look after my grandparents so she kind of left it to my sister to bring me up. She's a good sort, Janet. I love her to bits.'

'Nephews? Nieces?'

'Alan's got one of each, aged five and eight. Janet and Bob have a boy they adopted, Christopher, he's nearly six. I bloody love that kid, he's so smart. I missed him like hell when I was away. I can't wait to show him this place. In fact they...' He pulled himself up. Perhaps leave off mentioning the weekend invitation for now. 'Do you like kids?'

'I don't really know any. I don't have much in the way of immediate family. Just Mother and, well – you saw for yourself. Or heard.' She brushed his cheek with her fingers. He put one of her fingers in his mouth momentarily, then kissed it.

'Is there a Mr Lonsdale?'

'There is a Mr Lonsdale. But he's in the Far East. I've not seen him in years.'

'Whereabouts?'

'Presently? Singapore, I believe. That's the address I have for him. But he hops around.'

'I was in Singapore last year. Just think, I might have sat next to him in Raffles.'

'You might.'

'What do you think he'd make of me?'

'I hardly know what he makes of me. But my mother dislikes you, so that'd be a start.'

They fell silent.

'I don't care how much money you've got,' he blurted. She arched an eyebrow but did not reply. 'I'm not interested in money,' he went on. 'You'd be amazed how little I lived on when I went travelling.' She looked wistful.

'I'd love to do the overland,' she said.

'Then let's do it!' The thought of travelling again, with Marianne as a companion, was extremely attractive. She laughed.

'It's not so easy.'

'Why isn't it?'

She gave no reply, though he could see she was taken with the idea.

'Erringby's rather a poisoned chalice,' she said eventually. 'You can't just pick it up and put it down again. There are too many things to take care of. One day, perhaps.'

He was twisting a strand of her hair round his finger.

'You must know you caused a bit of a stir when you moved in here,' he said. She shrugged.

'I don't listen to gossip,' she said.

'No. But wasn't there another cousin, a man?'

'Yes, Cousin Ronald, the heir apparent. But Ludo changed his will.'

'He died very soon after Harold, didn't he?'

'Matter of months.'

'Heart, wasn't it, for both of them?'

'You seem to know all about it.'

'It's a small village. People talk.'

'I dare say.'

'And then...'

'The mysterious relative with her strange London ways arrives,' she said.

'Didn't your cousin mind?'

'Nosy, aren't you?' He grinned at her. 'Ronald was rather relieved not to inherit, I think. He's got enough on with his own estate.'

Estate. He was going with someone whose family had estates. Col had the sense that opening up was something she seldom did and that he should press his advantage.

'How come you got everything and he didn't?'

'Oh, he was meant to. But Ludo changed his will after Harold died.'

'Your mum said something about... watercolours?'

'That's what she thinks. That I was nice about Uncle Ludo's pictures. You know, the ones in the library. But there was a bit more to it than that.' She pulled at the hem of the dress riding up her thighs. He looked at her, waiting for her to go on.

'It was at one of the summer parties, actually. The only time I was ever invited. In fact that was the last time I came to Erringby, until my inheritance.

'That summer Mother and I were getting along, believe it or not. I was fifteen and she seemed just to have noticed me, decided I'd stopped being a tiresome child concerned only with ponies and pashes. And that year I got invited to the party as well, and she bundled me onto the train to London to have me kitted out. I remember the dress – taffeta with velvet flocking. It was all the more amazing since we didn't have much money – Father had abandoned us by then and left us in the soup. He was supposed to send cheques but they had got more and more erratic. My school had started complaining.

'And suddenly here I was at a grown-ups' party. It was as if by simply putting on the dress I had become an adult. Several people remarked that I looked like Brigitte Bardot.'

By people she means men. Col pictured Marianne at fifteen – eleven years and another era ago – the sophisticated cocktail dress, hair put up, cosmetics, scent, dress watch borrowed from her mother replacing the schoolgirl Timex. The Erringby summer parties had been notorious. It wasn't Alan's throwing up on the living-room carpet that had scuppered his chances of working there again so much as his tales of debauchery among the guests, naked romps in the woods and all. His parents had been shocked.

'I'm guessing the party was a bit of an eye-opener,' he said.

It occurred to Marianne that she had never told this story, not properly. Certainly not to Susannah.

'It *was* an eye-opener,' she said. 'Mother told me on the way over that some of Harold's friends were rather louche and I shouldn't take them seriously. A woman called Olga Youssoupov was going round telling everyone that Harold was the headless man in the Duchess of Argyll photograph – you remember that?'

Col nodded and grinned.

'And was he?'

'I shouldn't think so for one moment. But he had this *I-can-neither-confirm-nor-deny* smirk. He loved the idea of it.

'I remember thinking, *If this is adulthood I don't much care for it*. All that air kissing and pronouncing themselves thrilled, then sniping and backbiting as soon as the person had left the room.

'Uncle Ludo saved me from an awful man who had been trying to chat me up. At that age I had no idea how to deal with it. He was looking like he was going to kiss me. Ludo whisked me away into the library.'

She paused, twisting her hair into a rope and putting it over one shoulder. Col was watching her intently. What she did not tell him was that before they had gone into the library Ludo had opened the door to the gun room, where they had come across a tableau that now made her think of a James Ensor or an Otto Dix. Daphne Hodgkiss and Olga Youssoupov were on the sofa. Daphne's shoes were off; they lolled on the floor as she sat with her feet tucked under her, facing Olga. Her blouse had been undone almost to the waist, her bra askew, exposing her breasts. Her nipples were very prominent, almost conical. She was leaning towards Olga with her mouth open as the other woman blew smoke into her mouth, cigarette holder dangling languidly from her hand. All of this Marianne had time to take in in the instant it took Uncle Ludo to exclaim, 'Ladies! I am so sorry!' and the women had turned to look at them, neither abashed nor annoyed. Ludo had backed away from the door as if it were wired to the mains, bumping clumsily into Marianne. She remembered the amused look on Olga's face as she turned back to Daphne. And she remembered her own shock, ice on sun-blasted skin. It wasn't so much the sapphic element that had intrigued her – she had known even then that she was heterosexual, her dalliance with her schoolfriend Alicia notwithstanding – as the sudden glimpse of the possible, of what adulthood might hold. Intrigue. Sex.

She would not tell Col this. He would pump her for more of what Olga and Daphne were doing and it would overshadow the story she wanted to tell, the real story of the evening. Like the cache of pornographic Victorian postcards she had found among Harold's things, Olga and Daphne was something she might share with Col in the future. When he had earned it.

'And then what happened?' Col asked.

'It was rather strange. Uncle Ludo took me into his confidence. It was as if he had forgotten I was fifteen. Started talking about how sorry he was about my parents – I hadn't realised he knew – and opened his heart to me about his own miserable childhood and what a swine his father had been. And what a saint his dear mother – Great-Aunt Elinor – was. How she had married beneath her because her family was broke, etc.'

'Great-Aunt Elinor. Is she the one all in black?'

'That's her. In mourning for the husband whom by all accounts she loathed.'

'Then what happened?'

'Ludo wanted me to see his paintings. Had them hidden in a port-folio. Harold wouldn't let him display them, of course. He preferred

39

the dead ancestors. I thought the pictures were lovely, especially the poppies, huge and smudged. They look as if they've been wept over. One of the first things I did when I moved in was to get them framed and on the walls. Ludo said, *I hoped you'd like them. You feel things, don't you?* I had no answer for that. Didn't everyone feel things?

'And then.' The memory amused her. 'He grabbed my hand, as if the evening couldn't get any stranger.' She gripped Col's own hand, fixed him with an overwrought expression straight out of Edward Fitzball. *'Promise me you'll marry for love, Marianne.'*

'Ha!' said Col. 'What did you say to that?'

'I can't remember. Only I realised that I hadn't seen Mother for hours, and it was probably time to go home. I looked all over but she was nowhere to be found. And then Uncle Harold told me she'd gone home without me. He'd told her I'd left with Anthony Cleaver.'

'Who was...?'

'The son of the local JP. Bad stammer and acne. It was all a bit of a muddle. I telephoned Mother but she'd just got home and wasn't inclined to drive over again. Erringby Hall was full to the gunwales, of course, with people staying over, so Uncle Ludo suggested I spend the night here.'

'Here?' said Col. 'In the gazebo?' She nodded.

'Harold said something like, *The poor girl, banished, like Mariana in the moated grange.* But he looked rather pleased with himself. He disappeared into the billiard room with the other men. Not Ludo, he didn't play. I think he took himself off to bed.

'I'd been given a nightgown to wear – one of Great-Aunt Elinor's. It was a ridiculous garment, buttoned up and fusty. It came down to the floor. I couldn't sleep. I found a book on horse breeds and was trying to read. Then I heard someone coming up the stairs.'

'Who was it?'

'At first I thought it might be Harold, come to quote more Tennyson at me. There was a tap at the door.'

'And…?'

'It was a man I didn't know. I recognised him from the party. He had been playing billiards with Harold.'

'Bloody hell,' said Col.

'His name was Mark Hardy.'

She thought now of Mark, who had been in his mid twenties at a guess, tall, with a fringe that flopped over his eyes. The black bow tie lying undone around his unbuttoned collar, another shirt button open midway down his chest. How his gaze had taken in her hair, tousled and falling over one shoulder, the nightgown, her dusty feet. How the way he looked at her had made her heart beat faster.

'When I introduced myself he said, *I know who you are. You're Harold's niece,* and I must admit I was flattered that he had noticed me. When I said that this had been my first summer party he said, *Thought so. I'd've remembered a pretty girl like you.*'

'What was he doing?' asked Col. 'In here, I mean.'

'I thought perhaps he'd seen me come here and followed me.'

'Bloody hell,' said Col again. 'Then what happened?'

'He found Ludo's secret whisky bottle stashed away in there.' She nodded at the desk. 'We got chatting. About… nothing, really. This and that. There was just the one glass that we passed between us. We got a bit tipsy.'

'And…?' Col leaned towards her, hands on her knees.

'And nothing,' she said. 'All he did was kiss me. Once he found out how old I was. I was a bit disappointed, to be honest.' She thought of Mark's hand on her breast, first over and then inside the nightgown. How he had pinched her nipple, startling her. His hand on her knee, rucking up the ridiculous nightdress. How the fabric bunched up under his hand, there was so much of it. 'I fell asleep on this sofa next to him. When I woke in the morning I was alone.'

'He'd gone back to the house to sleep.'

'So I thought. Only when I went in for breakfast I found out he'd left. And the people at the breakfast table, all Harold's friends, were vile. Sniggering and giggling.'

Her fifteen-year-old self at the breakfast table, in her party dress and her soiled shoes, her hair unbrushed and her eyes smudged with mascara. The adults, Harold's friends, watching her in amusement as they smoked their cigarettes. The arch looks they had exchanged.

'Then Uncle Ludo came in and told me how *mortified* he was. Kept saying he had no idea, that if he had known what was going on he would have done something to stop it. That was when I realised that they all thought Mark had...'

'Screwed you?'

'Well, yes. I remember looking round at their faces. They all looked so gleeful and cunning, other than Ludo, who looked distraught, and I hated them all; I even hated Uncle Ludo for being so ineffectual. Then I remembered I'd been telling people – Bill Hobson, the man who'd been pestering me, for example – that I was going to be an actress. I was furious with Mark Hardy as well, for going off without saying goodbye. I thought, *Let people think the worst of him*. I turned to Uncle Ludo...' She looked at Col again, face pulled into an expression of mock earnestness. '*It wasn't so bad, Uncle Ludo. Really it wasn't.*' She gave Col a brave smile, a facsimile of the one she had produced at that breakfast table.

'Ha!' said Col.

'After breakfast Ludo dragged me into the library to apologise all over again. I kept on with the plucky wronged-maiden act – I was rather enjoying myself, actually, and Ludo was so upset it was funny – until Mother arrived to collect me. Ludo grabbed my hand again as I was leaving and said, *I shall never forgive myself for this, never.* It was only afterwards that I realised Harold must have set me up, told Mark that there were easy pickings for him in the gazebo.'

'Fucking hell,' Col said. 'What an arsehole. Why did he do that?'

'It was the kind of thing he did.' She shrugged. '*Wreakful*, Ludo once called him. *Harold can be terribly wreakful.* I think he was getting back at Mother – they hated each other.'

'And then…?'

'And then nothing. Until Ludo died and left the entire estate to me.'

'So if Ludo had gone first then old Cousin Ronald would have copped the lot?'

'That's right.'

'Blimey,' said Col. 'So you inherited Erringby all because Uncle Ludo thought you'd popped your cherry at his party. Ha!'

'It's a good story, isn't it?'

'And your mum thinks it's to do with watercolours. *Ridiculous!*' he said, in good mimicry of Susannah, making Marianne laugh. He looked at her for a moment.

'Mark Wotsit doesn't know what he missed.'

'I console myself with that.'

'*The sex soon wears off, you know.*'

She laughed. 'Does it?'

'Let's find out.' His hand slid beneath her dress.

3

June 1975

Christopher was under the table. They all thought he was outside playing with the cousins, but he had quickly bored of them. Ian wanted to climb the wisteria in the walled garden and Joanne trailed behind him, teasing him and telling him off at the same time, and Christopher thought that what was going on indoors at this, his first wedding, would be more interesting. Most of the house was out of bounds; a man with shoulder-length hair and shoes with big platforms had barred the way earlier when Christopher tried to climb the huge wooden staircase, saying, 'Oh no you don't, sunshine,' a cigarette dangling from his mouth, not listening when Christopher tried to explain that he wouldn't get lost, he had been to the house before. The staircase was very wide, almost as wide as the entire front room at home.

He had slunk back into the big hall where the reception was taking place and, unseen, crawled under the table at which his parents sat with a couple he didn't know, whose names were Roger and Eileen. The tablecloth hung down to just a few inches above the floor and was made from a sort of stiff white material; it swallowed Christopher up and then fell back into place as if he had never been there. There had been another couple at the table, but they had gone off somewhere.

'I do think,' Christopher heard his mother say, 'that we could have been nearer the top table. We are the groom's family after all.'

'Keep your voice down,' said his father.

'It doesn't matter,' said his mother. 'Her lot have got such braying voices that no one's going to hear us.'

The woman called Eileen giggled. Christopher's mother had slipped off one of her sandals and was wrapping her bare foot round the other ankle. The strap of the sandal had left a bright red stripe and her feet were swollen and puffy, with blue veins that stuck out like ropes. Christopher wondered what would happen if he speared one with a cocktail stick. Would blue blood ooze out? Would it spurt?

'They are very posh, aren't they?' said Eileen.

'Stuck up, more like,' said his mother.

'Janet,' said his father. 'You're drunk.'

A waiter came up to the table. He wore black lace-up shoes, very shiny.

'Oh, you are a stick-in-the-mud, Bob, sometimes,' Christopher's mother said. 'How often do I get to let my hair down?'

Eileen giggled again. There was the sound of wine being poured and the waiter went away.

'Well, they're paying for it all,' said his mother, and Christopher wondered who *they* were. He settled under the table and hugged his knees, away from the restless crossing and uncrossing of ankles.

'How did the two of them meet, anyway?' Eileen was saying.

'He made it his business.' Christopher's father chuckled.

'Bob,' said Christopher's mother. 'That's not very nice. You know Col, Eileen, he knows everyone. Always made friends easily. Right from being a boy.' She wasn't talking how she usually talked. She talked very quickly, as if she was worried about running out of breath.

'Are you going to eat that wedding cake, Bob?' was what she said next. 'I'd say let's wrap it in a serviette and take it home, but they're not paper ones. I dare say Marianne'd notice if we took one of these linen things. Probably counts them every night.'

Eileen gave a nervous laugh and said, 'You're close, aren't you? You and Col.'

'Oh yes. He's my baby brother.'

'He's twenty-eight, Janet,' said Christopher's father.

'He'll always be your baby brother,' said Eileen.

'What will they do,' said Roger, 'the two of them rattling around in this old place?'

His father started to say something but his mother jumped in.

'Oh, Col has loads of ideas. Open it to the public, tea rooms, drama school...'

'Drama school?' said Eileen.

'Oh yes. She's an actress. Or was. Didn't you know?'

'Would I have seen her in anything?' Roger asked.

'I shouldn't think so,' said his father.

'I do think,' his mother went on, 'that she could have worn a proper dress. What with this being a formal wedding and all.'

'She's bohemian,' Eileen said, a word Christopher didn't recognise, though from the way Eileen said it he guessed it wasn't anything good, and their conversation turned to wedding dresses. His father and Roger started talking about cricket. This was boring. Christopher looked at his fingers, grubby with food and grass stains. He didn't like having dirty hands, but even though he knew about the downstairs cloakroom and could find it easily, he would blow his cover if he crawled out from under the table now. He thought about Marianne, who he was now to call Auntie Marianne. She was very pretty in Christopher's opinion. And he didn't know what was supposed to be wrong with the dress. His mother had also not been happy that Uncle Col and Auntie Marianne had arrived at the town hall together in Uncle Col's car, a Triumph Toledo the colour of Heinz tomato soup. She had said, 'It's such a shame not to observe the old traditions, don't you think? Not even a ribbon on the car,' and his father had cleared his throat in the way that meant he didn't really agree with her but wasn't going to say so.

'The caterers might have some paper napkins, if we asked,' said Eileen. 'For the cake.'

'Christopher's just eaten the icing off his,' said his mother. 'Typical of him.'

'He's not terribly like either of you, is he?' said Eileen. 'Your son,' and under the table Christopher sat up straight to listen.

'Well, no,' said his mother. 'He's adopted.'

'Really?' said Eileen. 'I didn't know. How brave of you.'

Why was it brave?

'We tried for years and years, didn't we, Bob, but there was nothing doing. The doctors think it's Bob.'

'*Janet*,' said his father, and Eileen gave a funny laugh. What did the doctors think was his father? Christopher sat very still.

'Did he come to you as a baby?' Eileen was asking.

'Oh no,' said his mother. 'He was two and a half years old.' This was news to Christopher. He tried not to make a sound. Under the table his mother was rubbing the top of her bare foot against her calf. He wanted, very much, for the grown-ups to go on talking about him.

'We got him from a church mother-and-baby home,' his mother said. 'In London.'

She made it sound like they had bought him from a shop.

'What had happened to his parents?' Eileen asked.

'They died,' said his father.

'Car crash,' said his mother. This was more news to Christopher, who had been told that they didn't know anything about his real mother and father. His stomach went funny, as if it had dropped several feet.

'Does he remember them?'

His mother and father spoke at the same time. 'No,' his mother said. 'I don't think so,' said his father. Christopher sat very still.

'Well, he possibly remembers something about them,' his father said. 'Subconsciously, at any rate.'

'It'll be why he's so difficult,' his mother said. 'I dare say.'

'How good of you,' Eileen said. 'To take it on.'

'Well,' said his mother.

'He's a good boy, really,' said his father, who sounded as if he didn't believe what he was saying.

'He's forever getting into scrapes at school,' his mother said. 'His teacher says he's very bright, but he can't focus.'

'He gets into trouble and he gets other children into trouble,' said his father.

'The school have had us in several times, haven't they, Bob?'

'Yup.'

'Goodness knows what he's up to now. Bob, do you want to go and check on him?'

'He'll be all right,' said his father. 'He's playing with his cousins.'

'He's a very good-looking little boy, I must say,' Eileen said. 'Not that... I mean...' She sounded flustered, but everyone else laughed.

'None taken,' said his father.

'That's the thing with adoption,' his mother went on. 'You never know how they'll turn out. And I swear I do not know where Christopher came from.' Her other sandal was off now, her broad feet flat on the floor, the discarded sandals lying on their sides.

Christopher was holding his breath so tightly his lungs might burst. If he could keep from breathing long enough, his mum would spill out more secrets about his real parents.

'This car accident, then,' Roger said. 'Was—'

But he was interrupted by Christopher's father saying, 'Ah! Hello, Mr and Mrs Greenfield.' Uncle Col and Auntie Marianne had come up to their table.

'Hello there,' said Uncle Col. 'Are you enjoying yourselves?' There was a general murmuring of yes, they were.

'Lovely day,' said Christopher's father. 'Lovely... speeches.'

'Ah, well,' said Auntie Marianne. She and Uncle Col were standing very close together. 'You got a little carried away, didn't you, darling?' Uncle Col laughed. He was wearing tan slip-on shoes with a heel. The shoes were something else that Christopher's mother didn't think were right. Christopher liked Uncle Col a lot. He couldn't remember much from before he went away travelling but he remembered the letters, red and blue stripes round the edge of the envelopes like a maypole, exotic stamps that he cut out to paste in a scrapbook. His mother would read out bits from the letters, funny stories, at the breakfast table. Uncle Col had adventures. Then when he came back he lived with them at Flatley Close until he fell in love with Auntie Marianne and moved to Erringby.

'Can't a man declare his love for his own wife?' Uncle Col said now, and everyone laughed. 'We're all far too buttoned up in this country.'

'It's a big old place you've got here, Marianne,' Roger said. 'How many bedrooms?'

'Twenty-one, I think,' said Auntie Marianne.

'She thinks!' Christopher's mother seemed to find this very funny.

'It depends whether one counts the staff flat or not,' said Auntie Marianne.

'And we plan on filling some of those bedrooms,' said Uncle Col. 'Don't we, Marianne?' He would be tipsy. If they were all at home Christopher's mother would have said, 'You're tipsy again, Col!' Auntie Marianne's weight shifted towards Uncle Col as if he were cuddling her.

'Ooh!' said Eileen. 'Lovely.'

'Marianne, we wondered if we could get some paper serviettes to take the cake home in,' said Christopher's mother.

'Do stop going on about the cake, Janet,' said his father.

'Oh, they'll come round with boxes for it,' said Marianne.

'See?' said his father.

'Pity your dad couldn't make it, Marianne,' Roger said. 'Where is he again?'

'Singapore,' said Auntie Marianne.

'Nice he sent a telegram,' said Eileen. There was a silence.

'I'll get to meet him finally,' said Uncle Col. 'We're planning a big trip to the Far East for our honeymoon.'

'Yes,' said Auntie Marianne. 'We—'

'Oh Marianne!' Christopher's mother cut across her. 'I was saying to Eileen. Your table in the whatchamacallit, the library. It's a bit dusty. I could pop over with a can of Pledge if you like.' Her laugh was very loud. It died in the air.

'You shouldn't clean antiques often, actually,' said Auntie Marianne. 'Over-cleaning causes damage.' The grown-ups fell silent. Auntie Marianne was wearing sandals with no back. *Mules*, they were called, which was a funny name for a shoe. Her feet were tanned, their skin very smooth, the veins on them thin like threads of cotton. Her toenails were painted bluey pink, a shiny, shimmery colour. Like the picture of the inside of an oyster shell in one of the books Uncle Col had brought back from his travels. Christopher liked the colour very much. Auntie Marianne's feet were close to where his hand rested on the floor.

'Are these waiters coming round enough?' Col was saying. 'Do you want any more wine?' Christopher stretched his hand out beyond the tablecloth and gently touched the painted nail of Marianne's little toe.

She looked down. Christopher pulled his hand away, but she had seen him. She took a step back. Christopher, looking out from under the tablecloth, could see her face.

'I'll get you some more wine,' Uncle Col said, as Christopher's father was saying, 'Oh, we've had more than enough, Col, thanks.'

Marianne and Christopher looked at each other. She made a tiny movement with her head to show that she had seen him. Christopher shrank back and hugged his knees.

'Christopher must come to Erringby to play,' Auntie Marianne said. 'As often as he likes.' His mother gave a shrill laugh, as if Marianne had said something very funny.

4

April 1980

Christopher had the unfamiliar experience of being woken by his father, even earlier than his mother woke him on a school day, and being bundled into the new company car without having had his breakfast. He was savouring this drive through the countryside at dawn, scarcely hearing his father's lecture on how he must behave himself.

He'd had the dream last night. He was a little boy again, and it was a party, for there were coloured streamers decked around the room and an enormous cake had been cut into slices and put onto plates. But there were no other children and Christopher sat alone at the table. He wanted to grab the slices of cake, the ones meant for the children that weren't there, but he couldn't because he had jam all over his face, and a lady came up to him and was sad, and said something about wiping off the jam, but he couldn't do that either. He was sticky with jam round his nose and mouth. There was jam on his fingers, too. At least this time he didn't start crying in the dream, which meant he would wake up feeling upset. Christopher had been having this dream for as long as he could remember.

Something running along the lane ahead of the car brought him back.

'A hare!'

'Oh yes,' said his father. 'My goodness.' The creature ran on ahead as if challenging them.

'Dad, don't run it over.'

'I'm not going to run it over,' his father said. 'You'll see all kinds of wildlife at Erringby, I dare say.' The hare ducked into a hedgerow and reappeared a moment later, bounding across a field.

'I need my bird spotter book,' said Christopher. 'Did you pack it?'

'Sorry, son,' said his father. 'We'll pack it tomorrow.' Christopher looked at him.

'Am I going to Erringby every day, then?'

'Well...' said his father. He had said, as he rushed round the house – he didn't know where any of Christopher's things were, which was funny – that this was a 'stopgap measure'. When Christopher asked, his father said that it meant Uncle Col and Auntie Marianne would be looking after him today. If 'Well...' meant that he would be going to Erringby every day, Christopher didn't mind. His mother was in hospital and his father had said that he didn't know when she would be coming home.

The car pulled into the gateway to the Hall. Christopher jumped out to open the gate, waited for his father to drive through, then closed it again and got back into the car. They bounced and lurched along the driveway. To one side of them cows grazed in a paddock. At the top of the field the driveway curved off to the right. Bob drove along the front of the house and pulled up near the front door.

They got out of the car and his father rang the doorbell. There was the sound of dogs barking from inside.

'Come on, Marianne,' he muttered, Christopher's sports bag dangling from his hand. He looked at his watch. 'Oh Christ. Look, they're in, just...' With one hand he smoothed his son's uncombed hair, an action as fruitless as it was unfamiliar. 'They'll come to the door. Tell Auntie Marianne that I'll phone her when I'm leaving work. Remember not to be a nuisance and... just be good, will you?' He plonked down the bag, got back into the Morris Ital and drove off at speed, his hand waving over his head in farewell.

Christopher watched the car disappear. Still no one came. He wondered about ringing the doorbell again. The bell was nothing like the one at Flatley Close. It was set right in the middle of one of the doors for one thing – there were two doors, side by side, that was another – and you pushed a big cream button that, unnecessarily in Christopher's opinion, had PRESS written on it in black letters. A cat appeared and wrapped itself round his legs.

He pressed the button. The bell was loud and rackety and he pictured chandeliers quaking. The doorbell at home played chimes like Big Ben on the radio. The dogs set up another volley of barking.

He was about to give up and go and explore the outbuildings when he heard Uncle Col shouting at the dogs.

'All right. Shut up, you. Jesus Christ.'

Uncle Col opened the door. One of the dogs – Christopher hadn't seen it before but he recognised it as a springer spaniel – barged past him and made a dash for the paddock. Col was holding the collar of the other, an enormous Bernese mountain dog. The cat slipped inside.

'Christopher,' said Col. 'What the f— What are you doing here?' He craned his neck, as if Christopher's father might be hiding round the corner.

'Hello, Uncle Col,' said Christopher. 'Dad had to go. He's late for work.'

His uncle stared at him. His hair was even messier than Christopher's and he was unshaven.

'You've just got your pants on,' said Christopher, who found this funny. Col looked down at himself and laughed. He was wearing a pair of nylon briefs, rather small.

'That's because you've got me out of bed. What time is it, for the love of God?' He scratched his head vigorously, making his hair stick up even more. Christopher looked at his digital watch, a Christmas present.

'Seven eighteen... no, seven nineteen.' The dog licked his hand. Christopher stroked his head. 'Hello, Arlo.'

Auntie Marianne appeared from round the side of the house, carrying a wooden basket full of knobbly bits of branches.

'Christopher!' She didn't kiss him or ruffle his hair as other relatives might. 'We weren't expecting you so early. Where's your father?' Christopher explained about having to get to Birmingham for nine o'clock.

'Well, let us in then,' she said to Uncle Col, and pushed past him to lead the way indoors. 'And put clothes on, darling. You look half asleep.'

'Were we expecting Christopher?' Uncle Col asked as they went into the kitchen.

'You know we were,' she said. Uncle Col looked blank.

'Right,' he said. 'OK.' He gave a big yawn and stretched. He was much hairier than Christopher's father. The hair, thick and dark, ran from his chest down his stomach, tapering slightly before disappearing into his underpants.

'Have you had breakfast?' Auntie Marianne asked.

Christopher said he hadn't. 'I'm not hungry, though,' he added, keen to go exploring.

'Nonsense,' said his aunt. 'Col will make you a proper breakfast once he's dressed.'

Uncle Col went out of the kitchen. Christopher sat at the scrubbed wooden table while Auntie Marianne halved oranges and squeezed their juice into a glass.

'There. That'll keep you going for now.'

Christopher had never had freshly squeezed orange before and the tang of the juice, pulp and pips included, was a long way from the Rise & Shine his mother mixed up at weekends.

'Can I wash my hands?' he asked.

'Of course,' she said. 'Use the sink. There's soap somewhere.'

'What are those things?' he asked as he dried his hands on a tea towel, pointing at the lumps of wood she had brought in.

'Jerusalem artichokes. From the kitchen garden.' She was pouring herself a mug of strong-smelling coffee from a kind of metal jug.

'What do you do with them?'

'Well. *I* don't do anything with them. But your uncle makes them into soup.'

'What do I do?' Uncle Col had reappeared, wearing jeans and a shirt that was faded and old.

'Make soup,' explained Christopher. 'From those.' He pointed again at the artichokes.

'Oh, do I now?' Col said. 'That's very presumptuous of you.'

Auntie Marianne said, 'Well, if I asked very nicely, you might.'

'I might,' said Uncle Col, and kissed Auntie Marianne's cheek and squeezed her bottom. Christopher wasn't sure what was going on, only that it perhaps wasn't anything to do with the soup.

Col put sausages into a cast-iron dish that was the blackest thing Christopher had ever seen and put the dish in the oven, which itself looked as if it should be in a museum.

'Don't you cook sausages in a frying pan?' asked Christopher.

'Not in this house,' his uncle said.

'We saw a hare on the way,' said Christopher. 'Running down the middle of the road.'

'Did you clip it?' Uncle Col asked. 'We could have had it for dinner. Jugged, with a nice Cabernet. And lots of its own blood, of course.'

'Col,' said Marianne.

'That sounds yukky,' said Christopher happily.

'Do you know where the chickens live?' his aunt asked him.

Christopher did know. He had seen the chickens on a visit. Usually Uncle Col came to see them at home without bringing

Auntie Marianne, but this time they had gone to Erringby for Sunday lunch. Uncle Col had roasted a rack of lamb, which came out looking like a wigwam made of cutlets. Christopher wasn't sure about the lamb, which was much pinker than they ate at home, but his father had been enthusiastic.

'Do you cook, Marianne?' He had spoken with his mouth half full, and Christopher's mother had admonished him.

'Oh, I could burn water,' Auntie Marianne had said, and they all laughed, but on the drive home Christopher's mother said, 'Poor Col. He does everything round that place. I don't care what she says about antiques, the house is filthy. You'd think the least she could do would be to rustle up lunch occasionally,' and his father had said, 'Well, I dare say she makes up for it in other ways,' and his mother had admonished again, this time laughing, and Christopher had said, 'I do know you're talking about S.E.X.,' and his mother had stopped laughing and called him precocious, and then said, 'Anyway, that's that for the time being.' Christopher had been sad, because he loved going to Erringby, and he also knew that Auntie Marianne did a lot around the house and grounds, was always working, in fact – her hands, even at the dinner table, were lined with dirt – but he knew better than to bring it up. His mother disliked Auntie Marianne, though he didn't know why; the dirty hands were just the start of it.

'I do know where the chickens live,' Christopher said now.

'Do you want to see if there are any eggs?' said Auntie Marianne.

The hens lived in a rickety shed at the back of the house. They had been let out for the day and were wandering around, pecking at the ground. They were the shape of tea cosies, like hens in a picture book. The cockerel strutted up to Christopher, glaring.

'Boo,' said Christopher. 'Go away.' He stuck his tongue out at the cockerel and kept going. He found five eggs, still warm, and put them in the wire basket he'd been given.

'Nice one, girls,' Uncle Col said. Christopher sat and watched him make the bacon and eggs.

'Where's Auntie Marianne gone?'

'Oh, she'll be off doing something. And listen, kid, it's Col and Marianne while you're here, OK? You can skip the Uncle and Auntie bit.'

'OK.' Christopher grinned at him. His mother wouldn't approve of this. She was very firm on the right way to speak to grown-ups.

Col asked him how his mum was doing. Christopher said she was poorly, which was the word his father used. And another remembered phrase. 'She had complications after the operation.'

'I'll swing by again for a visit,' Col said. 'But not today. Expecting a big delivery later.'

'What delivery?' Christopher's uncle was serving up eggs, bacon, sausages and mushrooms on a white plate with blue flowers on it. The plate was old and chipped – his mother would have binned it years ago. Col ate his own breakfast off another old plate that didn't match.

'Catering equipment,' he said. 'We're opening a cookery school. Didn't your mum tell you?'

'She says she can't keep up with your schemes,' Christopher said and Col smirked, as if it were a compliment.

When breakfast was finished Col showed Christopher one of the downstairs rooms – it had been a scullery, he said – Christopher wasn't sure what that was, but didn't ask – freshly painted and kitted out with several electric cookers and two new sinks, not plumbed in.

'Are you going to teach them cooking?' Christopher asked.

'Well, I could. But I'll probably just do the odd masterclass. We'll hire a professional tutor. I've got contacts. Anyway, listen. What music do you like?'

Christopher thought about the cassettes in his bedroom at home.

'Madness,' he said. 'Stuff like that.'

'Who?' said Marianne. She had joined them in the classroom.

'Marianne's unaware of any cultural event post the Beatles splitting up,' said Col. 'Aren't you, my darling?'

He grabbed Marianne round the waist and kissed her full on the mouth. Christopher looked away, embarrassed. The kiss went on for a long time.

*

Bob dropped Christopher off every morning at a quarter past seven. Marianne would be up but could be anywhere so she left the back door open and told him to help himself in the kitchen. She showed him how to slice the oranges in two and squeeze them for juice. Radio 3 would be playing. Col would appear sometime after eight o'clock, tousled and bleary, switch the transistor to Radio 1, and cook breakfast. By mid morning the radio would have been turned back to Radio 3. Christopher learned how to retune it to Radio 1, and Marianne would laugh and accuse him of treachery, of siding with his uncle against her.

There were lists of what Marianne needed doing pinned up in the kitchen. Christopher quite liked it if there was something he could help with – depending on what it was – but if there wasn't he spent the days exploring. He was familiar with the house from visiting with his parents but now he was free to wander as he pleased. Erringby Hall was huge. The ground floor alone had two sitting rooms, a library, a dining room and the big hall where Col and Marianne had had their wedding reception. Off the hall was an enormous room that had been for billiards but now didn't seem to be used for anything. There were two staircases, the main one that had seemed so wide when he was little and was still imposing, and a more secret set of stairs near the kitchen. There was a lift – Col told him it was called a dumb waiter – that went up to a storeroom on the first floor. He'd wanted to ride in the lift when he'd been little and his mother hadn't let him, and he was disappointed now to find that he was too big to fit inside. In the kitchen was a set of bells you could ring from the other rooms, but most of them didn't work. Beyond the kitchen was a whole set of rooms that had been workrooms in the olden days when there had been servants.

On the first floor Christopher counted twelve bedrooms and four bathrooms. Most of the bedrooms were full of old things, furniture and boxes and trunks of clothes. Marianne's Uncles – they weren't actual uncles but cousins once removed, she explained, then explained what that meant – had left loads of clothes when they died. Some were still in their original wrapping. They must have had a hundred pairs of shoes between them. There were tea chests full of magazines, some from the 1800s. In a bedroom that had been the Uncles' nursery were some of their old toys: painted soldiers, a box of blow football. On the second floor were more bedrooms and bathrooms. There was a loft you reached via a special ladder. Col told him to be careful up there as the floorboards weren't safe.

There was an enormous garden and woods to explore. There were outbuildings full of rusting machinery and ancient jerry cans of petrol. Christopher slipped off an old tractor while scrambling onto its seat and cut himself on a rusty shard of metal. Marianne bathed the cut and put Savlon on it and a fabric plaster that smelled nicer than the plastic ones at home. She threw away his ripped and bloody shirt and gave him an old T-shirt of Col's to wear. His father did not notice the T-shirt, nor the plaster on his arm.

The house was so big that Christopher couldn't always hear them calling him. Marianne would ring a big bell, like a school bell, if she wanted him or Col. Col grumbled about the bell and sometimes ignored it and got Christopher to ignore it too, which was funny.

He had thought, after Col's huge breakfasts, that he wouldn't want any lunch, but by midday he was always hungry again. Lunch was usually bread and cheese, not the coloured cheddar they had at home but stuff Col bought from a local farm shop. 'Did you know there used to be a dairy at Erringby, Christopher?' he said, and Marianne had said, 'Don't you dare.' The bread, baked by Col, was brown with bits in it.

'I didn't think I liked brown bread,' Christopher admitted. 'The stuff Mum buys tastes like an old sponge.'

'Now, now,' said Col.

One morning, after being dared to by his uncle, Christopher had some of the coffee from the metal jug. Col topped it up with lots of milk and a bit of sugar, and Christopher found he loved it.

On Easter Monday Bob and Christopher arrived with bad news. Janet was not doing well at all. She'd been moved to another ward – the psych ward – and Christopher was not allowed to visit. His father said she was on so much medication it didn't make any difference, and to make things worse, the Birmingham factory was struggling; he was having to put in long days, and what with that, plus the hospital visits... Col told Bob that it was no problem having Christopher to stay for the rest of the holidays.

They put him in Room Seven. He had helped Col screw brass numbers onto the bedroom doors one afternoon. The cookery school was going to be residential, which meant that people would stay at Erringby while they learned to cook. Room Seven had been where Marianne's Uncles had slept when they were little boys. The wallpaper was very old with patches that had been peeled away. Christopher, digging at it with his own nail, wondered if the Uncles had done this when they were bored. In the wardrobe the shelves were labelled – *Hats, Pyjamas, Shirts*. The few clothes his father had packed for him looked lost in there. And the bedroom had its own bathroom, which Marianne said was just for him. It seemed unbelievably grown up to have what amounted to a suite of rooms – there was an adjoining door from the bedroom to Room Eight, the old nursery.

On the first night it took him a long time to get to sleep. At home the only sounds as he lay in bed were the television, then the footsteps of his mother and father coming to bed. Sometimes a car turning round in the Close. Erringby Hall had a life of its own – creaks and groans, banging pipes, something loose outside his window that rattled in the wind. And beyond that, the hooting of owls and the yowling of cats and the unsettling shriek of some other creature. Foxes, most like, Marianne said the next morning. It took a bit of getting used to.

At lunch one day Col asked him if he wanted to come with him to Ledbury to sell some antiques.

'Marianne's finally letting go of some of the relics,' he said. 'I'm going to see if I can't flog a few bits to this chap I know.'

'I still don't see why James can't come here and look at the things *in situ*,' said Marianne. 'And then if he wants them, he can take them. On his own time and expense.'

'Oh, blah blah,' said Col. 'It's loads easier if we go there. You up for it, Christopher?'

Christopher was, and after lunch helped his uncle lug the items down two flights of stairs and strap them into the back of the battered Ford van.

On the drive over Col talked about Christopher's mum. He had been to see her in the hospital the day before. The ban against Christopher visiting remained in force, which he was secretly and shamefully relieved about.

'When she comes home,' Col said, 'you must be very kind to her.'

'What do you mean?'

'You know people go to hospital because they've got something wrong with their body?' Christopher nodded. 'Your mum's got something wrong with her mind.'

'I do know what a psychiatric ward is,' said Christopher. 'I'm not a little kid.'

'I know you're not,' said Col. 'And look… it's normal for families to have arguments. But you need to be very grown up and patient with her when she comes home.' He looked at his nephew. He was being deadly serious for once.

Rows at Flatley Close were nearly always between Christopher and his mother; he and his father hardly ever argued and his father usually went along with whatever his mother said. And in the run-up to the holidays Christopher and his mother had had some screaming fights. It had seemed that whatever Christopher said or did was wrong. His dad must have told Col about the fights. He felt annoyed with him for that.

He didn't know what to say in response to Col now. He didn't like thinking about his mother in the hospital. When his father telephoned in the evenings he didn't ask about her and his father told him very little. It had been fun, the past few days, to pretend he lived at Erringby Hall all the time. He felt relieved that it was the school holidays and no one could tease him about his mum being in the loony bin. He hoped no one at school would find out. He didn't want to think about the holidays ending and having to go home.

'Your mum's not great,' said Col. 'They've got her doped up to the eyeballs, poor old girl. And not even good drugs, either.' He laughed at this. Christopher didn't join in. 'This whole thing has really shaken her up.'

'What whole thing?' Christopher didn't understand. All he knew was what his father had said, that it was a big operation, having your womb taken out.

'Well…' Col shot another look at him. 'She'd never quite given up hope.' Christopher was perplexed, so his uncle went on, 'She wanted a baby of her own, Christopher.'

'Oh.' This prospect had never occurred to him. He'd always assumed, indeed his father often joked about it, that he was more than enough for his parents. Sometimes his mother got upset when his father laughed about Christopher being several kids' worth of bother, and would go out of the room and up to their bedroom, and once or twice his father had gone up after her. And now, the idea that he might have had a brother or a sister had been presented to him only after all possibility had gone.

'Not being able to have kids... it's the worst thing, you know,' said Col.

'Oh.'

Was that why his mother was in the bin? Did that happen when you couldn't have kids?

'They were so made up when you came along. You saved... you made them very happy, Christopher.'

'Did I?' he said. 'Sometimes I just seem to make them cross.'

'Only because they love you so much,' Col said, bafflingly. 'Marianne and me – we're still trying for a baby.'

Christopher didn't know what to do with this information. He hoped his uncle wouldn't see him going very red. Col switched the van's radio on. 'Dance Yourself Dizzy' was playing.

'I hate this fucking song,' said Col.

'Me too,' said Christopher. He didn't dare ask if not being able to have a baby meant that Marianne would get ill in the head as well. The song ended and UB40 came on.

'Uncle Col,' said Christopher. 'Col, I mean.' They were dawdling along the A449. Something ahead was holding them up. Col was craning his head out of the window to see.

'Yeah?'

'What happened to my mother? My real one.'

'She died,' said Col. 'When you were just a nipper. Your dad, too. Road accident.'

'Was I in the car with them?'

'No, you weren't.'

'Where was I?'

'I don't know, Christopher.'

'Swear to God, is that what really happened?'

'Swear to God.'

'You'd tell me?'

'I'd tell you,' said Col. 'Don't you trust me, squirt?'

'Don't call me that!' Christopher punched Col on the arm and the van swerved.

'Hey,' said Col. 'If I have a prang and this furniture gets smashed up, you'll be the one to square it with your aunt. And she's not to be trifled with, let me tell you.'

The shop was on the high street. Col parked up outside.

'Shop!' he yelled as they walked in. The place was crammed with antiques and smelled of furniture polish and flowers. Christopher was wary of knocking something over and getting told off. A man appeared from a room off the main showroom.

'Col, you old bastard.' He was older than Col, with a red, angry-looking face, and he wore a green tweed jacket with a yellow waistcoat. The men did something between a handshake and a hug, clapping each other on the back.

'Who's this, then?'

'My nephew, Christopher. Christopher, this is James.'

James shook him by the hand.

'Pleasure to meet you, sir,' he said.

'Hello,' said Christopher uncertainly.

'Shall we unload?' Col asked. 'I'm parked on a double yellow.'

'Don't worry about that,' said James. 'The cunts never bother me.'

Christopher looked at his uncle in shock. He knew the word but had never uttered it, even secretly. *Fuck* he was used to, he heard it a lot at school of course; he was careful never to say the word at home and his uncle's liberal use of it was eye-opening, but *cunt*, he knew, was in a different league. Col didn't seem bothered, however. They went outside and brought the stuff in from the van. Christopher helped carry the two mahogany dining chairs. There was also a pair of carved bedside cabinets and a small writing desk, which James called a bonheur du jour. It meant 'daytime delight', he told Christopher.

'French, this,' he said. 'See, it has a decorated back, because it would have been moved around the room. It wasn't designed to sit against a wall. And the drawer would've been used for toiletries rather than writing things.'

Col nodded, as if this were all obvious.

'Nice piece,' James went on. 'Surprised she doesn't want to keep it.'

'Just clearing some space,' said Col. 'We've got this cookery school opening in the summer.'

'Oh yeah.'

'So – we said two-fifty, right?' said Col. James opened the cash register and counted out a handful of notes and gave them to him. Col folded them up and stuck them in the back pocket of his jeans.

'Let's move this stuff into the back,' said James. The back room of the shop was a jumble of items not yet priced up.

'Nice doing business with you,' said Col.

'Always,' said James. 'Since you're here, though, how about a snifter?'

'Don't mind if I do,' said Col. James fished out a bottle of brandy and three glasses from a cabinet. He made a gesture towards Christopher with the bottle, Col shook his head and James went off and returned with a glass of rather weak squash.

The men sat down on a sofa with a high back and carved wooden legs. Christopher sat on a battered leather armchair that sank beneath him.

'So,' said James. 'How's the old bonheur du nuit?' Col laughed. 'Hard work, I imagine.'

'Oh yeah,' said Col.

'But worth it?'

'Oh yeah.' The men laughed and clinked their glasses.

'You're a lucky bastard,' said James, and winked at Christopher.

'Are you still seeing that woman?' Col asked.

'Nah. The bitch went back to her ex, after stiffing me for two grand.' Col said he was sorry to hear that. 'Fucking losers,' said James.

'Better off without them,' said Col.

'You got that right.' James tipped his glass again at Col. He looked at Christopher, who was fidgeting on the armchair. 'You're sure he doesn't…?'

'Christopher, why don't you go over the road and get yourself something?' Col pulled out a five-pound note and handed it to him.

He went to the newsagents across the road and bought a copy of 2000 AD comic, a can of Coke and a Double Decker. At the cash desk his attention was caught by a sketchbook on display. On impulse he bought the sketchbook and some HB pencils, intending to give Col the money for these extra items, but Col, who was on his second glass of brandy, told him not to bother and, moreover, to keep the change.

The men looked set in for the afternoon. Christopher flicked through the comic but wasn't in the mood for it. He picked up the sketchbook and looked for something to draw. He settled on a four-masted barque in a bottle on a wooden stand. Once the shop bell went and James made a face before leaving the room. He came back ten minutes later. 'Fucking time-waster,' he said, and poured himself and Col another brandy.

It was five o'clock before Col stood up unsteadily and said they had better be going.

'Hey, that's pretty good,' said James, looking at Christopher's drawing.

'Yeah, he's got a lot of talent in that direction,' said Col.

'Doesn't take after you, then,' said James.

'Fuck off,' said Col.

'I'm adopted,' said Christopher.

Col drove back very fast. He turned up the volume on the radio. 'Call Me' by Blondie was playing. Col sang along, tapping his hands on the steering wheel.

'What do you think of Debbie Harry?' he shouted over the music.

'She's nice.'

'Does she remind you of Marianne?'

'Marianne's nicer,' said Christopher. Col laughed. The van wavered and lurched. He kept crossing over the central line.

'We've had fun, right?' he shouted at Christopher. The van swerved dangerously and Col laughed again, and Christopher had to agree; this journey back to Erringby, bouncing along the country lanes in the late-afternoon sunshine, songs playing loud on the radio, in fact the whole of these school holidays, felt like the most fun he had ever had. Perhaps his mum would never get better and he would have to live at Erringby with Marianne and Col all the time. No, that was a horrible thing to think.

'Two hundred,' said Col, handing the money to Marianne. Christopher opened his mouth to correct him but Col winked at him and he fell silent.

'I suppose you only went all the way to Ledbury so you could drink with him.' Marianne looked at the money as if it were toxic. She put the cash in an envelope that was already full of notes and shut it away in a drawer.

'Oh, don't start,' said Col. 'Where's dinner?'

'In your imagination.'

'Fucking great.'

Dinner – Marianne called it supper – was a let-down after the fun of the afternoon. She heated up some baked beans and toasted slices of the homemade bread on top of the stove. They didn't have a toaster. Col had disappeared, so they ate on their own. After dinner she said Christopher could choose a video to watch, which was a novelty – she and Col had the first video cassette recorder Christopher had seen. He sat in the gun room on his own and watched *Dawn of the Dead*, which Col had taped off the television – a film that he most definitely would not have been allowed to watch at home, even if they had anything to watch it on. The film was spoiled, though, by the sound of Col and Marianne arguing upstairs. Christopher shut the door against the noise. Marianne was screaming. Something about the bonheur du jour. Christopher turned up the volume on the TV.

When the film ended it was ten o'clock. Usually Marianne came and told him it was time for bed but tonight there was no sign of her. He went into the kitchen for a glass of water. Col was sitting at the table with a glass of wine, the open bottle next to it. On his cheek was a scratch, beads of blood starting along its length. He glared at Christopher.

'What do you want?'

Christopher froze.

'Just a glass of water.'

'Well, take it and fuck off.'

Christopher grabbed a tumbler from the cupboard and ran upstairs. He filled the glass from the washbasin in his bathroom. He couldn't get to sleep, so he switched the light back on and read 2000 AD until he fell asleep, exhausted, at just after midnight.

In the morning there was no sign of Col. Marianne made toast and the two of them ate it with jam that tasted of real strawberries. After breakfast Mrs Lonsdale, who was Marianne's mother, came to the house. She looked strict and she had a posh accent, like a lady in an old film. When she asked after Christopher's mother he didn't like to say that he hadn't seen her in over a week. After Mrs Lonsdale had left, taking with her some seedlings from the greenhouse, Christopher asked Marianne where Uncle Col was.

'Oh, he's getting over yesterday,' she said dismissively. 'I shouldn't bother him.' Christopher had no intention of bothering him, still less of mentioning the argument, nor how Col had been to him in the kitchen afterwards, but it was strange when he had still not appeared by lunchtime.

After they had finished eating the usual bread and cheese Marianne said she was going to spend the afternoon sorting through some old clothes.

'Can I help?' asked Christopher, and was disappointed when she said no. It would have been fun going through the Uncles' clothes with her.

Instead he got his sketchbook from his room. He tried drawing one of the dogs but it wouldn't keep still for long enough, so he went round the house in search of inspiration. On the first-floor landing there was a large, ornate cupboard – an armoire, Marianne had told him it was called – on which stood a pair of vases, ruby-coloured cut glass with extravagant handles made from an alloy that was called ormolu. He thought they would be interesting to draw and went to pick one of them up for a closer inspection. The handle was loose and came away in his hand. Christopher tried to grab the vase and missed and it crashed to the floor and broke into several pieces. He stared at it, appalled.

'What have you done now?' came Marianne's voice, and there she was on the landing. Christopher stood in shock, still holding the vase's handle.

'I'm really sorry.' His voice cracked. When he broke things at home and his mother shouted it didn't bother him, but now to his consternation and fury there were tears pricking his eyelids.

'Oh,' said Marianne. She looked down at the pieces.

'Can... can it be mended?' asked Christopher. He desperately didn't want her to see him crying. Nor to send him away and tell his father he couldn't visit again.

'No, not really,' said Marianne. To his amazement she didn't seem angry with him.

'I'm sorry,' he said again. 'Is it... was it very valuable?'

'Oh, probably,' she said. 'But it's only a thing.' She put her arm round him and squeezed him. Christopher had thought he didn't like anyone hugging him, would squirm away from the embrace of other relatives, but this was different. Marianne's head rested against his. He found he didn't want the hug to stop. Her body was soft and warm. She kissed the top of his head and he felt the tears well up again.

'Is that a sketch pad?' she asked. He nodded mutely, blinking against the tears. Gently, she took it from him. She glanced at the failed picture of the springer spaniel, then flicked back to the drawing of the ship in the bottle.

'Christopher, that's really very good.' She was looking at him. 'Did you do this in James's shop?' He nodded. 'Well, at least something good came out of yesterday.' Then, as if she had just thought of something, she said, 'Come with me.'

She led the way down the big staircase, almost at a run. They went into the library, Marianne still holding the sketchbook. 'May I?' she asked.

'Yes,' said Christopher, with no idea what she was asking for. Carefully, she tore the drawing of the ship from the sketchbook, took down a framed photograph of Mrs Lonsdale in an evening gown, removed the photo and replaced it with his drawing.

'There.' She hung the frame back on the wall, where it sat next to a painting of some big poppies. 'Much better. And now...' – she turned to Christopher – '*I* need to sort clothes and *you* need to carry on drawing.'

In one of the top-floor bedrooms – it didn't have a number – there was a miscellany of items in storage. Christopher could just squeeze through the doorway. Among the jumble he found a tailor's dummy that looked very old. It was made from canvas and wood and was shaped like a woman, but with an improbable figure. Surely no woman had a waist that small? Marianne certainly didn't. The dummy had a hooped skirt of wooden struts, as if it were wearing a farthingale. Christopher rooted in a steamer trunk for something for it to wear. He found a silk smoking jacket and a top hat and arranged them on the dummy. It looked completely absurd. He removed the top hat and put it on his own head. After more rummaging he found a fox fur, complete with head, tail and paws, which he draped round the dummy's headless neck. The dummy still looked ridiculous, and yet great. Christopher perched himself on the trunk and started drawing. In the next-door room he could hear Marianne humming.

He heard footsteps and the creak of floorboards and looked up from his sketchbook but the person went into the room next door. Christopher went on drawing. Sunlight was spilling through the room's grubby windows. He liked the way the dust motes danced in it like atoms, the way the sun showed up all the colours in the fox fur. The fox stared dolefully at him from its one glass eye. The room smelled of warmth and dust and a smell he was able to identify as mothballs.

There was murmuring coming from next door. Christopher made out Col's voice, sounding as if he wanted something very much, then Marianne's, gasping. Col's voice grew louder and more insistent.

'Yeah,' he was saying. 'Yeah, like that. Oh Christ, you are so fucking beautiful.' Marianne's voice was more of a sob. 'Tell me what you want... tell me,' Christopher heard Col say, and then, 'Oh Jesus!' Marianne made a funny kind of moan.

Christopher, still wearing the top hat, felt the blood drain from his face and through his body. His penis stiffened against his pants. He put his hand over his crotch but didn't dare move it. He didn't dare move at all, but waited for it to finish. After what seemed like an age he heard the door open and the creak of the floorboard, and a set of footsteps moved along the corridor.

He realised he had been holding his breath. The air came out of him in a huge sigh. He had to stay put, in case whoever was still in the room next door realised he was there and had overheard. To his intense relief the door opened and more footsteps made their way briskly towards the main staircase.

He was too shaken to carry on drawing. The picture would have to be finished some other day. He left the room and made his way to the back staircase, avoiding the creaking floorboard.

In the kitchen he found Col, chopping onions.

'All right, kid?' His uncle grinned at him. He had on his usual jeans and the same shirt as yesterday and his feet were bare. 'I thought I'd make curry tonight. Fancy giving me a hand?' Christopher took the knife he was handed and chopped garlic and ginger root. He felt light-headed, scarcely pinned to the floor, as if he might float out of the kitchen and out of the house. He barely heard his uncle talking about his plans for the cookery school. Something about adverts in *The Lady* magazine. How could Col be so calm, so normal, after what had just happened?

'We'll make it sound like we've been going a while, you know?' His uncle winked at him. 'Established.'

After they had cleared away the dinner things Col suggested they go and sit in the drawing room for a change. Christopher didn't really like this room, which was chilly and formal and nowhere near as cosy as the gun room.

'Marianne, why don't you play for us?' said Col.

So Marianne played the piano and sang; old songs, Christopher didn't recognise any of them, but she had a lovely voice. Col couldn't take his eyes off her. He was smiling.

'Play... you know.' And Marianne played and sang a song about how the woman was going to go on loving the man come rain or come shine, and to Christopher it seemed a bit mournful, but Marianne smiled at Col as she sang and he kept on looking at her and smiling at her as if his heart would burst. Christopher looked at Col's face. The scratch had scabbed over. And was his uncle crying?

5

April 1986

The car, a fin-tailed Chevrolet, is travelling at night along a desolate
highway through a desert basin, somewhere like Nevada. The man,
or the woman, is driving; the other, the woman or the man, dozing
in the passenger seat. An FM radio station plays soft-rock hits.
They are on their way to collect him before journeying on to San
Francisco. Or Mexico. Lulled by the unstinting monotony of the
landscape the woman, or the man, falls asleep at the wheel. The car
careens off the highway and into a gulley, where it lands on its roof.
There will have been a screech of car tyres and the sickening noise
of the crash, but the only sound now is the laconic voice of the DJ
coming from the radio that somehow has survived the impact.

Or: their sports car malfunctions at a critical moment as they
hurtle round a hairpin bend. They have been driving too fast of
course, one goading the other on with delighted whoops. Would
there be, for a freeze-frame millisecond, a rush of pure exhilaration,
a final moment of shared elation as the car spins out of control
and tumbles down the precipitous slope towards the coast of the
French Riviera?

Christopher liked the Americana of the first scenario, the Grace
Kelly-esque glamour of the second, but neither was very probable.
His adoption certificate gave London as his place of birth. His
parents are on a motorway, the M1, part of a huge pile-up in the
hulking English fog, sandwiched between two vehicles, their car, a
Triumph Stag or an E-Type, concertinaed at both ends, his father
prostrate on the wheel, motionless, blood dripping from his head

onto the floor of the car, his mother barely conscious, heart and liver crushed against broken ribs, life seeping from her, her last thoughts of what would become of her little boy, himself...

No. He didn't want her to suffer. Better that she die instantly, even if it meant she did not die thinking of him.

Christopher lay on his single bed at Flatley Close. A pad of paper next to him held half a page on the condition of Prussia and Piedmont in 1848. He was supposed to be revising. Instead, and though it made his heart feel as if it were being wrung out, he couldn't stop killing his already-dead parents, over and over again. Had they died instantly, or had one or both survived long enough to be scooped into an ambulance, transported to a hospital and wired up to machines that hummed and beeped, only to succumb to their terrible injuries a short time later? Did either know that the other had died? Had a relative been notified, sat with his father, or with his mother, held their hand as the life support machine was switched off and the beeping flatlined? *Were* there relatives? Why had they not taken him in?

And how had his parents' genetic material distributed itself? Whose eyes did he have? In rest, his left eyebrow was at a slight tilt – Marianne had remarked on it – giving him a quizzical air – where had that come from? What about his mannerisms, not copied from Bob or Janet – his fastidiousness about keeping his hands clean, his tendency to sneeze three times in a row, his habit, when concentrating, of fondling his earlobe?

He had satisfied himself, over the course of several rows, that his adoptive parents really did not have any more information; the story he had overheard at Col and Marianne's wedding was in essence all they knew. That the mother-and-baby home in Lambeth that arranged his adoption and from where he had been collected at the age of two years and seven months had provided no further information regarding his circumstances.

'That's just how things were done then,' Bob had said. 'They probably didn't know any more themselves,' and Christopher believed him.

And the blank canvas meant that he could give his imagination full rein. His real parents had been young, attractive and glamorous, their social circle cultured and bohemian. There would have been trips to art galleries, museums, theatres; his schooling liberal and progressive, his artistic side nurtured and encouraged. What a brutal twist of fate, for his parents' lives to have been ended so suddenly and so violently, for him to have been uprooted and exiled to this dull city. He had been reading Thackeray's *The Rose and the Ring*. 'My poor child,' said the Fairy Blackstick, 'the best thing I can send you is a little misfortune.' She must have been at his christening, too.

In the next room Christopher's adoptive mother slept, or rather lay in the coma-like state brought on by the psychiatric drugs to make her sleep. There were other drugs that made her awake in the daytime. This was the worst episode for some time, as bad, almost, as the Easter holiday of the hysterectomy. Her acceptance of her mental ill health, the way she seemed almost to welcome it, was immensely frustrating to Christopher. She defined herself as an ill person, like Mrs Bennet with her nerves in *Pride and Prejudice* but without being funny. It was infuriating, having a mother who could not be relied upon to fulfil even the most unambitious of family plans. It was shaming not to be able to invite friends to the house.

Things might go on as normal for months and then the signs would appear. Christopher felt he was better at spotting the almost imperceptible changes in his mother's behaviour than his father, whom he suspected of being in denial, of not wanting to accept that his wife was becoming ill again, of making excuses, allowances, right up until the point at which it became impossible to ignore.

Her housekeeping, rigorous enough when she was well, would ratchet up to aseptic standards. Nothing could be clean enough. She would mop the floor obsessively, wash curtains, stand on chairs to run the hoover attachment over the ceiling. Stockpiles of random items, tins of spaghetti and jars of Marmite, would appear in the cupboards, as if she feared imminent nuclear apocalypse. Until one afternoon Christopher would come home from school to find the situation had, seemingly in the course of that day, flipped onto its head – his mother on the sofa where she had remained all day, still in her pyjamas, breakfast things unwashed in the sink. Only then would his father make an appointment with Dr Malik and book an inconvenient day off work to take her.

Downstairs Uncle Col was talking to his father. They were drinking beer, Col probably drinking three cans for every one of Bob's. He would have been well over the limit even before the drive over. There had been another row at Erringby Hall and Col would end up spending the night.

Col's turning up unannounced was a variant on the marital brawling and had happened a few times. If Christopher's mother were around she would sympathise and pour balm on Col's wounds, metaphorically speaking – though she was careful not to be too critical of Marianne, even while Col railed against her – but tonight she had taken to her bed prior to her brother's unscheduled arrival.

Christopher had witnessed several of Col and Marianne's rows at first hand. It was mind-blowing how they would ignite, seemingly from nothing, burn in a white, candescent heat – the violence! the insults! – then exhaust themselves. He had to admit he found the fights exciting. His aunt and uncle were the gold standard for what romantic love should be, the rows needed for it to flourish in the way that fires were needed for forest regrowth. That was what he wanted, Christopher had decided, for a woman one day to love him as Marianne loved Col. How totally unlike the affection between his parents, in normal times, which was anodyne. He had recently discovered the word. He was pleased with it.

He heard his father coming up to bed, heard him use the bathroom then creep into the master bedroom for fear of disturbing his mother, though the drugs she had swallowed several hours previously meant that this fear was unfounded. His father had taken to sleeping in the spare bedroom, but tonight he couldn't because of Col.

Half an hour later there was the unsteady tread of footsteps on the stairs as Col came up to bed. On the landing outside Christopher's bedroom he stumbled heavily.

'Shit,' he muttered, and went into the spare bedroom and closed the door.

The next morning was a Saturday. Christopher came down to find his father and his uncle drinking mugs of instant coffee at the kitchen table. His mother was not up, but this was to be expected.

'Hey Christopher,' said Col. His clothes were rumpled from being slept in, his hair was uncombed and he hadn't shaved and the smell of stale booze emanated from him.

'Hey,' said Christopher.

'Your aunt threw me out again.' Col was grinning.

'I know,' said Christopher. 'I let you in, remember?'

'So you did,' said Col, who probably didn't remember.

'You can't go on like this, Col,' Bob said. Col shrugged, in a way that suggested that going on like this was exactly what he intended doing.

They probably do it deliberately, just so they can have make-up sex. Christopher filled the kettle for his own coffee. He had never again overheard them but understood, as he grew older, that it would have happened; after a row the atmosphere would thrum with unarticulated lust. He peered into the bread bin.

'Dad, this bread is mouldy.'

'Oh hell,' said Bob. 'Is there something else you could have for breakfast?'

'I wanted toast,' said Christopher.

'You poor mite,' said Col, and winked at him. Christopher decided not to be aggrieved, and laughed.

'How's school?' Col went on.

'It's OK.' In fact school had been enjoyable this year; he had found a group of kindred spirits, a cabal whose penchant for the arts set them apart from the hearty rugger-bugger ethos that dominated his sixth-form college.

'He needs to pull his finger out, though,' his father said. 'If he's going to get the grades for university.' Christopher rolled his eyes.

'Oh, he'll be all right,' said Col. 'I always winged it at school.'

'Don't let Janet hear you say that,' said Bob.

Christopher helped himself to cornflakes and poured on milk.

'Have you heard, Christopher?' Bob sounded excited. 'Uncle Col's film has got the go-ahead.' Christopher looked up from his cereal.

'Really?'

Col was trying not to look smug.

'Not *my* film, exactly. But I am an executive producer.'

'They're shooting it at Erringby!' Bob was grinning at Christopher.

'Wow.' Christopher, in spite of his best efforts, was impressed. 'The film scouts liked Erringby, then?'

'*Ideal location*,' Col said. 'And they're doing loads of repairs as well to get it ready.'

'Now that is good news,' Bob said. 'All of the repairs?'

'Well. A lot of it. I still need to crack on. Tiling the first-floor bathroom this weekend.'

'My bathroom?' asked Christopher.

'No, one of the others. D'you fancy giving me a hand?'

'Yes – take Christopher with you,' said Bob, and then, as if he realised he had sounded overeager, added, 'I mean – if you've got no homework, Christopher?'

'I've done it,' said Christopher, which was a lie.

'OK,' said Col. 'Do you fancy staying over?'

'Sure,' said Christopher.

'If it's no bother,' said Bob.

'Of course it's no bother,' said Col.

Christopher knew what was going on; knew why his father was keen that he spend the weekend at Erringby, knew why Col had suggested it. Christopher's mother would emerge eventually from the fug of the master bedroom, its windows shut tight – insect life was a new phobia – and come downstairs in her housecoat, hair unwashed and matted, and stare at Christopher as if she barely recognised this cuckoo in her nest, found him puzzling. Christopher's removal from the house meant that his father could focus on his wife without worrying that his son was antagonising her further by merely existing.

Col was in a good mood. He sang along to the Dave Lee Travis show on the van radio.

Christopher stared out of the window.

'Can I come and live at Erringby for a bit?'

'How would that work?' Col asked. 'How would you get to school?'

'I'd get the bus.'

'That's not very practical, is it?'

'You could drop me off in the village in the morning.' He looked at Col. Col gave him a look in reply. Christopher threw himself back in his seat and sighed.

'I know it's tough,' Col said. 'But she'll be better soon. You know how it goes.'

'And then she'll just get ill again. And again.'

Col was silent for a moment.

'I can get you a job on the film, if you like.'

'Really?'

'Course. I'm executive producer. I'll talk to them. And you can come and stay after your exams. Help me get everything ready.'

'So I'd be staying all summer, then?'

'Well... yeah.'

'Will Marianne be OK with that?'

'Course she will. She loves you. Luuuuurves you.' He made a cooing sound. Christopher rolled his eyes, but suppressed a smile.

He felt instantly cheered. The holidays were only a few weeks away. And a job working on a film! And in the meantime there was this weekend. Christopher knew, and knew that Col knew, that there was no prospect of his doing any tiling of any bathrooms, or anything else of a manual nature. Hopelessly impractical, he was ill-suited to anything on Marianne's lists, with the exception of a few gardening jobs or, and then only under Col's strict supervision, chopping vegetables for lunch or supper. Marianne often teased him about his aversion to getting his hands dirty.

He hopped out of the van to open the gate and close it behind them. The van chugged and jerked up the pockmarked drive.

'I love Erringby at this time of year,' he said. A group of cows watched from the water trough in the paddock as they drove by, their tails swishing indolently at flies. Warmed by the sun, the sandstone of the Hall gave off a roseate glow.

'I might sunbathe on the roof if this weather keeps up.' His uncle looked at him, amused.

'You do that.'

Col parked up at the back of the house. A dog came to meet them at the door.

'Arlo!' Christopher bent down and buried his face in the creature's fur, making a growling sound and shaking him.

'Careful,' said Col. 'He's an old man now.'

Arlo licked Christopher's face in spite of the roughhousing.

'Have you missed me?' Christopher asked the dog. 'I've missed you.'

'I think he has, actually,' said Col. 'No one else makes such a fuss of him.'

'Who's there?' A voice, sharp, female, came from inside the house. Christopher had forgotten that Marianne's mother had moved in. Had moved herself in, apparently, with little consultation, declaring Cormorants, Marianne's childhood home, a frightful bother.

'It's me,' his uncle called. 'I've got Christopher with me.'

Mrs Lonsdale was at the door to what had been the staff apartment.

'Hello,' said Christopher.

'So, you have returned,' she said to Col.

'Yup,' said Col.

'I've never in my life heard such a fracas,' said Mrs Lonsdale. 'That teapot was Sèvres. It was part of a set.'

'Oh well,' said Col.

'This place is like a lunatic asylum.'

'I'm used to mad people,' said Christopher. Only now did Mrs Lonsdale appear to notice him.

'Why are you here?'

Christopher laughed, taken aback.

'Janet's not well,' said Col.

'Again? What's wrong with her?'

'What indeed?' said Christopher. Mrs Lonsdale looked at him.

'Well, I hope you at least can conduct yourself with a modicum of propriety.'

'I'll try,' said Christopher.

'Where's Marianne?' asked Col.

'I'm sure I've no idea,' said Mrs Lonsdale, retreating into her apartment and closing the door. Col and Christopher looked at each other and laughed.

6

August 1986

'Uh-oh.' Andrew affected a transatlantic drawl. 'Mommy and Daddy are fighting again.' There was a yell and an object sailed past the window, landing on the ground with a thump and closely followed by another.

'You bitch,' they heard. Col must have been leaning out of the bedroom window. Christopher went over and looked out.

'Col's boots,' he reported. 'She's thrown them out of the window into a big patch of mud.'

'Uh-oh,' said Andrew again and for the benefit of Nicola, who had come into the room, 'You've just missed the defenestration of the boots.'

'Crikey.' She helped herself to coffee from the machine kept on the go – it was part of Christopher's job – from 6am right through to when shooting finished for the day, which might be after midnight.

There was shouting and banging from above. Nicola raised her eyes to the ceiling.

'Their rows are mega, aren't they?'

'This one's a doozie.' Andrew was enjoying himself.

'What do they row about?'

'Money,' said Christopher. 'Col's drinking. Those are the recurring themes.'

'And maybe Lois.' Andrew sounded a little pleased with himself.

'Lois?' said Nicola. Lois was the assistant art director, tall and willowy, a curtain of sleek dark hair falling over one shoulder, dramatic eye make-up and lips painted very red.

'Well... I'm guessing Marianne's twigged,' said Andrew.

'Col and Lois?' said Christopher.

'I saw them on the back stairs,' said Andrew. 'And the body language was very much we've-just-fucked.'

'Poor Marianne,' said Nicola. 'Mind you, Col is very sexy, don't you think?'

'So's Marianne. I'd fuck them both,' declared Andrew.

'So would I,' said Nicola. Christopher laughed and she turned to look at him. 'Christopher. That is such a very long name for such a very young man. Do you ever shorten it?'

'No, never.'

'I've got something for you.' She pulled out an eyeliner pencil. 'Hold still.' Christopher submitted to having eyeliner put on him, Nicola holding his chin in her left hand. 'There,' she said, and showed him his reflection in her hand mirror.

'What a pretty young man you are,' said Andrew.

'I'll give you a full makeover when I've got time,' said Nicola. 'You could definitely carry off more make-up, with those cheekbones.'

'Yes, please.' Christopher liked very much the attention he got from Nicola. She was about five years older than him, had a mass of red curls and always smelled nice. He wasn't sure if she *liked* him, or thought of him as an exotic pet. He hoped it was the former, then felt a stab of guilt at the thought of his girlfriend stacking shelves in Hereford, a thousand miles away. They were trying to earn money while waiting for their A-level results, but while she had the unglorious occupation of shifts at Tesco, he had hit the jackpot with his film job. His girlfriend had asked, hopefully, if there might be a job found for her on the film; there was not, but he could, he knew, have pressed harder, petitioned his uncle. He phoned her every so often and was finding the desperation of her hints – could he not get back to Hereford? surely he must have *some* evenings off from work? – problematic. Of course he loved her, he assured her. She had to understand that working on a film wasn't your standard nine-to-five. He could be called upon, theoretically, at any time. Privately, he had decided to let the relationship wither on the vine once they had gone away to university. He knew she could visit him at Erringby – in theory they might even achieve the consummation of their relationship for which, until very recently, he had been desperate – although he was sharing a tent with several other crew members and a venue would need to be found – the gazebo, he had wondered – but now he was glad he had not invited her. She was part of the old life – school, Flatley Close, Hereford – that he was shucking off like a chrysalis. She would not fit in here.

Marianne watched Col fish his boots out of the mud from her bedroom window. Increasingly, she was finding catharsis in their fighting. This morning he had taken a swing at her, as he occasionally did, and she had flown at him, fingers curled, ready to claw and scratch. He had grabbed her wrists and pushed her onto the bed and she had laughed at him scornfully.

'Come on then. Fuck me. I want you to!' And when he looked at her in disgust she had leaped up, grabbed the nearest thing of his to hand – the boots – and lobbed them through the open window.

She had mixed feelings about the film. Though Col was taking the credit it had begun with her, with a remark in a Christmas card from a friend from her drama school days who had since become a film executive. She had telephoned the friend – he was an old boyfriend, actually – and learned that he was looking for a cheap location for a film he had in pre-production. Col, hearing this, suggested Erringby Hall; the friend visited along with a location manager, declared Erringby perfect and a deal was struck. That the house and grounds could accommodate many of the crew was a bonus. Every usable bedroom had been pressed into service, the more junior crew members doubling up. Tents were erected on the lawn to house personnel further down the chain, Christopher among them. The leading actors had been put up in hotels. A catering van, seemingly staffed twenty-four hours a day, was stationed at the front of the house, since their kitchen couldn't cope with the numbers. Portaloos appeared, along with trailers and rigging lorries.

She had had no idea who Darren Fenby was, only that rumours of his being one of the leading actors had caused a buzz in the surrounding villages. His star, apparently, was in the ascendant since his role in *EastEnders*. Fortunately for this film's budget, he had appeared in the soap after he had signed the *Strassburg Pie* contract. Henry Melville she had heard of. He was also considered a bargain but for different reasons entirely: he had been *persona non grata* since a scandal involving a swimming party in Weybridge and some underage girls a dozen or so years ago. The case had never gone to court and had been kept out of the papers, the girls having been paid off by Melville's lawyers, but his fall from grace was an open secret and he was seen as too much of a liability for most British and American directors. His recent career had been cameo parts in small, European films.

She had not read *Strassburg Pie*'s script, which in any case seemed to be subject to continuous amendments, large and small – the photocopier installed by the production company was in almost constant use – but she gathered that it was set in an unspecified time period, nominally the 1930s, and was a dark comedy in which people impersonated other people and chased an elusive inheritance of some kind. A cat met a grisly end in the first reel and its ultimate fate, as Marianne understood it, was that it might or might not have ended up in the titular pie.

Erringby, apparently, was standing in for the destination where Henry Melville and Darren Fenby's characters, purporting to be uncle and nephew, had tipped up in their quest for this inheritance. A series of key scenes were being filmed in the hall and the billiard room, the setting for a New Year's Eve party that was, she gathered, very problematic to shoot. Certainly everyone seemed to be in a very bad mood about it, including – and this was funny, for what had it to do with him? – Col.

They weren't getting much in the way of a fee but the film company was making a contribution to the electricity bill and had carried out the promised repairs; the potholes in the drive, which had threatened to banjax the heavily laden trucks, had been filled and the boiler overhauled. They would also redecorate the rooms in which they were filming. And Col was convinced that further rentals of Erringby as a location for films or TV programmes or modelling shoots would be forthcoming, and – who knew? – perhaps for once his confidence was not misplaced.

The film company had commandeered the old staff apartment as their production office, meaning Susannah had had to move out. She now occupied one of the larger bedrooms on the top floor. Refusing Col's cooking or anything from the catering van, she had meals on wheels delivered every day instead and it was a surreal sight, sturdy WRVS volunteers making their way up the back stairs with their foil trays of food, squeezing past crew members a third their age.

Marianne found it strange having her home not just full but teeming again. The shooting of this part of the film, originally scheduled to last five weeks, was already a week behind, which apparently was normal. It was certainly intrusive – everywhere one went someone was jabbering into a walkie-talkie, or applying make-up to an actor, or adjusting a costume, or laying track for a camera dolly, or sticking tape on the floor as a marker for the actors – blocking, it was called. Frequently, she had to get away, taking Arlo, the dog, for long walks along the river.

There was something pleasurable, though, about seeing Erringby once more *en fête*, buzzing with activity from dawn until gone midnight, the lawn an encampment of canvas tents. *The field of the cloth of whizz*, Andrew had called it.

Col came into the bedroom with the boots and she turned from the window.

'Marianne...'

At thirty-nine he had filled out since the day they met, his bulk a little more ponderous, but he still had that hair and those eyes and he was in his element this summer, revelling in the busyness of the film, in the sense of himself being at the centre of it all, buzzy from the attention from the women and the men, many of whom were clearly beguiled by him, and yet he belonged to her still.

She went over and kissed him. He pulled back from her slightly but then, as if she had twitched a thread, he moved towards her, returned the kiss. She reached for his belt buckle. It was not yet 8am.

*

Christopher and Nicola sat in the kitchen. The director and the lead actors and the production office seniors were in the drawing room watching the rushes. Col would be with them.

The crew weren't meant to use the kitchen, one of the areas of the house being treated as a private space, but Christopher thought he could get away with it. He had reminded Nicola of her promise to make him up and he sat now with his chair turned to hers, eyes closed, offering her his face. She sat square to him, her perfume – he must find out its name – filling his nostrils, her breath on him as she dabbed and sponged and brushed. He was very keen to see the end result, while at the same time not wanting the touch of her fingers on his face to end.

'There,' she said finally, and he opened his eyes and looked at himself in her mirror.

'Wow.' She had made him into a china doll, his face a flawless mask of pale foundation, his cheekbones defined with coral blusher, his eyelids heavily smudged with kohl, his lashes mascaraed, his mouth a cupid's bow of scarlet. He turned his face to look at himself from several angles. 'Wow.'

'You need gel in your hair.' She ran her fingers through his fringe so that it stood up momentarily. 'I'll see if one of the girls has got any.'

'Oh my *God*.' Lois was at the kitchen door. 'Can I come in?'

'Sure,' said Christopher, playing host.

'Christopher, you look amazing.' Lois, too, ruffled his hair. 'You should wear make-up all the time.'

'Can you teach me?' he asked Nicola.

'Definitely,' she said. 'We could do some tomorrow, if we have time.'

'Stunning,' said Lois.

'Is that you?' Nicola pointed to his school photograph on the dresser and Christopher nodded. 'Adorable,' she said.

'How old are you there?' Lois asked him.

'Nine, I think.'

'What a cutie,' said Lois. 'Anyone fancy some whizz?' She pulled a baggie from her jacket pocket and rooted for something to snort it through.

There was the sound of throat-clearing and they looked round. Col was at the kitchen door, staring at his nephew, a painted butterfly, and at the two women with him, laughing and shiny-eyed.

'You shouldn't be in here,' he said.

They looked at him. Col walked away and Lois, with a glance at Nicola, got up to follow him.

'Oops,' said Nicola.

'He's all right,' said Christopher.

'She's left her speed,' said Nicola.

They took turns snorting lines through the plastic casing of a biro.

'Here,' said Nicola. 'You've got some on you.' She licked a finger and removed a trace of powder clinging just below his nostril, then put her finger in her mouth. She smelled very nice. He took hold of her wrist. She smiled at him, then leaned forward and kissed him.

'Don't want to spoil your make-up,' she said.

'No.' He was still holding on to her wrist.

'You look very beautiful,' she told him.

'You've made me beautiful.'

'Do you want to get out of here?'

He caught her meaning at once. The drug had emboldened him.

'Where can we go?'

'My room,' she said. 'Suzy's gone to the pub with some of the lighting crew. She won't be back for hours.'

They took the back stairs. She had one of the second-floor bedrooms; it was the room from which he had overheard Col and Marianne having sex, years ago. He thought of telling Nicola the story, how he had stood there, rigid with shock and with the sensations he didn't yet fully understand. It felt fitting to be back in here. Nicola had a mattress on a futon base provided by the film company. Suzy, another make-up artist, had a similar bed, piled messily with clothes and make-up and magazines.

They sat on Nicola's bed, and she turned to him and smiled, and he pulled her towards him and kissed her again, properly, their tongues meeting.

'You always smell so wonderful,' he said. 'What is that perfume?'

She told him that it was Chanel No. 5.

'Christopher,' she said, as if trying out his name again. She was pulling at his T-shirt, which had Sigue Sigue Sputnik on its front. 'I'm going to give you cat's eyes next time I make you up.'

'Cat's eyes,' he said, kissing her again. 'Yes please.' He lifted his arms and stopped kissing her so that she could pull the shirt over his head. Her hand was at the zip of his jeans. He felt shy, quite unlike he did with his girlfriend, but Nicola knew what to do. He didn't like to tell her it was his first time; was glad he had practised putting on a condom while alone at home. Tonight he managed it with only a little fumbling. Nicola lay back and guided him into her. He just had time to savour the long-anticipated sensation of being inside a woman, feeling her grip him, when she tilted her pelvis so that he went in deeper and, gasping, he felt himself coming.

He moved off her and they lay together. Her bed was narrow so they were on their sides, her back to him, his arm over her. She reached behind her for the condom on his detumescing cock, pulled it off him in one move, tied a knot in the top of it and lobbed it into the bin.

'Was that OK?' he asked.

'It was great.' She patted his hand. He wasn't at all certain that it had been; she had seemed to enjoy it, but he was pretty sure she hadn't come. That he hadn't given her enough time.

'What about your girlfriend?' she said, as if she had just thought of it. A bolt of guilt shot through him.

'Oh, we broke up,' he lied. 'Do you have a boyfriend?'

'Sort of,' said Nicola. 'But he's in New York. We don't see each other very often.'

He was grateful for the sort-of boyfriend. It evened up the sides a little, made his deceit seem less treacherous. He cupped her small breast, which was bluey-white, as pale and freckled as the rest of her.

'I suppose we'd better get up,' she said. Neither of them moved. He looked at his watch.

'Hey, it's my birthday in ten minutes. I'm going to be eighteen.'

'Eighteen!' She turned to him, awkwardly. His hand got caught underneath her body. He pulled it free. 'We should celebrate.'

'I just did.' He pulled her to him and kissed her. They cuddled for a while but he couldn't get hard so they lay there instead. Nicola asked him about his plans for university.

'I've got a place at Lancaster to read law,' he said. 'But I want to go to art school in London. My parents won't let me, though, so it's not going to happen.'

'You could always go later,' she suggested. 'Take some time out, earn some money.'

'No, I have to get away now,' he said. 'Else I might end up killing them both.' His mother had seemed to recover from her last bout of being unwell but all the energy that had gone into becoming ill and then recovering from being ill had, it seemed to Christopher, been poured into him, into obsessing over exams, UCCA points, grades. She was adamant that he should go to university only to study for a profession, of which law was merely the least unpalatable. His father, as he always did, backed up whatever she said.

'Yeah, I get it,' said Nicola. 'I love my mum and dad, but...' She rolled her eyes. How lucky she was, twenty-three and with a job and a flat share in London and financial independence.

'Actually, they're not even my parents,' said Christopher. 'I'm adopted.'

'Really?' She looked at him. 'From what age?'

'I was two.'

'So they are your parents, really. They brought you up.'

'I suppose so,' Christopher said sulkily.

'What happened to your real mum and dad?'

'They died in a car crash.'

'Oh shit, I'm sorry.' He shrugged. 'Were you in the car with them?'

'No.'

'Do you remember them?'

'No.'

'I'm sorry,' she said. 'I don't mean to upset you.'

'It's fine,' he said, but he kissed her on the mouth, hard, so she wouldn't say anything more about his parents. Then he looked at his watch again.

'Hey!'

Nicola took hold of his wrist to look at the watch herself.

'Happy birthday, Kit,' she said, and kissed his nose. 'That's a much better name for you. Kit the Cat.'

*

It pissed Col off, seeing his nephew transformed and peacocky, two peahens paying court, though he couldn't have said why, only that his mood was bad generally.

Marianne was behaving as though the film were nothing to do with her, absenting herself for hours at a time with the dog, leaving all the niggly queries from the assistant location manager to him – could the farmer please be asked to move the cows from the paddock, as they would spoil the background of the shot? would it be all right if they re-covered the window seats in the billiard room? actually *could* they use the kitchen, as one of the gas burners in the catering van had stopped working? – when he would far rather be involving himself with Dennis, the production manager.

And the sight of Marianne's open box of tampons lolling on their bathroom floor had triggered another row. She was thirty-eight, Col told her again, time was not on her side. Already they were probably too old to be considered for adoption by social services. Again he begged her to talk to their GP, ask to be referred for fertility treatment. And Marianne, as ever, had flat-out refused even to consider it. It would happen, or it wouldn't, was what she always said, infuriatingly. Then she had lost her temper, flown at him, which was when he had pushed her onto the bed. She had been scornful of him, taunting. *What's the matter, Col? Can't you get it up?* And then the incident with the boots. They had made up as they usually did, with sex, but it had been a joyless encounter, his mind full of Lois and when he might be able to see her.

It had not been a good day on set. The New Year's Eve scene, expensive to set up and complicated to shoot, was not going well. The rushes, said John Starr, the director, were terrible. The sound quality was poor, meaning the actors would have to come back to London and overdub the scenes. They absolutely had to be away from Erringby by next Friday. They were already ten days behind schedule. And there had been an unfortunate incident during the day's shooting.

'Cut!' John Starr had roared, followed by, 'Who the *fuck* is that?' Susannah, in search of Marianne, had wandered into the shot. Everyone gaped at the elderly woman who, though dishevelled, was very much the grande dame, had met John Starr's gaze with an imperious look of her own so that he had been, momentarily and uncharacteristically, speechless.

Col had stepped in. 'It's my mother-in-law. I'll take her upstairs.' He took Susannah's arm. 'Come on. Let's get you home.' She leaned on him as they took the stairs together, slowly. He steered her into the room they had set up for her on the second floor. Moving her from the staff flat downstairs where she had seemed settled, even happy, had been a terrible idea, but it was too late to change now. They would move her back once the film crew had gone.

He sat her down in the wing chair she had brought with her when she moved in.

'This place is full of young people,' she remarked.

'Yes it is,' he said. 'We're making a film, remember?'

'Oh yes,' she said, but as he was looking for her radio – she liked the afternoon plays – she went on, 'Are you having a party, Harold?'

He looked at her. 'I'm Col, Susannah. Harold died in 1972.'

'Are you sure?' She was querulous, as if accusing him of making it up. Col found the radio and switched it on. An adaptation of *The Castle of Otranto* was in progress.

'Oh, I like this,' she said in satisfaction. 'Thank you, Harold.'

'Good,' said Col. 'I have to go downstairs now, but I'll look in on you later.' She didn't reply; she was listening to the radio. The actors were hammy, clearly relishing their roles. It was a shame he didn't have time to listen to it with her.

As he was leaving she seemed suddenly aware of him again.

'Tell Marianne...' She tailed off.

'Yes?'

'Tell Marianne that I was wrong about you.' She went back to her play.

Susannah's appearance in the rushes raised the only laugh of the evening.

'This is supposed to be a fucking comedy,' John said. 'These scenes are about as funny as cancer.' Julia, the assistant director, made soothing noises; it *was* funny, it would all come good in the editing, but John stood up abruptly and stalked off to the production office – Susannah's former home – which was the sign that they were done for the day.

Col, in search of Lois, heard her voice coming from the kitchen and was discomfited to find her sitting there with Nicola and his nephew. But of course she followed him to the old brushing room, the place they used now. He undressed her without speaking; she was dark haired, small breasted and slim hipped, lithe as an eel, the anti-Marianne. He sat back on the ancient and collapsing sofa and she straddled him and unbuckled his belt. He lifted himself up to allow her to pull down his jeans and his underpants. Her cunt was already wet, which pleased him; he liked the thought of her anticipating him as they went about their day, apart but tantalisingly aware of each other's presence. She slipped onto his cock without preamble. He closed his eyes and felt himself go very deep.

She came vigorously but quietly, as was her practice, and he finished soon after. She got off him and fished for two Camel cigarettes from her jacket pocket, offered him one, sat next to him on the sofa. His jeans were still undone, a drop of moisture shining at the end of his cock. He zipped himself up. She was still naked.

They smoked in silence for a while. Col felt his mood lifting. Lois was very keen on him; he was used to that in women, but she was too smart to push him on it. When she had asked him whether he still had sex with his wife and he said that he did, she had not seemed particularly upset. Still the prospect of what would happen after the wrap party, which was next week, following which the film crew would pack up and leave, hung between them, unspoken. He was hopeful that business on this film and then others, perhaps, would take him to London fairly regularly, giving him an opportunity to see her. She rented a flat in Kentish Town by herself.

As usual they left separately. She went in search of Nicola, who had her speed, and Col thought he would sit outside with the production crew. Someone had a bottle of absinthe smuggled in from a corner of Europe. But John Starr called to him as he passed the office.

'Got a minute, Col?'

In what had been Susannah's bedroom John and Julia sat smoking at the trestle table that served as a desk. With them were Dennis, the production manager, and Larry, who was from the film company and had flown in yesterday. Col gathered his unscheduled arrival was not good news but hadn't had a chance to discuss it with Dennis.

John and Julia were tense and frowning. Larry, almost a parody of a movie executive with his Cuban cigar, was grim-faced, but Dennis was avuncular, smiling; he poured Col a whisky and asked after Susannah. Col said that the move upstairs had unsettled her a little.

'Sorry to hear that,' said Dennis, 'but we'll be out of all of your hair soon.'

'Very soon,' put in John Starr.

'Get on with it,' said Larry. He had an accent that Col couldn't place; it hovered somewhere over the American Midwest.

'So here's the thing, Col,' said Dennis. 'We're going to have to do a lot more overdubbing of the dialogue than we planned to...'

Col nodded.

'...We're also going to have to redo one of the London scenes, the permits from Westminster Council are all going to have to be renewed – you know we had to close off a street, don't you? The actors are going to have to be brought in specially, we're having to fly Darren back from Budapest because he starts filming there in two weeks.'

'Right,' said Col, 'so it's all running a bit late.'

'Thing is, *chum*,' said Larry – he was out of patience with Dennis – 'we've got sweet Fanny Adams left for post-production. The bottom line is that we're over budget to the tune of a hundred and ten K.'

'Oh,' said Col.

'Pounds,' said John Starr. 'Not dollars.'

'So we wondered,' said Dennis – he was smiling a little too broadly; his hand hovered with the whisky bottle, Col nodded and Dennis topped him up – 'if you wanted to come in with us. As a co-financier.'

John Starr said, 'Of course, you'd need to discuss it with... with...'

'Marianne,' said Julia.

Col's mind flipped open. A possible future as a film executive, with an office in London and perhaps eventually a small house or a flat, where he'd be able to go on seeing Lois, presented itself.

'This little film,' said Dennis. 'It *needs* to be made. Don't you agree?'

'Oh yes,' said Col. 'It definitely does.'

'You'll get a percentage of box office receipts,' said Larry. 'We can do you quite a sweet deal.' Col hesitated. A hundred and ten thousand pounds was a great deal of money. John and Larry looked at each other.

'He needs to think about it,' said Larry. Col heard an implied weakness, that Larry thought him not capable of a bold decision.

'You'll need to discuss it with Marianne,' said Julia.

'Count me in,' said Col. 'I'd need to see the details, of course.' He took a drink from his glass. Julia was looking at him. 'Count us in,' he said.

7

August 1986

Kit and Marianne lay on her bed, smoking a joint. A film played on the black-and-white portable television and Arlo was sprawled at their feet, panting softly.

Kit was feeling strange. One of the crew had given him a tab of acid and he wasn't sure he liked it. When he had used the bathroom the room had tilted, as if he were on a ship; it seemed that the space were filling with stagnant bilge water. Afterwards he had scrubbed his hands so hard with the nail brush that they stung, raw.

Marianne, coming across him swaying and uncertain, one hand on the wall, had invited him to her room to watch a film while she ran a bath in her en-suite bathroom. Kit lay on her bed and tried to focus on the film while she bathed. A young man with a seventies counter-cultural haircut like Peter Fonda in *Easy Rider* was stealing a small plane. Marianne had left the interconnecting door open and the bathroom was full of clouds of scented steam so that the shape of her, lying in the bath, getting out, drying herself, was only hazily made out. She came into the bedroom in a man's silk dressing gown, her hair wrapped in a towel.

Kit had hoped that the dope would take the edge off the acid. What he felt, lying on her bed, was a sense of immense well-being, a lightness in his head coupled with a feeling of extreme torpor. It was all he could do to prop himself up on one arm. The prospect of standing up and leaving the room, much less going downstairs, outside, seemed onerous beyond belief.

She passed him the joint resting in its ashtray. They were using an oval shell lined with iridescent shades of nacre. It was called a paua shell, Marianne told him. Col had brought it back from his travels. The colours inside the shell shimmered and jumped and Kit couldn't stop staring at it.

'It's too beautiful to use as an ashtray,' he managed to say.

'Everyone in New Zealand does, apparently,' she replied.

He realised what it was it reminded him of.

'You used to have nail polish that colour.'

'Did I?'

'Yes. Don't you remember me touching your toenail at your wedding?'

'Oh yes,' she said. 'What a funny little thing you were.' She unwound the towel from her head and shook out her hair. Damp strands, dark with her bathwater, hung around her face and clung to the silk of the robe.

An idea formed in Kit's mouth. 'I should like to paint you, Marianne,' he announced without thinking.

'Really? No one's ever wanted to do that before.'

'I can paint you tomorrow,' he said. 'It's my day off; they said they don't need me.'

'Oughtn't you go and see your parents?'

'They're not my parents.' She said nothing. He hadn't gone back to see his father and mother, or his girlfriend, since starting work on the film. The night of his eighteenth birthday had been spent drinking whisky with Col and several crew members at the Three Hares. They'd come back to Erringby at 3am and he'd needed a bump of whizz to get going for work the next morning.

'I slept with Nicola,' he said suddenly. It seemed important to confess.

'Did you?' said Marianne. 'Which one is she?'

'The make-up artist with the red curly hair. She wears Chanel Number Five.'

'Oh, the Pre-Raphaelite stunner.'

'I don't love her, though.'

'No.'

He was too shy, even in his current state, to admit to Marianne that it had been his first time. He assumed she thought he had had sex with his girlfriend. His mother certainly did. It had been the subject of several harangues. He was a little disappointed in Marianne's response, though he couldn't have said why.

'Are you looking forward to the wrap party?' he said, to change the subject. Though the film wasn't quite finished, this would be the last time the full crew would all be together and Erringby, it was felt, was a fitting party venue.

'Oh, my partying days are over,' she said.

'You must come. It's your house. I want you to come.'

She laughed.

'I'll leave it to the young people.'

'That's stupid,' he said. 'Loads of people are older than you. John, Julia, Andrew...'

'That's really not what I meant,' she said. 'Don't be so literal.'

He had the sense of melting, as if all his insides were gently deliquescing. Marianne's face was near. The dressing gown, which was large on her, gaped slightly. The swell of her breast was visible.

'You're so very beautiful, Marianne.' He couldn't help himself, he had to say whatever came into his head. She laughed, not unkindly.

'You're stoned, dear boy.'

Disinhibited by the acid and by the dope he leaned over and kissed her on her mouth, his hand on her arm, on the damp, worn silk of the absurd dressing gown. Its paisley pattern was ludicrously fusty on this woman who, it was now obvious, was and always would be the most beautiful he had ever known. He pulled away from her.

'Oh shit,' he said, and laughed.

'It's all right,' she said. She took his hand and kissed it.

'Are you stoned?' he asked her. 'I'm really stoned.'

'Yes, I'm a bit stoned,' she said. 'I don't smoke dope very often.'

They lay in silence. On the TV the man who had stolen the plane was in the desert with a woman about Nicola's age, with hair that reached all the way down her back. She was pretty, thought Kit, although he was barely following the film, had no idea who the couple were or what they were doing. On the diminutive screen of the black-and-white TV the desert was all stark shapes like origami. The couple began making love, rolling around in the dust. Other figures appeared as if they had emerged from the rock and the horsts, dressed and undressed, in groups of two or three or four, writhing and playfighting and kissing, getting so covered in dust and sand it was as if they were returning to the desert. Kit felt his cock stiffen. In normal circumstances he would have been embarrassed. He wondered if Marianne was turned on as well. He didn't dare ask her. He had kissed her. Kissed his aunt.

'When I think of you...' Kit's words were fuzzy, his voice coming from somewhere else. '...I think of a painting by Renoir, or Bonnard.' She laughed. The dog lifted his great head, looked at them quizzically, went back to sleep.

'I should have thought Rubens, if anything,' she said.

'Don't laugh at me, Marianne.' He wasn't sure he had said the words. He said them again. Suddenly he had never been so serious about anything. Absurdly, there were tears pricking his eyes. The memory of the broken vase on the landing came to him; how she had hugged him. How he had wanted her to go on hugging him.

'Oh dear,' said Marianne.

'I feel... I feel weird,' said Kit. 'Woozy and... a bit sick.'

'Do you want a Valium?' He nodded. She went into her bathroom and came back with a pill and a tumbler of water. The water tasted of toothpaste.

A tear rolled down his face.

'Oh dear,' said Marianne.

'Sorry.' He wiped his eyes with his sleeve. He felt very young suddenly.

'Come here.' She opened her arms, drew him to her, held him there for a time. They settled back on the bed to watch the film. It was hard to concentrate. To Kit it seemed as if the same scene, that of the figures writhing around in the desert, had been looping round and round for a long time. How long had he been on the bed? He lay against her, his head resting on her arm. Her robe gaped open. His head was very close to her breast.

The film ended and Marianne got up to switch the television off. Kit's feeling of extreme lethargy continued. His feet were concrete blocks; he couldn't have got up if he wanted to. He didn't want to. She got back on the bed. She put her arm round him. His cheek rested on the swell of her breast. There was a kind of grey sinking as the Valium did its work.

He was woken by the sound of someone in the room. He sat up and squinted at his uncle scrabbling in a dresser drawer. Marianne, beneath the covers, did not wake. Col found what it was he had come in for and at the door turned to take in the figures lying on the bed, his wife and his nephew. His eyes met Kit's, but he left the room without speaking.

Kit leaned over Marianne to check the time: just before six. It was his day off. He didn't need to be on set for seven, not today. He leaned back against the headboard and looked at her. It was unlike her to sleep on, not to be woken by movement in the room. He knew her to be a light sleeper. They had smoked a lot of dope, that was it. She was unused to it, she said.

He was on top of the bedspread and it dawned on him what Col would have seen: his shirt unbuttoned to the waist, his unbuckled belt, the open zip of his jeans. He slid his hand into his underpants and felt drying semen. He had had strange, troubling dreams, the birthday party and the cake but also of Marianne, Marianne comforting him, wiping him down.

He lay back. He should be feeling acute embarrassment, not only at his nightfall, right next to his sleeping aunt, but also at his uncle seeing the aftermath. But he felt oddly and utterly at peace. He watched Marianne sleeping, her tumble of hair on her pillow hiding her face. It felt as though his entire life had been building up to this moment. He wanted the day never to begin.

She woke at six thirty and did not seem surprised to find him there. She went to the kitchen and came back with two mugs of freshly brewed coffee, remembering he drank it black with no sugar, like her. She got back into bed to drink it.

'Sorry about last night,' Kit said.

'Sorry for what?' Was this her being deliberately obtuse?

'Did Col come up to bed?'

'No idea,' she said. 'He wasn't here when I woke up, was he?'

'He came in,' said Kit. 'Around six o'clock. He got something from a drawer.'

'Well then,' she said. 'You just answered your own question.'

Col not coming to bed was probably a regular occurrence. He wondered: what did she know about Lois? He was determined that he would not be the one to tell her, but didn't women always know these things?

'I've decided,' Marianne said, drinking her coffee. 'You may paint me. I rather like the idea of it.'

It was as Kit drove to Flatley Close in Marianne's Morris Traveller to collect his paints and brushes that the weirdness of last night fully hit him. He had made the briefest attempt at clarification –

'What happened?' he had asked as she moved about her bedroom, picking out the clothes she would wear that day – but she had given him no reply. He left the bedroom to give her the privacy to dress, and after his breakfast – an indifferent burger served up by the catering van – he looked for her but she had disappeared with Arlo. Kit had the sense of being part of an elaborate chess game, the rules of which were unfathomable. He liked that analogy: the queen was the most powerful piece on the board, capable of sweeping moves in any direction, the king one of the weakest, his power mostly symbolic. What did that make him? A rook? A knight?

At Flatley Close he gathered the things he needed quickly, though not quickly enough.

'Christopher! You didn't tell us you were coming.' His mother arrived home as he was leaving. Her pleasure in seeing him, when he had expected her to be angry at the lack of communication, at not spending any part of his birthday with them, wrong-footed him.

'I just came to pick up some things.'

'Uncle Col rang,' Janet went on. 'He says you went to the pub on your birthday with some of the crew. Did you have a good time?'

'Yes,' he said. 'It was all right.'

'How's the film? It sounds ever so exciting. Col was telling me all about it. I can't wait to see it, though Col doesn't know if it'll come to the Classic; it's a shame, isn't it?'

'It's going OK,' said Kit. 'We're a bit behind schedule, but that's normal.' He edged towards the front door.

'Oh, can't you stay longer?' said Janet. 'Your father'll be so sorry to have missed you.'

'No, I have to get going.'

'Well, let me give you your present at least.' She disappeared upstairs and came back with a box-shaped parcel. She looked at him expectantly as he tore off the wrapping paper.

It was a pewter beer tankard, with *Happy 18th Birthday Christopher With Much Love from Mum and Dad* engraved in italic script.

'It's great,' he said. Her entire face dropped.

'You don't like it.'

'No, I really do.' He tried to conjure enthusiasm.

'We try so hard, your dad and me, and you just push us away. Don't roll your eyes at me...'

He tried to arrange his face into neutral.

'I need to be getting back. I'll be late for work.'

'Col said you had a day off today.'

Fucking Uncle Col. Thanks for that.

'Change of plan,' he said. She didn't believe him.

'The present's great,' he said. 'Thanks, Mum.' He dropped a kiss on her cheek and left before he had to deal with any more of her anger and disappointment. He tossed the gift onto the back seat of Marianne's car, where it rolled off and into the footwell as he pulled out of the Close. He never drank beer.

For his A-level Art portfolio he had worked on large canvasses of coloured geometric shapes against a grey background – 'It looks a bit like Pacman,' had been his mother's assessment – but for this he wanted to do something different, 'more Neo-Expressionist,' he told Marianne.

'Whatever that means,' she said, waving away his attempts at explanation.

Since the house was teeming with film crew, cameras and equipment there were not many places where she could pose undisturbed.

'How about my bathroom?' she suggested and Kit felt his face colour. Though he had seen baigneuse paintings where the subject wore clothes – Alfred Stevens came to mind – this would not sit with the realism he wanted. He said, as casually as possible, 'How do you feel about posing nude?'

'Absolutely fine,' she said. She sounded surprised, even a little affronted, that he might suggest otherwise.

Her bath stood in the middle of the room, an immense tub of a thing on claw feet. He decided to paint her from behind, as if the viewer had just happened on her.

'You might get cold,' he warned. 'I'm going to need you to pose for a few hours.' Fortunately the day was warm and, said Marianne, hot water was plentiful, possibly for the first time ever, thanks to the film company's new boiler.

The bathroom had two doors, one from the landing, the other from her bedroom. She locked the door to the landing and ran the bath while he set up. She was wearing the paisley dressing gown, her hair piled messily on her head.

'Should I wear my hair down?'

'No, it looks great like that.'

'Are you ready?'

'We're ready.'

With her back to him she slipped off the dressing gown and stepped into the bath. He had just time to take her all in. She was beautiful, fleshy but not fat, *junoesque* was the word that came into his head and also – he thought he had remembered it right but he would have to look it up in the library when he got a moment – *zoftig*. Marianne was built from such words, not the lexicon of the sixth-form common room, or the words James had used that afternoon in the shop in Ledbury when he had talked and talked about women; women he had fucked, women he wanted to fuck, women he would only fuck while drunk, and Col had laughed, and Christopher had concentrated very hard on drawing the ship in the bottle. It had been his first experience of total immersion in creating a piece of art. He was aware, keenly aware, of the transgressive nature of what he and Marianne were doing. He had told no one else about the project and was certain that neither had she.

'How do you want me?' she asked, turning to look at him, and something inside him flipped and twisted, almost painfully. He was eleven years old again, drawing in the top-floor bedroom, overhearing them next door. *You dirty little bitch.* His heart hammered in his chest. He needed to control the situation.

'Just get comfortable – lie back against the side of the bath – OK? You need to be able to stay in the same position, this might take a while.' He was John Starr, he was directing.

'That's OK,' she said. 'There's nothing else I should be doing.'

On the landing outside two technicians were discussing lighting silks. In the bath Marianne was idly rotating her left hand. The water came up to her breasts. Her nipples were visible, softer and lighter than Nicola's tight chestnut buds, larger and less pink than Sally's. He could have called in on his girlfriend that morning and it had entirely slipped his mind. He started sketching.

For several minutes neither of them spoke. Kit worked quickly, sketching an outline of the bathtub and of Marianne. Elsewhere in the house the making of the film was going on. Irritable shouts came from the landing. Kit and Marianne were alone together in the eye of a storm.

'When is results day, again?' she asked eventually, not turning her head. He didn't reply; he was concentrating on the sweep of her left thigh. She shifted her position slightly.

'Keep still,' he said.

'Sorry.' She sounded amused; her voice had that teasing quality she often used with him, vaguely mocking, not taking him seriously, but she did as he asked and stayed still, and was silent. A rush of desire, quite unlike the quiet spark he had felt with Nicola, shot through him. His hand trembled a little and he fluffed the line of her leg and had to rub it out and start again.

'*Shit.*' An erection was straining at his jeans. He didn't dare ask again about last night. He needed to take control of the situation, be professional. He was an artist. He took a deep breath and spoke calmly.

'Next Thursday,' he said. 'The exam results.'

'And then it's off to Lancaster.' She had remembered. She seemed to be barely paying attention to the minutiae of your life when you talked to her, yet she took in everything.

''Fraid so,' he said.

She turned her head.

'You mustn't go, if you don't want to.'

'Don't turn round! I'm doing the back of your head.' Their eyes met for a moment. There was the hint of a smile. She turned her head back.

'Why don't you want to go?'

'I don't want to study law. I don't want to be a lawyer.'

'You could do something else with it. Human rights work, that kind of thing.'

'I'd rather study art.'

'Then do. Defer for a year and reapply.'

'My parents won't fund me. It's study for a profession or nothing. And I need to leave home.'

'Yes.' She had her back to him. 'I do see that.'

'I'll do a law degree, then do something else,' he said. 'Once I've got a job and can pay my own way I'll have more freedom.' She said nothing. 'I can always paint in my spare time.'

'I suppose you can.' She sounded doubtful, even disapproving, and a flash of anger ran through him.

'What choice do I have?' he asked hotly. She said nothing. Kit went on drawing. He sketched her breasts quickly, even carelessly, found that this approach, of not over-thinking it, produced a truer result. He felt calmer, and eventually he asked, 'What did you want to do, when you were my age?'

'Acting,' said Marianne. 'I was an actress for four years. Best years of my life, in hindsight.'

'What did you act in?'

'Theatre, mostly. A dreadful TV commercial for cigars that happily never saw the light of day.'

'Did you act in films?'

'No.'

'Did you want to act in this film?'

'God, no!' She spoke with so much vehemence that he was momentarily taken aback. He went on working in silence for several moments.

'It's Col's thing, really, isn't it?' he asked.

'Very much so. I let him get on with it.'

He wanted to ask her about Col, about Col's appearance in the bedroom that morning, but he couldn't.

'Marianne?'

'H'mmm?'

'If I find you a dress and do your make-up, will you come to the wrap party with me?' Nicola had made him a generous gift of cosmetics and he had been practising in front of the camping mirror in his tent, to the mild incredulity of the three young men from the production crew with whom he was sharing.

'Oh, for heaven's sake.'

'Is that a yes?'

'It's a get-on-with-your-work, and let me pose.'

*

Possibly Col had had too much coke, but right now he didn't care. He was dancing with Lois in front of everyone. For the party professional caterers had set up a marquee in the garden with a staffed bar and a dance floor had been made of part of the lawn. The hired DJ was playing Janet Jackson and Lois had her head resting on his shoulder. His hand was on her waist. At the edge of the lawn sat Nicola with three or four other women, and Col had the sense that there was some silent communion going on between Lois and these women. He was getting an erection.

Lois was wearing tight black jeans and a faux-crocodile-skin jacket. Her hair was glossier than usual.

'What about Marianne?' she was saying.

'Fuck her.' Col pressed himself to her, so that there could be no doubting his intentions. She moved away and looked up at him.

'You're not going to leave your wife, Col,' she said. But the way she said it, it was as though she didn't want him to.

'Shush,' he said. She was breaking the spell. The DJ put on 'Sexual Healing' and Col, grateful, lifted Lois's face to kiss. Others were dancing near them, other couples. She slid her tongue into his mouth and he tasted the spray of champagne on her breath. Everyone was watching. Marianne might be watching from an upstairs bedroom. Was she watching? He hoped so. Lois put both arms round his neck. The slim belt of her jeans was rubbing against the belt buckle of his own. She smiled at him.

'Do you want to go somewhere?' he said. One or two crew members had left already. There might even be a spare bed.

'Soon.' She touched his crotch momentarily, the lightest of pressure from her fingers. 'But not just yet.'

Then she looked over his shoulder, and he was aware of a commotion. Heads turned towards the house. A throng parted as if a traffic cop were directing it to let two figures pass through.

Marianne emerged, along with Christopher. He'd been at the dressing-up box, for he wore a purple velvet and brocade frock coat over pinstriped trousers, a grey homburg and black-and-white brogues, and he was heavily made up, but Col scarcely took in these details as Marianne snagged and then trapped his gaze, like a fly in amber. She wore a tight-fitting black dress, her hair teased into a bouffant and held in place by a black headband.

Col knew that dress. It was from her London days. He'd tried to get her to wear it once in honour of a special evening. Their anniversary? He'd intended an elegant meal in the dining room, both of them dressed up – he'd sponged his wedding suit – followed by drinks in the drawing room and her playing the piano. But she wouldn't. She'd turned up late to the meal he'd spent all day cooking, wearing her work clothes and tracking mud into the house.

'Sexual Healing' ended and the DJ put on a Michael Jackson song.

Marianne and Christopher – Kit – moved into the circle and started to dance. A cheer went up. Kit was a painted fop in his Edwardian frock coat. Marianne had her eyes made up with black kohl, dramatic cats' eyes. And she was wearing pale-pink lipstick. When was the last time she'd worn make-up? Kit was saying something to her. She laughed, and they advanced, retreated, shimmied and shaked, their movements fluid and graceful. Other dancers thronged round them as if drawn to them.

Col was unable to stop watching his nephew with his wife. He recognised the song now. 'Wanna Be Startin' Somethin''. He started dancing again with Lois, but more quietly now.

Andrew, one of the grips, had forced his way into the crowd round Kit and Marianne and was dancing next to her. He'd been slobbering over her since the day he arrived on set. He was yelling in her ear. *What?* she mouthed and Andrew shouted it again. Col could tell she hadn't heard and was unlikely to ask for it to be repeated a second time. But to his discomfiture she turned slightly towards Andrew so that she was dancing with the washed-up dipso, just for a moment, as the song ended.

She said what looked like *Golly! Phew!* Kit, looking pleased with himself, put an arm round her waist and kissed her cheek. She said something else, to Andrew, and he turned away, dispatched on an errand. As Andrew made his way to the marquee that was serving as a bar he looked over and saw Col looking back at him, and Col put as much venom as he possibly could into his answering glare.

Lois rubbed his arm. She understood what was going on. She was a find, this one. He smiled at her and they started dancing again.

He made sure to keep Marianne in his sights. She had now been snaffled by that puffed-up idiot Henry Melville who had his body very close to hers, his hips thrusting at her in a sexual parody that was meant to be humorous. And she seemed to be tolerating it. Meanwhile Kit was surrounded by a group of girls, all of whom looked delighted with him.

She seemed to tire of Henry; she said something to him, then turned and walked in the direction of the house. Col was pleased to see the actor so irrevocably dismissed. And she, having presumably made her point, would now be going to bed.

But then Col saw that Andrew had followed her. Had contrived somehow to intercept her by the back door, two glasses of champagne in his hands. They were talking.

Lois brought him back.

'Doesn't Kit look amazing? Like a butterfly.'

'Oh... yes.' He turned to her and smiled. 'Look, this is all a bit... Why don't we hook up later?'

'Sure.' She slipped away to join her friends.

The first place he looked was their bedroom. The door had been left ajar. Andrew and Marianne were not in flagrante on the marital bed. Of course they weren't, but the room was a riot of hatboxes and scarves and dresses and jackets, cosmetics scattered everywhere. Arlo, on the bed, was chewing what might be a make-up brush.

Which room had they put Andrew in? Col struggled to remember. Was it on the second floor? He went up the back stairs.

Room Eighteen, was it? He knocked on the door and a man's voice said, 'Yeah?'

It wasn't Andrew. Two lighting engineers were snorting lines off a bedside mirror. They turned towards Col.

'Want some?'

'You're all right,' said Col.

The drawing room had the best view of the lawn. The party was still in full swing, but there was no sign of her. He gave up and went to the marquee bar to drink several large Scotches with John Starr and Dennis.

It was perhaps half an hour before it struck him. Of course. He should have thought of it sooner. His footsteps clanged as he made his way up the steps to the gazebo, where a light was on. His hand shook as he turned the door handle. They were standing, together but a little apart, on the other side of the room.

'So here you are,' Col said. 'I might have known.'

'Might you,' she said.

He jerked his head at Andrew.

'What's he doing here?'

'I don't have to explain myself to you,' she said.

'We just came to talk, away from all the noise,' Andrew said. 'It's a perfectly innocent...'

He had that way with him, that way London types let you know they're more sophisticated than you. Col wheeled round and jabbed a forefinger into Andrew's chest.

'Let me tell you, *mate*... There's nothing innocent about her. She's a harpy. A she-devil. And as for you...' He jabbed at Andrew again. The London Wanker took hold of his hand and pushed it off him. Col squared up to him. '...as for you, sniffing round her like she's a bitch in heat, why don't you just *fuck off?*'

'Why don't you fuck off instead?' said Marianne. 'You disgusting drunk. You stink of alcohol.'

The London Wanker held up his hands.

'Look,' he said. Mr Reasonable. 'There's nothing going on here.

You've got the wrong end of the stick, Col. You've had a bit too much to drink, that's all. Why don't we all go back to the party?'

'Fuck you, you cunt,' said Col.

'Oh, that's nice,' said Marianne.

'Come on, Marianne.' Andrew took her arm and tried to steer her towards the door. Drunk as he was, Col realised he was in no state to fight Andrew who, though older, was probably in better shape.

'I was going anyway.' He turned and stumbled to the door, Marianne following. At the top of the staircase she gave him an immense shove and he tumbled partway down the stairs. His head made sharp contact with a wrought-iron baluster.

'Marianne!' said Andrew.

Pain seared into Col's head.

'Ow!' he said. 'You fucking bitch cunt.' Marianne laughed.

'And there we have it, the holy trinity of your extraordinary facility with language. He's used to it,' she went on to Andrew. 'He's so drunk he just bounces. He won't feel a thing in the morning.'

'Are you all right, Col? Mate?' Andrew had come to where Col lay sprawled across several steps. He wasn't going to be able to get up unassisted. He groaned and put out an arm. Andrew grabbed his hand and pulled him up, not without difficulty.

Col got unsteadily to his feet and limped down the rest of the stairs. Blood trickled from the cut on his forehead. He turned to look at them both.

'You've gone too far this time, Marianne.'

'Oh do shut up,' she said.

Col staggered across the walled garden and into the courtyard. Marianne was laughing. Andrew was not.

8

September 1986

'Trust fund?' said Bob. They were in the lounge bar of the King's Head, a venue Kit had selected precisely for its bland neutrality and lack of privacy, and where they had just eaten a mediocre lunch of chicken in a basket and prawn curry. Kit was enjoying the glances and raised eyebrows from other diners. Young men in make-up were a rare sight in the centre of Hereford, though he had toned it down today – just blusher, eyeliner and a hint of lip gloss. He wore a boiler suit picked up at a utility clothing shop, dyed pink and cinched at the waist with a belt.

He pushed the letter across the table. Bob picked it up and frowned at it as if it were written in Serbo-Croat.

'What is this…? I can't make it out… You've got all this money, Christopher?' His mouth hung open as he looked from the letter to his son. 'Nearly four hundred thousand pounds?'

'Give it to me.' Janet snatched the letter and scanned it quickly. She went very pale, her mouth compressed into a hyphen. 'What's this about, Christopher?'

'What it says,' said Kit. The letter, two closely typed pages from a financial services company in Jersey, contained the incendiary news that Kit had, on reaching his majority, come into a fund that had been settled on him on an undisclosed date and from which he was now entitled to draw upon as he saw fit, the only proviso being that the settlor of the fund wished to remain anonymous. Bob was reading over Janet's shoulder.

'Christopher, my goodness! All that money. I hope you'll

remember your old mum and dad when we've been put out to grass.' His laugh was forced.

'This is *her*, isn't it? Marianne?' Janet said. 'Who else could it be?'

Kit shrugged. 'My secret benefactor, I suppose.'

'It's very kind of your aunt,' said Bob. 'But does she really need to do this? We should talk to her, Janet.' She turned to look at him. 'It's... this is staggering news.'

'So, the thing is this.' Kit hoped that the shock of the letter would neuter the next revelation. 'I'm not going to Lancaster any more.' Janet lowered the letter. Both parents stared at him.

'What?' said his mother.

'I'm not going. I don't want to study law. I don't want to be a lawyer.'

'Now hold on, son...' Bob began.

'Oh yes, you are going,' Janet said quickly.

'No,' said Kit. He felt calm. He reached out to take the letter, folded it and put it back in its opulent envelope, cream wove and watermarked.

'Well,' said Bob. 'This does change things a bit, Janet, doesn't it? Why not have a year out, Christopher? I gather that's quite popular these days. Defer university for a year.'

'Defer?' Janet glared at him.

'Yes – he could go travelling. Like Col did.' He shot her a glance.

'I suppose he could.' Janet softened a fraction. 'And then go to Lancaster.'

'No,' said Kit. 'I'm going to London. I'm going to art school.'

'*What?*' said Janet. Bob stared at him.

'London?'

'Dad, don't just sit there repeating everything I say.'

'This is all her doing.' Janet's face reddened. 'You and she have cooked this whole thing up, haven't you?'

'Janet,' said Bob.

'She's done this out of spite! To get at me. To turn our own son against us. She's never liked us, Bob.'

'That's not true, Janet, you know she's been very good to Christopher.'

'To get at me!'

'If it is Marianne,' said Kit, 'she's done it because of me. You flatter yourself, Mum.'

'Christopher!' said his father.

'Of course it's Marianne,' said Janet. 'Who else could it possibly be? I'm going to ring Col, the second I get home.'

'And by the way, my name's Kit now. As I have told you repeatedly.'

'Kit!' His mother snorted. 'I never heard anything so ridiculous in all my life.'

'Where's that come from, son? The name?' His father was trying, really trying, to be placatory, to act as a conduit between him and Janet. But his appeasement was an irritant.

'From Nicola,' said Kit.

'Nicola? Who's she?' demanded his mother.

'A woman I slept with.' He took a sip of whisky and water.

'Keep your voice down!' Janet hissed, glancing round at the other diners who were indeed agog.

'She's your girlfriend, is she?' said his father. 'What's happened to Sally?'

'Oh, we broke up,' said Kit. His mother groaned, as if this were the last straw, although Kit had overheard her complain to Bob that she found Sally common.

'Christopher,' said Bob. 'Kit... whatever. Son...'

'Nicola's not a girlfriend,' said Kit. 'In fact she has a boyfriend in New York. It was just a fling.'

'Oh for heaven's sake!' Janet stood up and threw down her paper napkin. 'I can't stand any more of this. Take me home, Bob.'

'Can't I finish my drink?' said Kit. He took a pointedly small sip.

'You can stay and drink yourself under the table for all I care!' said his mother.

'Janet,' said Bob. 'Are you not feeling well? Christopher, you mustn't upset her.'

'Why, in all of this,' said Kit, 'does no one ever care if *I* get upset?' Janet was pulling on her coat.

'You're too immature, Christopher, to know what you want. And that's the truth of it. Your uncle gives you a job out of the goodness of his heart and you let it go to your head, you don't even come back and see us on your birthday... you get up to heaven knows what with women and come back with a stupid name and all painted up like a clown. You look ridiculous.'

'Mother,' said Kit. 'Adoptive Mother. Don't be a cunt all your life, will you?'

Janet gasped. Bob stood up and slapped Kit very hard across his face.

*

'Janet,' said Marianne. 'This is indeed a surprise.' Her sister-in-law had walked to the back of the house, looking for her.

'Don't act like you're pleased to see me.'

'What can you mean?'

Though it was eight thirty in the morning Marianne had been up for a couple of hours, had been putting away the roller and small tractor in the outhouse following a further attempt at repairing the lawn, one of the few things the film company had not entirely rectified. She wore yesterday's clothes and hadn't had a chance to wash yet. Janet would have showered and left her spotless house in her laundered and pressed clothes and driven to Erringby in her cleanly vacuumed and dry car.

'Where is Christopher?' Janet demanded.

'Do you mean Kit? I'm sure I don't know right now.'

'Oh, I think you do.'

'Whatever is the matter, Janet?'

'Don't play games with me, Marianne.' Janet's righteous indignation was puffing her up like a disgruntled hen.

'Very well, if you insist,' said Marianne. 'But let me at least offer you a cup of coffee.' Janet hesitated.

'All right.'

Marianne led the way through the back door to the kitchen. It had been some time since Janet had been at Erringby and normally she would have commented on how clean and tidy it looked, hoping, Marianne knew, to rile her; as it was, she said nothing until Marianne had poured two mugs of coffee from the percolator and sat down opposite her, when she said, 'I'll come straight to the point.'

'Please do.'

'What on earth do you think you're playing at,' said Janet – adding, before Marianne could interject – 'giving all that money to Christopher?'

'Ah yes,' said Marianne. 'The trust fund.'

'If you wanted to help him why didn't you come and speak to me and Bob?'

'You and Bob?' Marianne's eyebrows shot up. 'Kit's eighteen. He's a grown man.'

'He's not,' said Janet. 'Well, I suppose he is, technically... but it's too much for him. You'll ruin him.'

'Ruin him?' Marianne tried not to smile.

'You know perfectly well' – Janet's attempts to modulate her voice, calm it, had been only partially successful; now it cracked open – 'that Bob and I want him to study to be a lawyer.'

'Yes,' said Marianne. 'I did know that.'

'What right do you have to ride roughshod over our wishes?'

'What right do you have to ride roughshod over his?'

For a moment it seemed Janet might fling her cup of coffee at Marianne.

'We're his parents,' she said. 'He's a bright young man. With a good future. He's clever at art, I grant you, but it's a hobby, not a career. We're not all like you, swanning around in our big houses. Some of us have to earn a living.'

'Ah,' said Marianne. 'So that's it.'

'Why do you hate us?' said Janet. 'Bob and me. What did we ever do to you?'

'Nothing, I'm sure,' said Marianne.

'You don't deny you're the one who settled all that money on Christopher?'

'You seem to be certain that I'm not going to deny it.'

'Are you going to tell me where he is?'

'I have no idea,' said Marianne. 'Erringby's a big place.'

'So he *is* here.' Marianne shrugged. 'Answer me, Marianne: do you have Christopher?'

'*Have* him? What words you do use, Janet.'

'Oh my God,' said Janet. She stood up, her chair shrieking against the floor tiles. 'I can't stand any more of this. Where is he?'

'Would you like to look? You're welcome to go through the house. It may take you a while, however.'

'Oh, you and your big house, Marianne! Just tell me where he is.' Marianne raised her hands palms upwards in a gesture of resignation. Janet went on. 'You've done everything you could to turn him against us. Putting ideas into his head so that he comes home – when I'd been lying in my hospital bed, Marianne – sneering at us. Suddenly nothing's good enough. *We're* not good enough. The *bread*, the *coffee* – he comes back wanting coffee at the age of eleven – the *orange juice* – ooh, the things he gets at Erringby! Ooh, can't he have his own bathroom?'

'Do you not suppose,' said Marianne, 'that your doting brother might have had something to do with that?'

'Where is Col? I want to talk to him.'

'Now he I can account for,' said Marianne. 'Though I don't imagine he'll thank you for waking him. Another big night, you see. At the Three Hares.'

'Poor Col! What did he do to deserve you?'

'I can't imagine.'

'No wonder he drinks.'

'Indeed.'

Janet was standing over her, a Clarks-sandal-shod churel.

'Col's right – you *are* a bitch. You've tormented him from day one. You've got in the way of all his plans... putting him down... And you've stopped him from having children. The one thing he wants over everything else. That's unforgivable, Marianne.'

There was a sharp silence.

'Janet, you have no idea what you're talking about.'

'Oh don't I! Col talks to me, you know. Some families do. I know all about it. How you won't go for infertility treatment. How you won't even try. Won't consider adoption. I don't understand you, Marianne. As a woman. You're selfish, selfish beyond belief.'

'Maybe it's him. Maybe you're a family of duds.'

'Oh, how dare you!' Janet was shouting. 'How dare you, Marianne!' She ran out of the kitchen into the corridor. 'Col! Col!'

Marianne followed her into the hall, where Janet found herself face to face with Kit's painting. She turned and looked at Marianne, then back at the painting, disgust on her face. Then she ran up the stairs.

'Col!' She opened the door to one of the bedrooms.

'That's not it.' Marianne had followed her. She leaned against the wall, arms folded. Janet tugged the door closed, wheeled round, opened another. 'Nope, not that one either.'

Susannah appeared on the second-floor landing.

'Marianne? Who's that shouting?' She looked down at Janet. 'Are you the home help?'

'Col! Col!' Tears ran down Janet's face.

Another door opened and Col came onto the landing wrapped in a candlewick bedspread.

'Sis? What the hell's wrong?'

'Oh, Col!' Janet flung herself into his arms.

'Hey, hey,' he said. 'It's all right. Whatever's the matter?' Janet was sobbing. 'Shh, shh,' he said, holding her to him. Over Janet's shoulder he widened his eyes at Marianne, mouthed *What the fuck?*

Marianne looked up at Susannah.

'Good morning, Mother,' she said. 'What can I get you for breakfast?'

PART II

9

November 1986

A number 43 bus pulled out of its bay at London Bridge station, revealing Bridget at the entrance to the Tube. She had on her 1950s skirt and a cardigan over her blouse. Her shoes were flats, black and pointy-toed, and her legs were bare. Unaware of being observed, she looked not only cold but forlorn. Then she saw him and her face changed entirely.

'Kit!'

'So sorry I'm late, darling.' He dropped a kiss on her cheek. 'Thanks for hanging on.'

'My goodness.' She held him at arm's length. 'You're the lovechild of Tintin and Bertie Wooster.'

'Very much the look I was going for.'

'I like it.' His new hair, dyed bright blond that day, had been shaved at the sides and fashioned into a small quiff – more of a cowlick, actually – on top. Bridget ruffled it. 'Blond suits you.'

'I needed a change. And what do you think of the whistle?' He took a step back and opened his arms.

'Completely without precedent.' The suit, also new, was of burgundy tweed, the jacket short and fastened by one button, the trousers, tailored like baggy knickerbockers, ending just below the knee in a cartoonish parody of plus fours. He wore brown tassel loafers with no socks.

'Shall we?'

She took his arm and they left the station together.

'How was your day?' he asked.

'Less exciting than yours. Essay on business ethics. Two thousand words due on Monday.'

'Business ethics? Is that not an oxymoron?'

'No wonder I'm struggling to get over five hundred words. Do you know where we're going, by the way?'

'Of course,' said Kit, but it turned out he did not know where Turk Street was, exactly, and Bridget rolled her eyes and fished out her *A to Z*.

'I knew it was here,' he said, as they turned a corner to see the queue snaking halfway down the street. The queue was a harlequinade of fashionable youth, gorgeous daubs of colour against the concrete of an industrial building whose original purpose might have been bottle-blacking or carbolic soap production, so irrelevant had it now become.

'Did you say it was four pounds to get in?' she asked as they moved up the queue. 'Seems expensive.'

'I bet I can get us in for nothing.' At the head of the queue the doorman, whose painted-on eyebrows were thick black oblongs, the uncoupled parts of an equals sign, looked Kit up and down and pursed his very cherry-red lips.

'Nemeth?' he asked, in reference to the suit, and Kit nodded. 'Very nice. Welcome to Inge's.' Kit slipped inside. 'Whoa there, Betty!' the doorman said. 'I don't think so, love. Why don't you go back to the Home Counties?'

Kit turned to see Bridget crimson with annoyance. She had really tried, she did her best on her student grant, and it was too bad she wouldn't let him take her shopping, though he understood why. She was self-conscious about her weight, too, insisting that club clothes did not sit well on her.

'It's all right,' she said to Kit. 'You go on. I need to finish my essay in any case.' She looked entirely crestfallen.

The man with the eyebrows and the cherry lips actually

had his arm out, a physical barrier, as if there were a danger Bridget might leverage her extra weight and strong-arm her way in.

'Nonsense.' Kit squared up to him. 'She's with me. If she doesn't come in, I don't.'

The doorman looked from one to the other, weighing up their relative values. Kit was becoming used to this kind of assessment working in his favour. He saw the doorman make a rapid calculation and he lowered the barrier of his arm.

'Sorry,' he said. 'I didn't realise you were together.'

Bridget fished out her purse but the doorman waved her away imperiously, all the time looking at Kit and not at her.

'Prick!' said Kit loudly as they went inside. She managed a sort of giggle.

'Not to worry. Are you going to check your jacket?' She nodded towards the coat-check girl, an Amazonian in a black PVC sheath dress with an immense mane of backcombed white-blonde hair that made her look about seven feet tall.

'Absolutely not,' said Kit. 'It'd ruin the look.'

'I knew you'd say that. So... what do you think?'

They looked around them. Money had been spent on this club. The interior had been transformed into a mock-up of thirties Berlin: bare floorboards, varnished wood-panelled walls, small tables on which sat Tiffany lamps and candlestick telephones (these turned out not to work).

'Not bad,' he said. 'I assume Sally Bowles does her turn there?' He nodded towards the small stage on which sat the DJ. 'Party Freak' by Cashflow was playing.

'Drink?' Bridget said. 'Having got in for nothing the least I can do is boost their bar profits.'

'First things first.' They went to the Ladies where he chopped out two lines of whizz with his Access card on top of a lavatory cistern.

This went unremarked; there were at least as many men as women in the Ladies, all there for the same purpose.

Bridget went to the bar and bought a soft drink for him and a half-pint of beer for herself. The DJ was playing 'Word Up!' by Cameo and she jigged from foot to foot as she sipped her beer. She wanted to dance, but Kit preferred to watch. He knew this frustrated her.

'Is that Belouis Some over there?' he yelled in her ear.

'No idea,' she yelled back. 'Why don't you go and ask him?' He shot her an *as if* look. She got her chance to get on the dance floor when a group of people they knew from West End clubs arrived and she danced with them to a couple of go-go tunes that were unfamiliar to Kit. As he sat watching a man approached his table, a huge Nikon camera dangling from his neck.

'Excuse me,' he said. 'I'm from *Red Triangle* magazine. We're doing a feature on club movers and shakers.'

Kit did his best to hide his delighted surprise. *Red Triangle* had lately established itself as the number-one style publication. 'Your reverence for that magazine approaches zealotry,' Bridget had told him only the other day when he admonished her for nearly resting her mug of tea on it.

'Oh yes?' he said now, as disinterestedly as possible.

'Would you mind...?' The man lifted the Nikon. Kit made what he hoped was an *if you must* expression, lifted his chin and gazed into the middle distance. The camera clicked and flashed.

'Wonderful!' said the man. 'I'm Sebastian Scott. May I take a few details?' Kit supplied his name, age and the general location of his address. Bridget came back to their table. There were perspiration stains in the armpits of her cardigan and her make-up had smudged.

'This is Sebastian,' Kit yelled at her. 'Sebastian, this is Bridget.'

'Hellooo,' said Sebastian, and turned back to Kit.

'Sebastian works for *Red Triangle* magazine,' said Kit.

'Does he now!' said Bridget, and Kit permitted himself a sly glance at her. 'Have you had your photograph taken?'

Sebastian said, 'We're doing a photo feature on club movers and shakers.'

'Gosh. And which are you?' she asked Kit.

'Both. I move and I shake.'

'Fantastic!' Sebastian scribbled something on a notepad. 'Why don't you come and see us at our office, Kit? I think our fashion editor would be interested in meeting you.' He fished out a business card and laid it on the table. Kit and Bridget stared at it. 'And,' said Sebastian, 'if you time it so I'm there, I can take you for lunch.'

'You're on,' said Kit.

'Do you know Livonia Street?' Sebastian asked. 'We're just off Berwick Street.'

'Oh, I can find it,' Kit said. 'I'm in the West End all the time. I study at St Martin's School of Art.'

Sebastian straightened up and smiled.

'Course you do,' he said.

'Course he does,' said Bridget.

'He fancies you.' They were in a black cab, speeding up Liverpool Road. Kit was a little tipsy. He'd bought two bottles of champagne when some of his St Martin's friends had turned up at Kander & Ebb, allowing him a moment of schadenfreude over their annoyance at having missed Sebastian, who had vanished into the night in search of fresh faces.

'Can you blame him?' He gestured at himself with his hands.

'You're like a prize you just won,' said Bridget. 'You might be the vainest person I ever met.'

'Oh, do you really think so, darling?' He stretched an arm along the top of the seat. She snuggled up to him and her stiffly coiffed hair tickled his face. He smelled her high-street hairspray.

'Say you'll never never leave me,' she said.

'Of course not. We're going to have the most marvellous time when we're done studying. I'm going to buy us a flat in Little Venice – no! – Covent Garden.'

The taxi pulled up outside number 62 Crouch Vale, the run-down Victorian house they shared with six or seven others. All were asleep apart from Fabienne, awake in the kitchen with one of the four-year-old twins on her lap. She was a gloomy twenty-something Goth from Amiens whose English, despite her years in London, was rudimentary. Kit rather admired her stubbornness in refusing to master basic pronunciation and grammar and, now that her bilingual daughters could translate for her, her motivation for improvement had plummeted still further. She scowled at Bridget and Kit.

'Here.' Kit held out his arms to the infant Aurélie. 'Come and sit with me.'

'Bonjour, Kit.' The child wriggled out of her mother's arms. 'Have you been to a nightclub?'

'Yes.' He sat at the table and pulled her onto his lap. 'We've had a lovely time, and we're not even ready for bed yet.' Fabienne's scowl deepened.

'Why don't you go back to bed?' suggested Bridget from the sink where she was filling the kettle. 'We can look after Aurélie until it's time to get up.'

'Is no point,' said Fabienne flatly, but soon she had nodded off sitting up at the table, her coffee cooling in front of her. Aurélie scooped up a foxed and stained copy of *George's Marvellous Medicine* and read it to herself, or rather told herself a story from the pictures, since the text was too old for her.

Bridget joined them at the table. Every so often Fabienne woke with a start before her chin lolled back onto her collarbone. Kit was buzzing.

'Of course I *know* the fashion editor. Well, I know *of* him. Why do you suppose he wants to see me?'

Bridget mumbled something about her essay.

'Oh, screw that!' said Kit. 'You've got bags of time.'

'OK,' said Bridget. 'I am a bit tired, though.'

'You want more speed?' Kit felt about his pockets.

'No,' said Bridget.

Fabienne jerked awake. 'N'embête pas Kit et Bridget,' she admonished Aurélie, then promptly fell back asleep.

'She's fine,' Bridget assured Fabienne's inert form.

'Why do you think they want to see me?' repeated Kit. 'Do you think they want me to model for them?'

'Perhaps. Who knows. Yes. You're pretty enough.'

'Why, thank you.' Kit batted his eyelashes at her. He remembered, suddenly, an incident of a few weeks earlier: following a night out, amphetamine still zinging in their blood vessels, Bridget had put her arms round him and kissed him and asked him up to her room. He'd moved her away from him as gently as he could.

'I prefer older women,' he had said, which seemed to him the perfect get-out, making it somehow appear his fault and not Bridget's, but he had seen her upset, seen too her efforts to hide it. She had laughed off the incident and it had never been mentioned again and he hoped she had forgotten.

Now she pushed her chair away suddenly from the table and stood up.

'I'm going to bed,' she announced, and held his glance a split second too long. No, she had not forgotten. She was in love with him, Kit supposed.

*

Col was surprised by the venue Kit had selected, a café round the corner from Angel Tube that was part of a run-down row of shops, each seeming to prop up its neighbour. When he went in he understood a little better: sixties Mod decor, black-and-white floor tiles, seven-inch singles dangling from the ceiling, a huge Italian coffee maker on the counter behind which stood a woman with a blonde bob and pink beret, who grinned at Col as he came in and said hi, a Muddy Waters track playing on the sound system.

Kit was not there but that was to be expected, in fact Col had counted on it, to gain the advantage of being there first, poised and ready, and to give him time to collect his thoughts. He took a seat facing the door.

'How you doing?' The woman came up to him and slid him a menu.

'Good, thanks,' said Col, which was a lie, but his old habit of pleasing won through; he looked the waitress in the eye and smiled at her and she flushed slightly and looked down; she was older than she had appeared at first sight, perhaps nearly as old as he was.

'I'll just have a coffee for now,' he said. 'I'm waiting for someone to join me.'

'Sure,' she said.

The café was not busy, just a scattering of students and a rockabilly couple. They were all in their twenties and Col felt a further connection with the woman serving. She glanced at him once or twice as she made his coffee.

'Here you go,' she said, putting down his drink, which came in a black cup with a black-and-white chequerboard saucer, a little like the floor, the milk in a yellow melamine jug. 'There's sugar on the table.'

'You're American,' said Col.

'That's right,' the woman said. 'We're from Chicago.'

He caught the pronoun immediately; she was married, then, or similar. A pity.

'Chicago,' said Col. 'Nice city,' though he had never been.

'I'll leave you with the menu while you wait for your friend.' She went back to the counter.

It was as well, thought Col, he was not here to flirt but to think, very seriously, about how he was to patch up the damage done to his family by the series of hand grenades Marianne had lobbed into it.

She had presumably arranged the trust fund for Kit – Christopher – some time ago, but had not seen fit to consult her husband. This, though humiliating, was not untypical; she was secretive about her financial affairs and this had established itself as an item of contention very early on in their history of marital rowing. He did not know, had never known, how much money she actually had. There were investments managed by City brokers and she had mentioned a property portfolio once, almost in passing, but these might have been sold for all he knew. It was like her, too, to make Kit's settlement anonymous, then adopt a sphinx-like attitude whenever the subject was broached. That her prime motives were not only to scupper, irrevocably, her relationship with Janet, but also to drive a wedge between Kit and his parents, both of which his sister was convinced of, was far less certain. He didn't believe that even Marianne was that Machiavellian; it seemed an extraordinarily expensive and elaborate way to prime a family feud, even if that was her intention. But a distraught Janet on the first-floor landing at Erringby and afterwards, during the long, long conversations he had, or tried to have with her, would not be disabused.

Janet, that awful morning, had been so noisily insistent that Col had eventually, and despite having assured him that he would not, given Kit up, disclosed his location in the gazebo, where another showdown had taken place. Kit, to his credit, had remained calm, stating and then repeating that he would make one visit to Flatley Close to collect his belongings and would then be leaving for London. He had an interview at art school set up through clearing.

Kit had been angry with his uncle for what he evidently construed as a betrayal but he was a young man, thought Col; passion flamed brightly but briefly at that age, and perhaps he *was* mature enough to appreciate the position his uncle had been put in. But since leaving Herefordshire Kit had made no contact with his parents, had provided no address or telephone number, his parting shot being that he didn't want to see them. Col, via Lois, had discovered that Kit had found accommodation through someone Nicola knew; he called Nicola and managed to get a phone number off her. When he telephoned the house Kit answered and, rather to Col's surprise, agreed to meet him.

The one positive outcome from the whole unholy mess was that he and Marianne were getting on better than they had in a long time. It seemed that, having done her worst, wreaked as much damage as she possibly could on his family, she was calmer, happier. Certainly she became a lot more cheerful once the film company had left and the promised repairs and redecoration had been done. Erringby was, in fact, in the best condition he had ever known it. He had loved having the film company there, revelled in the frisson of his affair with Lois, but had to admit that his domestic life was vastly improved now that they had all left.

He was angry with Marianne, both about the ludicrous secrecy of the trust fund and for her treatment of Janet, and yet it was nothing new; it was in a sense an extension of her behaviour for as long as they had been together. Day to day their lives were not much changed, Col acknowledged; he had long been in the habit of visiting Flatley Close alone and Janet scarcely ever came to Erringby, so in that sense things would go on as before. Col did feel sorry for Bob, who felt the estrangement of his son very keenly; Janet, though much angrier, was convinced that it was an adolescent tantrum and that Kit would come round. Bob and Col had been terrified that the stress would trigger another bout of ill health but this had not happened; instead her energies were expended in hurling invective at the subject of Marianne, whenever Col saw her.

But while the details of Col's life might be relatively unchanged, the wider damage was seismic. Janet and Marianne would never speak to each other again, would probably not suffer even being under the same roof. There was little Col could do about that, but perhaps he could mend the relationship between Kit and his parents.

The café door opened and it took him a second to recognise his nephew. Kit's bleached fringe jutted out from beneath a black military-style cap.

Col stood up, unsure how to greet him. Kit solved this by sticking out a hand to be shaken, rather formally. Col clapped him on the arm with his other hand. His nephew had toned down the make-up and was wearing just eyeliner as far as Col could see. Col could also tell that, though Kit's clothes were self-consciously casual, even scruffy, they had cost a lot of money.

'Kit,' he said. 'How's it going?'

The American woman came up to their table.

'Hey, Kit.' They kissed each other on the cheek.

'How are you doing?' Kit fixed her with a dazzling smile.

'I'm doing great,' said the woman, and handed him a menu. The men sat down and Kit's smile vanished.

'Well, Uncle,' he said. 'This is a surprise.'

'I'm in London on film business,' said Col – this was actually true, he had just left the production company's Berwick Street office – 'so I thought I'd look you up.'

'Right.' Kit was looking at the menu and not at Col. 'So in no sense are you checking up on me, nor attempting to be an emissary between me and my adoptive parents.'

Col decided to play a straight bat. 'Yes, that's exactly why I'm here, of course it is.'

Kit looked up, half smiled. The woman came back for their order. Col realised that he had not looked at the menu despite having sat at the table for twenty minutes. The menu consisted of combinations of drinks and sweet and savoury items, all named after jazz and blues singers: the Billie Holiday, the Chuck Berry, the Etta James.

'I'll have a Sarah Vaughan,' Kit told her. Col, picking at random, ordered a Muddy Waters – a cappuccino plus two banana muffins with peanut butter.

'So... how's life?' he asked.

'Pretty good.'

'You've dyed your hair.'

'Well spotted.'

'It looks nice.' Kit looked sceptical.

'You're living... where?'

'Haringey,' said Kit.

'Oh... north London, is it?'

'Yes, just north of Finsbury Park.'

'Right,' said Col, not sure where that was. 'You sharing?'

'Yes. It's in a housing co-op.' Col nodded, as if the concept were familiar to him.

'And how's college?'

'It's fine.'

'How many days do you have to go in?'

'Oh, it's not about how often you go in,' Kit said, as if his uncle were being very obtuse.

'Right,' said Col. The American woman came with their order. Kit's Sarah Vaughan was a toasted cheese and ham sandwich and a Coke.

'Enjoy!' Her smile took in the two of them. *Fancies us both,* thought Col, and wondered how he felt about that.

'So. Look.' Col took a bite of his muffin. It was surprisingly good. 'Your parents...'

'They're not my parents.'

'Come on, Kit. Don't muck about.'

'Janet and Bob,' said Kit. 'What of them?'

'They love you very much,' Col began. Kit rolled his eyes.

Col, for the first time in his life, felt a surge of anger towards his nephew. 'They want to know you're OK.'

'As you can see, I'm fine.'

'Are you going to let them have your address?'

'Nope.'

'Are you going to let me have your address?'

'What would be the point of that?'

'So Marianne and I can keep in touch with you.' Kit looked up from his sandwich. Col had played his trump card.

'I've written to Marianne,' Kit said. 'She knows how to keep a secret.'

Col curbed the urge to hit his nephew.

'You need to understand the position I've been put in,' he said, trying to keep his voice in neutral. Kit said nothing, so Col went on, 'I'm stuck between the three people I love most in the world.' Kit rolled his eyes again.

'You watch too much daytime TV.'

'I don't watch daytime TV at all, you little fucker, don't you realise that? I'm too busy trying to keep the ship from sinking. Keep the wheels from falling off.'

'Interesting mix of metaphors there, Uncle.'

How like Marianne he had become! It was if he had been studying her all these years and only now, having got it down pat, was he playing the part of her. It took an effort of will on Col's part not to start shouting. The meeting was not going well, but he needed to broach one further topic. Janet had insisted.

'What about Christmas? What are you going to do?'

'Christmas,' said Kit, as if it were months and not four weeks away. 'Can I spend it with you and Marianne? At Erringby?'

Col was surprised. Kit sounded eager, even a little desperate.

'Of course you can. We'd love to have you. But only if you promise to go and see your parents.'

'Forget it, then,' Kit said sulkily. 'I'll stay in London on my own.'

'Oh, Kit, you can't... it'll be miserable for you all by yourself.'

'No it won't. Fabienne'll be around. Probably.'

'Fabienne? Who's she?'

'None of your business.'

'You are being careful, aren't you?' said Col. 'I mean you do use condoms? You can't be too careful. These days.' Kit looked at him scornfully.

'Fabienne's a lesbian, Col. It means she doesn't want to have sex with men, if you can understand such a concept.' He stood up and pulled out his wallet, threw down a ten-pound note. 'Here, to pay for lunch. Keep the change.'

'Kit...'

Kit was pulling on his coat. 'I suppose you gave Bob and Janet my phone number?'

'No,' said Col. 'I didn't.'

Kit said nothing, but turned and made for the door. 'Bye, Suzy,' he said to the American woman, and he was gone.

Col's head pounded. The meeting had been a disaster. He had promised Janet that he would extract as much information as possible from Kit: what courses he was studying, who his friends were, the ultimate trophy being an actual address. As it was he had very little to report back, only that Kit had dyed his hair and bought new clothes. And he had lied to Kit about the phone number, though he had made Janet swear she would not ring it until he'd had this meeting, prepared the way for a reconciliation. As it was, he had probably made things worse. And Janet would certainly phone anyway. Col closed his eyes for a second.

Thank goodness he had his night with Lois to look forward to; straightforward, sexy Lois who understood what he wanted and made no demands of him.

He waved at Suzy to get her attention.

'Can I get the bill, please?'

*

Lois threw herself back onto her pillows.

'Whew.'

It was the first time they had made love in a bed and they had made the most of it, luxuriating in the vast horizontal plane of available space, the privacy, the lack of urgency. They'd screwed for what felt like hours until finally he came while on top of her, her head hanging over the side of the bed, her hands bent behind her on the floor, supporting her weight. He'd had to clutch at her slim sides to stop her falling. There were red marks on her body where his fingers had been. She'd shown signs of wanting to be dominated by him, which intrigued him; she was a forthright and confident person outside the bedroom, but Col was up for a little sexual theatre. He began to calculate when he could get to London again.

He lay next to her, the sweat on his body starting to cool. He pulled the duvet over them both.

'Here, don't get cold.'

'You needed that, didn't you?' She smiled at him knowingly.

'Fucking right, the day I've had.'

'What happened?'

They had barely spoken since he'd arrived at her flat; she had opened a bottle of Beaujolais and straddled his lap as he sat at her kitchen table, and started kissing him.

'Missed me?' she had murmured into his neck, and he had buried his face in the sleek curtain of her hair that smelled wonderful – she had changed her shampoo – and cupped her small breasts in his hands and said, 'Yes. Very, very much,' and she had led him to the bedroom.

Now Col said, 'I saw Kit.' He had, in the course of their furtive telephone calls, told her a little about the ructions in his family.

'Really?' She reached over him for her cigarettes, lit one and offered him one. Col waved his hand in refusal. He'd managed to give up a year or two ago, had relapsed seriously during the stress and excitement of the film shoot and wanted to break with it now for good if he could. 'How is he?'

'Living the high life, as far as I can tell. Dyed his hair, new clothes. I'm not sure how much college work he's doing.'

'Did you find out where he's living?'

'He wouldn't tell me. Just that it's in Haringey. Where is that?'

'North London.'

'He says it's in a housing co-op,' said Col.

'Oh yeah, Nicola said something about it. I think she might have put him in touch with the co-op, actually.'

'Would Nicola know where he is?'

'She probably knows which co-op he's in. But they have dozens of properties.'

'Could you ask her?'

'Not really, Col. She's in New York right now. I'm not sure when she's back.'

'Oh.'

'This has really got to you, hasn't it?' Col gave a rueful smile. 'Poor old you.' She leaned over and kissed him.

'I don't know, Lois. It's all fucked up. I don't know what I'm going to tell my sister. Bloody Marianne. It's all her doing. Why couldn't she just give him money a bit at a time, or wait until he'd finished university?'

Lois fell silent. He didn't often talk about Marianne with her. Ten minutes ago he'd been having exciting sex with his London girlfriend. Now he was a married man complaining about his wife to his mistress.

'I'm sorry, Lo,' he said. 'Let's talk about something else. Let's *do* something else. Are you hungry?' She shook her head. He put his hand beneath the covers, started moving it up the inside of her thigh. She put her own hand over it to stop him.

'There's something I need to say to you.'

'M'mm?' He kept his hand where it was, pressing against her thigh to open her legs. He moved on top of her.

'I'm pregnant.'

All the warmth, all of the light, drained out of Col's body.

'What?'

'Do you want me to say it again?'

He moved off her.

'I thought you were on the pill. You told me you were taking the pill.'

'That day I had a tummy bug, remember? That must have been it.'

Involuntarily he looked at her stomach.

'It's too early to show,' she said.

He was suddenly angry with her, for thinking that he wasn't familiar with basic gynaecology. And for getting ill, and not being clever enough to realise what might happen. He rolled over, sat up against her headboard. He didn't look at her.

'Is it mine?'

'Fuck you, Col! How *dare* you ask me that.'

'Shit, shit, shit.' He put his head in his hands. 'This is not good. This is not good.'

'I'm sorry. Shit happens. What can I say?'

He scratched his head violently.

'Let me think. Let me think.' Could he leave Marianne for Lois, shack up with her in London? They'd need a bigger flat. Rents were expensive here. And he had very little, scarcely any resources of his own. Virtually all the wealth was in his wife's name. Their joint account was topped up by her to a humiliatingly low level.

The only money he had of his own was the proceeds from odd jobs he'd done for neighbours, a bit of cash-in-hand work for James. And she had smart London lawyers, who would make it their business to ensure he emerged from a divorce with nothing. What about *Strassburg Pie*, though? When would his share of box office receipts come through? Lois would presumably be giving birth in May, June. But, in any case, did he want to leave Marianne? And Erringby? He'd had it worked out, commute between his wife and his London girlfriend as he went back and forth on film business. If Marianne found out she probably wouldn't care much. And now Lois had ruined it.

'You were the one who wouldn't use condoms.' She reached for her cigarettes again.

'Don't *smoke*!' Col cried in horror. He snatched the packet from her and she looked at him incredulously.

'I'm not going to have it,' she said.

'What?'

'I can't have a baby. I've got too much work lined up. I've got three months in New Zealand next year with Ron Howard.'

'Fuck Ron Howard, Lois, this is important.'

'My career is important! I've already been to see someone. Made an appointment.'

'Without speaking to me?'

'Col, you were at home in your great big house. *With your wife*. What was I meant to do?' She mimed holding a telephone receiver. '*Oh hello Marianne, could you possibly get a message to Col? He seems to have knocked me up.*'

'Jesus fucking Christ!' he shouted. 'Lois, this is so fucked up!'

'God, Col, don't get in such a state. It's hardly the first time this has ever happened to anyone, is it?'

'Have you thought about having it? And giving it up for adoption?' The notion, just at the very margins of possibility, that he and Marianne could adopt Lois's child. His child.

'Col, I'm not having a baby,' she said. 'Not now, maybe not ever. I don't know.'

Col got out of her bed. He left the room, walked across the tiny entrance hall to the living room. He came back with the bottle of wine and a glass. Some of their clothes were on the armchair. He threw them off and sat down, poured himself a large drink.

'Fucking hell, Lois,' he said eventually. 'I don't know what to say.' She shrugged. 'Why tell me at all? Why not just go ahead and get rid of it, since you've apparently made up your mind?'

'I wanted to give you the opportunity to do the right thing,' she said.

'What right thing? Ask you to marry me?'

She looked at him disparagingly.

'Don't be ridiculous,' she said, and when he didn't reply she said, 'A gentleman would offer to go halves on the abortion.'

'Oh. Right.' Col barely heard her. This trip to London had turned into an epic nightmare.

'But then, maybe you can't.' Her voice was chilly.

'What?'

'Well. You haven't much cash, have you?'

'What?'

'Marianne has it all, doesn't she?'

He stared at her.

'What are you talking about?'

'Col, everyone knew! You and Marianne, screaming. In a house full of people. *You control the money, you dole it out like pocket money, you emasculate me.* Well, the last bit at least isn't true, it seems.'

Col stared at her in horror. She had quoted at him lines from the episodes of marital argument that had played on endless repeat at Erringby for the last ten years, lines that had become as stale and as worn out as those in a seaside revue, entertaining once, that went on playing at the end of a crumbling pier, long since fallen from favour as a place worth visiting.

10

May 1987

Kit met Marianne at Moorgate Tube station. She had not said what business took her to the City and he assumed it was to meet with someone regarding her finances, and perhaps his. When she saw him she gave an enormous wave and ran up to him and they hugged like old friends. She smelled of Erringby, of dust and earth and old wood. A wave of homesickness rolled over him.

He had thought to show her around the West End – his West End, he meant, for of course she knew London – but she had other ideas.

'I know where we can go,' she said, and led the way into the Tube station. On the train they were forced to stand, she looking straight ahead while he was crushed against her. An involuntary erection formed as he pressed against her leg. At Holborn they changed and he was disappointed when this train was emptier and they got seats next to each other. Wordlessly, they stared at a government advert warning of the dire consequences of AIDS.

Still she did not speak, and he would not give her the satisfaction of asking where they were going. At Marble Arch they got out and she led the way down Georgian streets to a gallery that was unfamiliar.

'I've not been here before,' he confessed as they went inside. It was the first words they had spoken since Moorgate.

Now she did turn to look at him, and raised an eyebrow.

'You know why,' he said, as if she had spoken out loud. 'Too busy among the living.'

She knew exactly where she wanted to go. He followed her to a temporary exhibition of black-and-white photographs. *Young*

London – Permissive Paradise, the exhibition was called; the pictures were of hippies and ban-the-bomb protesters and a Twiggy-esque woman in a see-through chiffon blouse with nothing underneath.

'Ah,' Kit said in spite of himself. 'So this was your London.'

'That's right. Sometimes I wish I had never left.'

'But then you would never have moved to Erringby, and would never have met Col, and I would never have met you.'

'Oh well then,' she said mockingly and he felt himself flush.

They were alone in the room with the photographs. He dared himself to reach out and stroke the side of her hand with his finger. She opened her hand and took hold, not of his hand, but of the finger. Her fingers closed round it but she did not look at him.

She nodded at a photograph of Mick Jagger.

'That picture was taken at the Rolling Stones festival in Hyde Park. Brian Jones had just died. Jagger recited from Shelley before they played.'

'I know,' Kit said. 'Afterwards they released hundreds of white butterflies. Col told me about it. He was there.'

'So he says.'

'You don't believe him?' She shrugged. 'But why would he lie?'

'Why indeed?' Still she held on to his finger. Her palm was dry. He had a strong urge to kiss her. They moved on to the next photograph. Two women sat on the roof of a house, a man sitting between them. The house was run-down but you knew that the women came from more exalted origins; were slumming it rather, with their long hair and coltish limbs, were playing at being the bohemian; the man, too, had a complacent air, as if he were in a hiatus between university and a career in something arty and profitable. Below the man and the two women an open window showed a third woman. She was naked; the camera had caught her in front of white tiles, as if she were about to step into the shower or the bath. One hand stretched behind her, frozen in the act of pushing the door shut. Her head was obscured by the ribbed glass of a windowpane. There was a faint tan mark at the top of her thigh; she had been wearing a swimsuit. Her left breast, generous and firm, was visible. You had the impression that, had she known the photograph was being taken, she wouldn't have given a damn, had perhaps even loitered in front of the open window deliberately.

'I like this one,' Kit said.

'Suppose I told you that was me?'

He turned to stare at her. Her eyes were looking straight into his. He felt a jolt of electricity.

'No? Is it you?'

'It might well be.' She read the caption out loud. '*No Loss of Face, Courtfield Gardens, London.* I lived in that street in the late sixties. South Ken. I'd just left drama school.'

'But then surely you'd know the people on the roof.'

'Jane Birley, Freddie Banducci, Pamela Williams,' she recited without hesitation.

'It's not you,' he said. 'Really?' He wanted to step into the photograph, peer at the headless body, see if it was possible it could have evolved into the woman he had immortalised in *Woman in the Bath.*

'You can't say it's not,' she said. Her hand was still round his finger.

They walked to Cambridge Circus and had a drink in the Spice of Life pub. He bought champagne cocktails without asking what she wanted; he saw that this amused her, he also saw her let it go unremarked.

'It's wonderful to see you, Marianne.'

'It's lovely to see you,' she said. 'I've missed you.'

'Have you?' he said eagerly, and when she made no comment, added, 'I want to take you to dinner.'

'That would be very nice,' she said. 'Though really I should be treating you.'

'It's the least I can do. By way of a thank you.'

She said nothing.

'I am so very grateful, Marianne. For everything.'

'I'm glad of it,' she said.

'If it weren't for you I'd be in some windswept prefab next to the M6 studying torts.' They were leaving the pub.

'Imagine!' she said.

'It can't be imagined.'

He chose Kettner's for its champagne bar, where he ordered more cocktails.

'Are you trying to get me tipsy?'

'I don't think I've ever seen you drunk,' he said. 'Really drunk, I mean. What happens then?'

'Oh, it's terribly dull,' she said. 'I fall asleep.'

'Then no more alcohol after this one,' Kit declared.

'Don't let me stop you.'

'I don't really drink much,' he admitted.

'No,' she said. 'You have other distractions, I dare say.'

He had done a line of coke in the Gents in the Spice of Life and had thought he'd been reasonably discreet but she had rumbled him, of course.

He gave her his best big smile and she smiled back as if indulging him. The head waiter showed them to their table.

'How are things at Erringby?' Kit asked as they sat down.

'Oh, not bad. The post-film transformation is wearing off, sadly, things are dirty again. Mother is getting crankier.'

'I'm sorry to hear that.'

'And you,' she said. 'How is art school?' Kit looked down.

'Well…' he said, and she caught his meaning immediately.

'All that fuss and palaver to get there, and now…' She was mocking him.

'It's true,' he said. She had anticipated him; she always did.

He just needed to say what she knew he was going to say. 'They're talking about me repeating a year. I'm a bit behind.'

'Ah.'

'I know what you're going to say.'

'Do you?'

'I'm squandering my talent.'

'Maybe art school was just a means to an end,' she said. 'A vehicle to get you away from home and living the life you were meant to lead.'

Kit liked that idea, which absolved him of the guilt that pricked at him at two thirty in the afternoon when he would wake up, faced with the unfinished paintings and scotched collages lying around his room. The more junior waiter who came to take their order seemed distracted, and afterwards turned back suddenly from his route to the kitchen.

'Excuse me, I know I shouldn't' – he glanced furtively at the head waiter, occupied on the other side of the room – 'but are you Kit Dashwood?' He was a couple of years older than Kit and looked vaguely familiar.

'Yes, I am,' Kit said, aware not just of sounding slightly pompous but of Marianne's arched eyebrows.

'I just wanted to say...' The man spoke very quickly and was blushing. 'I'm a huge fan of yours.' Marianne looked as if she might burst into laughter.

'Thank you,' Kit said, with all the grace he could muster.

'I've seen you... all over the place, actually,' the man said. 'At Heaven. I've seen you there. And I love your shoots in *Red Triangle*.'

'Thank you very much,' said Kit. 'What's your name?'

'David. David Goldney.' He lowered his voice. 'We're supposed to pretend we don't recognise famous people – but I had to say something.'

'David,' said Kit. 'I'll look out for you.' The waiter scurried off.

'My, my.' Marianne had thoroughly enjoyed this exchange. 'Famous. I had no idea.'

'Oh, hardly.' Kit did his best to sound dismissive, though privately he was thrilled. 'But I suppose I am a bit of a face in certain circles.'

'You've been in the magazine again?'

'A couple of times.' He tried to sound modest. 'And I'm about to sign with a modelling agency... I haven't got time for art school really, have I? At the moment?' And with that Kit bestowed upon himself the absolution he required. He laughed, suddenly free.

'Well!' she said. 'You have made a name for yourself. A different name, moreover. Where did you get Dashwood from?'

'*Sense and Sensibility*,' said Kit. 'It's my favourite novel.' And my favourite character of course is Marianne, he did not add.

'So Christopher Antrobus is gone?'

'All gone.' He raised his glass of Aqua Libra in salute. She clinked her own glass to his. 'And the most exciting thing... I was waiting to see you to tell you...' He paused as the waiter put down their starters, glanced at Kit, and left. 'I'm making a video with David Bowie – I know you know who that is, Marianne, so don't look at me like that. Well, I'm going to be in the video. In the background...'

He tailed off. She had the same half smile she had worn since the waiter's encomium.

'Say something, Marianne.'

'You astound me.'

'Don't make fun of me.' He moved pâté around with his fork.

'Don't sulk,' she said. 'It doesn't suit you. And I'm not making fun of you. I couldn't be more pleased for you.' This satisfied Kit, a little.

She asked him about where he was living and he told her something of 62 Crouch Vale.

'But you'll see it later.' It had been agreed that she would stay over in a bedroom that was currently unlet.

'Any romantic interest?' she asked him next; he had been anticipating the question since everyone, even she, was intrigued by his love life.

'Oh no,' he said. 'I've no time for it,' which was his stock response.

'I find that hard to believe.' She put down her fork and smiled at him. The waiter came and took their plates away, glancing shyly at Kit again. 'That gentleman, for example, seems taken with you.'

'I get hit on by men a lot,' Kit admitted.

'That's not so surprising, is it?'

'Gay clubs are the best fun,' he said. 'And I guess people draw their own conclusions.'

'As people will.'

'I'm a straight man who likes dressing up,' he said. 'What can I say?'

'You keep everyone guessing,' she said. 'I like that about you.'

'I like that about you.' He had replied without thinking. She looked directly at him again, and again he felt a surge of straightforward desire power through him.

The waiter came back with their main courses. Kit summoned the courage to ask her what he had been wanting to ask.

'How is Col?'

'I'm afraid your Uncle Col has been rather naughty.' She took a mouthful of fish.

Lois. Kit guessed that the affair had continued after *Strassburg Pie*, that she would have been Col's stopping-off point after his lunch meeting with him last year.

'Is that still going on?'

Marianne looked at him curiously.

'I went to see my bank today,' she said. 'To confirm a suspicion of mine.'

'Bank?' What had this to do with Lois?

'Col's been taking money out of one of my accounts. He's

forged my signature. They showed me one of the banker's drafts.' Kit put his knife and fork down.

'What? Can he do that?'

'The forgery was rather good, actually.' She seemed amused more than anything.

'What did the bank say?'

'Well, technically it's a criminal act of theft. But a little strange to prosecute one's own spouse, don't you think? Not great for marital relations.'

'How... how much money?'

'Rather a lot, I'm afraid. The drafts were made out to the film company. I think your uncle rather fancies himself as a mogul.'

'Have you said anything to him?'

'Not yet. I only found out for certain this afternoon.'

Kit's mind raced. 'Are you going to be OK?'

She looked at him.

'I mean...' It was hard to say this. 'Do you need any money back? From me, I mean?'

'Don't be silly. I don't need anything from you. Who knows, maybe *Strassburg Pie* will be a huge hit and we'll make lots of money from it.' Kit felt a hot flash of relief, then shame at being relieved.

'But...' He couldn't believe how calm she was. 'Don't... don't you and Col discuss these things? Why didn't he ask you about the money?'

'He would have thought I would say no, I suppose.' She went on eating.

Kit was in shock. Marriages could be unfathomable, he knew – just look at his parents – but Marianne and Col were in a different league. There was something about the casual way she had revealed this, almost as if she were pleased about it. That it gave her more ammunition in the long-running conflict with her husband. That this was just a skirmish in the ongoing war. Kit had the feeling he was straying into territory that was off limits and dangerous, a land riddled with incendiary devices and dark, unsanctioned corners, but he ploughed on anyway.

'Why do you stay with him, Marianne?'

She paused from eating to look at him.

'He's the love of my life, Kit,' she said simply, and went back to her trout.

The intensity of emotion hit him like a freight train. His heart seemed to skip several beats and his stomach lurched; he felt unsteady, as if he might fall from his chair.

'Are you all right?'

'Yes,' he said, trying to recover. 'I just feel a bit woozy – I don't know what came over me.' He took a bite of risotto. It turned to ash in his mouth. 'I'm not hungry all of a sudden.' He put down his fork and pushed his plate away.

She said nothing, but had she guessed the reason he had fallen silent, what had made him snap closed like a steel suitcase, the appalling realisation that he was sexually jealous of his own uncle?

Kit paid for the meal automatically, throwing down his credit card without even glancing at the bill, pulling out cash for a tip that, he could tell by Marianne's expression, was overgenerous even for him.

He was reeling from the onslaught of emotion he had felt in the restaurant and he barely spoke on the Tube and bus ride home, but she didn't seem to notice. Where had this come from? He felt blindsided, violently mugged by an epiphany he would far rather not have had.

'Here we are,' he said finally, pausing at the entrance to number 62. He saw his home through her eyes, a sprawling Victorian semi built for the expanding middle class, a house once prosperous and now down on its luck. He wondered what she made of it, then remembered the house in the photo. He thought of the naked woman at the window and his stomach lurched again.

Suppose I told you that was me?

'Here we are,' he repeated, and led the way up the pathway with its black-and-white tiles, many broken or missing, the spaces where they had been taken up with moss and algae. She followed, her canvas holdall over her shoulder. The house had its unique odour, familiar now, of stale food and damp and cigarette smoke. She put down her bag in the hallway and nodded as if in approval.

'Let's have a cup of tea,' he said, suddenly shy; it struck him that she was the first person he had actually brought here, though there were plenty, of both sexes, who were eager to go home with Kit Dashwood, whose propositions and entreaties he was becoming proficient at deflecting.

They went into the kitchen with its fug of old meals, windows steamy from the ascot heater. Fabienne was at the table with Élodie and Aurélie. Kit made the introductions.

'Bonsoir,' said Fabienne and Marianne replied with a stream of French that was, Kit could tell, very proficient. Even Fabienne looked impressed. She said something in response that he couldn't catch and the two women fell into an animated conversation in which Kit heard his own name mentioned at intervals; he made out the words for 'nephew' and 'painting'. Marianne wasn't describing *Woman in the Bath*, for heaven's sake? Aurélie, the more outgoing of the twins, piped up in her endearing mixture of French and English.

'Est-ce que Marianne is coming here to live, Maman?' and Marianne smiled at her and said, 'No, I'm here only for tonight. Malheureusement.' Fabienne actually laughed, something Kit didn't think he had ever seen her do.

Bridget came in as he was making tea. He had been spending little time with her lately; she came clubbing with him less and less often, citing essay deadlines and exams that seemed many and onerous. Their lives were on divergent paths, the more so, he realised, in the light of that evening's decision to quit his degree course.

'Oh, Bridget.' He tried to sound casual. 'This is Marianne.'

'Oh! Hello.' Bridget shot him a surprised look, lifting her hand in a greeting that was like a little wave. Marianne turned to look at her.

'Hello,' she said, and went back to her conversation with Fabienne.

'You didn't tell me Marianne was coming,' Bridget said. Kit caught a peevish note.

'Yes I did, of course I did,' he lied. He had not told Bridget about the visit, mainly from the fear, unfounded he now realised, that she would want to tag along when he wanted Marianne to himself, to luxuriate in her company without having to accommodate anyone else's needs or wishes. Bridget looked at him, saw the lie, and looked so downcast that he felt sorry for her. The Fabienne–Marianne conclave, with its interjections from Aurélie, was winding down; Élodie, the other twin, had declared that she wanted to watch *Cockleshell Bay*, a particular favourite, on the VCR in Fabienne's room, and since it was already past their bedtime the girls' mother made a graceful-sounding apology and left the kitchen with progeny in tow, the three other adults singing out their goodnights.

'How adorable,' said Marianne, watching them go. Kit found no trace of sarcasm in her tone.

'I gave Bridget that fur coat of yours,' he said, to bring Bridget into the circle. 'You know, the sixties one that fastens at the neck.'

'Did you?' said Marianne. 'Didn't you want it?'

'It looks loads better on her,' he said. Bridget, half smiling, blushed a little.

'Really,' said Marianne. A silence descended on the room.

Kit, desperate, said, 'Bridget's doing a Business Studies degree. At City Poly.'

'Uh-huh,' said Marianne. He felt a flash of fury at her, for her hauteur and her unfriendliness.

'She's been my partner in crime,' he said. 'We've terrorised all the clubs.' Bridget gave an embarrassed laugh.

And now Marianne did, finally, turn to take Bridget in, condescend to give her a modest portion of her attention. At that moment she reminded Kit very much of her mother, Susannah. How overweening the upper classes were, how secure in their innate sense of superiority, even those who professed, like Marianne, a form of socialism.

'And of course I spent last Christmas at Bridget's.' He bit off the words *in Bury* for fear of a sarcastic comment. 'Her family are lovely. They were very nice to me.' Bridget slid him a glance. He had pleased her, lauding her family to Marianne.

'Oh yes,' said Marianne. 'That was kind of them. Poor Kit was destined to be quite a hermit.' It had been a surprisingly good Christmas. Kit had been taken in by the extended Buckley clan as one of their own and made a huge fuss of. He'd had the piously Catholic Mrs Buckley eating out of his hand, having represented himself as Bridget's poor-little-rich-boy friend. He had substituted Bob and Janet for his real, dead parents and then killed them off, and told the Buckleys that he had been brought up by his dead mother's brother and his wife in a Victorian country house. Bridget had eagerly gone along with the fiction, almost as if she believed it herself.

'My family wouldn't let anyone be by themselves Christmastime,' Bridget said now. 'It's just not how they are.'

If there was bait there, Marianne did not take it. She merely nodded, as if this were to be expected.

'Anyway.' Bridget picked up her mug of tea. 'I've got this essay, so...'

'See you later, Bridge,' Kit said as she slipped from the room.

There was no gun room in this house, nor drawing room, nor library. There was only one place where he could entertain. 'Shall we go and sit in my room? It's a bit more comfortable.'

'By all means,' she said. He showed her into his bedroom.

'Oh yes,' she said, seeing the clothes and the antiques and the paintings, many unfinished, the vase of flowers in the huge fireplace, the unmade mattress on the floor, as if it were exactly as she had pictured it. He was annoyed with her, though, and said, 'You could have been a bit nicer to Bridget.'

'She's a very plain girl, isn't she?' She was looking at a strip of pictures of Kit and Bridget taken in a photo booth at Victoria Station and pinned to his mirror, and at that moment he hated her for her snobbishness and her thoughtlessness.

'Fuck it,' he said, 'I need to do a line, a line of coke... do you mind, Marianne?' For it seemed pointless, scurrying off to the bathroom.

'Of course not,' she said, and he got out his wrap, sat on the mattress and chopped out a line.

Marianne didn't sit down but moved around the room, taking it all in.

'I like him,' she said of a bronze bust that Kit had picked up at a Highgate antiques shop. It was probably the most expensive thing in the room. 'Do you know who it is?'

'Antinous, apparently,' said Kit.

'Antinous?' She looked amused. 'He was a favourite – and I believe that's a euphemism – of the emperor Hadrian. A very pretty young man. How appropriate.'

'Don't start with that again,' he said.

He was hungry for her approval and felt a private thrill when, without asking, she started going through the stack of paintings leaning against the wall.

'They're not all finished,' he said.

'Art is never finished, only abandoned.' She turned to smile at him.

'And some is more abandoned than others.' He was waiting for the coke to kick in.

'You'll finish them one day,' she said. 'I like this one.' She pulled out an abstract portrait of the twins, the girl that was Élodie staring fixedly at the viewer, the figure of Aurélie only sketchily drawn, both girls occupying frameworks of black lines that could be construed as cages.

'Thanks,' he said. 'I will... I will finish them one day.' He felt relief, euphoria even, at the decision to leave St Martin's. He would go into college this week to break the news to his tutor, a woman whose patience, Kit knew, he had taken to breaking point even by the standards of his fellow students, prone as they were to histrionics and erratic behaviour.

Marianne slid the picture back between its neighbours.

'Maybe you'll paint me again one day.' She looked at him and smiled. Cocaine soared majestically into Kit's system, emboldening him.

'I would love to paint you again. Just name the day. I guess we don't have time tomorrow?'

'No,' she said. 'I have an early train.'

'Too bad,' he said, and then, 'I like thinking of *Woman in the Bath* hanging at Erringby. But sometimes I imagine breaking in and stealing it back.'

'Oh no you don't,' said Marianne. She was standing at the bay window. She pulled aside a grimy net curtain to look onto the night-time street. A red London bus chugged past, the handful of passengers on the top deck looking careworn, transiting from their indifferent evenings to their indifferent homes. 'That picture belongs to me. To Erringby.'

Kit's picture had caused a stir among the *Strassburg Pie* crowd when it was unveiled, with some ceremony, by Marianne. It was clear to everyone that the subject, though enigmatic, was her.

'It does,' Kit said. 'I did give it to you. But it's a special painting for me. It's what got me into St Martin's.'

'Well, it's very special to me, too.' It hung in a prominent position opposite the stairs where anybody visiting would see it. 'You must come and see us – me and the painting – when you can.'

Yes. He needed to come to Herefordshire. It had been eight months since he had spoken to either of his parents, and guilt had been nipping at his heels. Col had given Janet the phone number for the house, as Kit knew he would, and when a housemate had tapped on his door one afternoon, saying a woman was on the phone who would not give her name, he had simply replaced the receiver in its cradle and walked away. She hadn't rung again.

Me and the painting, Marianne had said, as if they were a couple.

'What about Col, though?' he asked, and it was a wrench just saying the name.

'Col needs to understand that you'll do things in your own time,' she said. 'With or without his intervention.' She was offering him a staging post from where he could visit Flatley Close, or not.

'*You* always understand me, Marianne,' he said, and now she did come and sit next to him on the mattress. Though to ask meant a knife twisting in his guts, Kit said, 'What does Col think of *Woman in the Bath*?'

'What does *Col* think?' Col, as the picture was brought downstairs and hung in the hall, had said very little that Kit could recall.

She seemed to be pondering the question of her husband's response to a nude portrait of her.

'Do you know, he's not really said. I suspect at root it offends his petit-bourgeois sensibilities, but he's far too anxious to appear bohemian to admit it.'

Kit laughed; he liked hearing this disdain of Col from her, but then said, 'Hang on, if he's petit bourgeois, what does that make me?'

'Oh no,' she said. 'You're not of that family, remember? No one knows your provenance. You might be very special.'

The cocaine in Kit's brain meant that he liked very much what he was hearing.

'Marianne, I don't suppose you know anything about my real parents?'

'Only what you know. A car crash. You were two, you weren't in the car with them.'

'I once overheard Bob and Janet telling someone that maybe I remembered some things, that supposedly that's why I was "difficult".'

'I don't know anything about that. Maybe you were in the car, and they lied to protect you.'

'Maybe.' But it didn't feel right. It was something he had given a great deal of thought to and though, try as he might, he couldn't remember anything before Flatley Close and Bob and Janet, he knew that he had not been in the crash that had killed his parents, though he couldn't have said how he knew.

She shifted her weight on the mattress. It wasn't the most comfortable place to sit. He would get a sofa. Move some of the clothes out of the way and buy a sofa.

'What will you say to Col?' he asked. 'About the money.' He was straying into one of the marriage's dark corners, but at that moment he didn't care.

'Oh, I don't know,' she said, and then, 'What will *you* do now, instead of art school?'

'Well, the modelling agency seem to think I'll get a lot of work. So I guess I'll do that.'

'Do you enjoy it?'

'I love it,' he said. 'I love the buzz, I love the attention, I love the clothes. There. Now you know what a truly shallow individual I am.'

'You're not shallow,' she said. 'Far from it.'

'You don't think I'm wasting my life?'

'If I did, I should tell you.'

He reached out and took her hand.

'I love you, Marianne.'

'Dear boy,' she said.

Kit was soaring; he talked, garrulously, about the David Bowie video he was going to be in. She listened indulgently.

'Of course, I may not get to actually meet him,' he admitted finally.

'It's late, for me,' she said. 'I should be getting to bed. Where am I...?' He had not shown her to the empty room upstairs.

'You can always stay here with me, Marianne,' he said, emboldened. She gave no reply, but stood up, left the room, came back with the holdall she'd left in the hall.

They went up the staircase with its threadbare carpet and into the bedroom, empty save for a mattress on the floor. At the window an old blanket had been pegged up to serve as a curtain and a naked light bulb hung from the ceiling.

'Fuck, it's bleak!' He was almost laughing. 'Sorry, Marianne. Is this all right?'

'It's absolutely fine,' she said.

'Bedding, though. You need bedding.'

'It would be nice.'

He went down to his room, brought up his own pillow and a spare sheet and a blanket.

'Thank you,' she said.

'Will you be all right?'

'Of course. Why shouldn't I be?'

She stood before him, holding the bedding to her chest. Kit's heart was racing.

'Marianne...'

'Yes?'

'Can I stay here with you?'

'Sleep in bed with me, you mean?'

'I mean literally lie on the bed with you, and sleep.' She said nothing. 'I'm lonely, Marianne.' She smiled at him, a rueful sort of smile.

'But you're not going to be ready for sleep for a long time, are you?'

It was true. His habitual bedtime was four or five in the morning. And he was wired on coke.

He took a step towards her, put his hands on her upper arms and pulled her to him and pressed his lips against hers. She let him do it.

'Fuck, Marianne!' he gasped. They looked at each other, his hands still on her arms. Gently, she took his hands away, letting the bedding fall to the floor.

'Goodnight, Kit,' she said. 'Will I see you in the morning?'

'What time do you need to leave?'

'Early. Around seven.'

'I'll be awake.' He turned and left the room.

II

August 1987

There was a red Triumph Spitfire 1500 with its top down outside the house. It had a W registration, so it would have been one of the last off the Canley production line before it shut down. Col peered inside to admire the aluminium-spoked steering wheel, walnut dashboard, deep-piled carpeting. The odometer measured a few clicks under eleven thousand. Col had just arrived in the van with its malfunctioning wipers and leaking oil tank. This car would be a lot more fun.

They were in the kitchen, laughing and talking. The laughing fell away as he walked in. Kit and Marianne were sitting at the table, plates of half-eaten beef stew in front of them. They had started dinner without him, despite his telling her he wouldn't be late.

'Hi, hi, hi,' he said. 'Hey, Kit.'

'Hey, Col.' Kit got up to clap his uncle on the shoulder. Man to man. 'How's it going?'

'It's going great,' Col said. 'Has Marianne told you? We're getting Erringby used for locations, photo shoots, all sorts.'

'Well, perhaps,' said Marianne.

'Is that your car outside?' Col asked, and Kit said that it was, and that he had treated himself.

'Nice,' said Col. 'Be fun to drive, I dare say.'

'Yes, it is fun,' said Kit.

'I've always fancied one of those.' Col helped himself to stew and sat down. 'Torque's loads better on this model, I think.'

Kit giggled and said, '*Torque*,' and raised his eyebrows at Marianne.

'You've lost us,' said Marianne. 'Do you want a glass of wine?'

'Not right now.'

'I'm taking Marianne for a spin in it later.' Kit reached for his own wine glass. His fingernails were painted with black nail polish, his hair was still blond and he was wearing a white linen shirt and an expensive-looking pair of jeans. This was his first visit to Erringby, indeed to Herefordshire, in a year. Marianne had said that he would be staying a night or two and would drop in unannounced on his parents. Col, who had not seen his nephew since that lunch at the Angel, was under instruction not to forewarn Janet.

'A ride would be super,' Marianne said. 'Will I need sunglasses and a headscarf?'

'Naturally,' Kit said. 'You can channel your inner Bardot once more.'

'H'mm?' She raised her eyebrows at him.

'Well, you wore that Bardot dress to the wrap party. And the way we did your hair. Just like her.' Marianne smiled, as though pleased by the memory. She had been in a vile mood that morning, making Col spell out what was needed from the builder's merchant and how much it would cost, doling out the exact number of notes from her locked drawer in the library; now she was playing the coquette.

'You could come as well,' she said to Col. 'We could all go to the Three Hares.'

'Hardly.' Col talked through a mouthful of stew. 'Unless you were going to stick me in the boot.'

'Oh!' said Marianne. 'Oh well, never mind.' What Col wanted was to take the Triumph out by himself. Kit would probably let him, if he asked. He was carelessly generous with his wealth.

'Have you seen *Strassburg Pie*?' Kit asked. 'I saw it the other day.'

'I went to a screening in Wardour Street,' said Col. 'But I've not seen the cinema release.'

'I'd have to go to Birmingham to see it,' said Marianne. 'It's not coming to Hereford.'

'Oh, isn't it? Has it not had a widespread release?'

There was an eye flicker between Col and his wife.

'No,' said Col. 'Which is a bit disappointing.'

'It got good reviews, though,' said Kit. 'Kim Newman was very enthusiastic in *City Limits*.'

'Yeah,' said Col.

'Did you spot Susannah in the background of the New Year's Eve scene?' Kit said. 'It's hilarious.'

'Is she?' said Marianne.

'Blink and you miss it,' said Col.

'You have to know where to look,' said Kit.

'Heavens,' said Marianne.

'How is Susannah?' Kit asked.

'Oh, she's... how is she, Col? Have you seen her today?'

'Not yet.'

'Her meals on wheels lady's been,' said Marianne. 'I saw the van earlier.'

'Didn't she move back to the staff flat?' Kit asked.

'No, we thought it best not to disturb her again,' said Col. 'I'll go and sit with her. While you're at the pub.'

Col switched on Susannah's television set and turned the sound down, which was how she liked it. The stipulation was that it had to be a BBC channel but this was academic, for she never actually watched it as far as he could tell. The talking heads, the quiz shows, the sitcoms and the snooker were moving wallpaper, flickering away in the corner of the room, ignored.

She sat in her wing chair and drank the tea he had brought up. Col sat on the hard, uncomfortable sofa. He supposed that they should get a doctor out to see her. She was becoming increasingly disoriented, often not knowing where she was or who they were. Or rather who he was; he suspected Marianne, though she claimed otherwise, of not visiting Room Twenty very often.

'How was your day, Susannah?'

He wasn't sure if she had heard but decided not to repeat the question. Her response might well be an imperious *I'm not deaf, you know*, as if she were choosing to take her time to reply.

'I've been sitting here reading,' she said finally. Her hardback copy of *The House in Paris* sat on the mahogany side table. Col doubted this, as the bookmark never seemed to advance, but said, 'It's a good book, is it?'

She stared into the middle distance as if contemplating.

'You were more of a reader.'

'Not really,' said Col, who rarely read anything other than the headlines in the *Guardian* or, very occasionally, a mass-market paperback that had been remaindered in the Hereford branch of WH Smith.

'What's your book about?' he asked.

'Oh, it's terribly sad. Those children. That poor boy. His mother wouldn't come to visit. You've read it, of course.'

'I haven't, Susannah. It's not really my thing. Marianne probably has.' It would be nice, though probably a bit too much to hope for, if his wife came up here to discuss literature.

'You were more of a reader. Harold didn't bother.'

'I'm Col, Susannah. Your son-in-law.'

'I know who you are!' Her voice was sharp. Col decided not to push it. 'Do you still have parties?' She sounded wistful.

'Parties, not lately, Susannah. But we had one last year, remember? For the film.'

'Oh yes.' She fell silent. On the television a tenor sang soundlessly on the stage of the Buxton Opera House.

Col couldn't have said why these asymmetric discussions, punctuated with their silences, should be soothing. He not infrequently sought sanctuary in Room Twenty.

'We were never invited again,' she remarked.

'Oh?'

'You remember that party.'

'Which party do you mean?'

'Nineteen sixty-three, of course.' She looked over his shoulder at a rosewood wall clock brought from Cormorants, her old house. 'That thing has not told the time properly for twenty-five years.' He turned to look at it.

'You like it, though,' he suggested. She seemed not to have heard him.

'You must remember the atmosphere in the drawing room,' she said. '*Glacial*. Harold always hated me.'

'Did he? Why?'

She took a sip of tea.

'This is cold.'

'I'm sorry. Would you like another?'

'I met Mr Churchill, you know.'

'Really?' Susannah hardly ever talked about her wartime experiences.

'Does Marianne tell you nothing?'

'You know what she's like.'

'Indeed. Well, I met him. He came to see us at Number 10 Group.'

'What were you doing there?'

She looked at him incredulously.

'I was a plotter. Battle of Britain.' Col did not know this about her.

'Wow. And what was Churchill like?'

'Cold,' said Susannah, taking a sip of tea.

'You mean the tea, or...?'

'Cold,' she repeated.

'You were in the operations room?' The films of Col's childhood came back to him. 'Moving the counters round a map?'

'Of course.' There was pride in her voice. 'Best days of my life.'

'Wow,' said Col. He needed to ask her more about this, perhaps write things down, before the memory seeped away.

'She won't make you happy, you know,' Susannah said.

'Who won't?'

'Maud. Your mother was right to put a stop to it.'

'I don't know who Maud is, Susannah. I'm Col.'

'We were never invited again. His friends were a very fast set, you know. Not our kind of people.'

The things Marianne had told Col about that party came back to him. 'Why didn't Harold like you?'

'Didn't like women. And I had a good war, while he…'

Col thought of the portrait in the hall downstairs. Uncle Harold's green three-piece suit and his moustache and his brilliantined hair gave him the look of a Terence Rattigan cad. He had apparently avoided being called up on a spurious pretext, had in fact accomplished little in his sixty-one years beyond building an impressive wine cellar. Ludo on the other hand spent a miserable war serving in the 46th Infantry Division.

This was the root of everything, Col thought. Of Marianne's inheritance, of the three of them living here now. Ludo's guilt over Marianne's supposed violation in the gazebo, engineered by Harold out of spite and out of resentment of Susannah. It all went back to Susannah.

'The summer Marianne turned nasty,' Susannah went on confidentially.

'What?'

'She won't make you happy, you know.'

'Who won't? Maud? Or Marianne?'

'She never forgave me for not wanting her.'

A chill ran through Col. Susannah, in her semi-confusion, her synapses misfiring, had the potential to tell him things that were incendiary. It was wrong, exploitative, to push her.

'How do you mean?'

'Oh, mistake, mistake. Her father.'

'You mean… you didn't plan to have her?'

'Thought I tricked him. Never forgave me. Neither has she.'

Col's head was spinning. He had yet to meet the elusive Francis Lonsdale, living in apparent luxury with his girlfriend in Singapore. The planned honeymoon trip had never come about. There were birthday and Christmas cards addressed in a spidery hand, but nothing more. Col had the impression of a charming but ruthless man. He risked an outrageous question.

'Did you have to get married, Susannah?'

She seemed to look right through him.

'Not the motherly type. Like me.'

'That's all right,' said Col. 'I've got enough love for both of us.'

'Love,' said Susannah.

They sat in silence for a while. Susannah sipped at her tea and pulled a face.

'Col,' she said. 'Cold.'

He stood up. 'I'll get you a fresh cup.'

'No!' It seemed she didn't want him to leave. He sat back down.

'Erringby Hall,' Susannah said after a while.

'Yes?'

'Needs money spending on it.'

'Yes.' Col did not mention his own part in their current financial woes.

*

'Is that all true, then?' Kit asked on the drive back. 'What Derek was saying?' The landlord of the Three Hares had left his post behind the bar to join them, uninvited, at their table. Kit had been unsure why Marianne tolerated Derek, who was a boor, but he seemed to amuse her.

'You caused a bit of a stir, moving into the Hall like you did.' He had the local accent, its West Country burrs tinged with Welsh inflections. 'Everyone knew them two – the Fentimans – weren't leaving behind no children but no one had heard of you, see? And word gets out there's this slip of a girl moved in by herself. Next thing we know she's got rid of all the staff that's been there for years.'

'Did you, Marianne?' Kit had been all mock-eyed wonder. 'How brutal of you.'

'Yeah,' said Derek. Marianne had continued to look amused. 'That didn't go down too well, I have to say. And then she moves a whole bunch of young people in.'

'A commune?' said Kit.

'Hardly,' said Marianne.

'And I remember when Col come in here, asking after you.'

'Me?' said Marianne. She had removed her dark glasses but retained her headscarf, knotted under her chin like a fifties fashion plate.

'Yeah, when he was back from all his travels, some hippy place. India or something. Like – you know – the Beatles. Been gone a few years. He always was a good-looking chap, but now he's filled out. Brown as a berry. Says he's heard about them two brothers, Mr Fentiman and the other one, dying so sudden and so close together, and that some cousin no one's heard of, some woman from London's moved in, and then – you remember Pete, don't you? Pete Walkey?'

'No,' said Marianne.

'Well, he remembers you. He used to help out in the garden sometimes up your way. With Bert Allenby. Before you got rid.'

'Oh yes.'

'He says to Col, *Yes, there's a woman running things now. And she's drop-dead gorgeous. You should see her. She looks just like Ann-Margret.*'

'Who?' said Kit.

'Ann-Margret. From the films. Pete says, *She's got...* I shan't tell you what he said next. *Anyway, Col,* he says, *you should check her out.* And Col says *I will, I'll go tomorrow and check her out. Bet you I can get her to go out with me.* And Pete says, *Ten bob says you can't. She's a bit of a snooty one.* That's what he said, Miss Lonsdale...' Derek had looked at Marianne apologetically, as if he had no choice but to report the conversation verbatim. 'And Col says, *You're on.* And a week later he comes in here and says he's fallen in love and he's getting married.' The landlord had sat back in satisfaction, and been called back to his post at the bar by a thirsty local shortly afterwards.

'I suppose it may be true,' Marianne said now, in the car. 'I hadn't heard it before.'

'So Col went after you for a bet? That's not very romantic.'

'That's not really how it was.'

'How much *is* ten bob?'

'Fifty pence, in new money.'

'Fifty pence!' He grinned at her. 'That's what you were worth?' He caught his breath. It was easy to overstep the mark, however unwittingly, with Marianne. But she was inclined to indulgence.

'You need to take inflation into account. It was thirteen years ago, after all.'

Kit laughed. 'Do you like him? Derek, I mean?'

'Why, don't you?'

'He's a bit creepy. Plus he's stuck so far back in the closet he's in Narnia.' This made her laugh.

'And the other stuff,' he went on. 'About you sacking all the staff. Why did you do that?'

'You ask a lot of questions, don't you?'

'Well, you fascinate me, Marianne.'

He needed to get a couple of things straight in his mind before they got home.

'Has Col stopped drinking?'

'No, but he's cut right down. Takings at the Three Hares must have halved.'

'Did you talk to him about the money?' Kit was making a right turn into the dark lane on what was a notorious blind corner. The car's headlights picked up the stripes of a dead badger on the verge. Marianne looked at him. 'I know it's none of my business...' She said nothing. 'But you did tell me about it. In London.'

'Yes, so I did. He knows that I know about it.'

And the silence that fell in the car was such that Kit knew not to push it. He had the sense of Col having been brought to heel, chastened, by the uncovering of his financial misdeeds, and knew that she would be enjoying this. What had he expected, coming here? That the night they had spent together on her bed, both stoned, she in her dressing gown with her damp hair, was a precursor to something? That she would honestly let him kiss her again, let him sleep on or in her bed, her husband under the same roof? He had been deluded to dream of it. The car pulled into the driveway of Erringby Hall and he hopped out to close the gate behind them without speaking to her.

12

August 1988

'Hello, Kit.' Anthony flung himself onto the banquette. 'Show us your cock.'

'He doesn't have one,' said Emile. 'He's a hermaphrodite.'

'Don't you mean a eunuch?' Anthony was drunk and there was a messy fumbliness to him, a contrast to the crystalline edges of Kit and Emile who had done several lines before setting out.

'Fuck you both very much,' said Kit. They were sitting in the VIP section of Salvage, Leo Woodcott's new club. Anthony lurched at him, alcohol-breathed and panting, wanting to settle the question of his genitalia once and for all. Kit shoved him away but he came back at him, trying to push his hand inside Kit's spandex leggings.

'Ooh, fight!' said Emile. Kit was forced backwards by Anthony who lay on top of him and mimed sexual intercourse.

'Get off me, you little pissant.' Kit pushed at Anthony, who was heavier than him and refusing to shift. 'This is a Galliano jacket. I'll sue your sorry white arse.'

'Anthony, don't be a bore,' Emile said. 'Just because you've had enough cock to build a handrail round the Isle of Man. Oh God, she's coming. Quick, sit up!' Anthony turned to look and sat up hurriedly. Kit straightened and gave him another hard shove.

'Wanker,' he said, and adjusted his jacket and smoothed his hair, for Leo Woodcott himself was bearing down on them. 'You really are tiresome.'

'Boys,' said Leo Woodcott severely. He was resplendent in a flowing black cassock and a klobuk, like an Eastern Orthodox archbishop.

Even when not dressed up his height was imposing, six foot five or six in his socked feet, and tonight his platform shoes, along with the headdress, meant that he towered over them. 'This is not a rumpus room.' Emile giggled.

'Sorry,' said Anthony, sounding like an eight-year-old. Leo arched an immaculately groomed eyebrow. Kit, relieved that Anthony seemed to be getting the blame, nodded and arranged his face into a stern expression.

'Come,' Leo said to Kit. 'Leave these barbarians behind. There is a person that I should like you to meet.'

Trying not to look gratified at being singled out, and shooting Anthony another look, Kit stood up. Leo placed a splayed hand between his shoulder blades and piloted him away from Anthony and Emile and towards the other end of the VIP section.

'I do so enjoy whatever it is you do, Kit,' Leo said as they walked. 'What do you do, by the way?'

'Ask my agent.'

'I see.'

Seated round a table were the editor of Italian *Vogue*, who Kit knew by sight, and three women, all models. Kit was on nodding terms with Ella Sharp from encountering her at one or two fashion parties; the other two he had not met, though he recognised them both.

'Georgina Garvey, meet Kit Dashwood,' said Leo. 'I cannot believe you two do not know each other already.'

Georgina put out her hand. She was even more striking in person than she was on the page. Her heart-shaped face had very little make-up other than some lip gloss and mascara, and instead of the outré outfits for which she was famous she wore a simple black dress. Her hair was a mop of platinum curls and the only jewellery was a pendant of white gold, amethyst and diamonds resting on her chest. Kit shook her hand and said hello.

'So this is the famous Kit Dashwood,' she said, though Kit was nowhere near as famous as she was. He knew of her, of course; she was one of the world's top models, but she was notoriously private, an infrequent attendee of parties and nightclubs. Leo held up both his hands in a gesture that, because of his outfit, was like a benediction.

'And so,' he said, and went away.

'Do join us,' said Franco Moretti, the *Vogue* editor.

'Yes – please do,' said Georgina. She made a sign to Nikki Healey to move up and Kit squeezed in between them. The others introduced themselves.

'Champagne?' Franco beckoned to someone. A glass appeared and was filled with Dom Pérignon.

'Thank you,' Kit said.

'I've wanted to meet you for a while,' said Georgina. 'I love your column in *Red Triangle*.' She had the transatlantic twang of her profession although Kit thought he detected traces of Home Counties.

'Thank you very much,' he said. To admit that he had been hoping to meet her, too, would be gauche in the extreme. 'I really liked your shoot in *Vogue*. The Idolatry Collection.'

'Oh, that,' she said, and frowned, a tiny line of vertical discontent flashing between her eyes. 'It was awful. Sandflies. My God! They were plastering camouflage make-up on me as fast as they could but the little brutes kept coming at me. I must taste like an insect banquet. By the end of the shoot my legs looked like red porridge.'

'You were molto coraggiosa,' Franco said appeasingly.

'Well, you looked fabulous,' said Kit.

'Thank you,' she said. 'I like your stuff too.'

'Oh... it's nothing.' This was not just false modesty; his modelling career was an amateur affair compared with her international catwalk shows, Italian *Vogue* and all. 'Although did you know Leo's planning a men's fashion show here?' She shook her head.

'With any luck I'll get to be in it.' Georgina nodded, as if there were no question of Kit's being excluded.

'Have you heard,' Franco was saying to the other women, 'about Jackson?'

'No,' said Nikki. 'Not him.'

'It's too awful,' said Ella.

'And Crawford as well,' said Georgina. 'I heard the other day from Vanna.'

'No!'

'Oh God, it's so grim,' said Nikki.

Kit did not know these people, but guessed what they were talking about.

'They reckon at least a quarter of the people we know will have it,' he said.

Georgina nodded. 'I heard they're turning people back at US Immigration if they find medication on them.'

'No!' said Ella.

'How awful,' said Nikki.

Georgina shook her head as if to jettison the topic.

'Let's change the subject,' she said, and to Kit, 'What are you doing at the moment? What projects?' He had a good answer for this.

'Well,' he said. 'I'm not supposed to talk about it' – he lowered his voice conspiratorially and Georgina's solemn nod assured him of her discretion – 'but *Red Triangle* and my agent are talking to a publisher about turning my magazine columns into a book.' Her dark grey eyes widened.

'Really? How exciting.'

'Shh,' said Kit, looking around him.

'Oh, strictly *entre nous* of course,' she said, and continued in a stage whisper, 'but you will let me have a signed copy, won't you?'

'Of course.' He smiled at her and she smiled back, a guileless smile quite unlike the moues and pouts she affected for photographs.

'Oh!' she said suddenly and looked towards the dance floor, 'I love this song.' 'Pump Up the Volume' was playing. 'Do let's dance,' she said to the whole table, but Ella was talking intently to Franco and shook her head and Nikki had melted away somewhere. 'Ohhhh...' said Georgina in what sounded like real frustration. She turned eagerly to Kit.

'I don't really dance,' he said.

'Oh, pleeeease! This is my big night out. I'm flying to Miami tomorrow for a shoot.' She was play-acting, but there was a hint of real desperation in the mock-beseeching eyes.

'Then of course,' he said, and stood up and offered her his arm.

Kit was used to being looked at, but taking to the dance floor with Georgina Garvey was something else entirely. It was extraordinary, the effort people made not to stare at them. Or more correctly at her: Kit registered eye flickers and sidelong looks. In his circle, death was preferable to acknowledging the presence of a celebrity.

He found, to his surprise, that he enjoyed dancing, had missed it even, as he surrendered himself to the music. He realised he was competent but not dazzling on the dance floor and this was one reason for his reluctance; in the VIP lounge or bar area of any club he would be one of the best-looking people present; as a dancer he was a valiant runner-up. Georgina, he saw now to his surprise, was not exceptional either, the grace she exhibited on the catwalk for some ineffable reason not translating here, but what she did have, what set her apart from virtually everyone around her, more even than her looks, was her obvious and almost childlike enjoyment of it. She smiled at him and took his hand, so that they were dancing hand in hand but apart, and this was another infringement of etiquette, the tangible delight in each other's physical presence. Kit had not enjoyed a dance so much since taking to the lawn at Erringby with Marianne. The simple pleasure of dancing with a woman was something he thought he had left behind.

The song ended and another came on, less recognisable; the dance floor emptied a little. They were still holding hands.

'I might sit this one out,' Kit said in her ear. 'Do you fancy a line?'

'Oh! I don't really. But you go ahead.'

'And leave you here? That wouldn't be very gallant, would it?'

'It wouldn't,' she agreed. 'So...?'

'Let's dance,' he said. This was a slower number and she put her free hand on his shoulder, so that it was natural for him to put his other hand on her waist, and they danced together almost formally, like a 1930s couple who had just met at a dance hall. She rested her head on his shoulder for a moment and her hair smelled of something fresh, like grass or hay. And she wore a perfume that was familiar: Kit couldn't place it but something stirred in recognition and he felt himself hardening. He moved his body slightly away from hers.

When the song ended they went back to their table to find that Franco and the others had left. A half-full bottle of champagne sat in a pail of melting ice.

'Shall we?' He lifted the bottle. She looked at her wristwatch, which he was able to identify as a Tiffany.

'Just a very quick one. I have to be up early tomorrow.' They sat side by side and drank. At the other end of the VIP section Anthony and Emile were trying not to look. In a flagrant breach of every unwritten rule that governed his social life, Kit lifted his glass at them in salute. Both men's eyes widened. Emile whispered in Anthony's ear. Kit laughed.

'What is it?' asked Georgina.

'My friends over there.' Kit actually pointed at Anthony and Emile, who looked discomfited. 'Trying very hard not to stare at us. At you.'

'Ohhhh...' said Georgina. 'This is why I don't come out much. I know it sounds ridiculous coming from someone who's made a career out of being looked at, but I don't very much care for being looked at.'

'Sorry,' said Kit.

'It's not your fault,' she said.

'It sort of is.'

'But I've had a lovely time.' That guileless smile again, as if he had given her a huge and unexpected birthday present.

'So have I,' he said. She looked again at her watch.

'I know it sounds silly...' she began.

'It doesn't,' he said.

'You don't know what I'm going to say,' she said teasingly.

'Yes I do.'

'What am I going to say, then?'

'You're going to say...' Kit, in fact, had no answer ready. 'You're going to say... *I thought you were gay.* You thought I was gay, I mean.'

'No I wasn't,' she said. 'I know you're not gay.'

'Do you?'

'Everyone knows.'

Everyone. Kit liked the idea that he had been a topic of conversation, however fleetingly, in Georgina's circle of 'everyone'.

'Most people think I'm asexual, actually.'

'Golly.' She seemed to have no answer for that.

'So what were you going to say?'

'Oh yes. I was going to say...' She took a deep breath, as if preparing herself. 'Would you mind terribly leaving with me? I know it sounds babyish but I'm not meant to be by myself in public.'

'Of course,' he said.

'You can go straight back in,' said Georgina. 'My driver will be waiting outside.'

'Let's go, then,' said Kit. He was unable to resist a little wave to Anthony and Emile as he escorted her to the exit. They came out of the club and there was a roar, as if something feral had been unleashed; he could just hear Georgina saying, 'Oh hell,' at the same time as he was dazzled by the glare of light bulbs popping and flashing at them. At her.

'Georgie! Georgie!'

Kit automatically put an arm over his eyes. With his other hand he groped for hers. Only the red velvet rope at the entrance to the club was keeping the photographers at bay. It was impossible to see how they could move away from the building without walking straight into them.

'Georgie! Over here!'

Kit was aware that she had dipped behind him, that she had found his hand and was gripping it tightly, but he did not see the figure to their right, who seized Georgina and lifted her completely off her feet; she kept hold of Kit's hand so that he was dragged along with her and the two of them were bundled into the back of a car, its windows blacked out.

His immediate thought was that they had been kidnapped and he felt a surge of adrenaline as a man got into the driver's seat. There was banging on the car windows as the paparazzi surrounded them. But Georgina was OK; she sat back in her seat, panting a little, and she knew the driver, who turned over his shoulder to look at her quizzically.

'Oh hell,' she said again. 'I was not expecting that.'

'Sorry, Miss Garvey,' the driver said.

'It's not your fault,' said Georgina. The hammering on the windows got more insistent. The car rocked. 'Can we just get out of here?' The car edged away from the club. There was a final thump of frustration on the rear window as they rounded the corner into Charing Cross Road.

'How on earth did they find out where I was?' Georgina said; this seemed to be rhetorical, since the driver didn't reply and Kit certainly didn't have an answer. 'I can't have just one night out for myself, can I?' She looked as if she might cry.

The driver said nothing, so Kit said, 'It must be an occupational hazard for you,' which was lame but the best he could come up with.

'It's... it's... it's maddening.' She shook her head vigorously and almost growled in frustration. Then she looked at him.

'Oh! You need to get back in. Mike, can we drop Kit somewhere?'

'Um...' Kit, much as he had enjoyed the club, did not want to go back in. He wanted, very much, to spend more time with Georgina Garvey.

The driver was looking at him via the rear-view mirror.

'Um...' he said again. He was, uncharacteristically, tongue-tied. He was used to others doing the propositioning.

'Oh,' said Georgina, as if suddenly both realising his shyness and interpreting it. She took his hand and squeezed it. 'Would you like...' She was tentative, almost bashful. 'Would you like to come back for some champagne? Or some tea? If that doesn't sound too granny-ish.'

Kit glanced at the driver, whose eyes were now fixed on the road. The limousine was turning into Regent Street.

'Yes please,' he said. 'I'd like that.'

They held hands for the rest of the car journey. Mike pulled up at the private entrance to Claridge's and they were whisked inside by uniformed doormen. A lift took them to the second floor where they were escorted along a thickly carpeted corridor to her suite. A door opened and it was as if Kit had stepped back into the last century.

A young man met them at the door. They walked through an entrance hall – Kit had time to take in a bowl of white tea roses on a round rosewood table – and into a vast sitting room, where there were sofas covered in Regency stripes and a marble fireplace and armchairs and luxuriant floor-length curtains drawn against the West End night. Pictures of what might have been French aristocracy hung on the walls. A woman was speaking Italian into a phone. She hung up as they walked into the room. Georgina made the introductions.

'Kit, this is Dijon' – the young man gave a little wave, said 'Hiyaaa' – 'and this is my wonderful assistant Vanna.'

Vanna, an unsmiling woman in her mid twenties with a red Louise Brooks bob and dramatic eye make-up, said hello and turned her attention to Georgina.

'What happened? I tried to get word out to the club but it was too late.' Her English was heavily accented.

'Oh... the usual.' Georgina dropped onto one of the sofas. She sounded resigned.

'How did they find out?' said Vanna. She glanced at Kit. He opened his mouth to retort. She wasn't implying... surely?

'God knows,' said Georgina. 'They're like a pack of rabid dogs. I just hope it's nothing to do with R.P.'

Kit had the feeling he shouldn't ask who or what R.P. was.

'I knew I should have come with you,' Vanna said.

'Oh no,' said Georgina. 'It was your night off. What are you doing here, anyway?' Vanna shrugged. 'How was your father? Did you have dinner with him?'

Vanna pulled a sour face, shrugged again.

'Oh dear,' said Georgina. Vanna looked at Kit, rather pointedly. 'We'll talk about it tomorrow,' Georgina said. She sounded appeasing.

'You have everything you need?' Dijon asked. 'For tomorrow. Your bags are packed.' He was a fine-featured African man, short – perhaps five foot four – and around Kit's age. He wore an exquisitely tailored suit.

'Yes – thank you,' said Georgina. 'Mike's picking us up at six.'

'You want some Perrier?' he asked. 'Or perhaps I make a pot of tea.'

'I'll sort myself out,' Georgina said. 'I've kept you up late enough.'

'I go now?' Dijon suggested.

'Yes, of course. Go and get some sleep.'

'OK, goodnight. It is nice to meet you, Keet.'

'Nice to meet you,' said Kit. 'And I love the suit. Is it Givenchy?'

'You have a good eye,' said Dijon, and left.

Vanna on the other hand showed no sign of wanting to leave.

'Can I possibly use your bathroom?' Kit asked.

'Of course,' said Georgina. 'It's as you come in but straight ahead.'

Kit washed his hands carefully in the marble basin in the bathroom and dried them on a fluffy white towel. As he came out of the room he could hear Georgina and Vanna in earnest-sounding conversation. He dared himself to peep into the bedroom. On a huge bed with a mahogany headboard were propped two pillows in crisp-looking white cases, the bedcovers turned back neatly. A vase of calla lilies stood on a side table. Her suite was larger than the whole of the flat he had recently bought.

'So...' Vanna was saying as he walked back into the sitting room. She stopped talking abruptly as he came in. Georgina leaped to her feet.

'Kit, you haven't anything to drink. Champagne...?' She hovered in front of a lacquer cabinet with an intricate Chinese pattern that presumably masked a fridge.

'I'll have Perrier,' Kit said, since that was what they were having. Georgina opened a small bottle and poured it for him. He sat on the other sofa. Georgina and Vanna went on talking about people he didn't know. He looked around him and wondered about doing a line of coke. It seemed as if Georgina might not, which was surprising, and he got the impression that Vanna would be disapproving. He should have done a line in the bathroom. It would be too obvious if he were to excuse himself again. He sipped at the Perrier and tried not to fidget.

Georgina glanced at him.

'So...' she said to Vanna.

'H'mm?' said Vanna.

'I'm keeping you up. It's not fair, on your day off.'

'Oh!' said Vanna. Georgina looked at her with meaning. 'I go to bed then,' Vanna said reluctantly, and stood up.

'Buona notte,' said Georgina, and stood up as well. The women kissed each other on both cheeks. Vanna disappeared, not out of the suite's main entrance, but down the corridor past the bedroom. Presumably she had a connecting room.

Georgina kicked off her shoes and lay with her feet on the sofa, scrunching a cushion to rest her head on. She smiled at Kit, wrinkling her nose.

Kit wondered what to say next. He was about to ask her about Miami, but instead she said, 'Thanks for looking after me back there.'

'Oh – it was nothing.'

'This is why I don't come to London very much. The tabloids here are the worst.'

'Where do you live?'

'I have an apartment in Milan but I'm not there very often. I'm mostly in New York or LA but I stay in hotels. I wish I could come to England more but, well… you saw for yourself.'

'Yeah,' said Kit. There was a pause.

'Do you—' she said.

'Where—' he said. They spoke over each other. They both laughed.

'Go on,' he said.

'You first,' she said.

'Where do your family live?' he asked her.

'Tenterden,' she said. 'In Kent. Do you know it?' Kit shook his head. 'It's a lovely place. It's where I grew up. I go there as often as I can, which is *hardly ever*.' She rolled her eyes. 'How about yourself?'

'Hereford,' said Kit.

'I've always liked the sound of Hereford. But I've never been.'

'It's a hick town,' he said. 'Full of yokels.'

'Oh.' She seemed not to know what to make of this. There was a pause. 'But you go back to visit?'

Kit had scarcely been back to Hereford since moving to London. There had been the fugitive trip from Erringby, the day after he had driven to the Three Hares with Marianne, then a brief Christmas visit... was that it? He found he wasn't able to lie to Georgina.

'Not often,' he admitted. 'My parents and I... we don't get on so well.'

'Oh no.' Concern was writ large on her face. 'That's so sad. Do you have any family members you're close to?'

'My uncle and my aunt,' said Kit. 'Well... more my aunt, really. They sort of brought me up.' This *was* a lie, but he thought if he could suggest as much to Georgina she might understand a little better. And he found himself, very much, wanting her to think well of him.

She nodded.

'My best friend at school lived with her grandparents most of the time. Because her mum had... well... problems.'

'Yeah,' said Kit, hoping to imply the same. It made him sound more interesting.

Georgina yawned.

'I'm stopping you from going to sleep,' he said. 'And you've got your early start.'

'It's all right,' she said through the yawn. 'I don't feel like going to bed yet. And I like you being here.' That smile again. Kit felt his heart do a kind of flip. He needed a boost.

'Is it all right if I do a line of coke?'

'Sure.'

'Do you fancy one?'

'No... but you go ahead.'

Kit chopped out a line with his Amex card on the coffee table. He snorted it through a rolled-up fifty-pound note. She watched him intently.

'Actually...'

'You want one?'

'If I start with that...'

'It's not addictive,' he said.

'Go on then. Just a little one.'

'Move up, then.' This was his excuse to sit next to her. She shifted her legs so he could sit down. Kit chopped her out a small line. She picked up the rolled note and grinned at him. Again that childish excitement, which made him want to protect her.

She fluffed snorting it, chasing the powder around the table surface. She sat up, wiping her nostril with her finger, and laughed.

'Whew!'

'OK?'

'It tastes funny.'

'Metallic? Dripping down your throat?'

'Yes.'

'You've really never done it before?'

'Oh, I get offered it all the time. And harder stuff. But I don't like the idea of losing control.'

'You won't lose control.'

'Promise?'

'I promise.'

'It's a bit late now really, isn't it?'

'You'll be fine.' This was his chance. He sat back, stretched his arm out on the top of the sofa. As he had hoped she rested her head on his shoulder. Her hair was close to his face. 'Your perfume,' he said. 'Chanel Number Five?'

'That's right.' She tilted her face to his. He could easily kiss her now. 'Well identified.'

'I recognised it,' he said. 'Someone I know used to wear it. Well, I imagine she still does.'

'A girlfriend?'

'No. Not really. She was my first time, though.'

'What was her name?'

'Nicola.'

'Where were you?'

Kit told her about the filming of *Strassburg Pie* at Erringby and going up to the top-floor bedroom with Nicola. Georgina said she hadn't seen the film, though it had played briefly at the movie theatre round the corner from her New York hotel.

'I wish I'd seen it now,' she said.

'It's out on video. I'll buy you a copy and send it to you.'

'It won't work in the States.'

'Oh.'

'Not to worry,' she said, 'I'll catch it when I can. Ohhhh...'

'Are you feeling something?'

'Yes, I am,' she said. 'Ooh. It's nice.'

'Told you,' he said, and she smiled at him again. 'So who was your first time?'

'Well, I haven't really told many people about it...'

'Oh, but you can tell me,' said Kit. Cocaine had restoked his confidence, and the thought of Georgina Garvey confiding in him was a marvellous one.

'Well,' she said again. 'It was Mr Nielson. My piano teacher.'

'Your piano teacher? How old were you?'

'Fourteen.'

'Fucking hell,' said Kit. 'I'm sorry.'

'Don't be.' Her head lolled on his shoulder, she was gazing at the ceiling. 'I knew what I was doing. Well, I thought I did.'

'But even so... how old was he?'

'Oh, I don't know... about forty.'

'Did you tell anyone? Your parents?'

'God, no! They would have been furious with me.'

'That doesn't seem fair.'

'It's just how it was,' she said. 'We only did it a couple of times.'

'That's all right then,' said Kit. She looked at him.

'Do you disapprove terribly?'

'Not of you.' How was he to match this? He wanted very much to impress her, which would involve shocking her. 'Can I tell *you* something?' She turned her grey eyes to his.

'Ooh, a secret. Yes please.'

'I had sex with my aunt. Well, I think I did.'

'What? The aunt you were telling me about?' Her eyes widened still further and immediately he wanted to take the words back; even with the cocaine jangling his synapses and loosening his tongue Kit felt that he had made an appalling error, sharing his deepest secret with a woman he barely knew, something that was special and private and should have remained so. *Fuck it*, he thought.

'Let's do another line.' He sat up and picked up his credit card.

'Isn't that illegal?'

'What, coke?'

'No, silly, your aunt.'

'Well.' Kit was desperate now to downplay it. 'She's not a blood relative – actually I don't have any blood relatives, I'm adopted. She's the wife of the brother of my adoptive mother.'

'Even so,' said Georgina; she looked shocked and excited at the same time.

'I'm not even sure what happened,' he said. 'I was completely stoned. All I remember is lying on her bed, next to her – then everything goes fuzzy. The next morning... Can we kind of forget I said anything?'

'It's a great story, though,' she said. 'It totally trumps Mr Nielson.' She actually looked impressed. *Fucking hell*, thought Kit.

'Have you tried to find your real parents?' Georgina went on.

'They died. When I was too little to remember them.'

'Oh, that's so sad.'

There was a silence.

'I should go,' he said. 'Will they get me a taxi downstairs?'

'Kit.' Her hand was on his arm. 'Don't take this... I mean...

I'm off to the States tomorrow, for a couple of weeks. What I'm trying to say...'

Extraordinary, that someone so fêted, whose image was of ultra-confidence, should be so diffident. *We're like a couple of kids*, he thought.

'Yes?' He put his hand on the hand on his arm.

'Please stay,' she said.

'All right,' he said. 'I'd like to. I can sleep on the sofa.'

'I would like it,' said Georgina, 'if you slept in the bed with me. We don't need to do anything.'

'Sure,' he said. Her face was very close. They kissed, chastely. Something inside him gave way and melted. He gave in to kissing her.

Kit went into the bathroom to clean his face of make-up and get undressed. He came into the bedroom wearing just his boxers. She was sitting up in the bed wearing white linen pyjamas. She'd taken off her make-up too and her denuded face made her look younger, still very striking but a little less empyreal, as if she might just be someone you could encounter in everyday life. She had the radio on.

'Do you mind?' she said. 'I need it to help me sleep.'

'I don't mind.' The World Service was broadcasting a programme about China. He got into bed with her. He put his arms round her and kissed her again.

'Actually, would you mind terribly if we didn't do anything?' she said.

'Not at all,' said Kit. He thought he sounded rather chivalrous. In fact he felt relief. He had invited a few women back to his flat, as much for the company as anything else, and typically they would stay up talking and doing coke before tumbling into bed and typically, he would find he was unable to sustain an erection for very long. He would laugh it off, blaming the coke. The women never seemed to mind.

'Have you got a girlfriend?' Georgina asked him.

'Not really,' he said. 'Nothing serious.' And then, 'How about you?'

She sighed, and the vertical frown flashed between her eyes for an instant.

'There's someone in Italy,' she said, 'but he's married and it's all got horribly complicated. He's… oh, it's quite boring, but he's very high up in Italian politics and he's terrified of the press finding out. I can't tell you his name.'

'Is it… is it R.P.?'

'Shh,' she said, as if she feared the room might be bugged. 'It's fizzling out, in any case.'

They were lying with their heads on the pillows, facing each other. He could feel her breath on him. He was very tempted to say that he was glad about the fizzling out of R.P., whoever he was.

'Do you enjoy modelling?' she asked.

'Sure. Yes, I love it. Don't you?'

'I hate it. I want to retire, as soon as I can.'

'Retire?' Kit was amazed. 'And do what?'

'Lead a normal life. Like a normal person. In a normal town – no, a village in the country, that would be best. When my contract's up with my agency I'm getting out. I haven't told them, though. Don't tell anyone, will you?'

'No, of course not,' he said. *But you could never be normal,* he did not say.

'I'm getting a bit old for this, in any case.'

'What? How old are you?'

'I'm twenty-five. How old are you?'

'Twenty.'

'You're a baby,' she said, and he smiled. 'You've got a gorgeous smile.'

'Thank you.'

'Can I ask you something else?'

'You can ask me anything.'

'I'm back in London in a couple of weeks. Would you like to meet up?'

'I'd like that very much,' he said.

'I mean... on a sort of date.' She was looking at him intently. On the radio 'Tell It Like It Is' by Aaron Neville was playing.

'Yes please,' said Kit. They kissed again.

At about four o'clock she fell asleep. Kit thought he would watch her sleep until she had to get up, but he must have drifted off, for he was woken at ten to six by voices in the suite.

He was alone in the bed. Someone came into the room and he sat up, but it was Vanna.

'Excuse me,' she said shortly, and retrieved something from a drawer, and left. After the drowsy intimacy of the night before the noise from her sitting room, the raised voices – there were several people in there, not just Dijon and Vanna – was jarring.

Georgina came into the bedroom.

'Hey,' said Kit, and smiled at her.

'Hi,' she said. She had showered and made herself up, she wore a short skirt with a fitted jacket. She was fastening an earring, bustling round the room, grabbing her purse, her make-up bag.

'Hey,' said Kit again. He reached his hand out towards her.

'I have to dash.' She slipped into a pair of heels. 'My car's waiting. You can stay here, if you like. Get room service to send you up some breakfast. They know you're here.' She was all business. She kissed him on his cheek, squeezed his hand briefly.

'I had a great time last night,' he said.

'Me too. Write down your number...' – she handed him a notepad and a propelling pencil; Kit wrote it down. 'I'll call you when I'm back,' and then she was gone, and all the voices were leaving as well, and the door to the suite closed behind them.

Kit rolled over to her side of the bed and rubbed his face in her pillow. It smelled of her perfume.

13

August 1988

He walked into his flat to hear the telephone ringing. It was his agent.

'Have you seen the newspapers?' Murray was in a state of some excitement.

'No,' said Kit, yawning. 'I just walked in through the door.'

'I've been ringing and ringing,' Murray said with a note of irritation; the insistent flashing of Kit's answer machine confirmed this. 'The papers – you're in them.'

'Huh?' Kit felt more tired than he had done in an age. He hadn't had the nerve to ring for breakfast from the Claridge's suite but found, when he came down, that they did know who he was; a car was procured for him and charged to Georgina's room.

'You didn't tell me you were walking out with Georgina Garvey!' Murray was too excited now to be petulant.

'Oh... yes, I got papped last night. I didn't think. Is it in all the papers?'

'The ones that matter. The red tops.'

'Gosh,' said Kit.

'Yup. You and the Garvey leaving Salvage. Couple of good ones of you actually.'

'Wow.'

'Excellent timing, Kit, I have to say. A splash in the tabloids'll do your PR no end of good.'

'Really? Wow. They don't know who I am, though, do they?'

'Ned Cargill knows who you are.' Murray had a triumphal air, as if he were responsible for the coup. Ned Cargill was the gossip columnist for the *Daily Mail*. '*Georgina Garvey leaving Salvage last night with model and party boy Kit Dashwood*,' Murray read out.

'*Party boy?*' Kit wasn't sure whether or not to feel offended.

'Yeah, yeah. You're a serious journalist. So, Kit...' There was a silence; he would be lighting a Peter Stuyvesant. 'You and Georgina...'

'Murray.'

'I know. It's none of my business.'

'It is none of your business.'

'But...?'

Kit sighed.

'We were introduced by Leo Woodcott. She's very nice. I might see her again when she's in town.'

'Good.' Murray was probably literally rubbing his hands together. 'If you're not actually going out, pretend to be. Because the publicity will do you no harm at all.'

'OK.'

'Georgina Garvey! I wonder what she wants with you.'

'What she...?'

'She's fucking some Italian MP, is what I heard.'

'Oh! How did you...?'

'It's out there,' said Murray. 'Listen, Kit.' He sounded more cautious. 'Don't put her in your column. You can allude to her, just don't name her. Her people are Rottweilers.'

'I've no intention of putting her in my column.'

'There's a joke there.' Murray was amusing himself. 'About putting your column...' Kit was silent. 'Never mind. And you can't put her in your book either, worse luck.'

'I've no intention of putting her in my book. I just met her, Murray.'

His agent would have been in his office since early morning, perusing the newspapers for mention – preferably, although not necessarily, favourable – of his clients. Today he had struck pay dirt. Kit had been in the newspapers before, in the background of photographs of London's night-time goings-on – half his head had been visible in a shot of Boy George a month ago – but never like this.

'*About* your book, Kit.' Murray would be taking a drag from his cigarette, pouring himself a coffee from the machine he had perpetually on the go.

'Yeah?'

'I had the publishers on yesterday. They're going to love the angle with G.G., but Kit...'

'What?'

'They feel there isn't quite enough for a compelling read. It needs... spicing up.'

'Spicing up.'

'Yeah. Some kind of personal revelation. You know – *my abusive childhood, my brushes with the law.*'

'I haven't had any brushes with the law.'

'It's just an example, Kit. Something the readers can get their teeth into.'

'I don't know, I...'

'Something outrageous. Make it up, if you have to.'

From his pocket Kit pulled out a tablet of Chanel No. 5 soap he had taken from her bathroom. He put it to his face and inhaled, closing his eyes.

'Uh-huh,' he said.

'The Garvey, eh? I wonder what she wants.'

'She might actually like me, Murray.'

'M'mm. Well, it's very, very good news for us. I'm already getting calls about you. See you next week.' He rang off.

Kit dropped onto his sofa. He loved this flat. His friends had expressed surprise at his choice and he had looked at bigger apartments in supposedly better locations, but for him it was a positive that Craven Street backed on to Charing Cross Station.

He liked the constant noise of trains coming in and out over Hungerford Bridge. It soothed him. London, his birthplace and the setting for his metamorphosis into Kit Dashwood, was pivotal to who he was, and where better to live than its epicentre, Charing Cross, the point from which distance was measured?

*

'To be honest I'd rather stay in and watch telly,' Georgina said. 'Can't we just stay here instead?'

They were at Craven Street. Mike had brought her straight from Heathrow, which was extremely gratifying. Kit had the date of her return etched on his mind and had hardly dared hope when the telephone rang but it was Dijon, calling from the airport. Would it be all right if Miss Garvey called on him? Yes, it would be all right, Kit had said.

She was wearing jeans and a T-shirt. Her hair was still platinum but the curls had gone, replaced by hair that was straight and brushed back from her face and tucked behind her ears. She wore no make-up.

'What a dinky flat,' she said. She was walking around his living room, looking at the magazines and the ornaments and the photographs. Kit with a group of friends at the Café Royal on his twentieth birthday. Kit dressed up like David Bowie in his *Ashes to Ashes* period. Kit with Leigh Bowery at Madame Jojo's. She took it all in without comment.

'I'm a bit self-obsessed,' he admitted, seeing the photographs suddenly through her eyes.

'You are rather, aren't you?' she said teasingly. 'Don't you have any photos of your family?'

'I actually do.' Kit went to his bedroom and brought back a framed photograph of Marianne. 'My aunt. On her wedding day.'

'*The* aunt?' She widened her eyes at him. She had remembered, and he nodded. 'She's gorgeous. What year was that?'

'Nineteen seventy-five.'

'I loved the seventies,' said Georgina. 'What a great dress.'

'I remember my mother being most disapproving,' said Kit.

'How old were you at the time?'

'Six or seven.'

'Ah... I bet you were a gorgeous little boy.'

'I was adorable,' said Kit.

'So... Auntie...? What's her name?'

'Marianne.'

'Marianne.' Georgina stood the photo on the coffee table.

'So, tonight.' Kit was buoyed by several factors; the fact of Georgina Garvey being on his sofa at all, her being delivered to the flat straight from the airport and, not least, the two lines he had snorted prior to her arrival. And he was far more confident here on his home turf than in the Princess Louise suite at Claridge's.

'You saw what happens when I go out,' she said. 'And I just got off a plane, remember? I'm jet-lagged.'

'I've got just the thing for that.'

'...and besides, I've got nothing to wear. All my stuff's at Claridge's.'

'I've got stacks of clothes,' he said. 'Something's bound to fit you.'

'You've an answer for everything.'

'I try.' He drew her to him, kissed her properly for the first time, her lips parting to admit his tongue. They kissed for some time.

'I'll be recognised,' she murmured.

'We'll disguise you,' he said. 'Clothes, wig, make-up, everything. Come on. It'll be fun!'

'Oh, I don't know,' she said.

'Come on, it's Saturday. We can't stay in.'

'What sort of wig?' She was kissing him again, her breath a

little heavier. Kit felt himself hardening. His hand moved onto her breast, surprisingly full and firm. 'M'mm,' she said.

'I tell you what.' He sat up, his hands on her upper arms. 'Compromise. We won't go out for dinner. I'll get food sent in instead. And then we can go to Swoop. It's a nice little club. Intimate. It'll be fun. Come on. You don't want to stay in. Really?'

'You're a terrible influence.'

'Good.' They both laughed.

'I'll need a nap first,' she said. 'Long-haul flight, remember? My body thinks it's eight thirty in the morning after a night of no sleep.'

'Course,' he said. 'Would you like a nap now?'

She was grinning at him.

'Is that a euphemism?'

'It could be.'

'Come on then.' She led him to the bedroom where she undressed, throwing her clothes to the floor, and got into his bed.

'Brrr!' she said. 'Hurry up.' He pulled his clothes off and got under the covers with her. He was happy to let her take the initiative. His cock stirred in her hand, responding to her ministrations. She had done this many times, with other men. He closed his eyes.

'Now who's a bad influence?' he murmured. In reply she pushed the covers aside and moved down his body, parting his legs and kneeling between them.

'Oh God,' said Kit, as she took his cock into her mouth, much deeper than anyone had before. If he wasn't careful he was going to come straight away. He tapped her head.

'M'mm?' She raised her head and looked at him. 'Not good?'

'A bit too good.' He pulled her up, put his hand between her legs; she was shaven, just a landing strip of hair. Her pubes were dark. He looked at his hand, two of his fingers buried inside her.

'Not a natural blonde, then?' he murmured.

''Fraid not,' she whispered back.

'I'm shocked.' He was whispering too.

'Neither are you, though,' she said, looking down at him. 'So there.' She was wet, wetter than Nicola had been, much wetter than Sonia or Annelie or any of the others. 'Ooh, that's good. That's right, wiggle your fingers... Oh God,' and she was coming, writhing and jerking, tightening round his fingers.

'Wow.' Kit was a little taken aback. He was also more turned on than he thought he had been in his entire life. He pulled his hand away and moved on top of her.

'Hey.' Her hand was on his chest. 'No party hat, no party.'

'Huh?'

'Condoms,' she said. 'I don't have any on me.'

'Oh.' He felt a brief hot flash of shame for not having remembered, for not talking about it first like you were supposed to. 'Hang on.'

He leaped out of bed, scrabbled in his dressing-table drawer until he found the pack of Durex, open, two remaining.

'Here.' She was sitting up, hand held out. Obediently, he handed her the condom. She made a tear in the foil wrapper with her small white teeth and opened it. He lay on his side next to her. The latex was cold on his cock, he felt himself wilt slightly, but she knew what she was doing; she pinched the teat end between her fingers and slid the condom down his shaft.

'Ready?' she said.

When dressed up, primped and ready to go, Kit was the master of any night-life situation, supremely confident. Now, naked but for the condom, he felt gauche next to Georgina's self-assurance and her toned body. Her extremely, publicly, famous body. Of course, she had done this loads of times.

Outside his window the trains rattled by.

'Uh-huh.' He moved on top of her. He wasn't quite hard enough, the end of his penis flattened against her, but she took charge, moved her hand up and down him, fondling his balls; she lifted her knees, parted herself with her fingers...

I'm fucking Georgina Garvey, Kit thought.

Suddenly, unbidden, an image of Marianne filled his head; Marianne in her bath, turning to look at him, naked, smiling.

'Shit!' He ejaculated before he could stop himself.

Georgina laughed and in doing so pushed him a little way out of her.

'Oh my.'

'Sorry about that.' Kit, rolling off her, did his best to sound nonchalant. 'Got carried away. You're too sexy.'

'It's always a bit crap the first time,' she said. He didn't know whether to feel mortified by her verdict or bolstered by the implication that there would be a next time. 'You could do something for me, though.'

'Again?'

'Of course. Don't look so surprised.' She took his hand, put two of his fingers in her mouth and licked them, put his finger on her clit. Her orgasm came quickly again, in huge, powerful waves. Kit was astonished.

Georgina yawned and stretched. She saw that he was watching her.

'What are you looking at?' She smiled at him.

She likes me. She does like me.

'I'll leave you to your nap, shall I?' He tried to sound brisk.

'That would be lovely.' She yawned again.

He got up, pulled the condom off, threw it in the bin. He went into his bathroom to shower. When he came back into the bedroom she was asleep, her arms above her head like a small child.

14

November 1988

'There's the church,' said Kit, unnecessarily. 'Ooh look, we're just in time.' The limousine pulled up behind the undertaker's vehicles.

'What a lovely church.' Georgina peered out of the window. 'Is it in the Italian style?'

'Yes, something like that. Let us out, Mike.'

Mike got out and opened the rear door. Georgina, wearing a tight black dress that ended at mid thigh under a short jacket, got out first. Her hair, worn in curls again, was shiny bright against her clothes. She had on a black straw cocktail hat with a net veil encrusted with crystals that came down to just below her nose. A black silk flower, half the size of her head, was on the front of the hat, arrowhead quills sticking from it. She wore black stockings and totteringly high heels.

Kit followed her out of the car, the Victorian tailcoat over his Paul Smith suit a foppish burlesque of the undertakers unloading the coffin from the hearse. In his buttonhole was a green carnation. His hair was slicked back from his face and he had made himself up to look vaguely ghoulish, pale, with dark grey shadows around his eyes. From the car in front Marianne and Col got out. Kit grabbed Georgina's hand.

'Marianne!' he called. Several of the mourners, all elderly, who were milling near the church, turned to look.

'Kit.' Marianne went up to kiss him. 'I thought you were meeting us at Erringby.' She, too, wore a black dress but hers was longer, and was under a black wool coat that had been expensive in its time but was old, and she wore thick tights and boots.

'Oh, well, you know,' said Kit. 'Can I introduce you to Georgina? Georgina Garvey?' The women shook hands. Georgina stepped forward and kissed Marianne's cheek.

'Oh!' said Marianne. People were looking. '...*really Georgina Garvey?*' someone murmured. '*Who?*' someone else whispered back.

'It's nice to meet you,' Marianne said. A smear of Georgina's very red lipstick was on her cheek.

'Lovely to meet you, too,' said Georgina. 'I've heard so much about you.'

'And this is my Uncle Col,' Kit said. Col was in a dark suit, also showing signs of age.

'Hello, Col,' said Georgina. Kit looked from one to the other and grinned.

'Hello,' said Col. They shook hands.

'How nice to meet you,' said Georgina, but did not kiss him. Col held on to her hand a moment too long. He looked slightly stunned.

'Right. Yes. Hello,' he said. Kit giggled.

'It's a lovely day for it,' said Georgina. It was a bright winter's day, very crisp, and very cold.

'Yes, trust Mother to summon the weather gods,' said Marianne.

'I'm so sorry I didn't get to meet her,' said Georgina. 'She sounded like a real character.'

'Yes, she was,' said Col. The undertaker was hovering.

'Whenever you're ready,' he said to Marianne. Susannah's coffin had been hoisted onto the shoulders of four liveried men, their faces pulled into expressions of blank solemnity. They began the procession into the church, Marianne following with Col.

'Come on.' Kit tugged at Georgina's hand.

'Are you sure?' Their voices were loud, they clanged in the wintry air. 'I mean, we're not family.'

'Of course you are,' said Marianne, and so they followed behind her and Col into the church where Kit, after a second's hesitation, took his place in the front pew next to Col. Georgina joined him.

'I am the resurrection and the life,' intoned the vicar. 'He who believes in Me, though he may die, he shall live. And whoever lives and believes in Me shall never die. Welcome, everyone, to this celebration of the life of Susannah Avril Lonsdale. Please stand for the first hymn, "Immortal, Invisible, God Only Wise", number thirty-eight in your hymnals.'

There was shuffling and coughing as people stood up and opened hymn books. Kit and Georgina were sharing. The church organ wheezed into the opening bars and Kit giggled. He couldn't find the hymn, and Georgina took the book from him, found the page and tapped her finger on it. The vicar looked at them, aware that these gorgeous creatures were going to attract more attention than himself.

Kit, no singer, mumbled through the hymn, which was in any case unfamiliar to him. Col's voice was serviceable. Marianne's rang out tunefully, her head up, not needing to look at her hymn book. The vicar met her eye gratefully. Georgina knew the tune and most of the words. She had a pretty voice.

'Hey, you're really good,' Kit said to her as the second verse began.

'Shush!' said Col, sounding annoyed.

'*Sorry*,' said Kit.

Everyone sat as the vicar gave a reading from Lamentations.

'God, this is depressing,' Kit whispered loudly.

'It is a funeral,' Georgina whispered back. Col glared at them.

After reciting a prayer the vicar asked them to be silent for a minute or two for their own private recollections of Susannah.

Kit broke the silence.

'It's freezing in here. Are you warm enough, G?'

'Have some respect, for Christ's sake!' Col hissed. Kit smirked. Marianne looked amused. The vicar tried not to look dismayed.

During the eulogy, in which the vicar talked about Susannah's childhood in Kidderminster and her war years in the Women's Auxiliary Air Force, Kit nudged Georgina to point out Col, dabbing his eyes next to him.

Marianne remained dry-eyed throughout both the service and the burial in the churchyard that followed. Kit managed to get through the committal without commenting or giggling, though he wasn't going to miss the opportunity to throw a handful of soil onto the coffin with a theatrical flourish.

'What the hell do you look like?' Col demanded of him as they walked back to the waiting cars. Georgina had gone ahead with Marianne. 'This is a funeral, not a fucking pantomime.'

'Oh, don't be so provincial.'

'Are you on drugs?'

'We had a few toots on the way down. Christ, lighten up, will you?'

'It's really inappropriate.'

'Come on, Col. At least it gives these fossils something to talk about.' He gestured at the mourners following them, some of whom were looking at him and shaking their heads. 'They'll be talking about this funeral forever.'

'For all the wrong reasons.'

'Well, they'll be following Susannah soon enough.'

'*Kit!*'

'Oh, la-di-da,' said Kit. 'Marianne agrees with me. Don't you, Marianne?' he called.

'Don't I what?' Marianne turned round. Kit skipped ahead and linked arms with her and Georgina, leaving Col behind.

Erringby Hall was also freezing. The funeral reception was in the drawing room, the only room that seemed to be heated, a rueful wood fire burning in the grate. The radiators had all been turned off.

It had been agreed that Kit and Georgina would stay the night and call in at Flatley Close the next day before driving back to London. Marianne had offered for Mike to stay over as well, but he preferred to make his own arrangements and was putting up at a local hotel.

Kit had taken one look at Susannah's mourners – Ronald the surviving first cousin, a couple of more distant relatives and a few former neighbours – sitting on sofas huddled near the fireplace, and declared that he was going to give Georgina a tour.

'Come on.' He took her into the library. 'Let me show you an example of my juvenilia.' He pointed out the pencil drawing of the ship he had done in James's shop. 'There.'

She peered at the boyish signature in the bottom right-hand corner.

'It says *Christopher Antrobus*. That's not you.'

'It was me,' he said. 'Bob and Janet are the Antrobi. I emerged as Kit Dashwood over the summer and autumn of 1986. I'll show you what I mean in a sec.'

She was perusing the books. '*The Thoughts of a Man of Mode*,' she read from one of the spines, and went to take the volume from its shelf, but Kit was at the door.

'Sounds riveting,' he said. 'Come on, I want to show you my next significant work.'

'God, you're egocentric,' she said.

'Naturally.' Kit took her by the hand and led her out of the library. Next door, in the drawing room, someone was saying, 'Of course, one hadn't seen Susannah in years.'

'Shouldn't we be socialising with them?' Georgina whispered. 'It's a bit rude.'

'Oh, we can show our faces in a bit. I want you to see... there!' They were in front of *Woman in the Bath*.

'Wow,' she said. 'I like this one.' Kit, pleased, stood by as she went up to the painting to scrutinise it. 'Is it supposed to be Marianne?'

'Supposed to be?'

'I mean… it is, isn't it?' He nodded. 'I love it,' she said, taking a step back from the painting. 'It's very sexy.'

Kit looked from Georgina to the painting.

'You're sexy.' He pulled her towards him and kissed her. She was still wearing the hat. The veil tickled his nose. 'Stupid hat,' he said, and pulled it off her head and dropped it.

She returned the kiss, throwing her arms round his neck. One of the mourners – he had the look of a retired colonel – made a grumbling sound as he passed them on his way to the downstairs cloakroom. Georgina watched him go.

'Where's our bedroom?' she whispered.

He took her up to the first floor. They were in his old room, Room Seven.

'This is where I stayed as a kid, when my parents had had enough of me. They used to pack me off here.'

'It's nice,' she said. In fact the room was shabby and drab, in serious need of redecorating.

'So what do you think?' he asked. 'Of my relatives?'

'She's great,' said Georgina. '*Very* attractive. I can see why… And she's obviously very fond of you. Well, she must be, to have given you all that money.'

'What about him?'

'Nice-looking. Fancies himself a bit, I think.'

'Bullseye.'

'But it was sweet the way he cried during the service. No one else did. You want to have someone cry at your funeral.'

'Oh, he's always crying. Especially when he's pissed. He's an old soak. I don't know how Marianne puts up with it.'

'She must love him.'

'Must do. They're starting to show their age, though. I don't know why Marianne doesn't dye her hair.'

'Can't a woman age naturally?'

'I suppose. Christ, it's colder than a witch's tit in a brass bra in here. Why doesn't she put the heating on?'

'It is a bit chilly.' Georgina sat on the bed.

'Jesus!' Kit jumped up and down and rubbed his arms vigorously.

'Come here,' she said. 'I want to warm you up.'

'Only if I can keep all my clothes on,' he said.

'Uh-uh. The clothes come off.' She slid off her spike-heeled shoes and started unbuttoning her jacket.

'You're a sex beast,' he said, but did as he was told and undressed. They slid under the sheets, which were nylon, cold, and with a suspicion of damp.

'Fucking hell,' complained Kit.

'Shh,' she said. 'Stop moaning.'

Matters progressed, until she whispered, 'Did you bring condoms?'

'No,' he whispered back. 'I thought you did.'

'Shit.'

'It'll be all right just this once,' he said.

'Not really.'

'Come on, G. I'm OK. I've hardly had sex with anyone – and no one since you. There. I've said it.'

'I've not had sex with anyone else since you, either.'

So R.P. had gone, thought Kit.

'Well then,' he said.

'That's not the point, though, is it?'

'We'll be OK.'

'You think?'

'Nothing's going to happen to us. Come on, G. Don't you want to?' She let out a small sigh.

'You know I do. Feel that. See?'

When they dressed and came back downstairs the reception had ended and everyone had left.

'Oh no,' said Georgina. 'We missed the party.'

'Not to worry,' said Col. 'We managed without you.'

'Col,' said Marianne.

'I do like your picture,' Georgina said. 'The one Kit painted of you.'

'Oh yes, everyone does,' said Marianne. 'Now, what are you two going to eat? We've been stuffing ourselves with sandwiches and cake but I dare say you didn't even have lunch.'

'Not hungry, Auntie,' said Kit. 'And by the way, what's with the heating? Our bedroom's like a fridge.'

Marianne and Col exchanged glances.

'We could light a fire in your room,' said Marianne. 'But the chimney smokes rather badly. We've lots of hot-water bottles. And extra blankets.' Kit looked unimpressed.

'We're out of oil,' said Col. 'Waiting for a delivery.'

'Bollocks!' said Kit. 'You'd never let that happen, Marianne.'

'Well...' she said.

'Oil's very expensive, Kit,' said Col. Marianne shot him another look.

'Oh!' said Georgina.

'Oh, *that*,' said Kit. 'Why didn't you say something? I could've paid for your oil. Why don't you send the bill to my accountant?'

There was a silence. Georgina stood up and poured herself a cup of tea and took a slice of fruit cake.

'There's really no need, Kit,' said Marianne.

'We're waiting for a delivery,' said Col. 'It got overlooked, what with the funeral and everything.'

'I'm sure Kit would love to help out if he could,' said Georgina. She sat down with her cup of tea and cake. 'Especially seeing as...' The sentence tailed off.

'We're fine,' said Col. 'Thanks.'

'You're allowed to eat cake, Georgina?' Marianne asked.

'Oh, she eats anything,' said Kit.

'I don't put on weight,' said Georgina. 'But I hate the way I look, actually. I'd much rather have a figure like yours, Marianne.'

Marianne looked surprised and pleased.

'I don't suppose your modelling clients would be very happy, though,' she said.

'Oh, it's ridiculous the way we have to look,' said Georgina. 'I so wish they'd use bigger models. Half the girls I know absolutely starve themselves.'

'With a bit of help,' Kit put in.

'Well... yes,' said Georgina. 'That does help keep your weight down.'

'Ah,' said Marianne. 'So you take drugs for professional reasons?'

Kit and Georgina laughed.

'What's your excuse, Kit?' said Col. Kit glared at him but didn't reply.

'Anyway,' said Marianne. 'What have you been up to, Kit? I haven't seen you in so long.'

'Oh, tons of stuff,' said Kit who, despite his claiming not to be hungry, was wolfing down sandwiches. He talked with his mouth full. 'My book's coming out for Christmas.'

Georgina laughed uncertainly.

'What?' said Col.

She looked at Kit.

'It's rather explosive,' she said.

'How do you mean?' Col asked. 'I thought it was just stuff from your magazine columns.'

'There's a bit of... context added in,' said Kit. 'To round it out. I'll get the publisher to send you both a copy, don't worry.'

'And we haven't told them about the ad campaign.' Georgina had the air of someone changing the subject.

'Oh yes,' Kit said. 'Did you bring the magazine?'

'I'll go and get it.' She ran out of the room and came back presently with a copy of Brazilian *Vogue*.

'It's come out earlier in Brazil,' she said. 'Heaven knows why.' She started flicking through its glossy pages.

'Oh, give it here.' Kit took it from her. 'There!'

With a flourish, he presented the magazine, folded open at the chosen page, to Col and Marianne. Col fumbled for the glasses in his pocket and put them on.

'Goodness me!' Marianne exclaimed.

In a full-page ad for a women's and a men's version of a fragrance was a full-length photograph of Kit and Georgina. They had their arms round each other, Kit grinning cheekily at the viewer, Georgina looking enigmatically at Kit. They were naked, their modesty preserved only by some strategically placed drawings of garlands of flowers and leaves superimposed onto the photograph.

'Bloody hell,' said Col.

'Isn't it great?' said Kit. 'It's a big campaign in all the glossies. And it's going to be on billboards in London as well.'

'And buses,' said Georgina.

'I'm going to be on the side of a bus!' said Kit. 'Stark bollock naked. Isn't it a scream?'

'Is it... I mean, are these actual photographs of you?' asked Marianne.

'Course they are,' said Kit.

'They were airbrushed a little,' Georgina admitted. 'Me more than Kit, actually. It's something when your boyfriend is prettier than you are, don't you think?'

Marianne laughed.

'It's kind of a John and Yoko thing,' said Kit. 'That's the idea, anyway.'

'John and Yoko,' said Col.

'What's the scent like?' asked Marianne.

'Oh, it's all right,' said Kit. 'We've gallons of it. I'll send you both some.'

'The photograph is extraordinary,' said Marianne. 'I'm flab-bergasted.'

'You like it, though?' Kit asked her.

'Of course. You both look incredible. Don't they, Col?'

Col didn't seem to be able to stop looking at the image.

'What?'

'I said, don't they look incredible?'

'Best not show this to your mum and dad,' said Col.

'Yeah, perhaps you're right,' said Kit. 'It's OK, Col, you can keep the magazine.'

'Won't they see it, though, eventually?' asked Georgina.

'Not unless Janet's taken a subscription to *Vogue* or *Tatler*,' said Kit.

'That seems improbable,' said Marianne.

'And it's hardly going to be in the *Daily Mail*,' said Kit. He, Georgina and Marianne all laughed.

'Quite the celebrity couple, aren't you?' said Marianne. She sounded pleased, as if it were her doing.

Supper was lasagne made by Col, who opened two bottles of Bordeaux and drank most of the contents himself. The kitchen, thanks to the range, was warmer than the rest of the house.

'We could sleep in here, G,' said Kit. 'Marianne, that's never a microwave oven.'

'Yes,' said Marianne. 'He would insist. My one concession to modernity.'

'Oh, I love all your old things,' said Georgina. 'It's so homey. I'd adore a house like this.' She looked wistful.

'Maybe one day,' said Kit, and smiled at her.

Afterwards they went back into the drawing room where Marianne stoked up the fire. Col disappeared and came back with a cobwebby bottle of port.

'I've been saving this,' he said. 'Nineteen eighteen, the year of Susannah's birth.'

'Golly, has it been in your cellar all this time?' said Georgina.

'Yes, would have been,' said Marianne. 'I hardly touch the stuff. Mother was rather partial, so I suppose it's appropriate.'

'Is there much booze left in the cellars, Col?' Kit asked.

'Some,' said Col. Kit snickered.

Col poured out four glasses of port.

'Just a little one for me,' said Marianne.

'I adore these glasses,' said Georgina. 'Are they antique, Marianne?'

'Everything in this house is an antique,' said Kit.

'Including me,' said Marianne.

'Oh no, Marianne!' Georgina remonstrated. 'You look wonderful.'

'Why, thank you,' said Marianne. Kit and Georgina sniffed their glasses of port dubiously.

'Well, here's to Susannah,' said Col, raising his. The others joined in the toast. Col took a drink. 'Not bad,' he said, swilling it round his mouth. 'Nice finish. Although apparently 1918 wasn't a great year.'

'People had other things on their minds, I dare say.' Marianne sipped at hers. 'It's not bad, is it? This glass'll do me, though.'

Kit, copying Georgina, had taken the tiniest of sips and put his glass down. He made a face.

'Not really my thing, I'm afraid.'

'That's all right,' said Marianne. 'It's just symbolic really.'

'Was that the oldest thing in your cellar?' Georgina asked.

'Do you know, I'm not sure,' said Marianne. 'I've never had a proper look.'

'I bet you have, Col,' said Kit.

'Oh shut up,' said Col, but he had become less irritable with his nephew since the wine at supper and sounded almost fond of him again.

'How did she die, anyway?' Georgina asked. 'Susannah.'

'Alzheimer's,' said Marianne. 'She declined very quickly. Terrible, really.'

'It was horrific,' said Col.

'Oh dear,' said Georgina. 'My granny's got that. She's in a home. It's awful, isn't it?'

'Very upsetting,' said Col. They all fell silent.

'Marianne.' Georgina sat at Kit's feet, an elbow hooked round his knee. 'Can I ask you something?'

'Of course.'

'Is your piano in tune?'

'Why, do you play?'

'I haven't for ages, but...'

'Please do go ahead.'

Georgina went over to the baby grand, selected a piece of music from the piano stool and, after a fumbled beginning, made a fairly good fist of a short classical piece. Kit, watching her, looked pleased and proud.

'Mozart's *Allegro in B Flat Major*,' said Marianne when it had finished. 'I haven't heard that in ages. You play well, Georgina.'

'I studied piano to Grade Eight.'

'Yes, so did I.'

'Why don't you both play?' said Kit.

'Have you got any duets?' Georgina asked.

'In the library, perhaps,' said Marianne. 'Hang on while I look.' She went out of the room.

'I didn't know you still played, G,' said Kit.

'I haven't for ages. It was fun. Do you know, I'm going to get a piano when I get home.'

'Where is home, Georgina?' Col asked.

'Milan,' she said, and Kit scowled. 'Oh, don't pull faces. He wants us to move in together,' she explained.

'Blimey,' said Col. 'Isn't that a bit soon?'

'You shacked up with Marianne pretty damn fast from what I hear,' said Kit.

'That was totally different.'

'Was it?'

'Oh, don't squabble,' said Georgina. 'We're having such a lovely time.' Col helped himself to more port. Marianne came back into the room, brandishing sheet music.

'Found these,' she said. 'Budge up.' She squeezed next to Georgina on the piano stool. They looked at the music, Georgina's head of platinum curls close to Marianne's long honey-blonde hair, streaked with a little grey.

'What do you think?' Marianne said. 'The Brahms? Fauré?'

'Marianne,' called Kit. 'Is it OK if I do a line?'

'Of course,' she said, looking up. 'You don't need to skulk away in the toilets here.'

'G, do you want some?'

'In a bit,' said Georgina, and, to Marianne, 'How about this one? Respighi.'

'Yes, let's give it a whirl,' said Marianne.

'Uncle Col?' said Kit, with meaning. Col shook his head.

Kit chopped out a line on the marble mantelpiece while the women started playing. There were a couple of false starts, Marianne shaking her head and laughing, but they got through the piece.

From the fireplace Kit applauded. He sniffed loudly and rubbed at his nose.

'Let's do it again,' said Marianne, and they repeated it, this time with no mistakes.

'That was pretty,' said Col. He was the only one still drinking the port.

'How about something more modern?' said Georgina to Marianne.

'Ha!' said Col.

'You'll be lucky,' said Kit.

'Do you like Joni Mitchell?' asked Georgina.

'I do, as a matter of fact.'

'I used to be able to play some of her songs from memory,' said Georgina. 'I bet I still can. Hang on…'

And Marianne stayed next to her on the piano stool as Georgina played 'Free Man in Paris' and they sang it together.

Kit, sliding onto the sofa next to Col, was grinning. He looked sidelong at his uncle, who was watching the two women, who were looking at each other and smiling, as if they were singing to and for each other, the men forgotten. Col watched transfixed, until he became aware of Kit looking at him and the two men locked eyes for a moment. Col gave Kit a half smile and went back to watching the women.

By 1am Georgina had crashed out on a sofa and was asleep. Marianne was sitting on another sofa, her boots off, her feet tucked underneath her. Kit sat next to her. Col had disappeared. Earlier he had put a record on in the gun room and 'Shine On You Crazy Diamond' was coming through the speakers.

'G?' Kit called softly. Georgina shifted slightly in her sleep. She gave a little snore.

'Aaah,' said Marianne.

'So what do you think?' Kit spoke quietly, so as not to wake Georgina.

'Now her I do like,' she said. 'You make a very handsome couple.'

'Oh, good.' He was whispering. 'I really wanted you to like her.'

'And I do. I like her very well.'

'I'm really glad. But I don't think Col does, much.'

'No, perhaps not.' They kept their voices low.

'He doesn't like her but he'd like to fuck her.'

'Oh, that's a given.'

'He's drinking a lot again?'

'Oh yes.'

'And is he... does he still play around?'

'There's a woman in the village he sees sometimes, after the pub. It's been going on for years.' She was dismissive.

'Don't you mind?' She shrugged. 'I'd hate it if Georgina slept with someone else,' he said.

'What will your parents make of her, do you think?'

'Bob will be so in awe of her he won't be able to speak. Janet will hate her.' Kit and Marianne exchanged smirks that were almost identical. 'In fact I bet Col's already phoned them. To "warn" them.'

'Yes, quite possibly so.'

He got up and went over to the mantelpiece.

'How much of that stuff are you doing, Kit?'

'Oh, I don't know... A gram or two, maybe.'

'A week?' He looked up, smiled at her naivety.

'No, Marianne, a day.'

'Oh.' He snorted the line and sat back down next to her. 'So... is this it, do you think?' she asked him.

'Georgina? I think so. I love her, Marianne.'

'Have you told her?'

'Not exactly.'

'Maybe best keep your powder a little dry, if you know what I mean,' she said.

'You reckon?' He smiled at her.

'I think the two of you will do very well together.' They watched Georgina sleeping for a while. 'She's exquisite,' said Marianne, as much to herself as to Kit.

'Oh, Marianne,' he said, turning to look at her again. She raised one eyebrow but didn't reply. 'I'm so happy, and it's down to you. All of it. I do love you, Marianne.' He stretched himself full length on the sofa and rested his head on her lap.

'I love you too, dear boy.' She began stroking his face with one finger, his cheek, his brow, his lips. 'Such a beautiful young man.' He closed his eyes. 'Such lovely long lashes.' She bent and kissed his forehead. She kept her lips pressed to him for a while.

Col had come into the room. Georgina stirred but did not wake. Kit opened one eye to see his uncle standing a few feet away, staring at him. Marianne's hand was in Kit's hair.

'Oh, hello Col,' he said, squinting up at him.

'I don't want to even think about what goes on between you two,' said Col, and then he was gone. Kit closed his eyes again.

PART III

15

January 1989

It was four in the afternoon and Kit had been awake for an hour. He was on his sofa, riffling through a gift bag he'd been given the night before at a fashion party. The bag contained a pocket television set as well as the usual items. Only the Acqua di Parma fragrance, the mints and the Rifat Ozbek pendant were of much interest. He already had a Filofax and several wallets and rarely watched television. It really did seem that the less you needed stuff, the more they gave you.

To his annoyance, Georgina had been in Italy for two weeks and had not, despite promising to, flown to London to see him that weekend. His attempts to telephone her had been frustrated; he could only ever reach Vanna, who would tell him that he had *just* missed her, she had *only now* gone shopping, or to see a magazine editor, et cetera, et cetera; *of course* Vanna had asked her to phone him as soon as she possibly could, but...

His book had been published at the beginning of December. Kit, with a deadline looming, had unprecedentedly stayed at home for sixty hours to finish it – Georgina had been in Thailand, being photographed by Annie Leibovitz. He'd gone on a cocaine binge – *if it was good enough for Robert Louis Stevenson* – and written fifteen thousand words on his childhood. He'd remembered the lie he'd enjoyed telling Bridget's family that Christmas of two years ago; the story of being brought up by Marianne and Col at Erringby. It had been fun to fantasise about and so, fuelled by the couple of eight-balls he had got in specially, he'd given himself free rein and had effectively recast his childhood, inventing an estate and changing names, depicting himself as a heterosexual Stephen Tennant in the making, opulent costume parties and the rest of it. He'd taken a few details from Marianne's stories of her Uncle Harold. He also hinted heavily that his relationship with his aunt – 'Annabelle' – had gone well beyond what was appropriate. Kit liked the notion of himself as a member of a bohemian set for whom normal mores didn't apply. He had put the floppy disk into the hands of a cycle courier before he could change his mind and edit. The publishers declared themselves delighted; this was just what they wanted, and sales had been buoyant.

Which was why it was annoying, now, that some of the shine had been taken off by more current blether. Murray had been on at him again about some of the headlines: *Georgie's £500 a Day Habit* (this was nonsense); *Armani Threatens to Drop Georgina Garvey after Cocaine Pictures Circulate* (this was not). Although the theory of no publicity being bad publicity held true, it only held true up to a point; when lucrative contracts were at stake it became a different matter entirely and Georgina's people – 'the Rottweilers' – took a very dim view of this particular strain of notoriety. They had a go at Murray and Murray had a go at him.

Kit felt it was extremely unfair that he seemed to be getting the blame – as if Georgina wasn't a grown woman, five and a half years older than he was, actually. No one forced her to do drugs. Neither was it his fault that they could barely step outside without being papped. It had been fun, in the beginning, to disguise her – for their first outing as a couple, that day they first made love, he had dressed her as a boy and himself as a girl and given them both harlequin make-up – aquamarine eyeshadow and black painted brows and tiny heart-shaped mouths over deathly pale foundation – but the press had quickly cottoned on and now it was hard to go anywhere together.

He had never been to Milan, her putative home; despite the heavy hints he dropped she remained evasive. Occasionally, at 6am, say, wired and unable to sleep, he would convince himself that the reason for this was the supposedly erstwhile lover, R.P., that the affair had not in fact ended – he pictured a private jet flying her to Rome for an assignation – and he would phone, only to have her castigate him sleepily for waking her.

The telephone rang. Kit sat up but didn't immediately answer it. If it was her, he didn't want to give the impression that he was waiting by the phone, even if that was precisely what he was doing. The phone rang twice and then stopped: this was the signal that it was Jonathan calling. When it rang again Kit picked up.

'Kit.' Jonathan's drawl elongated the vowel. He lived, apparently, in some sequestered part of Hampstead Garden Suburb. Kit had never visited, transactions taking place with Jonathan's couriers, primed to turn up at Kit's flat at any time with an hour's notice, less if they were already in the West End. Which they usually were.

'Hey, Jonathan.'

'I'm not disturbing you.' This was a statement rather than a question.

'No.'

'Good. Because I hope you don't mind my telephoning you about a rather delicate matter. I have been trying, you will be aware, to reach you for some time.'

'Uh-huh.' Kit was looking at the large painting of himself, a triptych, hanging above the fireplace: Kit in semi-profile flanked on either side by Kit looking at the viewer. He had had it commissioned specially and it had arrived a few days ago. The artist had given him an ethereal look that he was pleased with. He was looking forward to showing it to Georgina.

'It is the tiny matter of your account, you see.'

'Oh?'

'My terms, as you know, are normally flexible. But twelve big ones, Kit.'

'Crikey, is it as much as that?' He was examining his finger-nails. He needed a manicure.

'It is indeed as much as that. Now, Kit...'

'M'mm?'

'My terms are normally flexible. But a sum of this size... there are implications. Supply chain. You understand me.'

'OK, I get you. I'll sort something out.' Kit tried to recall his last conversation with Ray, his accountant. 'I'm a bit illiquid at the moment, or something. Something's not flowing.'

'May I assume that my courier will be able to collect the amount due from you on Monday?'

'Monday? Bloody hell, that's a bit soon. Can I not...?'

'Monday. Or I'm very much afraid that I will have to suspend your account.'

'Jonathan!'

'Monday. You have a good weekend now.' He rang off.

'Fuck's sake!' Kit said to the telephone receiver. A sum that size, in cash, was not that straightforward to come by. He probably had about a thousand pounds in the flat. He was going to have to phone Ray, and then go to his bank, if Ray were able to transfer the money in time. In the meantime he would have to score coke from friends. It was very inconvenient.

He wondered about tonight. There were a couple of parties he'd been invited to, a gallery opening. Going out alone was far easier. Though his book had generated some heat, the press were not much interested in him unless there was an angle relating to Georgina – *Lovelorn Kit Parties Alone* – but he enjoyed being one half of a couple. She was a part of who he had become. And he missed her.

Another irksome thing was the letter from his father. It sat on the coffee table a few inches from his foot where it seemed almost to pulsate, as if it were radioactive. Kit had scanned it quickly. The gist was that his parents were horrified, both by the newspaper reports of his drug use and by his book. *Your mother and I are at a complete loss as to why you would write those terrible things about us, about your aunt.* The letter made reference to Janet's mental health dipping as a result, which Kit thought was a bit low. Having urged him to get help, go to rehab and then come back to Hereford to recuperate, Bob signed off by assuring Kit of their love and support. Kit had stuffed the letter back in its envelope. He wanted to throw it away, but couldn't bring himself to.

*

Georgina telephoned at eleven o'clock on Monday morning. He was too sleepy to be annoyed with her for waking him. It was a bad line and she sounded distant, her voice fading and then brightening so that it was hard to follow her. He tried to picture her in her apartment, which he had never visited. He imagined something grand in the palazzo style: high ceilings, Gothic windows, marble terrazzo floors. She was apologising for not calling sooner.

'I wish you'd come home,' he said. 'I miss you.'

'I miss you too, sweetie.' He wanted her to say *I am home; this is my home*, so that he could chide her for it, insinuate that her home was with him, in London, but she did not rise to it. Instead she broke into a volley of Italian with someone in the room with her; Vanna, he assumed. Georgina and her assistant had a compact whereby they spoke English together in London or New York and Italian when they were in Milan. He used to find it charming, now it felt like one more way in which she excluded him from her life.

'Is Vanna there with you?' He felt impatient with her, for waking him when she could have waited until she was alone before calling.

'She just got here; she's going straight out again – ciao, ciao...' And Kit did think he heard a front door closing.

'I need to talk to you,' she said. 'It's rather serious.'

'It is serious,' he said. 'Have you talked to Armani? Are they really going to sack you?'

'Oh, I don't give a monkey's about Armani. They can go and stuff themselves for all I care. No, it's something else. Something I just found out.'

'What is it?'

'I went to see my doctor,' she began.

'Are you ill?' A flutter of panic rose in his chest.

'No. No, it's not that. I'm just going to come out and say it. I'm pregnant.'

There was a pause.

'Oh fuck!' A reflex response, something he might have said on receiving a minor piece of bad news; a friend losing their wallet, or breaking their ankle. His immediate thought was that she was telling *him*, *he* had got her pregnant; this cemented the fact that he was her boyfriend and that she had not lied, that R.P. had indeed been booted into the long grass. But... fucking hell. Fucking, fucking hell.

'Hello? Are you still there?' Her voice was going faint.

'I'm here, G.' There was a slight echo on the line.

'Well... say something.'

'Are you sure?'

'Yes, I'm sure.' She had her business voice. 'I saw the doctor at eight o'clock this morning. There's no question about it.'

'So... God... We must have...'

'It was that time at Marianne's house. Remember? We forgot to bring condoms.'

It had been, paradoxically, probably their most successful act of love. He found he preferred sex without a condom, and despite or perhaps somehow because of the fact that she was under the same roof, pouring cups of tea for the bereaved, Marianne had not made her presence felt in his head, and he had managed to keep his erection, stay the course, Georgina's heels on his shoulders as he felt himself go deeper. And the conversation about condoms, his persuasion of her, had been about HIV and his insistence that he was safe, was unlikely to be a health risk to her. So focused had he been on that, he had forgotten the chance of pregnancy. But so, presumably, had she.

'Kit? For God's sake, say something.'

'It's... I'm in shock, G. It's a shock.'

'Well, it's happened. I'm up the duff.'

'Are you OK? Do you feel OK?'

'Well. Listen. Here's the thing. *I'm* OK. But the doctor says there's a problem. Possibly. Because of...'

He caught her meaning immediately. They never referred to drugs explicitly over the phone. It wasn't, in the circles they moved in, considered prudent.

'Oh. Right. Can't you...?' He meant, *Can't you just stop doing coke? Go cold turkey?*

'This is the thing, Kit. Roberto and Simon think I should go into rehab. To sort myself out.'

'*Rehab?* But you're... you're not...' He couldn't say the word *addicted* over the phone.

'They say I am.'

Kit thought of Bob's letter and almost offered to go into rehab with her but something stopped him, the shameful and selfish relief that he didn't have to.

'Hang on,' he said instead. 'You talked to Roberto and Simon?'

'Yes.'

'Before you talked to me?' She had discussed this, her most intimate and private business, with her agent and her publicist before she thought to ring her boyfriend. The man who had fathered her child. She hesitated, as if she knew she had miscalculated, should have at least pretended that the conversation had not yet happened, phoned him back later to relate it.

'Well... yes. They're my people, Kit.'

'I thought I was your people.'

'Well, you are. Of course you are. But...' She sounded as if she might cry. 'Shit, I'm fucked up, Kit. Hormones, plus...' She would be desperate for a bump. Or perhaps she had done one already today, something to get her through the doctor's appointment, then another to get through the conference call with Roberto and Simon, and was now consumed by guilt.

'Oh God, G, I miss you so much. I wish you were here. Or I was there.'

'Oh, Kit...' She was fading again; he thought he heard muffled voices in the background.

'Is someone there with you?'

'No. Of course not.'

'So when are you...?'

'They want me to go straight away.'

'Where?' Kit was thinking he would visit. Would he be allowed to visit?

'Roberto knows somewhere... some of his other clients go there apparently. It's in the mountains. It sounds beautiful. Switzerland. The Italian-speaking part.'

'Switzerland? Not the UK?'

'Yes. Because of the British press. It's much safer there.'

'And they want you to go straight away?'

'This week, really.'

'I'm coming over, Georgina. I'll get a flight today.'

'No! Don't come over!' Her vehemence took him aback.

'What?'

'Don't come. It's for the best.'

Why was it for the best? He felt too stupefied to argue with her. He needed to get something straight, though.

'So... you're having it, then?'

'*It?*' Her voice had a slight chill.

'The baby. Our baby.' And the enormity of the words crashed over him in a huge wave. *Fuck.*

'Yes, of course I am.' Again she sounded as if she were in a business meeting.

'What about your work, though? Your assignments?' She had a great deal lined up, much of it in London.

'Well. Here's another thing. There's a clause in my contract. *Force majeure*, or something. They're going to have to give me a leave of absence. The agency, Armani, everyone. Armani are quite happy about it, actually. It sort of gets everyone off the hook.'

'Hang on...' Things shunted painfully into place in Kit's mind. 'You've talked to *Armani?*'

'Well, Simon has.'

Arranged that morning. Pregnancy confirmed, deals struck, clinic booked. All before the minor matter of informing him that he was to be a parent. It sounded as if she might be crying.

'Kit?'

'I'm still here, G.'

'Oh fucking hell, Kit...' That little-girl voice that had so beguiled him, that continued to beguile. He thought of the first time he kissed her, of burying his face in hotel sheets to smell her perfume after she'd left.

'When can I see you?'

'I'll come to London as soon as I can. As soon as I'm... you know. Better.'

'How long will you be gone?'

'I'm not really sure. Maybe a couple of months.'

'A couple of *months?*'

'I don't know, do I? I've never done this before. Don't be angry with me. I need you to support me.' She really was crying now, in hiccupping sobs.

'You'll write to me, though. And you'll phone me every day.'

'If they'll let me. I don't know how these things work.'

'Get Vanna to sort out a plane for me. I'll fly over today and come to Switzerland with you. See you get settled in.'

'Oh, Kit, you can't. They... they told me not to see you.'

'*What?*'

By early afternoon Kit had done more than three grams of coke. Jonathan's courier was due any time and he had only about eight hundred pounds to give him. *Shit.*

Georgina. Georgina pregnant. Kept from him. He thought about the things she'd told him. She professed to hate modelling. Talked about stopping a great deal. *I want to retire, as soon as I can... When my contract's up I'm getting out. I haven't told them, though...*

Had she done this deliberately? Engineered it? Yes, it had been he who had urged her, after Susannah's funeral, in the freezing Room Seven, but had her mind been working as they made love? He thought back to that afternoon, how she had squirmed and writhed as she came, her nails digging into his back, how shortly afterwards he had ejaculated deep inside her, and she had sighed, and smiled up at him...

He needed to get out of the flat. He had to think. And he had no appetite for a visit from Jonathan's courier and the petty negotiations that would ensue. He would go and see Ray and have a proper meeting, get hold of the cash and settle up with Jonathan.

For now he would score off friends. There was any number of people he could ask to tide him over. He dressed quickly, without showering, pulling on the most anonymous clothes he could find. He put on sunglasses, though it was grey and chilly outside.

In Trafalgar Square he found tourists getting themselves photographed feeding the pigeons, an army of Japanese schoolchildren with green rucksacks sitting on the steps of the National Gallery, busy Londoners making their way to Charing Cross Station, none of whom paid him the least attention. Kit sat on the wall surrounding one of the fountains and took several deep breaths. This was his London: the traffic, the commuters, the whirl of commerce. Go back to Hereford! *You ridiculous man, Bob, how little you know me.*

A number 11 bus rumbled along the south side of the square and was held up in traffic, chugging and wheezing. On the vertical advertising space at the bus's rear was the picture of Georgina and himself. How strange that this was the first time he had seen himself like that, in daylight hours. He stared at his own image, full-sized, grinning at him. He recalled the fun of the shoot, the two of them giggling like schoolchildren as they undressed. How much shyer than he she had been, how she had sought assurance after assurance that this depiction of her would not be salacious, would not tarnish her image. On the side of the bus a life-sized and naked Georgina Garvey looked at Kit, or rather at the image of Kit. For the first time – and he had looked at the photograph a great deal – he discerned something else in her expression, a certain wariness perhaps. And now they were to be parents. He and she. He tried to picture it, tried very hard to imagine holding a baby, changing its nappy, and found he simply could not.

The bus moved on its way down Whitehall.

He stood up and walked along Whitcomb Street. In Leicester Square he stopped to buy a newspaper. He had not had a call today from Murray; that might mean no bad press regarding Georgina, but it was best to be sure. As he paid at the kiosk he became aware of a group of four men, ten feet or so away. One of them was looking at him intently. Kit did his best to stare stonily back, even while his heart banged in his chest. The man actually nudged his companion, who turned to look. Panic fluttered in Kit's throat. Who were they? The one who had been staring at him first, who seemed to be the ringleader, took a step towards him. These men were not from London. Londoners were too cool to stare in this way, too wary of strangers, too wary of any kind of connection for fear a person might be dangerous, or mad, or just plain weird; they would do anything to avoid eye contact even when crushed right up against a person on the Tube – not that Kit had recent experience of this.

'Bender,' the man said to the one standing next to him, who sniggered.

Kit almost laughed out loud. He was so used to being thought gay, right from the days of school where his looks and his aversion to sports automatically placed him under suspicion – even now people suspected Georgina of being his beard – that it had become a badge of pride. These men had not been dispatched to harm him. They were just a bunch of bigoted oiks from somewhere unspeakable like Gravesend or Burnley or even Hereford, homing in on Leicester Square like the lemmings they were. They would have been drinking, too, overpriced, tasteless bitter in characterless pubs. The pinnacle of their trip was going to be a visit to the Hippodrome, where they would try and get inside the boob tubes of women who had stiffly sprayed hair and too-tight miniskirts and white shoes and who danced round their handbags to Rick Astley. Kit considered blowing the man a kiss. He took off his sunglasses and stared boldly at him, daring him to say something else.

'Fucking AIDS queer,' the man said, and the rest of them laughed.

One of the men, not the leader, took a step towards Kit. This man had on a navy shell suit and very white trainers, and wore his lank hair short at the front and sides and long at the back.

'Hey!' He pointed at Kit. 'I know who he is. It's that cunt from the advert.'

Kit looked directly at the men, all of them.

'That's right,' he said pleasantly. 'I am that cunt from the advert.'

He was walking home along Charing Cross Road with the *Daily Mail* tucked under his arm when he heard his name being called, and now his heart did thump in his chest, for a woman was walking towards him, looking straight at him; he saw she was wearing a cheaply cut business suit and that her plump feet were stuffed into navy court shoes, just as she was saying, 'Kit! Oh my God!' and he recognised her.

'Bridget!'

On another day he would have professed himself thrilled to see her and then moved on, leaving her with vague promises to get in touch, but that afternoon it was a relief to see a friendly face. They went for a coffee on the Strand. Despite the vastly divergent paths their lives had taken she was still easy to talk to. She had stayed at 62 Crouch Vale until graduating last summer, she told him, and was now living in a house share in Bromley and training to be an accountant with one of the big firms.

'More exams,' she said, rolling her eyes.

'I think you always liked exams, secretly, didn't you, Bridge?'

And she smiled and shrugged and stirred sugar into her cup and he could tell, by the way she blushed a little and looked down, that she liked him calling her Bridge, like he used to, and also that, despite being a little intimidated by him, she still liked *him*. Buoyed up by the small thrill of squaring up to the thugs in Leicester Square who had called him a cunt, it mattered, for some reason, that Bridget should form a good impression of him.

'I read your book,' she told him. 'My God!'

'Did you like it?' He would get her to bring her copy along if they met again, so he could sign it for her.

'Well, yes. But that stuff about your aunt… is that meant to be Marianne? Did she *really*…?'

'Oh, artistic licence,' he said airily.

'I called you a couple of times,' she went on, 'and left a message.' She was trying not to sound reproving.

Kit nodded. 'M'mm,' he said, pretending to remember her messages. 'Sorry about that.'

'And then the next thing I know, you're in the papers going out with Georgina Garvey!'

'Oh, well.' Kit tried to sound modest.

'What's she like?' The first thing that the commonalty, with their nine-to-fives and their mortgages, people who had to do their own laundry, always wanted to know.

'She's wonderful,' Kit said brightly, and a knife twisted painfully in his heart. 'She's in Milan, though, so we don't see each other as often as we'd like.' The official line, Georgina had schooled him this morning, was going to be that she was getting over glandular fever and taking a break from modelling.

Bridget chattered on. 'Milan's great. I went there when I was Interrailing. The cathedral's amazing, isn't it?'

'M'mm.'

'And you've seen *The Last Supper*, of course?'

'Yes.'

'You can imagine Mum when I told her I'd seen it in the flesh, as it were.'

'How is your mum?' He was grateful of the chance to change the subject. 'And everyone else?' A recitation of the trials and tribulations of the Buckley family followed. Kit was only half listening. He interrupted her by putting his hand on hers and she flushed and fell silent.

'It's really good to see you, Bridge.'

'It's lovely to see you, Kit,' she said. The effects of the coke he had done in the coffee-shop toilet were falling away vertiginously; he had only had enough for a tiny bump off his house key. He needed to get home and put in some urgent phone calls. When Bridget suggested he come out clubbing with her and a friend he found himself agreeing in order to get away. When that Saturday came he had intended to call her to cancel, but curiosity got the better of him. It might be good to try something new. Meet different people.

*

A couple of weeks later, to distract himself from both worrying about Georgina and the comedown from his last coke binge, Kit turned on the television.

'We live in a peaceful, prosperous time,' George Bush was saying in his post-inauguration speech, 'but we can make it better.' Kit flicked channels. A documentary about rave culture was in progress. Footage from a club very similar to Cameleo was being shown.

His trip to the nightclub with Bridget and her work friend Doug had not been a success. He had thought he was making a point to Georgina Garvey, ridiculous as it might seem and holed up as she was in her Swiss bunker. By showing her, proving to himself, that he didn't need her. That he had a life that pre-dated her, Leo Woodcott, Anthony and Emile and everyone else. That he could strike out and have an anonymous night out in a grotty Vauxhall club that she could never in a million years go to.

But as soon as he had walked into Cameleo he had realised that, though he had thought himself dressed down in his Paul Smith suit, he was not just overdressed but ridiculously so, as he took in the baggy jeans and T-shirts, dungarees, Kickers, Converse sneakers. Smiley-faced logos pinned up everywhere.

He had felt magnanimous at turning down the pill Bridget had offered him – at twenty-five pounds a pop, it would be expensive for her on her trainee accountant's salary. He had been offered ecstasy many times but the few occasions he had taken it had either left him feeling unpleasantly panicky or had had no effect at all. In the Gents at Cameleo he had been confronted by a throng of saucer-eyed loons sitting on the floor, holding hands and swaying, blocking his way to the cubicle. God, happy people were so *stupid*. He made his escape soon after, the blessed cab that appeared outside the club door whisking him efficiently back to his West End.

On Kit's television a man wearing a baseball cap and a long-sleeved white T-shirt with a large pink heart on the front was being interviewed. He was several years older than Kit.

'There's a revolution in progress. Young people are sick of the tired old London club scene. Where you can't get in unless you're wearing Vivienne Westwood. When you can't go to the football and then go clubbing without a change of clothes. That whole scene's run by a St Martin's art school clique. It's over.'

The programme shifted to the free mass raves that had popped up in various parts of the countryside the previous summer. An aerial shot showed a shambolic mass of tents, tepees and camper vans and what looked like a big top, with people, people everywhere. Kit watched, with fascination and horror, as throngs of ravers stumbled around in broad daylight, laughing and swaying and gurning.

'Not everyone comes away unscathed, it seems,' a voiceover said primly, as on-screen a young man and his girlfriend staggered round a field. The woman tripped and fell onto the ground, pulling the man down with her.

Kit realised he had no interest whatever in that scene. Acid house, rave culture, ecstasy – it all left him cold. He had no appetite for the oversized T-shirts and dirty jeans, the industrial buildings, the soggy fields scores of miles from anywhere. For asking horrified locals the following morning, 'Which way's London?' He felt, inexplicably, too old for it all, as if somehow it had passed him by. He turned the television off.

16

March 1989

Marianne was wondering how much longer she could realistically string the meeting out. The prospective business partners were looking decidedly peeved. She had got to the restaurant early but they had trumped her; they sat side by side at the oval-shaped table in its faux-opulent booth. This meant that they had the padded banquette seat, leaving her one of the Rococo-style dining chairs, high-backed with no arms and designed deliberately to be uncomfortable, or so it seemed to Marianne; the men were also seated fractionally but discernibly higher than her. They had chosen the venue, of course; her knowledge of London restaurants suitable for a business meeting was decades out of date.

She disliked Oliver Cottrill immediately, with his too-white smile – like an American – and prominent canine teeth; also the way he looked her up and down, not bothering to hide his assessment of her – she had been a looker once but had let herself go, allowed herself to run to seed in her agrarian backwater. Philip Langham she was less certain about; his handshake was entirely boneless and unlike his colleague he seemed unable to look her in the eye.

'Do you mind if I smoke,' said Oliver Cottrill, not as a question, and proceeded to chain-smoke a pack of Rothmans.

A dinner-suited flunky came to their table.

'We're waiting for someone.' Philip looked pointedly at his watch, an arrangement of stainless-steel links and dials so bulky and cumbersome it was a wonder he could lift his scrawny wrist. In terms of their appearance men had fewer opportunities to display their wealth, Marianne supposed, once suits and shoes had been taken care of. The two men had made it clear that this meeting had been sandwiched between more potentially lucrative propositions.

'Let's order,' she suggested, 'and my husband can catch up when he arrives.'

'Langoustines,' said Oliver, 'and veal carpaccio.'

'I'll have the same,' said Philip. Marianne scanned the menu with its fussy italic font and chose whitebait followed by a caesar salad, the first acceptable items on which her eyes settled, although she noticed that neither langoustines nor veal were on the menu.

'And to drink...?'

'Perrier,' declared Oliver on behalf of them all. The waiter nodded his solemn approval of Oliver's choices.

'Why don't we begin?' she said, in an attempt to wrest a small amount of control from Oliver. They glanced at each other: they were waiting for the man to arrive, the one with whom they might do business. *I'm the one with the property*, she wanted to say, but bit the words back. Women, to these men, were either secretaries scurrying to do their bidding, typing contracts, booking restaurants and laughing at their jokes, or girlfriends for display at bars and nightclubs, hotels and lidos. The two groups were doubtless not mutually exclusive. They were too young still for trophy wives, probably. It was galling, and she would have taken pleasure in quashing them, but they held the cards, those cards being the prospect of a substantial investment in Erringby, not just the house but the whole estate. These two men, ten or perhaps fifteen years younger than her and emblematic of the staggering amounts of money sloshing around the capital, were her last hope. She prayed that they did not realise this.

'OK,' said Oliver, the more alpha. 'We liked your business plan. We think the site has a lot of potential.'

'With a lot of work,' said Philip. 'To the house, especially. We'd be looking at a complete rewire and a full refurbishment judging from the information you've sent us.' Marianne nodded.

The waiter brought a bottle of Perrier and began pouring. Oliver put his hand over his glass.

'This is a red wine glass,' he said. 'Can I have my water in a water glass, please.'

The waiter removed the offending item. Oliver pulled a folder of papers from his briefcase and unfolded the A3 plan of the estate that Marianne had submitted to Lancot Properties. She had wondered, on meeting the men, about 'Lancot'; it was surprising that Oliver had stooped to allow his name to provide the suffix, but presumably euphony had won through.

Oliver moved aside a set of heavy and monogrammed cutlery and spread out the plan to face Philip and himself. The plan was much annotated in a cramped, scrawly hand. She tried and failed to read the upside-down comments.

'This, then.' Oliver tapped at the part of the plan depicting the wood with an expensive-looking fountain pen. 'It's currently underutilised. Would you object to a change of use?'

'Change of use?'

'Yes,' said Philip. 'We're thinking we'd get rid of the trees and make this bit of land part of the golf course.'

'I see.' She had strenuous objections to woodland that had been in existence since Saxon times being razed. But the purpose of today was to get an in-principle deal and to argue the detail once money was secured.

'How likely is the neighbour to sell?' asked Oliver. Marianne was on surer ground here. Bill Carter, the farmer who had grazed his cows in Erringby's paddock since the 1950s and who owned the adjacent farmland, was recently widowed and had declared an intention to sell up and leave. He would, she knew, have no qualms about ancient agricultural land being turned into greens, fairways and hazards, being completely unsentimental about such matters. Marianne assured Oliver that Bill was amenable.

'For the right price, of course,' she added and the men nodded; this was talk they understood.

'Let's talk about the money,' she went on, since the subject had been introduced.

'Shouldn't we wait for your husband?' said Philip. She swallowed her anger.

'I think we could agree a few principles. The assets are all in my name, actually.' Oliver and Philip looked at each other. 'The submission is from both of us,' she went on. 'Our suggested terms are in the document.'

'You'll want to discuss this with your husband,' said Oliver. 'Is he coming, by the way? Because if not—'

'He'll be here,' said Marianne, far from certain. Col had taken a train to London the day before – she had driven from Hereford that morning – and was supposed to have met her at the restaurant prior to this meeting.

'So just to clarify,' said Philip, 'you and your husband would be responsible for the day-to-day management of the hotel and the golf club. Have you any experience of the hospitality industry?'

'Col has.'

If one counted running a glorified flophouse in Kathmandu in the seventies.

'Because you would be the face of the project,' said Oliver. 'We're in London, we wouldn't be able to oversee it. We'd need to know we were in safe hands.'

'It's all about the people, this type of project,' put in Philip.

The heck it is, thought Marianne.

'So we have to know we can really work with you both,' said Oliver. Their starters arrived.

'Shall I take these away?' The waiter hovered over Col's place setting.

'No, we're expecting someone else to join us,' Marianne said, as if saying it again might conjure him up.

'And you'd be prepared to give up the whole house?' Oliver was saying.

'Yes!' she said. 'Absolutely.' Her plan was that she and Col would move into a new house that would be built at the end of the east wing.

More exchanges, about planning permissions and building regulations, followed as they ate their starters. The whitebait was desiccated and tasteless.

'Good.' Oliver looked at Philip. 'So I guess the next thing is for you and me to take a trip out to Herefordshire to see for ourselves. And then, if we're happy, to have heads of terms drawn up.' The men pulled out bulging Filofaxes bound in expensive leather.

'Excellent,' Marianne said. 'Just name a day.' She smiled at Oliver Cottrill, saw him reappraise her as more toothsome. His returning smile held a suggestion of desire. She allowed herself to imagine what he would be like to have sex with. Small cock, no doubt.

The men busied themselves with their Filofaxes and after much conferring settled on a date. Marianne fished out her Letts diary, the pages of which were almost entirely blank, and pretended to juggle a few things before agreeing.

'Excellent.' Oliver smiled again. He was staring at her tits.

He looked up as there was a noise at the other end of the room; the door had opened, slammed shut and then opened again. Marianne turned to see Col coming into the restaurant.

'Ah,' she said, 'here's...'

It was immediately apparent that Col was extremely drunk. He made his way falteringly, grabbing at an empty chair to steady himself. People looked, then looked away. It seemed to take a very long time for him to cross the room. At one point he lurched badly and it seemed he might fall, but he righted himself in time.

'Oh my God,' Philip murmured. Col came to a meandering halt at their table. Oliver and Philip looked at each other in distaste.

'Gentlemen.' Col leaned across the table, offering them his hand to shake. With the other he clutched at Marianne's shoulder. 'Sorry I'm late. Late.' He exuded beery fumes. His shirt, partly untucked, had drink stains on it.

Oliver stared stonily at him. Philip proffered the boneless handshake. 'Philip Langham,' he said primly. Col tugged at one of the Rococo chairs and sat down heavily.

'Phew!' he said, and laughed. The waiter arrived to take their plates away. 'Ah!' said Col. 'What're we all drinking?'

'We're not,' said Marianne.

'Oh, come on,' said Col. 'How about some wine? Can I see the wine list please?'

'We're good, thanks,' said Oliver.

'Ah,' said Col. 'Oliver. I presume. You look like a man who enjoys a drink. Château Lafite? Do you have Château Lafite?' This to the waiter. 'You know Erringby used to have an excellent wine cellar. Used to.'

'Not for me,' said Oliver. 'We're driving to East Sheen straight after this meeting. In fact, Philip...' He looked at his watch, another piece of spectacular over-engineering.

'Can I have one of these?' asked Col, helping himself to one of Oliver's cigarettes.

'Col, why don't you have a coffee?' said Marianne.

'Coffee!' Col started laughing. 'That your Porsche outside?'

'The Carrera?' Philip said. 'Yes.'

'Fuck me, the insurance on that thing must be a motherfucker. What are you, twenty-five?'

'Twenty-six,' said Philip. 'The insurance is affordable, thanks.'

'I'll have a bottle of Château Lafite,' Col said to the waiter.

'Do you know, I think we're done here,' said Oliver. 'Waiter, can you cancel our main courses? And bring me the bill.'

'What?' said Col. 'Oh!'

'Thank you for your time, Mrs Greenfield.' Philip was reaching for his jacket.

'What?' said Col.

The waiter returned with the bill.

'You're not going?' Col demanded. The men had gathered up the Erringby site plan, the Montblanc fountain pens and the Filofaxes.

'Goodbye, Mrs Greenfield,' said Oliver. 'I think you can appreciate that our offer is no longer on the table.'

'Christ!' Col started laughing again. 'Lighten up.'

'Well, *my* offer is no longer on the table.' Marianne stood up. 'Erringby's not for sale to a couple of prigs who are scared stiff of women. As if I'd hand ownership of my home over to you. And have you never seen anyone drunk before? And by the way, that woodland is ancient, at least a thousand years old. You really think I'd let it be turned into a golf course?'

'Well!' Oliver said to Philip. 'This was a waste of time.' The two of them left the restaurant and got into the Porsche parked outside. They drove away with much revving of the engine, as if the car itself were making its displeasure known.

She was spared the humiliation of getting him home on a train, since she was driving. He slept on the back seat, snoring and belching, for much of a drive that was long and arduous, an incident on the A40 causing a monumental tailback that would have been avoided had she chosen the motorway. At Erringby she parked in the garage and left him sweating and snorting in the car, and went to bed, locking the door to the house behind her.

She didn't know if he would have remembered his key and didn't much care, but presumably he had, for when she got up the next morning the car was empty and he had spent what remained of his night in Room Four, where he often exiled himself, sometimes for several nights at a time. There were more of his clothes in the armoire in that room than there were in the marital bedroom.

They encountered each other late that morning. She was fixing a dripping tap in one of the bathrooms and he shuffled into the room, lowered the lid of the toilet and sat down. He was still in yesterday's clothes, his good shirt rumpled and stained by drink. His face, haggard and dehydrated, blotchy and spider-veined, made him look older than his forty-two years. The reek of stale alcohol rose from him. Marianne was unscrewing the tap valve with a spanner. She ignored him.

'Sorry,' he said eventually.

'You're sorry.' She unscrewed the washer and replaced it.

'What else can I say?' He shrugged, as if what had happened was little to do with him. Perhaps it wasn't, since he wouldn't remember most of it.

She reassembled the tap.

'How did you manage to get so drunk? That's what I can't understand.'

'I only had a few,' he said. 'With Dennis.'

'A few.'

'OK. Four pints. Maybe five.'

'Five pints? You were a lot drunker than five pints.'

'OK, so Dennis and I made a night of it the night before, and this was the hair of the dog.'

'Right,' she said. 'So basically you didn't go to bed.'

He sat and waited. The pattern was this: she would lose her temper and scream at him, he would scream back, accusations and counter-accusations would be lobbed to and fro, things would escalate, often into a physical scuffle, until they were both spent with screaming and scratching and pushing and sometimes punching and would retreat to their different corners of the house, avoiding each other for hours or days – Col sometimes seeking sanctuary at Flatley Close – and eventually both would recover enough equanimity for some sort of uneasy truce to prevail; sex was involved less often these days.

But today she felt becalmed, stalled in the marital doldrums with raging storms distant on the horizon. The magnitude of what Col had done had not properly sunk in; she had not had time to think about what she might do next. The Lancot deal, which had had the potential to inject Erringby with the investment it needed, restore her parlous finances while allowing them to carry on living there, albeit in a new house and not in Erringby Hall itself, had felt like the last chance. No other investor had shown sufficient interest.

She would not give Col what he was expecting. She would wrong-foot him by not screaming at him.

'This was our last opportunity,' she said. His head sagged; he had the grace at least to look a little sheepish. 'It's as if you went out of your way to sabotage us.'

He lifted his head to look at her.

'It's all off then, is it?' His very blue eyes were bleary and shot with congested veins.

'My God,' she said. 'You really don't remember, do you?'

'I'm sorry, baby.' He looked so abject that fury rose in her.

'Yes, you're sorry – for yourself. You have no conception of how crucial that meeting was. Why did you have to get drunk? *Why?* I truly do not understand you.'

'I guess I was anxious.'

'Anxious!' She picked up the tools and made to leave, but at the door she turned round. 'Yeah, well, I'm *anxious*, Col. I'm anxious about the rates bill. I'm anxious that half the window frames are rotting. I'm anxious that when this tank of oil runs out there's no money for any more. I'm anxious that there's a bucket on the top landing because of a bloody great hole in the roof. I'm anxious, Col, that not only does my husband not support me when I work my behind off chasing money and schemes to sort it out, sucking up to yuppie schoolboys in overpriced restaurants, he sabotages me by turning up as drunk as a skunk. I was completely humiliated, Col. So I'm sorry about *your* being anxious. I really am.'

His expression was an old one, part sullen, part martyred. It was a look that had driven her to hit him in the past, and she was determined to keep her temper. But his silence infuriated her.

'So?' she snapped, loitering in the doorway, not going.

'Are things really that bad?'

'Yes, Col, they really are that bad.'

'What about the money from your mother's house?'

'That'll barely pay for the roof. You really don't have a clue, do you?'

'Can we not ask Kit for some of his money back?'

'No. Of course we can't.'

'I didn't know things were that bad,' he said. 'How could I?'

'*Because you never tell me anything* – I know. It's my money, Col.'

'Fine. Your money. Your fucking house, tower, garden, woods, riverbank, fucking gazebo and every fucking thing else. So you sort it out.'

'I was trying to!' She was shouting. 'I was trying to sort out this deal. You were meant to help me. We were meant to be a team. A husband-and-wife team.'

His laugh was brittle.

'That's a joke, Marianne. We've never been a team. We're two people who've existed in this mausoleum of a house for fifteen years. Separately.'

'Because you won't work with me. You were always off with your own hare-brained schemes. Cookery schools. Campsites. Film sets.'

'Which you never helped me with, ever.'

'Because your ideas were stupid!'

'Oh, now we're getting to it.' Col stood up, took a step towards her. Even with the appalling hangover he must be experiencing he had the advantage of height and bulk over her. She retreated very slightly, in spite of herself. 'Why did you marry me, Marianne?'

'Is that a serious question?'

'Yes, it's a serious question. Why? I want to know. I really do.'

'You know why. I loved you,' she said.

'Huh.' The sound was dismissive, an exhalation more than an utterance. 'This house is a morgue,' he said. 'A monument to your fucking dead ancestors. It's obscene that only two people live in it. I always thought we would create something worthwhile. Something to leave behind.'

'Oh, we're back on that, are we?'

'Yes, we're back on that, Marianne.' He grabbed her hand before she had a chance to move away. 'There's still time. We could go to a private doctor. Sell... I don't know, sell the paddock or something. Or use your mother's money. Fuck the roof. Women your age can have kids. You still have periods. Chances are it might work.'

'We've been through this. I don't want to be meddled with. Having children isn't a right. If it was meant to happen, it would have happened.'

'We could foster. We could foster a bunch of children here. Think about it, Marianne! A whole crowd.'

'I don't want to foster children. I don't *like* children, Col.'

'What?'

'I don't like children. I never have.' He was gripping her hand, so tightly that her wedding ring dug into the next finger. 'Ow!' she said. She tried to tug her hand away.

'What?' he repeated. With her free hand she pulled something from the back pocket of her jeans.

'Here.'

He stared at the blister pack, the top row of russet-coloured pills half used up, the shorter row of white pills and the longer row of beige pills beneath still intact.

'What? What is this?'

'I'm on the pill, Col. I've been taking it the whole time.'

He dropped her hand, reeled backwards, as if he might fall.

'Oh no. Oh no no no, Marianne.'

'Col, I...'

'Get away from me!' He pushed her aside and ran from the room.

She heard retching from another bathroom.

He was crying, leaning heavily on the washbasin. Spittle and a darker-coloured liquid clung to the bowl. He wiped his mouth with the back of his hand.

'Col.' She put a hand on his shoulder.

'Don't touch me.' He pushed her off.

'OK,' she said, more gently. 'Can we just talk about this for a moment?'

'The whole time? You've been on the pill the whole time we've been together?' He was perspiring with the effort of retching and with the alcohol. His face was wet, too, with tears.

'Yes,' she said.

'Oh, you bitch,' he said. 'You evil, evil bitch. Leave me alone.'

'Col,' she said. 'It's my body. I've never wanted them. I thought you'd get over it, that it would go away...'

'Well, it hasn't, has it?' He rounded on her, rage pumping him up so that he seemed to dwarf her. 'It's never gone away. You know what it means to me. You always knew.'

'I'm sorry,' she said.

'Sorry? You think sorry will make this better? That we'll go off to our separate corners and come back together and fuck and it'll be like this never happened? Not this time, Marianne. Not this time. I can't... I can't deal with this. Our whole marriage has been a lie.'

'Let's talk about it.' She put a hand on him again.

'I said get away from me!' He grabbed her by both wrists, pushed her backwards out of the room. In doing so he tripped and they fell heavily onto the landing floor together, Marianne banging her head hard on the skirting board. For a second they lay like that, he on top of her, pinioning her wrists over her head, Marianne panting. Col's breath was heavy and hot on her face.

He got up and went away, stumbling as he did so, leaving her lying on the carpet.

His van had gone from the garage. She knew he would have gone to his sister's, knew, too, that he was certain to return. She passed the day in a fugue state, unable to settle to anything. On the back of her head was an egg-shaped lump.

He came back at around 9pm. She was in the kitchen, a mug of tea cooling in front of her.

'I came back to tell you I'm leaving,' he said.

She said nothing, nor did she look at him.

'All those times, so many times, I used to think *Maybe this'll be it... maybe this'll be it.* You used to say it too, remember?' His voice trembled; he was struggling not to cry. 'And it was all lies. Every time we made love was a lie.'

'Oh, don't be so melodramatic.'

'You've gone too far this time,' he said. 'I can't come back from this.'

'Do you want a divorce?'

'Yes, I want a fucking divorce! What do you think?'

'You won't go through with it,' she said. 'You can't.'

'What's that supposed to mean?'

'You're too bound up with me.'

'Christ! Your arrogance... Do you want to know something, Marianne? Shall I tell you? I could've had a baby. With Lois.'

'Who?'

'Don't give me that, Marianne. Lois, Lois from the film. I got her pregnant.'

'Oh.'

'Christ, I knew I should have left you then! If only I'd had the guts to go through with it. I could have had a son or daughter by now.'

'Well, good for you. At least you know your pencil's got lead in it.'

'My God, you are a vile, vile woman.' He was standing behind where she remained at the kitchen table. She stared ahead, still not looking at him. 'I was never a husband to you. We've never shared things. You've never let me into your life, your finances...'

'You did a good enough job letting yourself in there.'

'Christ, one mistake.'

'Mistake! As well as emptying the coffers, well now, let me see.' She pretended to count on her fingers. 'The cookery school. The campsite. The bed and breakfast. The money you wasted, Col, on what? Nothing. Not only that, you stole my money. I could still have you prosecuted, you know.'

'Yeah, well, go ahead! Prison would be better than living here with you.'

'Don't think I won't!'

'You've eaten me up. You've chewed me up and shat me out. You've kept me as your toy. A sexual plaything. It's over. I've come to pack my things and I'm going.'

She did turn, now, to look at him. His eyes, red from a day of crying, were watery again.

'You'll be back.'

'You think I can't live without you?'

'No,' she said. 'You can't.'

'Just watch me!'

He left the room. Marianne stood up stiffly. She poured away the mug of cold tea and put the kettle back on the hob. It occurred to her that she had had nothing to eat all day. She made toast but her throat closed before she could swallow. She heard him come and go from the house a few times. Eventually, he came to the kitchen door. He had on his coat and was carrying an old duffel bag. He was crying again.

'Bye then,' she said.

'Do you know, Marianne, something's only now just occurred to me. I've never seen you cry. Do you cry? Are you even capable of it?' She said nothing. 'Anything I've left behind, burn it on a big fucking bonfire. I don't want any of it.'

'Fine,' she said.

He stood there as if waiting for her last words.

'So go on and leave, if you're going.'

'You have no heart. You say you loved me, but you have no idea what the word means.' His voice shook.

'Yes I do, Col,' she said. 'I do know what it means.'

'Just answer me one thing.'

'What now?'

'Did you fuck my nephew?'

'What?'

'You heard me.'

'I'm not going to dignify that with a response.'

'So why is he putting it about that you did?'

'I can't help what he writes. He likes being sensational.'

'You fucked his family right up. Me included. Why wouldn't you go the whole hog? I wouldn't put anything past you. Are my family just toys as well? Give a boy a load of your money, ruin his relationship with his parents. Screw him, fuck him up forever. He's going to crash and burn.' He came forward, leaned over her, his face close to hers. 'You say you don't like children, but you *liked* Christopher, didn't you, Marianne? Oh yes, you liked him *a lot*. Didn't you? Didn't you!' He was shouting, right in her ear, making her wince.

She stood up.

'I've had enough of this. Go and do whatever you have to. Come back when you've calmed down.'

'Calmed down! You think this is just a tiff? I'm leaving you.'

'Well, fucking go then.'

She walked past him, out of the kitchen, without looking at him, leaving him standing there with his bag. She went upstairs. The window from her bathroom looked out over the garages. He walked to his van, opened the door, threw his bag onto the passenger seat. He looked back at the house as he got in. If he saw her at the window he made no sign of it.

17

March 1989

The taxi dropped Kit off at the address he had been given, a house tucked away in a cobbled mews near Knightsbridge. He rang the bell.

It was several minutes before he heard the clack of heels on hardwood floor and Vanna answered the door.

'Hi Kit.' They touched cheeks briefly and kissed the air. Vanna's hair had been dyed a deep cherry and she wore a tailored suit with a peplum in Black Watch tartan. She had never liked Kit much, tolerated him at best. Possibly she resented his claims on Georgina, for her relationship with her employer was more like that of old schoolfriends. Vanna, who was the same size as Georgina, did a lot of her shopping. Kit would arrive at Claridge's to find them giggling in front of a full-length mirror in their underwear, the bed and the sofas piled high with dresses, shoes, hatboxes. When Vanna had run errands for Kit in his capacity as Georgina's consort – or rather caused errands to be run by Dijon or another lesser employee – she had done so with an unsmiling hauteur. And Kit knew that she, Vanna, had visited the clinic in Brunescio while he had not. The notion of an assistant of his own being added to Georgina's payroll had been mooted but had never come about. Today was probably not going to be the day to raise it.

'I like the hair,' Kit said now.

'Thank you,' Vanna said. 'She's upstairs.' She led the way to the first floor. In a huge, sparsely furnished drawing room Georgina sat on a cream-coloured sofa. She turned her head as they came in.

'Oh, hey, Kit.' Her hair was what he assumed was its natural colour, mid brown, brushed back from her face. She wore jeans and an oversized turtleneck jersey.

'Hey.' It was the first time he had set eyes on her in over two months. He went over and kissed her.

She smiled brightly at him, a smile she would have given to a press conference.

'How are you?' he asked her.

'I'm great.'

'You look great.'

Vanna was hovering.

'Shall we have some tea?' Georgina said.

'Sure,' said Vanna. 'Earl Grey, lapsang...?'

'Ooh,' said Georgina. 'Do we have any more of that gunpowder tea?'

'I can go check.'

'Gunpowder if we've got it, if not, Earl Grey. Kit?'

'Oh... anything, I don't mind,' he said.

The women looked at him. Clearly, he had to make a choice.

'Earl Grey,' he said, though the fact was he didn't care for tea, had stopped drinking it years ago.

Vanna left the room.

'Can I sit down?' he said to Georgina.

'Oh! Sure. Sorry.' She shifted up to make room for him. He sat down next to her.

'G...' he said, and took one of her hands. She pulled the hand away, used it to smooth her hair. She looked nervously towards the door.

'It's so great to see you,' he said.

'You too,' she said.

'So... you're all better?' he asked her, as if she'd been ill.

'Oh yes,' she said. 'I feel fantastic.'

It occurred to him that Vanna was behaving like a social worker sitting in on a supervised access visit, and that this might be his only chance to be alone with Georgina.

'G,' he said again, and put his hands on her arms and, before she could object or move away, pulled her to him to hug her. He buried his face in her neck, smelled her perfume. 'I've missed you so, so much.' She relented enough to put her arms round him and hold him tightly for several moments.

'Me too,' she said.

'How's...?' He put a hand on her stomach, felt the swell of it under her jersey.

'Oh, it's cooking.' They heard Vanna's footsteps on the landing. Georgina peeled away from him and sat up. 'Ooh, lovely,' she said, on seeing that Vanna had brought in a plate of Penguin biscuits, along with the tea, on a tray. Kit looked at her quizzically.

'It's my latest thing,' she said. 'With some women it's lumps of coal, with me...' Vanna put the tray down on a coffee table and took a seat on another sofa. Georgina busied herself with the tea.

'Milk or lemon?' she asked Kit.

'Oh... lemon.' He guessed that this was the more sophisticated choice.

'And do you want a green Penguin or a red one?'

'I think they're basically the same.'

She looked up and gave her *Oh, don't spoil the fun* smile, and in that moment he was transported into the latter months of last year, before the pregnancy and all the horrific complications it had trailed in its wake.

'I think you should have first dibs on the Penguins,' he said. 'Given your condition.'

She giggled and pretended to dither, her hand hovering over the plate before selecting a biscuit in a green wrapper. Vanna looked unimpressed.

'Would you like a Penguin, Vanna?' Georgina asked.

'No, grazie.'

'All the more for me,' said Georgina.

'So,' said Kit, sipping his tea and hating it. 'This is a nice house.'

'Isn't it?' Georgina said. 'It belongs to Crawford. You heard?' Kit nodded. Crawford Pennington, a theatre director, was in an AIDS hospice. Kit, who had met him a few times through Georgina, had thought of visiting, then had not been able to bring himself to.

'So you're going to stay here?' he asked. Crawford would not be asking for his house back, that much was obvious.

'For the duration, yes,' she said. 'I'm having the baby at the Portland.' This meant nothing to Kit.

'Oh, good,' he said. 'And it's all going OK?'

'Swimmingly.' Kit knew that the pregnancy was progressing well, that Georgina had detoxed with no ill-effects to either mother or baby, from the brief and rather bland letters she had written to him from Brunescio. There were other things he wanted to know, more pressing matters.

'And then are you going back to modelling?' He had asked her this once or twice in his letters to her and she had not responded.

Georgina and Vanna looked at each other. Vanna said something in Italian, and Georgina replied. Irritation washed over him.

'Speak English, Georgina.'

'I'm not sure, Kit,' she said. She tore the wrapper of her Penguin with her teeth and he was reminded, ludicrously, of their first time at Craven Street, and how she had opened the condom wrapper the same way. He felt a pang in his chest.

'I wish you could be straight with me,' he said.

She looked again at Vanna, who shrugged.

'Possibly not,' said Georgina. 'Going back to modelling, I mean.' A silence fell on the room. Georgina ate her Penguin biscuit.

'How's the new book, Kit?' Vanna asked, rather pointedly.

She had never shown the least interest in his writing. Kit was perfectly sure Vanna had not even glanced at his last book. She couldn't know... surely? Couldn't know about the lacklustre meeting Kit and Murray had had with his publisher just days earlier? Murray had pitched their new idea: Kit's exploration of rehab clinics and facilities, from the high end – admittedly not as high-end as Brunescio, it was unlikely his advance would stretch that far – to street projects run by councils and charities. The hook was that it would be set next to his own drug recovery. When Murray had proposed this it had seemed a brilliant way of earning money, getting clean and impressing on Georgina his suitability as partner and father, in one fell swoop. But enthusiasm had shrivelled away in his publisher's tiny office as Murray talked on, even before Lorraine McIver screwed up her face as though the room contained an unpleasant smell.

'I'm feeling some resistance to this,' she had said finally, as Murray stubbed out another Peter Stuyvesant and Kit wished fervently that he could do a line. '*My drugs hell and my road to recovery* – it's been done to death, Murray.'

'Yes,' Kit's agent had said, 'but the angle on this is...'

Lorraine had held up a manicured hand, nails filed into magenta points.

'We loved your first book, Kit. That stuff about your childhood – wonderful! And as for your aunt...'

'Yes, but...' Kit had said.

'What we really would like,' Lorraine had said, leaning towards them, elbows on her desk, 'is more of that kind of thing. What we need is another scandal, Kit.'

In Crawford Pennington's sitting room now Vanna said, 'H'mmm?' The imprint of her black cherry lipstick was on the china cup that she set down in its saucer. Kit detected a trace of malice. Vanna must have set spies on him, found out that he and Murray had left Lorraine's office with nothing.

'Oh, nothing's agreed yet,' he said. Georgina smiled blandly. 'Early days.' He tried to sound breezy.

'Huh,' said Vanna.

The telephone rang from a table at the other end of the room. Vanna got up to answer it.

'Do you want to speak to Simon?' she asked, her hand over the receiver.

'Oh, I suppose so.' Georgina got up to go to the phone, leaving Kit on his own. He added milk to his cup of tea, hoping it would make it more palatable, but the lemon just curdled it.

'I don't know... not really,' Georgina was saying into the phone, looking at Vanna, who shook her head. 'No. It's a no. Yes, maybe then. Bye.' She hung up.

'I'm just not in the mood for it right now,' she said to Vanna as they walked back across the room.

'You have to tell them sometime,' Vanna said.

'Tell them what?' Kit was fed up at being excluded.

'Oh, Simon wants me to go public about the pregnancy,' Georgina said. 'Obviously I need to at some point, unless I'm not going to leave the house for five months. There's rumours out there already. What on earth have you done to your cup of tea?'

'Yes, I think the press might be on to you,' he said. This was something else he had wanted to raise.

'Oh, you mean *Paris Match*,' said Georgina. Murray had called that morning to tell Kit that the magazine had published a photograph of her in which her bump was visible. What troubled Kit, however, was the additional information that the photograph had been taken in Paris and was of Georgina and an unnamed man sitting outside a café on the Place de l'Opéra. What had she been doing in Paris? And who, moreover, was this man?

'That's it,' said Kit. 'Do you want me to do the press conference with you?' He liked the idea of publicly cementing his role as her partner and the father of her child.

'Oh, that won't be necessary.' Georgina unwrapped another Penguin biscuit. 'I can't stop eating these.'

He looked at Vanna. 'Do you think I could have a moment or two with Georgina? In private?' Again, the shared glances. He felt impatience rise in him. Vanna was indeed playing the role of chaperone. 'Look, I'm not going to do a line off this table in front of you, if that's what you're thinking.'

'Oh, Kit,' said Georgina, as one might to a tiresome child. 'Maybe...?' She held up a hand to Vanna, the fingers splayed. Five minutes.

'I will wait downstairs then,' said Vanna with obvious reluctance, and stood up. Kit waited for the sound of her footsteps on the spiral staircase.'

'G. I hate this. I really do.'

'Don't make a scene,' she said.

'Look, just tell me one thing.'

'What's that?'

'Am I still your boyfriend?' How juvenile that sounded, as if he were back in the sixth-form common room in pursuit of Sally Leyland.

'You're the father of my child.'

'That's not what I meant.'

'Oh, Kit,' she said again. 'Yes, of course you are.' But she wouldn't look him in the eye.

'Can I stay here tonight?'

'Not tonight,' she said. 'Soon.' He made a sound of exasperation. 'I can't be around you if you're still using. Are you still using?'

Kit hesitated. He had made sure he was not at all high before setting out, had taken a Valium earlier to take the edge off his comedown from last night.

'You want me to be truthful?'

'No, Kit, I want you to lie... Yes, tell me the truth, obviously.'

'I'm working at it, G. I really am. And I'm cutting down.'

'OK,' she said dubiously.

The absolute truth was that he had made a half-hearted attempt to quit, had, at Murray's suggestion, booked himself into a health spa in Surrey, where he had spent several days in his room watching TV and doing line after line of coke.

The telephone rang again and was answered, presumably by Vanna, elsewhere in the house. Kit seized Georgina's hand. She made a slight attempt at pulling it away, then stopped.

'G...' He leaned forward and kissed her mouth. She made no response at first, then pouted her lips fractionally in answer. He sat up. 'I won't do drugs around you, I promise. I love you, Georgina.' She looked down and said nothing. 'For fuck's sake!' he said in frustration. She looked alarmed and pulled her hand away. 'Sorry... sorry...' he said. 'It's just...'

'It's a difficult time,' she said. 'I have to put my health first. You can see that. And I can't be around toxic people.'

'Toxic!' Fury rose into Kit's gorge. She flinched. 'G, I haven't seen you in two months, you wouldn't phone me, you barely wrote to me...'

'That was part of the treatment,' she said. 'Separation.'

'Look, I can give up the drugs, I know I can,' he said. 'If I just knew that we were together.'

'Don't make this about me,' said Georgina. 'You have to want to heal yourself first.'

'Oh, spare me the psychobabble!' She said nothing. 'You know what, Georgina? This whole thing... You were never an addict. It's pathetic. This was just an excuse to get away from me, wasn't it?'

'You're being ridiculous.' She sat up and tucked her hair behind her ears.

'In fact... yes! It's all becoming clear. This is about R.P., isn't it? Whoever the fuck he is. The press know, G, everyone knows. This was to take the heat off him, wasn't it? You and me. That's why Leo introduced us.' He thought of Leo Woodcott delivering him to her in her corner of Salvage's VIP lounge. The way he had said *And so...* as he walked away, hands raised. The way Franco Moretti and the other two models had melted away, leaving him alone with her.

'Oh, Kit,' she said, but would not look at him.

'I'm right, aren't I?'

'You're paranoid. The cocaine's made you paranoid. It's classic. You need to...'

'I'm so glad I was able to help out, Georgina. I'm so glad I was able to create a distraction from your tiresome scandal and knock you up into the bargain. You've taken the heat off what's-his-face *and* you've got yourself a very pretty baby *and* you've got an excuse to quit the career you claim to hate.'

'Kit!' Her grey eyes filled with tears.

'Oh God.' He pulled her to him. She didn't protest. 'I'm so sorry. Just say we're together. Please.'

'Of course we are,' she said into his neck. 'I told you that already.' He pulled apart from her.

'We're a couple,' he said. 'You and me. We're having a baby. We need to talk about what we're going to do. Where we're going to live.'

'I know,' she said, mollifying now, but Kit, still agitated, wasn't satisfied.

'Just tell me one thing. What were you doing in Paris? I thought you came straight to England.'

'I had to see someone,' she said. 'Givenchy. I couldn't put them off any longer.'

'Bullshit!' His voice was loud. 'And who was that man you were with?'

'Just a friend.' Kit made a sound of exasperation. There was the sound of footsteps.

'G, why don't you come to mine later? So we can talk properly, without the spectre at the feast hanging around.'

'Kit, that's rude.'

Vanna hurried into the room. Georgina was wiping her eyes on the sleeve of her jersey. Vanna's expression was one of concern but held, Kit thought, a hint of triumph.

18

May 1989

Kit lay on his sofa, wearing a flowered silk kimono. In the street outside, the gas company or the water company had been drilling all day, a noise that shook his bones and rattled his nerves. His flat was in some disarray since Adeola, his cleaner, had handed in her notice via a polite note in a copperplate hand left on the kitchen worktop – she was awfully sorry, but she could no longer go on cleaning a flat that was so untidy – and he had not got round to replacing her. He could scarcely blame the long-suffering Adeola, whose remit had shrunk week on week, so that latterly she had been stepping over the sleeping bodies of friends on the living-room carpet to get to the kitchen area to mop the floor and wipe down the scarcely used hob of his cooker, then making her way across his clothes-strewn bedroom floor to clean the bathroom, unable to change his sheets or make the bed as Kit would invariably still be in it. 'Untidy', really, was an understatement.

He was looking at a letter from Ray and trying to make sense of it. He had missed several scheduled meetings with his accountant, either by oversleeping or by simply forgetting to go. The gist seemed to be that he was short on liquid funds. Royalties from his book had dwindled to almost nothing and most of his investments had been sold, the letter explained, to meet his day-to-day expenses. It really was a matter of some urgency that Kit contact Ray to discuss his options. In the meantime, did he have any assets he could sell to raise cash? He wasn't sure he did. He had bits of jewellery, but nothing of huge value. His clothes, though expensive and legion, would not raise that much and besides, how did one go about selling them? The Triumph Spitfire languished in a lock-up garage after an unfortunate altercation with a taxi on Park Lane. Kit had kept meaning to get it fixed but had never got round to it, and its tax and insurance had lapsed. Craven Street, paid for in cash, was his only asset to speak of.

And modelling work had all but dried up. The world of fashion and media was not much interested in Kit minus Georgina now, it seemed, and she was most definitely out of circulation. He was going out less, partly because going out with her had been so much more fun, and partly because snorting coke was easier at home, where he didn't have to do it surreptitiously, and snorting coke was often all he felt like doing. Although – and he couldn't pinpoint the moment when it happened – doing cocaine had become something he did to alleviate the effects of not doing cocaine; it had ceased being fun in its own right.

And the night out with Bridget, appalling as it was, and much as he despised Cameleo and that unwashed, mindless, happy scene, had somehow taken the shine off Salvage, Swoop, all his old haunts; he hated to admit it but things *had* moved on, the dressing-up scene that he had loved so much seemed a little tawdry now, old, over. In his darker moments it felt as though he was, at the age of twenty, washed up. If only he had been born a handful of years earlier, hit London at the start of the New Romantic scene, been a Blitz Kid, got in at the beginning.

Sleep, often hard to come by, had become more elusive than ever. If he was lucky he might get an hour or two between 8am and midday. Kit, however, now did doze off; whether for minutes or hours he was not sure, for he was awoken by the shriek of the doorbell. Blearily, he stumbled to the intercom.

'Hello?'

It was hard to hear above the noise of the drilling.

'Hello... ...come in?' he heard over the door entry system. He pressed the button with the key glyph on it and from habit unlocked the door to the flat.

There were two of them; he heard the clatter of their feet on the stairs. But when a man pushed the door open and walked into the hall, followed by his companion, Kit didn't recognise either of them.

The first man wore a suit – tailored, Kit could tell – and very shiny shoes, patent. The other was considerably younger, perhaps mid twenties. He wore a very ordinary pair of jeans, trainers, and a Fred Perry shirt. His hair was shaven in a number two cut. They stood in Kit's hallway and looked at him.

'Sorry...? Are you...?' Kit said in some confusion.

'May we come in?' the first one said, and walked into the room without waiting for an answer. The other followed. They were perhaps something to do with the management company that owned the building. Some sort of survey. Maybe it was about the drilling outside, which continued.

'Was I expecting you?' It was very possible that an appointment had been made via a letter that he had overlooked, or simply forgotten about. But neither man spoke.

The three of them stood on Kit's oriental rug, a present from Marianne. It had come from her library. The men had tracked dirt in from the street onto it. It would need vacuuming, Kit thought automatically, then remembered that Adeola would no longer be coming to do it.

He had a sudden realisation of who the men were and why they had come, and an ice chill ran down his gullet to land in his stomach. He had heard of such people; had heard stories, whispers in dark corners of nightclubs. Shameful. And he had let them walk right in, like a gullible sap had even left his door open for them. He waited for them to speak, but neither did.

'I know why you're here,' he said eventually.

'Really?' said the older man pleasantly. 'And why are we here?'

'Jonathan sent you.'

The man did not answer, but looked round the room, taking in the mess of clothes, books and magazines, the photographs, the embroidered Indian cushions, the silk throws, the bust of Antinous. His eyes settled on the triptych of Kit. He walked to the fireplace to look at it more closely. Kit's heart was hammering in his chest so hard it must be visible. The man turned to look at him.

'A little hubristic, wouldn't you say?'

'You could say that,' Kit said unsteadily.

'You are a very handsome young man, though.' The man turned back to the portrait. 'I can see why you might want to indulge yourself. Isn't he handsome, Leonard?' The younger one shrugged and gave a kind of snort. 'You mustn't mind him,' the first one said to Kit. 'Leonard doesn't perceive beauty in the way that you and I do, Mr Dashwood. Doesn't have our eye, you might say.' He was standing before the fireplace, his back to the room. The one called Leonard was staring at Kit, his gaze unwavering.

'I can pay you,' Kit said. 'Pay Jonathan, I mean. I just need a little time.'

'H'mm?' The man turned to look at him. 'Time, Mr Dashwood?'

'I've got... maybe four hundred pounds in cash on me now.' Kit was calculating rapidly. 'And I can get the rest... soon... in two or three days. Just...'

The man said nothing, but walked across the room to the sofa. He was looking at the jumble of papers and statements that Ray had included with his letter. Kit seized up the paperwork to hide it from the man's gaze.

'Thank you.' The man sat down. 'Would it be too much to trouble you for a glass of water?'

'Yes, of course,' said Kit. In his kitchen area, visible from the sofa, his hands shook as he filled a tumbler.

'Leonard?' the man asked. 'Would you care for a glass of water?'

'Naah,' said Leonard. 'Thank you,' fronting the *th* a little. *Fank you.*

Kit handed the glass of water to the older man, who patted the sofa.

'Do please join me.'

Kit sat next to him. 'I've a car,' he said. 'A Triumph Spitfire. In a garage near here.'

'A Triumph Spitfire, Leonard!' The man made a show of pretending to consider it. 'Is that a nice car?'

'S'all right,' Leonard said grudgingly, and then, 'Yeah, it's a nice car, actually.'

'You can have it,' said Kit. 'I'll give you the keys.'

'And how much might this car be worth, Mr Dashwood?'

'Um...' Kit tried desperately to remember how much he had paid for it. 'Maybe ten thousand pounds?' The man shook his head, as if this were disappointing news. 'I can get you the rest... very soon,' Kit said.

'Mr Dashwood.' The man turned to face him. He leaned in. He had dark wavy hair, slicked back with gel. His breath smelled of something foul, as if his teeth and gums were rotting. Kit did his best not to recoil. The man placed his hand on Kit's thigh. 'Nice,' he said, as if to himself, rubbing the fabric of the kimono between finger and thumb. 'Raw silk.' He left his hand there. Every muscle in Kit's leg tensed. 'Mr Dashwood – may I call you Kit?' Kit nodded. 'My client is, as you know, a patient man. But I'm afraid that you, Kit, have worn his patience very thin indeed.' He moved his hand further up Kit's leg, rucking the kimono. The stories that Kit had heard, of knives, assault, humiliation, ran through his head. He was aware that he was perspiring heavily.

Leonard, as though bored, unwrapped a stick of Wrigley's chewing gum and popped it into his mouth.

'*She's* nice,' he said decidedly, pointing at a framed photograph of Georgina on the coffee table.

'Ah yes.' The other man turned to look. 'Miss Georgina Garvey.' He turned back to Kit, staring at him. Kit was unable to meet his gaze.

'This has nothing to do with her.' His voice came in a stutter.

'You're right,' the man said thoughtfully. 'It doesn't.' Kit felt a tiny rush of relief, that Georgina was too celebrated, too closely guarded, to be within reach of these people.

'And now she's in the family way, I understand,' the man went on. 'You must be *so* proud and pleased.' Kit said nothing. 'Isn't that nice, Leonard?' the man called. Leonard was moving round the room, looking at the photos and objects, just as his associate had. He picked up a vase, looked at its base, put it down again.

'Uh?' he said.

'Mr Dashwood – Kit – becoming a father.'

'Oh, yeah,' said Leonard.

'Now then,' the man said, turning back to Kit. 'Where were we?' His face moved closer. Kit forced himself to look back at him. The man's breath came a little heavily; it was rank, vile. His hand moved further up the inside of Kit's thigh. Leonard, following some cue, stopped looking round the room and came and stood by them, next to the sofa.

'Twenty-two thousand, four hundred and eighty pounds,' said the man. 'Does that sum sound about right to you?' Kit made a tiny sound of assent. 'With our fees and costs added on, of course, let's say... how about a round twenty-five? Keeps things simple, doesn't it?'

'OK.' Kit's heart was pounding. He had a very strong urge to pee.

'Otherwise...' The man gave his thigh a gentle squeeze. Kit was naked under the kimono. Just a fraction of an inch and a flimsy piece of raw silk stood between the man's fingers and Kit's balls.

Where the knife came from Kit couldn't have said, but suddenly Leonard was plunging it into the cushion next to him, slitting it down its middle. Stuffing oozed out of the huge gash in the red and green embroidered silk. Kit jumped, then sat perfectly rigid and shut his eyes. The other man squeezed his thigh again. The drilling outside had stopped.

*

He told no one about the visit. He sold the car, which in its condition and his hurry to sell raised the meagre sum of five hundred pounds, and prevailed on a few wealthy friends for what he assured them were loans. It wasn't enough, and the ultimate humiliation was having to ask Georgina – with Vanna in the room – to lend him the remaining five thousand pounds. He told her he needed the money to fix up the Triumph and get it back on the road. She didn't question the sum and he felt safe in assuming she would not remember to ask about the car subsequently, much less suggest he take her out in it. An anonymous aide of Jonathan's wordlessly collected the cash from Craven Street a day or two later. Kit had to change dealer, of course, and moved his custom to a woman his friend Stefan sometimes used. She was Mother Teresa in comparison with Jonathan but Kit wasn't taking any chances; he took a black cab to her north London council flat, paid in her in cash with the taxi waiting round the corner and came straight home again.

The handful of meetings – they could not be called dates – he had with Georgina, always at his instigation, were fraught. He told her that he had stopped doing drugs, but she didn't believe him. The pregnancy had been announced via a carefully choreographed press conference to which Kit was not invited. The newspapers and magazines reporting it scarcely mentioned him: only the *Daily Star* carried a picture of him, a thumbnail-sized photograph captioned *Kit Dashwood – father-to-be*. Several messages from Bob on Kit's answerphone followed.

He found out about her antenatal appointments only after the event. This was upsetting, but he tamped down his feelings and did his best to join in with Vanna's ooh-ing and ah-ing over the fuzzy photograph from which he was scarcely able to pick out a human form.

The press, by some tacit agreement, largely left Georgina alone. Occasionally a gossip column published a photo of her shopping for baby things, or sitting outside a café with Vanna. One snap in the *Daily Star* showed her coming out of the Ivy with the man she had been photographed with in Paris. The newspaper identified him as Giles Fitzsimmons, a merchant banker.

'Who's he?' Kit asked, as casually as possible.

'Oh, he was in rehab with me,' she said offhandedly. 'We supported each other a lot. You form a bond.' And Kit had suppressed the fury he felt with her, and with Giles Fitzsimmons, whoever the fuck he was, and cut short his visit to take a taxi to his new dealer on the Elthorne Estate.

He woke up on his sofa the next afternoon, following an hour or two of fitful sleep in which fearsome dreams crowded in on him – the party of his infancy, the cake and the jam, attended by appalling figures he knew to be himself, hideous, deformed, leering, a succession of portraits in the attic. He stumbled to his bathroom and scrubbed his hands with a boar-bristle nail brush until they stung.

Marianne. Marianne would understand his predicament. He needed to call her, but from a phone box. There had been the nagging suspicion for a while that someone was listening in on his calls. A phone box would be anonymous. Untraceable.

But people might be following him. This man, now, ostensibly browsing a bookshop window on the corner of Charing Cross Road and St Martin's Court, this man was waiting for Kit to move on so that he could follow. Georgina's people might have been sent to spy on him, prove he was using, give her the reason she needed to cut him out entirely.

He found a free telephone box on Charing Cross Road. The air inside was fetid, the hopeful smell of bleach no match for the stink of urine. The phone box, like every other in central London, was wallpapered with business cards advertising sexual services. As fast as the authorities tore them down they sprang up again like mushroom spores. He found himself staring at *Spanking Fun With Sexy 19Yr Old* as he dialled the number for Erringby Hall. He knew to let the phone ring a long time. There was a telephone in the vestibule, another in the library, a third in her bedroom. It could take her a while to get to the phone. She didn't have an answer machine. Perspiration trickled into Kit's eyebrows. Eventually the phone was answered.

'Hello?'

'Marianne?' He was cradling the receiver to his right ear. He dug the nails of his left hand into his palm, which stung from being scrubbed so hard. The pain helped him focus.

'Kit. What is it?' She sounded so familiar, voice tinged with impatience, that a flood of homesickness for Erringby and for her engulfed him.

'Oh, Marianne...'

'What?'

'It's G. Georgina. You know she's pregnant?'

He would have taken Marianne away from some important task, replacing a cracked tile, rehanging a door, unblocking a drain.

'Is she?'

Of course: Marianne took the broadsheet newspapers, the *Guardian* and – for Susannah – the *Times*, and rarely had time to read either of them. They would amass, still folded, in piles in the scullery, to be thrown out eventually. She was not a consumer of celebrity gossip.

'Yes. Seven months.'

Stern Dominatrix. 935 4752. PVC. Rubber. Leather.

'Unplanned, I take it?' She was probably talking to him from the vestibule; Kit thought he could make out the echo.

'Yes. Well. Unplanned by me. I think maybe she...'

'I see.'

He blundered on.

'She... she went to rehab. In Switzerland. They wouldn't let me see her.'

'*Rehab?* You mean, like a clinic?'

'Yes. The Italian-speaking part of Switzerland.' He realised the pointlessness of this last detail as he said the words.

'But she's better now?'

'Yes, she's in London, but Marianne, she never wants to see me. She treats me like a pariah.' He felt his chin wobble; he must not cry. Marianne wouldn't like it.

'Whatever for?'

'Because... because I'm still using. Cocaine.'

'Goodness,' said Marianne, as if she were feigning interest in a topic at a vicarage tea party.

'The thing is, I've got myself into a bit of a state over it.'

'Yes.'

'Should I... do you think I should ask her to marry me?' His nose was running, badly. He felt about himself for a handkerchief.

'I've no idea,' she said. 'If you want to, I suppose.'

'I need help, Marianne!'

She would be resting an elbow on the marble-topped console table.

With her other hand she would be absent-mindedly twirling the telephone cable backwards and forwards, straightening and then reforming its curls. Kit knew this direct appeal to her sympathy was the least likely way of getting any, but he was desperate. She would be impatient, wanting to get back to whatever it was she was doing. He had no handkerchief on him. He sniffed and wiped his nose with the heel of his hand.

'Have you done drugs today?' She had heard the sniff.

'Yes. But I want to stop. So I can be with her. With Georgina. And the baby.'

Belgravia Angels. Hotel visits possible.

Did he have enough change? He fed in more coins.

'What's happening with her modelling?'

'She's probably going to give up. That's a secret. Don't tell anyone, will you?'

'Of course not.' Again that rising impatience. *What do you take me for?* she did not say, but the words burned through the receiver. If there was one thing she was good at, it was secrets.

'Not even Col.' She said nothing. 'And... don't tell Col I'm still doing drugs. Please.' A tear trickled down his cheek.

Watersports! Hardsports! Foot Fetishers!

'Your Uncle Col has gone away, Kit.'

'What?' He wiped his nose on his sleeve, blotted his tears on the fabric of his shirt.

'I should have thought your parents would have told you. Since I assume he went running to them.'

'I haven't spoken to them. Not... not lately.'

'I see. Well, he went off a few months ago.'

Kit had a yearning so hard that it ached, to be at Erringby with Marianne. He needed her to tell him that everything would be all right. That he could come and stay for as long as he liked. That Room Seven would be got ready for him.

'He'll be back,' said Marianne. 'He always comes back.'

Kit was unable to process this information about Col. He was going to cry again.

'I don't know what to do.' His voice shook. He was unravelling. 'I'm losing her, I know I am.'

'Oh, come on now.' This time she made no attempt to hide her irritation. 'It can't be as bad as all that, surely?'

He had to plough on, ask her the other thing anyway.

'Marianne... I don't suppose you could let me have some more money, could you?'

There was a silence at the end of the line.

20yr Slim & Busty Mediteranian Girls.

'I'm afraid not, Kit.' Her voice was crystalline. Cold.

And Kit realised, with sickening clarity, that he was not going to get what he needed and wanted. Any of it.

'No... of course not,' he said. 'Forgive me. I'm going to go now. Bye, Marianne.'

'Goodbye,' she said, now sounding faintly amused. He put the receiver down. Before he had time to change his mind he put more coins into the phone and dialled the number for Flatley Close.

'Hel-*lo*?' His father's telephone voice, the emphasis as always on the second syllable, an optimistic upbeat, as if he were looking forward to the conversation already. 'Hello?' Bob said again, more warily.

Kit put the phone down. He thought he heard his father say, 'Kit?' as the receiver clicked into its cradle. The telephone spat out his surplus coins.

19

August 1989

When the phone rang Kit was alone, his swabs and his bag of coke and his spoon on the coffee table. He had done several hits with the same syringe, was struggling to get it into a vein. Angry bruises were forming on his upper arm. He'd been slamming coke – injecting – for... what was it? Three months? Four? It had been a friend of a friend who'd set him off. The three of them, Stefan, Luca and Kit, had been lounging around Kit's flat, when Luca, bored, had looked up from Kit's rug, where he lay with his legs in the air, balancing a cushion on his bare feet, and asked if they fancied taking it up a notch. Then explained what he meant.

Kit knew about smoking cocaine, how it gave you a rush that was supposedly orgasmic, but he'd never liked the idea of it. Only baking soda separated it from crack, which was what filthy junkies smoked. Injecting, however, notched things up a gear, meaning you were serious about your drugs and not just a casual party user, but why the hell not?

And so he had sat on his living-room floor with his fist clenched, feeling first the cold of Luca swabbing his arm and then the prick of the needle. Time had been suspended, everything reduced to this moment. Outside the house the trains had rattled by.

There was a slight burning sensation in his vein and then it hit him.

The rush was like nothing he had experienced before. He was thrown headfirst into a tunnel, moving at the speed of light. That lasted only a second before he was back in his room. His brain had burst open and he started laughing, found he couldn't. Never had he felt euphoria like it; it was better than his best time ever snorting coke. Better than Georgina in Room Seven. Nausea swelled in his stomach, but he didn't care.

'Good, huh?' Luca's voice was a juddering hiss. Bees swarmed in Kit's head. He stared at the cushion Luca had been toying with earlier. Its stripes and swirls were almost unbearably bright. He had grabbed Luca's hand and squeezed it, gasping for air. It was a struggle to get the words out.

'More,' he said. 'I want more.'

The phone was still ringing. Kit was going to ignore it, but then he remembered.

'It's Vanna.'

'Oh shit.' There could only be one reason for her calling, and he had got his dates in a muddle.

'Two hours ago,' said Vanna. 'You have a daughter.' She hung up.

Kit was disoriented. He had barely slept for what felt like several days, and the blinds were drawn. When he lifted them the glare of the street assaulted him. He was too preoccupied with his comedown, with the need to go out and buy syringes – he was going further afield to avoid suspicion, seeking out pharmacies in Marylebone, Lambeth, Vauxhall – and with the need to call one of his dealers – he was alternating the woman on the Elthorne Estate with a man Luca used, whom he had never met – to feel aggrieved that he had missed the birth of his child.

He went into the bathroom and splashed water on his face. Of late he had been avoiding his reflection and the face staring back was a jolt. But he recognised himself. He was as he had been at Susannah Lonsdale's funeral, made up to look like a consumptive, pale foundation and grey shadow around the eyes. Now he had achieved the look without cosmetics.

Outside rush hour was in full swing, crowds swarming down Villiers Street, into Charing Cross Station, over Hungerford Bridge. There were no taxis to be had and Kit, not having taken the Tube for the longest time, had developed a phobia of it – the mere thought that the train might break down, a hundred feet underground, every airless carriage rammed with passengers, was enough to bring on a panic attack. Could a bus take him there? He had no idea.

He started running up Charing Cross Road but almost immediately was doubled up with discomfort, pains shooting across his chest as sweat broke out on his face and neck and underarms. The noise of the crowds and the traffic was jarring. He alternated between a slow jog, his hand clutching his side, and the fastest walk he could manage. He kept looking over his shoulder for black cabs, but the one he saw that had its light on wouldn't stop for him.

At St Giles Circus he realised he didn't know where the Portland Hospital was. He'd assumed it actually to be on Great Portland Street, but maybe it was one of those geographical sleights of hand London was prone to, like Clapham Junction not being in Clapham. He headed west down Oxford Street, where it seemed that shoppers, commuters, tourists, all were united by their determination to impede his progress. There were too many people altogether. He darted down Berners Street, where it was quieter, and made his way by that route to Great Portland Street.

The hospital was at the furthest end, near Regent's Park. At the front desk a receptionist regarded him acidly as he struggled to get his breath back, aware of the figure he must cut, gasping, ashen-faced, covered in sweat and dust. She clearly did not believe him when he was able to get the words out that he was the father of Georgina Garvey's baby, here to meet his daughter for the first time. With reluctance she dialled a number and he saw the surprise in her face, the *oh* shape of her mouth, when someone at the other end of the phone – Vanna? a friendly nurse? – confirmed his story and he was buzzed through to the bank of lifts.

A ride in a lift was something else he was phobic about but the alternative, six flights of stairs in his current condition, was no alternative at all. He stared at the roof of the lift, willing it to deliver him as swiftly as possible. When the door opened onto the glaring whiteness of a carpeted landing he realised he had forgotten the name of the wing that Georgina was on, and none of the signs struck a chord. He very, very badly wanted some drugs right now. If he had had any on him he would have found a toilet and done a bump or, better still, slammed some coke. He leaned against a wall and tried to get his breath back.

'Are you all right?' A passing nurse looked concerned. Kit gave her the best smile he was able to conjure and explained who he was. To his surprise she believed him. He was recognised less and less frequently these days but it was just possible she remembered him from the perfume advert or the gossip columns. She knew where Georgina was.

'I'm going that way,' she said. 'Why don't you come with me?' and at the end of a corridor she tapped on a door and opened it and said, 'Here's...' and Kit was faced with a familiar scene: the birth celebration. The room contained a lot of people. Vanna was there and Kit recognised – from the framed photographs Georgina carried with her – her parents and her sister, who was holding a pink balloon and a teddy bear, and there were more people, but Kit did not have time to take them in, because his attention was drawn to the bed in which Georgina sat up, holding a tiny bundle.

'Hey!' she said, with forced brightness, 'Kit's here.' And her announcement, for the benefit of the people in the room rather than to welcome him, caused a tangible shift in the atmosphere, which had been festive and now tensed, and everyone's eyes were on him as he went up to the bed. They were staring at the bruises on his arm. He ought to have worn a jacket. He leaned over and kissed Georgina's cheek, clumsily, was aware of her very slight recoil, probably imperceptible to anyone else, and of her gripping the bundle more tightly.

'Well done,' he murmured.

'Well... here she is,' said Georgina, again a little too brightly. The baby was wrapped in a white blanket and wore a yellow woollen hat. Her livid face was screwed up, the eyes tightly shut, the dark brown hair not covered by the hat plastered to her forehead as if she were sweating.

'She's beautiful,' said Kit, since that was what one said, though he had never seen a newborn before, had no idea, really, *what* she looked like. 'Can I hold her?'

Georgina hesitated a beat too long before saying, 'Of course,' and handing her to him. Vanna was at his side in an instant.

'You have to support her head,' she told Kit unhappily.

'I do know that,' he said, and turned a little away from Vanna, and from everyone, towards the window.

'Hey you,' he said. The baby squinted more deeply. He shielded her eyes with the hand that was not cradling her head, trying to stop his hands from shaking. He couldn't make them stop. What should he feel? Wasn't he meant to have some kind of epiphany at this moment? He needed a hit. The baby opened her eyes – they were a deep blue – and seemed to regard Kit for a second or two. She had a solemn look, as if she were frowning. Did she look like him? There were no baby pictures of himself. Did she resemble his own parents? He realised suddenly that she would never know her paternal grandparents, would grow up with that side of her family tree a blank. He should say something to her. What should he say, with all these people in the room? The shaking of his hands worsened. He was aware he was perspiring very heavily. Vanna was right there: firmly she took his daughter from him. She made a kissing sound with her lips and said something to the baby in Italian.

'OK, you've seen her, now you can go,' said a man; he also spoke with an Italian inflection. It was Roberto, Georgina's agent, chief among the Rottweilers. Everyone looked at Kit, waiting for him to leave. Vanna handed the baby back to Georgina. There was the palpable sense of something having been got over and done with. Kit's palms were sweaty. He dug his fingernails into them.

'What will you call her?' he asked Georgina.

'Sophie Elise,' she said. 'After my sister and my grandmother.'

'It's pretty,' he said, and she gave him a half smile, as if in apology, and then Roberto was bearing down on him and he turned and left the room.

In the corridor he passed a man who he recognised, from the magazine photograph, as Giles Fitzsimmons. The man had a casual air, as if he were returning from a trip to the hospital café or shop. He would have been in the building a while, absenting himself from Georgina's room only to avoid a scene. He glared at Kit as they passed each other, but did not speak to him.

*

When the doorbell rang Marianne was in what had been the boot room, trying to sort the junk from the perhaps-not-junk stored in fusty cardboard boxes. The boxes themselves had originally housed forgotten foodstuffs like Heinz tinned salad and Pack-a-Pie filling. One had been chewed at by mice and contained not only droppings but an actual rodent, recently deceased. She needed more cats. When she'd moved to Erringby there had been a clowder (Manning, during her brief tenure as his employer, had taught her the word) living in one of the outhouses, practically a feral colony, but they had died away and the cats that she and Col had adopted had been house creatures, too well fed to bother much with mousing other than as a casual hobby. She would speak to Bill Carter; his farm cats frequently had kittens.

Another box contained electrical parts: old fuses, antediluvian pin plugs, twisted flexes covered in fabric, strips of cardboard wrapped in fuse wires of varying thicknesses. Sorting through the boxes was one of many jobs it had taken her decades, literally, to get round to.

The idea was to convert the boot room and the old dairy into tea rooms, one of Col's schemes that might, she had latterly admitted, have some merit. In warm weather she could serve teas to visitors in the walled garden.

Since John she had had something like a renewed energy for getting things sorted. He was from the village. Recently retired from his farrier business, he had turned up at her door one afternoon and declared himself bored and in need of a project. He had heard – he put this tactfully – that she had been by herself of late and was struggling. He was a practical man, at his happiest getting his hands dirty, fixing things. Why not let him come and help her with some of the bigger, messier jobs? He didn't expect a wage but she paid for his petrol and passed him fifty pounds now and again, which kept both of them happy. He was a man used to working on his own, not much given to conversation, which suited her; they left each other alone by and large. It was a good arrangement.

His current project was clearing dead trees and branches from the paths in the wood and pruning some of the canopy trees. Today he had drafted in two young men from the village to help him, but he'd had to make an unplanned trip to Hereford to buy a sharpener for the chainsaw, and had warned Marianne that the men might arrive before his return. Could she set them off on something else to do until he got back?

The young men now at her front door did not look well-suited to manual labour. She didn't go into the village often; since the closure of the shop-cum-post-office several years ago there wasn't much reason to, and her last visit to the Three Hares had probably been that time with Kit two summers ago. She supposed that the country-boy types she was used to had become as obsolete as those electrical parts. The young men on Erringby's casual staff when she had arrived in 1973 had not been much different from the youths that Uncle Harold had press-ganged into service for his summer parties of the sixties, bar longer hair and perhaps – if they were particularly *au courant* – flared trousers. But things had moved on, and these two men were perhaps representative of young people nowadays. They wore jeans from a high-street store and not the factory shop on the outskirts of Hereford. One had on a T-shirt that looked brand new, with the letters R.E.M. on it – a drug thing, she supposed – the other wore an expensive-looking shirt in a blue-and-white check. Both had on suede desert boots. They had brought work clothes to change into, perhaps.

Neither, if it came to it, did they seem particularly young. They might be as old as thirty.

They grinned at her expectantly.

'Sorry I'm late,' said the one in the T-shirt. 'I was bitten on the penis by a dachshund.' His companion giggled.

'Good heavens.' She was somewhat nonplussed. 'You're early, as a matter of fact.'

Check-shirt man looked a little nervous. He took a deep breath. 'This is…?'

'Erringby Hall, yes. You've come to the right place.' The men looked at each other.

'Could we… could we possibly come in?' R.E.M. asked.

'Of course,' she said. 'I was expecting you.' Check-shirt grinned at his companion. He was the better-looking; he had dark curly hair and eyes that crinkled at the edges when he smiled. The other one, R.E.M., was sandier, frecklier, sharper-featured. 'Follow me,' she said, and led them into the house.

'I'm Tony,' said the good-looking one.

'And I'm Martin,' said the other.

'And I'm Marianne.'

They peered around them as though struck by the house but she led the way briskly into the kitchen.

'Do sit down.' The men sat. 'Have you brought clothes to change into?' They looked at each other.

'Clothes?' said Martin.

'Oh, never mind,' she said. 'I could find you something to wear, I suppose.'

'Wow,' said Tony.

'Can I offer you both a hot drink?' she asked them. 'Before you get started.' They looked at each other and giggled.

'I'm rather partial to inspissated juice!' they said in unison.

'What?' she said. 'I meant tea or coffee.'

'Oh, OK,' said Martin. 'Tea, then.'

'Tea for me as well,' said Tony.

She filled the kettle from the sink and set it on the range. She was reaching for three mugs from a shelf.

'And I'm guessing you each have two sugars.'

'No.' Tony sounded puzzled.

'Me neither,' said Martin.

'Things are looking up,' she said, and saw again their shared glances.

'Does Col Greenfield live here?' Martin asked. There was a pause as she poured boiling water onto teabags.

'He's away,' she said.

'But this is his house?' Martin asked.

'It's *my* house,' said Marianne.

'Oh,' Tony said.

'Oh, right,' said Martin, 'so you are...?' She saw Tony try to kick him under the table, managing only to bang his own ankle on a chair leg.

'I'm Mrs Greenfield,' she said. Tony surreptitiously rubbed his sore ankle. 'Col's wife. You may call me Marianne.'

'Oh!' said Tony. 'So is it *your* mother who lives here?'

'She did live with us for a while, yes,' said Marianne. 'But she died last year.'

'I'm sorry,' said Tony.

'It's all right,' said Marianne. 'She was an elderly lady.'

'Yes, she was,' said Martin.

'You knew her?'

'Oh no,' said Martin. 'Of course not.'

'Well,' said Marianne. This was a very peculiar afternoon. 'I suppose that...'

Martin was nodding at Tony meaningfully.

'Would it be terribly cheeky of us,' Tony began, 'to have a quick tour of the house?'

'I suppose so,' she said. 'While we wait for John. If you don't mind a kind of self-tour. I'm rather busy.' Tony grinned at Martin, who grinned back. 'Take your mugs of tea with you,' she told them. 'And try not to spill anything. Oh – and please don't go into the dining room. It's out of bounds.'

'This is *amazing*,' she heard Martin mutter to Tony as they went out of the kitchen.

'She seems nice,' Tony said.

'Bit eccentric.'

'I would expect nothing less.'

She made to turn left out of the kitchen towards the workrooms but then loitered. For some reason these young men piqued her interest. They turned right and went back the way they'd come, towards the hall. She slipped, unseen, into the drawing room and left the door open.

'This is it...' Martin was saying. 'Wow, it's just how it was!'

'Check out the portraits,' said Tony. 'I remember this one.'

'It was on the other wall, I think,' said Martin.

'*Harold Fentiman, 1942*,' Tony read out.

'He looks a bit like Lord Lucan.'

'He actually does, doesn't he?'

'*Kit Antrobus, 1986*,' Tony went on. They were looking at *Woman in the Bath*.

'Never heard of him,' said Martin.

'Is that her? Marianne?'

'Dunno.' She heard them move into the hall. There came stumbling steps, as if the men were waltzing together, badly.

'I came late to wood pigeon,' Martin said.

'You unconscionable little turd,' Tony replied, and they laughed.

'Wow, the fireplace and everything,' said Martin.

'The deer's not wearing the hat,' said Tony.

'Shame.'

'I wonder who's got it?'

'*Industria et Spe*. What does that mean?'

'Industry and... something.'

'Let's keep going.' They went into the billiard room. Marianne, bored, went back to the kitchen to clear away the tea things. She heard them go into the gun room. She suspected that Col's LPs, gathering dust in ranks along the walls, might prove to be another attraction.

Presently she took up a can of furniture polish and a yellow duster and went to the dining room. The door was open. One of them had looked in, in contravention of her instruction, and annoyance flared up in her. At the door she stopped.

Tony was standing at the end of the dining table looking at the two place settings that had been made up. He had picked up one of the scallop-shaped plates with the pink roses for a closer look. She saw the room suddenly through his eyes, the contrast between it and the rest of the house. Sunlight spilled through the windows onto the cut-glass goblets and the cutlery, making them sparkle. There was a smell of furniture polish. Only that morning had she arranged mop-headed agapanthus blooms in the Chinese urn in the fireplace.

Tony put down the plate and sniffed at a posy of freesias, also fresh, in a silver vase. He reached out to touch one of the stiff linen napkins.

'I thought I told you not to come in here.'

He spun round.

'Oh shit,' he said. 'Sorry.' She stood in the doorway, regarding him. He looked embarrassed and younger than his probable years. 'Sorry,' he said again. 'We're sorry,' though it didn't seem very fair to implicate his friend.

'I bet you are,' she said.

'It's just... This is such a lovely room.' His eyes flickered to the ceiling, as if he realised he sounded a little pathetic. And now she did smile at him.

'Thank you,' she said.

'We only came for a look around,' he said.

'You're not here to clear the woodland, are you?'

'No! I think we've been talking at cross purposes.'

'I think we have.' He really was rather handsome, despite the puppy-dog demeanour. She looked him up and down and saw his blush.

'Um...' he said.

'And so? What brings you and your associate to Erringby Hall?'

'What... the film, of course. *Strassburg Pie.*'

'The *film*?'

'Well... yes. It's legendary. The classic scenes. The New Year's Eve party.'

'Good heavens!' said Marianne.

'We're not the first to come here, surely?'

'I believe you are. Unless there've been others, skulking around the grounds. One never knows here.'

'There's so many things I want to ask you,' he said. 'About the film.'

'I had no idea,' she said. 'You mean we're famous?'

'Not… I wouldn't say *that*, exactly. But sort of… cultish, I suppose.'

'Cultish!' She rather liked the idea. 'So, those strange things you and your friend were saying, about being bitten on the penis?'

'You have seen the film, haven't you?'

'Oh, a long time ago,' she said. 'When it came out. I don't remember much about it to be honest.'

He looked amazed.

'It was Col's thing, really,' she said.

'Anyway, I want to apologise,' he said humbly. 'You were generous enough to let us look around and this was the one room you asked us not to go in and I did.'

'Yes, you did.'

'I'm sorry,' he repeated. She looked straight at him.

'Come to bed,' she said, 'and we'll say no more about it.'

20

December 1990

On the morning of Christmas Eve Kit woke late on the Habitat sofa, duvet half pushed to the floor. He had as usual slept badly, listening to the rain fall on the laurel bushes beyond the bay window, pretending to doze through Bridget getting up, making herself breakfast. She no longer said goodbye when leaving for work.

He sat up, reached for his jacket crumpled on the floor, chopped out a line of speed with Bridget's Blockbuster Video membership card. He was not a fan of Christmas. The last good one had been two years ago with Georgina. Since then Christmas had served as a marker of his decline: his trust fund finally running out, having to sell Craven Street to pay off his drug and other debts, moving into Bridget's one-bedroomed flat in Bromley. Officially, he slept on her sofa; occasionally, if he was feeling lonely, he shared her bed. There had been, at the beginning, a few fumbled attempts at sex, relegated now to the back of their minds and never referred to. The arrangement was meant to have been temporary and he could tell, even through the selfish prism of the drug user, that she was more than a little fed up. The situation had become more urgent since her casual boyfriend, Doug – he of the dismal visit to the Cameleo nightclub – had of late become less casual. Though neither Bridget nor Doug had said anything, Kit knew that Doug for one would be happy if there was an absence of Kit. He, Doug, worked at the same accountancy firm as her and was also doing exams – tax, was it? Their work conversation was arcane and Kit could take no part in it. Sometimes, when Doug was coming over, Kit absented himself on one of his long walks to Beckenham or Sydenham, returning at an hour late enough to ensure that they had gone to bed, then lay on the sofa watching TV as he tried not to listen to their lovemaking, tried to remember what arousal felt like.

Impossible not to think of Georgina at this time of year, impossible not to remember their gilded Christmas: cocktail parties, an extravagant dinner with theatrical friends of hers in a Mayfair private dining room, cocaine passed round on a silver salver between courses, the New Year's Eve party in her suite at Claridge's.

That was the last time he had been truly happy. He had known extreme euphoria since then through taking drugs, especially slamming coke, but it had been, he now realised, delusive, chimerical. Still, he would have given anything now to have *those* days back, the days of injecting coke, the days before the money ran out. Speed in comparison was sordid, the high it gave you nasty and synthetic. He hated taking it but was incapable of stopping. The early highs of slamming coke had been revelatory, and hallucinatory. In the breathless exhilaration of those first rushes when the solution hit his vein he had once or twice encountered a woman with long dark hair, her face an oval of light so blinding he was unable to make out her features, but she was, he knew, his own mother, resurrected from the car smash to revisit his two-year-old self, and he had felt, for the briefest moments, entirely at peace. That happened only at the beginning; soon he was bingeing on cocaine, injecting gram after gram, so that by the time his daughter was born he was constantly chasing the raptures of those first times; occasionally he came tantalisingly close, but never close enough.

He saw no one now from the Craven Street days. Some friends had dropped him like a stone, once his impecuniosity became common knowledge. Others were very ill or dead. He'd stopped going to the funerals. The last had been Emile's at St Marylebone Church. Kit had timed his arrival to slip in just as the service was beginning and had sat at the back incognito, ignoring the card on the pew. *The family would appreciate it very much if you left your name and address.*

He had not seen his daughter again. He kept in touch with Georgina by letter – had allowed her to assume that the Bromley flat was in his name – and received the occasional note in return, sometimes with a photograph enclosed. The most recent showed Sophie sitting on a beach in Lampedusa, wearing a pink hat and pointing at something off camera. She looked very happy. She had his dark eyes but otherwise resembled her mother. He stashed the photo in the back pages of his battered copy of *Vanity Fair*. Looking at it was almost unbearably painful.

The wrapper of speed lay in his hand. There was enough maybe for two days. And it was Christmas Eve, and his next dole cheque would not come through until the New Year. Could he borrow from Bridget? She worked just off Eastcheap. He probably had enough for the bus fare. He could phone from a nearby call box, get her to meet him at a cashpoint. Then he remembered she had said she was finishing work at lunchtime and catching the train to Bury. There had been no talk of Kit spending Christmas with the Buckleys this year. He looked at the clock: a quarter to midday. By the time he got to central London she would be on her way to Euston and he would never find her.

She had left without wishing him Happy Christmas, had not troubled to ask how he was spending the holiday. The situation was far from ideal – staying with her had strained their friendship – but still, that felt callous. The Bridget of his earliest clubbing days, who had practically insisted she join him for her family Christmas, had gone, replaced by a Bridget with a boyfriend and a Next card, who wore suits to work and studied for an endless round of exams.

Kit walked into her bedroom. Like the rest of the flat it was unimaginatively kitted out: pine bed, sprigged duvet cover and matching curtains, fawn carpet, a framed Athena print of a couple embracing next to a steam train.

He found what he was looking for in the jewellery box in her scarf drawer. She'd said more than once that she didn't much care for it: a gold flower brooch with a turquoise stone standing in for the stamens, left to her by the Irish granny. He had been told the story of the brooch but had forgotten it.

There was a jeweller and pawnbroker's on the high street. Kit was surprised when the ugly little thing turned out to be good for a loan of just under three hundred pounds. He was making his way to his usual man, who worked out of a tower block just off the A21, when at Bromley South train station he found himself coming to a halt. A train was about to leave, and Kit got on it.

At Victoria he caught a bus to Regent Street. He had not been to the West End since moving to Bromley and the streets were packed with last-minute Christmas shoppers, a slow-moving phalanx of people clogging the pavement. He went into Hamleys toy shop where he was assailed by noise: piped Christmas music, fractious parents, the squealing and bawling of children, the whirring and beeping and exclamations of unseen mechanical toys. For several moments he stood, disoriented, with no idea where to start. He asked an assistant for help and she directed him to the second floor.

Kit bought indiscriminately: Barbie dolls, Polly Pockets, trolls, teddy bears, Lego, a train set, a clock from which to learn the time. Only the restriction on what he was able to carry stopped him buying bigger items – there was a doll's house he particularly liked the look of. He staggered onto Regent Street and hailed a black cab.

In the back of the taxi Kit sat surrounded by bulging carrier bags with their top-hatted, red-jacketed figures and watched the

West End's Christmas lights swirl by. He felt a surge of optimism, an emotion he'd thought he'd forgotten. He was doing something good, for once.

She lived off Heath Street in Hampstead. Kit paid the taxi driver and lugged the carrier bags out of the cab and up her front path. A blue plaque on the wall informed him that an Egyptologist he had never heard of had once lived in her house. He climbed a set of steep steps to the front door. It was the crepuscular hour, dark enough for the lights to be on, not dark enough to draw the curtains. An enormous Christmas tree, lit up and laden with decorations, filled an entire corner of the room. On a sofa sat his daughter, her back to him, playing something with a woman he didn't know. Kit felt as if his heart might stop. He couldn't see a doorbell so he banged the knocker and waited.

A man came to the door. He looked down at Kit on the doorstep. 'You,' he said.

'Hello, Giles,' said Kit. 'I don't believe we've actually met.'

Giles Fitzsimmons was holding a goblet glass of red wine. He stared stonily at Kit.

'I've come to see Sophie,' Kit said. 'I've got her Christmas presents.'

'You're not welcome here,' Giles said. 'I believe that was made perfectly clear to you.' Somewhere in the house a carol concert was playing on the radio.

'Five minutes,' said Kit. 'If I could see her for just five minutes.'

'Absolutely not,' said Giles. 'Now please leave.'

Though he realised it was pointless, Kit tried to get past Giles, into the house. 'Sophie!' he called. 'Sophie!' Giles, the bigger man, barred the way. He gave Kit a shove and Kit tripped over a bag of presents and fell backwards down the steps onto the gravel path. A Steiff teddy bear tumbled out of a bag next to him. 'Sophie!' he yelled. 'Georgina!'

'What's going on?' Georgina appeared in the hallway behind Giles. 'Oh my God!' The woman in the front room was hastily drawing the curtains, her shocked face briefly visible.

'He's just leaving,' Giles said. 'Aren't you?'

'G,' said Kit from his prone position. 'If I could just...'

Georgina, from behind her husband, shook her head, her face stricken. Kit crumpled.

'G...' He began to cry.

'Just go, will you?' said Giles. He closed the door.

Kit got up, stumbling over a carrier bag. He turned and walked back up the road, leaving the presents behind. At the corner with Heath Street he stopped to catch his breath. His face was wet with tears, his nose streaming. He wiped it on his jacket. The palms of his hands were badly grazed and smarting from his fall. Around him Hampstead was getting ready for its well-heeled Christmas, families following their old traditions or making new ones, putting out a snack for Santa and his reindeer, getting ready to watch a favourite video. In Bury Bridget and her family would be gathering in their tiny terraced house to play board games, their own Christmas Eve ritual. Maybe Doug had joined them. There were millions of these family units the length and breadth of the country doing pretty much the same, and Kit was excluded from all of them.

'Kit...'

He turned. Georgina was running towards him. He waited for her to reach him.

'I only wanted to see her, G. Just see her.' He started crying again.

'I know you did.' She reached out and touched his arm. She was wearing brown moleskin trousers and a caramel jumper. Her undyed hair, the same colour as their daughter's, was longer than she used to wear it. She was bigger than she had been, had kept some of the baby weight. It suited her. He recognised the familiar scent of Chanel No. 5.

'You look great,' he said.

'You don't,' she said. Kit half laughed through his sobs.

'I know.'

'I'm sorry about what happened there,' Georgina said. 'She wouldn't understand, Kit. She's still too little.'

'You will tell her about me, though? When she's older.'

'Of course I will.'

'Thank you.' He did his best to stop crying.

'But you need to get cleaned up.'

'I know.'

'Promise me?'

'I'll try.' She was smiling at him. 'I'm sorry I wasn't able to wrap the presents,' he said. 'Tell her... tell her Father Christmas came a bit early.'

'I will do,' she said. 'And I'm sorry about when she was born. I'm sorry there were so many people there.'

'We were outnumbered,' he said.

'We were.'

'That was always our problem.'

'I know. I'm sorry,' she went on. 'About everything. I allowed others to... My choices weren't always my own, Kit.'

They stood in silence for a moment, neither sure what to say next.

'Here.' She pushed something into his hand.

'What...?'

'Just take it.'

It was a wad of money, folded in half.

'I have to go.' She leaned forward to kiss his cheek, then turned and walked quickly towards her house without looking back.

Kit took another cab to Paddington. The last train to Hereford was packed and he spent the journey sitting on someone's suitcase in the space between the carriages. The last bus for the village had long gone so he took a taxi for the nine-mile ride to Erringby Hall.

He found her in the kitchen, sitting in front of the range with the oven door open to keep warm. She turned as he came in.

'Hello,' she said, as if it had been two days and not two years since she had seen him last.

'Marianne.' He felt he might cry again, this time with happiness and relief. Why on earth had he stayed away so long?

'Have you come for Christmas?'

'Yes. If you'll have me.'

'Have you? Of course I'll have you, dear boy.' She stood and took him into her arms. They hugged for a very long time. Her hair smelled of woodsmoke.

'Let me look at you, then.' She put her hands on his upper arms and held him at arm's length. Kit knew he cut a poor figure; pale, thin, haggard in his clothes, which badly needed laundering. But she was not wearing well herself. She was also thinner, had lost a little of her curvaceousness. Col had sometimes called her 'Voluptua'. It had suited her then. Her hair, now more grey than blonde, needed conditioning. Lines were starting to appear, around the eyes, around the mouth. She wore what had been an expensive sweater, cashmere, that was stained and holey, and old jeans. Her hands were filthy.

'You have grown up, haven't you?' she said.

'That's one way to put it.'

'You don't look at all well, though.' She moved to the sink to fill the kettle. 'Are you still taking all that cocaine?'

'Speed,' he admitted. 'I... I can't afford cocaine any more. I spent all the money, Marianne.'

'Well, I can't give you any money!' She put the kettle on the hob.

'No... that's not what I meant. That's not why I came.'

'You find me somewhat in Queer Street myself.'

'Oh, Marianne...'

'Quite a pair we make, don't we?'

'Oh, Marianne,' he said again, and a tear started in the corner of his eye. He wiped at it discreetly, so she wouldn't see.

They sat at the kitchen table and drank tea.

'Have you had anything to eat?' she asked him. He realised that he hadn't eaten since the fish and chips Bridget had brought home last night.

'No. I don't think I want anything, though.'

'Nonsense.' She found a tin of oxtail soup and put it in a pan to warm up. He drank it out of an old mug that had an advert for animal feed on its side.

'You've no luggage with you?'

'No,' he said. 'I don't have much any more.'

'I dare say we could root out some clothes for you.'

'Are you spending Christmas here by yourself?' he asked.

'By which you mean, where is your Uncle Col?'

'Well...' In fact that was not what he meant, but she went on, 'He's away.'

Kit knew that this, while literally true, was inaccurate; Col, he had gathered from a letter from Bob, forwarded from Craven Street – his parents did not have his current address – was last heard of in Littlehampton, where he was running a pub.

'OK.' He sensed it was better to let the matter lie.

'But – oh!' She had remembered something. 'I actually have something for our Christmas dinner. Come and see.' She stood up and led the way to the walk-in pantry off the old scullery. 'There!' she said in triumph. Hanging from a hook, its fur matted with mud and blood, was a dead rabbit.

'Crikey,' said Kit.

'John brought it round,' she said.

'Who's John?'

'He helps out from time to time. He doesn't really need paying, thank the good Lord. He's from the village. I think he knew your grandparents. Well, you know what that place is like. Anyway, he bagged this for me.'

'He shot it?'

'Well, I don't suppose it committed suicide at his feet.'

'I thought rabbits hibernated.'

'Dear me!' She looked at him. 'And here's me thinking we turned you into a country boy. We failed, didn't we?'

'I've been away a long time, Marianne.'

'Yes, you have rather.' She smiled at him. He felt the easy tears well again.

'Marianne?' In the scullery the cookers his uncle had bought for the intended cookery school, that Easter holiday when Kit – Christopher – had been eleven, still stood, never used and covered in dust and grime, along with the two sinks, not plumbed in.

'H'mm?'

'Is it OK if I stay here for a while?'

'Stay as long as you like.'

'I'd like... I want to...'

'Well?'

'I want to detox. Give up the drugs. I've got enough for tomorrow, and then on Boxing Day I'm going to stop.'

'Heavens.'

'I'll stay in my room. Mostly. Can I stay in Room Seven?'

'Of course. I'll have the butler make it up for you.' They both laughed. 'I'm not the Florence Nightingale type, you know that, don't you?' she went on.

'I don't expect you to help me, just... be there. It's something I need to do by myself.'

'Yes. Oh!' She had remembered something. 'I have people coming for the New Year.'

'People?'

'Yes. A kind of party.'

This was most unlike her. Kit was disconcerted.

'I'll tell them to stay out of your way.'

From the hall the tall-case clock struck the hour. They listened to it chime twelve times.

'Heavens, it's late,' she said. 'Are you all right to make the bed up? Help yourself to anything from the linen cupboard.'

'Of course. Happy Christmas, Marianne.'

'Happy Christmas, Kit.' They hugged again, and he pressed his lips to her cheek, and held them there for a while, and buried his face in her hair. Her hair still smelled of woodsmoke.

When he woke the next morning a watery sunlight was stealing in between the curtains, which he had forgotten to fully draw. He had fallen asleep warmed by the hot-water bottle Marianne had insisted on – 'You're so thin, you've no natural layers to keep you warm any more' – and by the blankets he had piled on the bed, topped with a full-length astrakhan coat (Uncle Harold's, doubtless) that he had found in the wardrobe.

He had only the clothes he had put on yesterday, in Bromley. Marianne had lent him an old pair of pyjamas – the Uncles again, probably Ludo this time – and he pulled the coat on over them to come downstairs. One of the dogs, a briard that was a couple of years old – Arlo was long gone – met him on the landing and followed him to the kitchen, where Marianne was making coffee.

'What do you look like?' she said when she saw him.

'A junkie in a fur coat,' said Kit.

'You look a little like Syd Barrett.'

'I can live with that.'

'Sit down,' she said, 'and drink your coffee.'

It was like old times. She had the transistor tuned to Radio 3. A presenter was waspishly complaining about the particular arrangement of a carol he was about to broadcast, 'ruined by flutes'.

'Well, he's not very festive,' said Marianne.

'I'm afraid I haven't brought any kind of present for you,' Kit said.

'Oh, pish and nonsense. I don't need a present. I've nothing for you in any case.'

Breakfast was eggs from the two remaining hens, on white toast. Kit managed to eat a little of it. Afterwards he sat and watched her skin and gut the rabbit. Two cats stationed themselves by the table in readiness. 'That's their Christmas dinner sorted,' she remarked.

'Christ, Marianne.' She was working her fingers into an opening she'd made in its back and dragging its fur apart.

'You had no idea I was such a hunter-gatherer, had you? It's really easy, actually. John showed me how.'

The mysterious John, again.

'He didn't want to join you for Christmas dinner?' Kit asked.

'Oh no,' she said. 'It's nothing like that. He's antisocial just like me. It rather suits us both, actually.'

'So how come you're having a New Year's party?'

'Oh, well...' she said vaguely. 'It was sprung on me, rather. But I don't really mind.'

'Who's coming?'

'Just some people.' She had turned rather coy. Was she actually blushing? He decided to let the matter drop.

'Now, then.' She pulled a last handful of guts out of the rabbit's cavity and set them to one side. 'I may be a skilled butcher now but I am still a dismal cook. But you will help me.'

'Me? I'm terrible, Marianne.'

'Oh dear! But help is at hand.' She washed the blood off her hands and took a book down from the dresser. 'Here we go.'

It was a crumbling volume, perhaps a hundred years old, entitled *The Gourmet's Guide to Rabbit Cooking, in One Hundred and Twenty-Four Dishes*, by someone calling themselves An Old Epicure.

'It's actually a woman called Georgiana Hill,' Marianne said. 'She was a contemporary of Mrs Beeton's, but while dear Mrs B was a rather fashionable journalist who I suspect rarely saw the inside of a kitchen, An Old Epicure knew how to get her hands dirty.'

They amused themselves for a while reading out loud extracts from the introduction to *The Gourmet's Guide*, in which An Old Epicure described her early fascination with rabbits in baroque terms. Marianne, eventually, selected a recipe for roast rabbit *à la française*, with a sauce made from its liver. Kit could tell that he was not going to enjoy this dinner: it smelled awful as it was cooking, and even if he had been in robust health, his appetite not decimated by amphetamine use, he would probably not have been able to eat it. She served it with roast potatoes and boiled carrots. The potatoes were hard and greasy, the carrots boiled almost to a pap. They sat at the kitchen table to eat it. Kit had not bothered to change out of Uncle Ludo's pyjamas and Uncle Harold's coat.

'M'mm!' said Marianne. 'I call that not bad.'

'Marianne...' He was toying with an undercooked shred of the unfortunate creature's leg. 'This is absolutely bloody awful.' She looked up sharply, fixed him with a hard stare. Kit met her gaze. He raised his eyebrows at her.

She burst into sudden laughter.

'It is, isn't it?' And Kit, as he laughed with her, realised that he barely knew the sound of his own laughter, had forgotten what it felt like to have it bubble up, uncomplicated and joyous, in his throat.

She pushed her plate away.

'Shall I make some toast instead?'

'Yeah.'

'Ooh! I almost forgot.' She went to a cupboard and produced two bottles of red wine with a flourish. 'Ta-da...'

'What is it?'

'This,' she said with emphasis, 'is wine that I actually bought. From an actual supermarket.'

'My God,' said Kit. 'You mean it's not a hundred years old?'

'No!' She looked at the label. 'Nineteen eighty-seven. Positively a nursling. One moment.' She disappeared and returned with two wine glasses.

'How come we're eating in here?' Kit had peeped into the dining room earlier and, seeing it set out for two with the best china and cutlery, had assumed it was in honour of the day.

'Oh – I'm saving the dining room.' She uncorked the wine and poured it.

'Not too much for me.' Kit put his hand over his glass. 'It's like it's in a different house, that room. It's so...'

'Clean?'

'Well...'

'I know I've let the place go, a little.' She took a drink of wine. 'It's not so easy, Kit, on your own.'

'I don't care,' he said. 'You should see how I've been living.' This was unfair, as Bridget was fairly fastidious, but he wanted to feel a connection to Marianne. 'The dining room, though... It's for Col, isn't it?'

She sat back in her chair. One of the cats jumped onto the table to help itself to the ruined dinner. She pushed it to the floor. Kit wondered if he was delving where he should not.

'He cooked me the most marvellous supper, right after we met,' she said. 'Fillet steak in a mushroom and wine sauce, and pavlova. We ate in the dining room, of course. Afterwards I played the piano for him and we made love on the rug. That was when I fell for him. I want things nice for when he comes back.'

Kit knew this made no sense. He also knew that, even in his current state, with desire as he had known it set to one side, atrophied and unused, the old jealousy of his uncle was still there.

That he still had feelings for Marianne that were unseemly. That he did not like the thought of her and Col having sex on the drawing-room rug. He did a line of speed off the kitchen table. He needed to ask the question. He lifted his head and wiped at his nose.

'You really think he's coming back?'

'He always does,' she said. 'All those times – when he used to go running to your mother – he always came back, didn't he?'

'Yes, but it's been a long time now.'

'We're too bound together, Kit. I know it sounds like mystical nonsense…'

'It doesn't, but… It must have been a really bad fight.'

'It was. I made a bad error of judgement. Oh, you don't want to be hearing about this stuff.'

'I actually do, Marianne.' He topped them both up with wine, took a drink. Col's departure had not registered much with him at the time, he had been too caught up in his own troubles: his lack of career, money, Georgina. In the course of Bob's letters he had gathered that Col had stayed at Flatley Close for a short time but, saying he needed to get away from Herefordshire, had drifted for a while, ending up on the Sussex coast. His contact with Janet and Bob had apparently become sporadic. *Poor Mum*, Kit thought suddenly, surprising himself. When he was better he would get in touch with his parents. But not now; they must not see what he had become.

'I'd love it if you could tell me,' he said now to Marianne, and the realisation, hot and shameful, hit him: he was feeling a selfless concern for someone else's situation for the first time in years.

There was a pause as she dealt with another recalcitrant cat and took a sip of wine.

'Your Uncle Col wanted children, you knew that, didn't you?' Kit nodded. 'Lots of them. He made it very clear, right from when we met, from before we were married. I thought… I thought it would go away. But it didn't. And that's why he went, in the end.'

'But that's not fair!' Anger at his uncle rose in him. 'It wasn't your fault you couldn't have them. Even if you wouldn't... get help.'

'This is the thing, Kit. It was my fault. I took the pill. Secretly. The whole time we were together. He thought we couldn't get pregnant. Until one day he found out.'

'What? So... you didn't want children?'

'No. I never did.'

'Why didn't you tell him? Right at the beginning?'

'He wouldn't have married me, Kit. And I wanted to marry him.'

'So you pretended, all those years?' Kit was incredulous.

'Oh, don't look at me like that. It happened. Now you know. How about that toast, then?' She stood up, cleared away the plates, took a loaf of sliced white from the bread bin. 'I made an error of judgement, telling him about the pills. I thought, as the years went on, that his need for children would diminish. I was wrong.'

Error of judgement... To her, the error was letting Col find out, not the years of deceit. Kit suddenly recalled the van ride with Col to James's shop in Ledbury. *Not being able to have kids, it's the worst thing, you know...*

'How come you didn't want them?'

She turned from where she was dropping slices of bread onto the range top.

'Do I need a reason?'

'No, but...'

'Did *you* want children?'

Kit flushed. It was the first reference she had made to Sophie. He recalled the humiliating sprawl on the steps of the Hampstead house, only yesterday, Giles looking down at him, Georgina standing behind. The look on her face.

'Marianne, that's hardly fair.'

'Isn't it?'

'Let's not fall out,' said Kit. 'I don't think I could bear it.'

'No,' she said. She put an arm round him, kissed the top of his head. He squeezed the hand resting on his shoulder.

'He'll be back,' Marianne declared. 'He always comes back,' and Kit didn't have the heart to challenge her.

Marianne got a fire going in the gun room. She had opened the second bottle of wine and they were both rather drunk. The television was on, a ballet, but neither of them paid it much attention. Kit lay on the sofa with his head on Marianne's lap, just like on the day of Susannah's reception, in the drawing room with Georgina asleep on the other sofa.

'This has been the best Christmas in ages.'

'I've enjoyed it, too.' She was stroking his hair.

'Marianne?'

'H'mm?'

'I'm sorry I spent all the money. I'm sorry I wasted it.'

'Shush. It doesn't matter.'

'Of course it does!'

'In the scheme of things – not really.'

'Can I ask you about something else?'

'I dare say.'

He twisted round to look up at her. The light from the fire illuminated her face, softening her wrinkles. Her greying hair was like a halo.

He couldn't bring himself to ask it. Instead he vocalised a thought that had popped into his head.

'I'm going to come and live with you. When I'm all better. I'll live with you at Erringby and help you.'

'Will you now,' she said, but she was smiling.

It was later, near to midnight, when he finally asked her. He had done his last line of speed, a big one, had been saving it: as the rush hit him, as his hands began trembling, he knew that if he did not ask now, he never would.

Last time last time this is the last time hammered in his brain.

'Marianne?'

'Yes, Kit.' They were still in the gun room, Kit slumped up against her. His teeth were chattering. Grinding. His heart banging in his chest seemed to rattle his ribcage. The briard and the other dog, a wolfhound, sprawled on the floor, taking up most of the room.

'That night that summer… the summer of the film… the night I stayed in your bedroom,' he began. Trying to stop his hands from shaking.

She's going to make it as hard as she can for me, he thought, *make like she doesn't remember*, but Marianne said, 'Oh yes?'

'I'm not going to use euphemisms. Did we have sex?'

On the television *Rear Window* had started. James Stewart, sweatily unwell, reminded Kit a little of himself.

'You don't remember?' She was staring straight ahead, watching the movie. *No doubt Grace Kelly is another blonde siren you've been compared to*, Kit thought.

'I was out of it, remember? Off my head.'

'Plus ça change.'

'Yes, I've been off my head ever since that night, Marianne. Maybe because of that night.'

She looked at him. *Do not dare to impute your problems to me*, the look said. Kit hugged himself, hands in his armpits to quell the shaking.

'So did we?' he asked.

'Oh, Kit,' she said, and went back to the film.

'You're not going to tell me?' She gave a tiny shake of her head. 'Please,' he said.

'No,' she said, very decidedly.

And Kit felt defeated.

21

December 1990

He was lying on the bed in Room Seven. He had woken on Boxing Day morning with the habitual urge, and it been several moments before realisation settled on him: he was at Erringby, he was detoxing, he had no drugs and no means of obtaining any. Even if he managed to get himself to Hereford he wouldn't know where to look, after all these years.

After *Rear Window* had ended Marianne had asked him if there was anything she could do for him over the next few days. She was being, Kit thought, as maternal as she knew how to be. Perhaps she felt compunction at the fractious exchange that had left him so frustrated.

'Just... be there,' he had said, with no real notion of what lay ahead, and on the first-floor landing they had hugged again, and Kit had said, 'This was one of the best Christmas days of my life – but the worst Christmas dinner I've ever eaten,' and she had laughed, and said, 'It's lovely to see you, Kit. Get well,' and they had gone their separate ways to bed.

Now he lay with Sophie's photograph in his hand. It had fallen out of the pages of *Vanity Fair.* He rolled onto his back and stared at the ceiling. There was a brownish stain from where the bathroom above it had leaked, a dozen or so years ago. The ceiling had an elaborate leaf cornice round its edge, broken in several places. As a boy he had counted the leaves when trying to get to sleep. A huge cobweb dangled from one corner of the room. In the photograph Sophie laughed at whatever was just out of shot. He hoped it wasn't

Giles Fitzsimmons who was making her laugh like that. He hoped she was as happy now, had had a magical Christmas. He propped the photo against the bedside lamp and waited.

Sleep came first, after the initial cravings died down. He was surprised to open his eyes and find it was four in the afternoon. He went on in that way for a while, sitting out the shakes and the cravings, reading, reading, until sleep came again. He found himself awake at 3am, groggy and achy, his head pounding. The sheets were damp. He was also hungrier than he had been in years. He pulled on the coat and went downstairs. The dogs watched him indifferently from their baskets in the hall.

He went through the kitchen cupboards. They had finished the loaf of sliced white bread, apart from the crusts. He found a box of stale cornflakes, filled a bowl and poured on milk and sugar. He ate it quickly and was still ravenous. He ate a second bowlful. There were three eggs in the wire basket on the table. He scrambled them, the only way he knew how to cook them, and ate them with the crusts, partly burned from being toasted on the range top. He finished the box of cornflakes, using up all the milk. His hands were shaking so much that he had, he was dimly aware, left a mess of milk and cornflakes and raw egg on the table. He left a note for Marianne – *We need more food* – and went back to his room.

At around six he woke with searing stomach pains. The milk had been off. Or the eggs. He spent a wretched hour sitting on the floor of the bathroom, clinging to the toilet bowl, at first dreading being sick – he had always had an aversion to it, had generally managed to avoid it in his drug-taking career – then longing for the release of puking up his guts. The nausea gradually subsided enough for him to be able to crawl back to bed, where he tore at his skin, which seemed to be infested with insects. They must have dropped onto him from the cobwebs. They had buried into his skin; scratching gave no respite. He stumbled back to his bathroom to scrub at his hands with a nail brush.

He spent the next day between sleeping and waking, beset by nightmares and hallucinations. He was in a fairground hall, like a hall of mirrors, only instead of mirrors he was surrounded by his own unfinished paintings, pulsating and swelling, the faces of people he'd painted – Bridget, Fabienne's twins, fellow St Martin's students – grotesque and leering. He was pursued by rabid dogs, which dragged him to the ground and tore at his clothes. He was a small boy, trailing after a pair of grown-ups across a sand flat. He knew there were quicksands, knew that he must not tread in one, yet at the same time was compelled to – the sediment swallowed him up instantly – he tried to call out to the adults to save him – they were his parents – simultaneously they were Janet and Bob and his real mother and father – but the sand constricted his chest, making sound impossible... He woke with the taste of vomit in his mouth and got to his bathroom only just in time. There were footsteps on the landing outside.

'Marianne,' he groaned, but she didn't hear him. He fell asleep on the bathroom floor, hunched over the toilet. He woke with the edge of the bowl cold against his cheek.

The next day, or was it the day after, was better; hungry again, he made it to the kitchen where he sat on the floor in front of the range to keep warm. The briard – its name was Balzac – came and sat with him. Kit hugged the dog, his face buried in his fur. Presently, he opened a tin of baked beans, the only food he could find, and ate them, cold, from the can. He was managing to keep them down, ignoring the pains in his stomach.

Marianne came into the room.

'Uh-huh?' she said. He looked up at her and saw her eyes widen. He must look truly dreadful. 'Do you have everything you need?'

'More bread,' he said. 'Soup. Crackers.'

'All right,' she said. 'I'll go when the shops open.'

He looked at her in bafflement.

'Are the shops shut? Is it still Christmas?'

'It's Sunday the thirtieth,' she said. 'In the evening.'

'Oh,' he said. There was a pause, then he got up and rushed to the sink, pushing her out of the way. He vomited copiously, almost doubled up.

'Oh good heavens,' said Marianne.

He stared at the sink in horror.

'Marianne!' It came out in a hoarse whisper.

'Whatever is it?'

She went over to where Kit stood, appalled. In the sink were the fat maggots in blood he had thrown up. They were still alive, twitching in their congealed goo. They must have hatched from the insects under his skin.

'Look!'

'At the baked beans you've just eaten?'

He was panting and sweating, gripping the edge of the sink.

'I don't... feel good,' he was able to get out.

'Would you like some sleeping tablets?'

'Yes please.' She disappeared and came back with an ancient bottle of Valium pills. He swallowed two straight away.

'I'll leave you to it, then, shall I?'

'No... please...' said Kit, but she had gone.

The Valium delivered sleep that was fitful and headachy but free of demons, just the sound of people in the house, up and down the main stairs, up and down the back stairs, shouting and laughing. He dreamed of voices coming from the room next door that had been the Uncles' nursery, part of his domain when he had stayed here as a boy. A couple, a man and a woman, laughing. He woke to find a plate of cold toast on the bedside table.

He sat up, ate the food, testing how he felt. The insane desire for speed, which had howled through his body and his brain for the past however many days it was, had quietened, but anxiety gnawed at him instead. What would become of him? What would he do now? Where would he go? Absurd idea, that he would stay at Erringby and help Marianne! He was hopelessly impractical. What possible help could he be to her?

There was a connecting door between his room and Room Eight. He heard the sound of something heavy being dropped.

'Shh!' said a woman's voice. 'We need to be quiet, remember?'

'Oh yeah,' said the man. 'I forgot.' Who were these people? Kit went into his bathroom and ran a bath. The water was little more than tepid and he bathed as rapidly as he could. When had he last had a bath or a shower? It would have been at Bridget's. With a jolt he remembered the pawned flower brooch. He would have to get it back, somehow. The pyjamas he'd not taken off since Christmas Eve were foul, reeking of sweat and toxins. He felt like burning them. Marianne must have come in and taken his own clothes to be laundered without his noticing. They lay, un-ironed but folded, on the chair in his bedroom. Kit put on his jeans and sweatshirt. He was still cold, so he pulled Uncle Harold's coat on over the top.

There were more footsteps on the stairs and the sound of dragging luggage. Someone was going up to the second floor. No, he was not hallucinating, there were people in the house. Kit didn't want to meet them, didn't want to talk to anyone other than Marianne. But he had to leave his room sometime. He was hungry, in spite of the toast. He pulled the door open and padded onto the landing. His spirits lifted when the door to her room opened.

But a man emerged, in his early thirties perhaps, wearing jeans and an Icelandic sweater. He wore no shoes and held an open bottle of beer.

'Oh, hey!' he said. 'You must be Marianne's nephew.'

'Hello.' Kit was entirely disconcerted.

'I'm Tony,' said the man.

'Kit.'

Though the man might be ten years Kit's senior he resembled a big puppy, energised and enthusiastic. He was obscenely healthy-looking. Kit, in comparison, was a wraith in an astrakhan coat who had experienced more pain in the last two years than this older man had in his entire life. *You don't know what trouble is*, Kit thought.

Tony seemed uncertain what to say next. His broad smile wavered slightly.

'That's a great coat,' he said.

'It actually belonged to...'

'Don't tell me – the famous Uncle Harold.' Kit nodded. Marianne appeared on the landing. She had on clothes that were smart and not full of holes, and her hair was washed and brushed.

'Oh, good,' she said. 'You've met. How are you, Kit?'

'Much better,' he said feebly.

'Excellent. Why don't you come downstairs and meet everyone?'

Kit could think of nothing he'd like less than to sit and make polite chitchat with hearty strangers. 'Marianne...' he said.

'What?'

'Could I...?' He pointed at Room Seven. '...have a word?'

She gave a sigh of exasperation and followed him to his room. 'Well?'

'I'm not feeling very sociable.' She said nothing. 'Could you bring up some more food for me?'

'I've got people here, Kit. I told you I couldn't be a nursemaid to you.'

'But...'

'Don't be so pathetic. I can tell you're much better. You don't have to come to the party. Just come and say hello.'

Very well, he would make himself some food as quickly as possible and scuttle back to his room.

'OK.'

'Come on then,' she said briskly. They went back onto the landing, where Tony was waiting. She actually *took Tony's hand* and they went downstairs together. Kit was poleaxed. Who on earth was this man?

The kitchen hummed with activity. Three women were busying themselves stocking the fridge, wiping down surfaces, chopping vegetables on a wooden board. They were around Tony's age; two also had bottles of beer on the go. Crates of beer and wine sat against the walls. A huge pan of something simmered on the range.

'My dear, you must be simply exsiccated,' said Tony.

'I'm a husk,' said one of the women, and laughed.

'This is Kit,' Marianne announced. 'My nephew.'

'Hi Kit.' Two of the women exchanged glances. They all smiled at him.

'Hello,' said Kit. The women introduced themselves. Caroline-Julie-Hayley. He wouldn't be able to remember.

'Kit needs feeding,' said Marianne.

'Ooh, of course,' said Caroline-or-Hayley, as if she should have known. 'What can we get you? Some bread and cheese?'

There was the sound of people arriving in the hall. 'Marianne?' a voice called.

'Do excuse me.' She squeezed Tony's arm. 'More people.' She left the room.

Tony sat at the table and helped himself to an orange from a bowl and began peeling it. He seemed very much at home.

'Do you want a beer, Kit?' he asked.

'No,' said Kit. 'Thank you.'

'Would you like some soup?' It was the woman who'd spoken to him before.

'Yes, please.'

'It's veggie,' she said. She dished up a bowl of soup and put it on the table. He realised he wasn't going to be able to take the food up to his room. The logistics of finding a tray, his shaking hands, the stairs.

'There you go.' The woman found a spoon and put it next to the bowl. Kit sat.

The soup smelled delicious, of tomatoes and spices and warmth. The sort of thing Col would have made for him. He felt a pang of nostalgia for the days of Col's cooking, the three of them eating together, the spats over the radio. He had an urge to drive these incomers, whoever they were, away from Erringby, reclaim it for his uncle. But best be grateful, and at least these people knew how to cook.

Tony caught Kit looking at him.

'You a fan, then?'

'Fan?'

'Of *Strassburg Pie*.'

'Oh!' Now Kit recognised the quotations. 'Is that why you're here?'

'Well… yes. Of course. Didn't Marianne tell you?'

'She tells me nothing.'

'That sounds like Marianne,' said Tony. 'An enigma wrapped in a conundrum, that's her.' He laughed indulgently.

Of course. The film. The New Year's Eve scene, now described as *iconic*. Kit had been dimly aware that the film had sold well on video, had become something of a cult with students.

'We're going to watch it on video before the party gets going,' said one of the women. 'If you'd like to join us.'

'You're all right,' said Kit.

The soup was flavoursome, warming and soothing. He thought it might be the best thing he had ever tasted. But still the hand holding the spoon shook badly. One of the women was watching him. She had a kind face.

'I worked on the film,' Kit volunteered. 'The summer I left school.'

Tony looked at him eagerly.

'Really?'

'Yes. Only as a runner. Nothing important.'

One of the other women, not the soup one, turned to him.

'So what was he like? Darren Fenby?'

'I was bitten on the penis by a dachshund!' the other two women said in unison.

'He was all right,' said Kit, trying to remember.

This was insufficient. All four looked at him to continue. *What was Darren Fenby like?* It was hard to recall clearly, hard to reconcile the soap-opera actor of four years ago with the Hollywood luminary he had since become. And Kit had been too bound up in himself that summer – being made up by Nicola, going to bed with her, spending the night with Marianne, painting her portrait, becoming Kit – to be starstruck by Darren Fenby.

'He was a bit of a prat, actually.' The third woman laughed.

'Ha!'

'How so?' asked Tony.

'He used to play practical jokes,' Kit recalled. 'One morning he stuffed cotton wool into his mouth and pretended to have toothache so he couldn't talk. John Starr went ballistic.'

'What was he like? John Starr?'

'Scary.'

Tony nodded, satisfied.

'What about Henry Melville?' Caroline-Julie-Hayley asked. Henry Melville's fortunes had been transformed by the film and he had acquired national treasure status, voicing animated films and reading children's stories on television.

'Very quiet,' said Kit. 'Spent all the time in his trailer. I don't think he liked Darren much. I think he thought the film was a bit beneath him. Oh, but at the wrap party he got really pissed and tried it on with all the women.'

'Ha ha!' said Tony. 'You must talk to Martin. He's writing a book.'

'Where is Martin?' asked the soup woman.

'Decorating the billiard room,' said the third woman. Kit recognised her voice; she was his neighbour in Room Eight, the one who had admonished her boyfriend for making a noise.

'Billiard room!' said the soup woman. 'It's like Cluedo, this house, isn't it? Colonel Mustard with the lead piping.'

'Are there any secret passages, Kit?' Tony asked.

'Not that I'm aware of.' Kit felt exhausted from the effort of coming downstairs and having to talk to strangers. He had socialised very little in the last months, he realised, other than the increasingly terse communications with Bridget. He excused himself to go back to his room. On the stairs he met Marianne.

'All right?' she said.

'Who's that man? Tony.'

'Just someone I met.' Her voice was crisp.

'Marianne, he came out of your bedroom. With no shoes on.'

She glared at him. He felt himself quail a little.

'Do you require me to live like a nun?'

'No, of course not...'

'Well then.'

Kit went to his room and flopped down on the bed. He felt wrung out. He tried reading *Vanity Fair* but the words leaped around the page. He lay down and closed his eyes but sleep wouldn't come. From the corner of the ceiling the cobweb drooped. He wished he could reach up and brush it away, but it was too high. He needed a duster on a long pole.

He was beset with anxiety, centring on, of all things, Col. What was she playing at? Suppose Col *was* to come back, after – what was it? two years? – to reassert his claim to her, only to find she'd taken up with this overgrown student. If she truly believed he was coming back, what was she thinking? Or maybe this was the point: Col would return to find her in flagrante, and be chastened, punished, for leaving her. Payback for Lois, for the woman in the village, for doubtless others that Kit didn't know about. But Tony was the most unlikely suitor. Surely she would tire of his puppy-dog cheerfulness, chew him up and spit him out, like an old bone. And what about her, anyway? Had there been other lovers? Had that been part of her and Col's casual cruelty to each other? There had been that grip – Andrew? – on the film, who had pursued her relentlessly. They'd gone off together at the wrap party and Col had followed them and there'd been some huge fight – Col had a nasty gash on his forehead the following day – had that been set up to provoke him? Perhaps this was what she fantasised about: a showdown between Tony and Col – not that Tony stood the glimmer of a chance – with herself as the trophy. But in any case, what right, really, did Kit have to admonish her about Tony, as if he were some prim maiden aunt himself? And, at the heart of it all, the question that would not go away, had never gone away, that rattled around Kit's head like a beetle in a cage: had they, he and Marianne, been lovers? Was that what disconcerted him so much – jealousy of Tony, not concern for his uncle?

Kit groaned. For the first time in what felt like months he was getting an erection. He pushed his hand into his pants to masturbate but couldn't make himself come. He wished he could take more Valium but that meant going to look for Marianne. He fell asleep eventually, his hand still on his cock.

He woke disoriented, taking several moments to place himself. Music was coming from the billiard room, directly below his bedroom, as were sounds of shouting and laughing. His head ached and he had a very strong yearning for a line of speed. He'd thought the worst was over; he felt like crying. To distract himself he tried masturbating again; he was able to wrench a climax but only by fantasising about Marianne naked beside him in the bed. And she was downstairs, with her new lover, at a party. He did cry now; tears of rage and frustration, his fingers clammy with semen.

He couldn't stay in his room. It was past midnight; the new year had been ushered in. Nineteen ninety had been so unremittingly awful that he didn't care that he had slept through its passing. He went into the bathroom and washed his hands, pulled on Harold's coat and padded downstairs.

The billiard room was full of people. More than could possibly be staying the night; there might be forty or fifty. The room, Kit realised, had been decorated to resemble its 1986 apotheosis when it had been set-dressed by Lois and her team for the 'iconic' New Year's Eve scene, the scene that had caused so much anguish and shortness of tempers, most noticeably John Starr's, but which had gone on to be plagiarised shamelessly by a couple of television adverts. At the time an army of extras had been drafted in to make up the numbers. Kit himself had been put in costume and stuck in the background of a shot but he'd not been able to spot himself and supposed he had ended up on the cutting-room floor.

The room was festooned now with red, white and blue garlands, the floor covered in balloons. On the day of the shoot the net suspended from the ceiling had malfunctioned at the pivotal moment, occasioning much swearing from John Starr and pinched faces on the set decorators.

The revellers were likewise dressed up in character. Kit made out Tony, wearing a false moustache and an army uniform decked in medals, an homage to Henry Melville's blimpish Ernest Scarlett role. Someone else had taken the Darren Fenby part and had the slicked-back hair and monocle of his character, Matthew Griffin. Two women, who possibly did bear a passing resemblance to each other in real life, wore identical cerise ball gowns and elaborate blonde ringletty wigs – they were the twins Vise and Versa, Ernest Scarlett and Matthew Griffin's primary antagonists. There were women in peacock headdresses and men in fezzes. There were people in pierrot costumes.

It was astonishing that they had gone to so much trouble. Kit wondered how they got to dole out the main parts and if they auditioned. The music piped into the room – via Col's hi-fi in the gun room, presumably – was also in keeping: 'Sing, Sing, Sing' by Benny Goodman came on as Kit hovered at the doorway. There were so many people that it took him a while to spot Marianne, sitting on the window seat in the far corner. She had not troubled to dress as a character from *Strassburg Pie* – how typical of her – and a coterie of admirers, male and female, surrounded her. Perhaps she was Susannah, there only by chance but very much mistress of the situation.

She spotted him and waved at him to come over. Kit did not feel like paying court. He acknowledged her but made his way slowly across the room. En route he encountered Tony – Ernest – and he tugged at the sleeve of his Pattern Service Dress tunic.

'Oh, hey, Kit.' Tony was swaying. He was very drunk. 'You made it,' as if Kit had travelled miles and not down one flight of stairs to get here. He put a hand on Kit's shoulder, as much to steady himself as anything else. 'You need to meet Martin. He's writing a book. Martin!' He waved at the man dressed as Darren Fenby dressed as Matthew Griffin. The man did not hear. '*Martin!* You need to meet him,' Tony told Kit.

'Yeah,' said Kit. 'I don't suppose you've any speed, have you? Or coke?'

'*What?*' Kit repeated the question, bellowing in Tony's ear. 'No, mate. Sorry. I think there might be some dope going round. You should meet Martin.'

Possibly Marianne had put them on guard. *Do not offer my nephew any hard drugs.* But more likely there were none to be had. It wasn't that sort of party. Kit couldn't remember the last time he had been around so many very drunk people. Tony's hand was still on his shoulder. From the corner of his eye he could see Marianne watching them. He felt a wave of hatred towards Tony, his bland cheerfulness, his casual appropriation of Erringby, of Marianne. *There were loads of drugs on the shoot, actually, if you really want to be authentic,* he felt like saying, but did not. Tony was yelling something in Kit's ear, something about John Starr and Darren Fenby. Kit pretended to agree with what he was saying, and shrugged Tony's hand from his shoulder.

He crossed the room, wading through a sea of balloons and pushing past several drunk people to reach Marianne, who remained on the window seat, surrounded by acolytes like Gertrude Stein at a salon. Someone moved up to let him sit next to her.

'This is my nephew, Kit,' Marianne said to the group at large. 'He's been hiding himself away like Anne Frank.' Several people Kit had no interest in meeting said hello.

'Are you having fun?' she asked him.

'Not really,' he said, but then felt he was being ungracious. 'It's all a bit weird, this, isn't it?' For someone who prided herself on her anti-sociability she seemed to be lapping it up.

'Oh, I don't know,' she said. 'It's only once a year.'

'You've done this before?'

'We had one last year. On a much smaller scale. But people have been tipping up on their pilgrimages. One finds them roaming the grounds or hanging around the outbuildings.' From Col's speaker system Rudy Vallée was singing 'Deep Night'.

There was a commotion on the other side of the room. A woman screamed, and a man in a maharajah costume shouted, 'Oh shit!' Smoke was coming from the opposite window.

'The curtain's on fire!' someone shouted. There was a collective gasp and more screams as flames shot up the floor-length curtain to the ceiling as if from a gun. Marianne was on her feet.

'Everyone needs to clear the room!' There was a jumble of confusion and panic as people stumbled over balloons and garlands towards the room's only door and out into the hall. The fire had spread to a paper garland draped across the wall.

'Fire extinguisher,' someone was yelling. 'Marianne, where's the fire extinguisher?' Rudy Vallée sang on.

'We don't have one. Someone call the fire brigade!'

Kit dialled 999 from the phone in the vestibule. He had to shout to make himself heard over the din of yelling and popping balloons. Someone had filled a bucket from the downstairs cloakroom and tossed it at the flames, to almost zero effect. He found Marianne.

'What should I do?' Everybody else was very drunk and the two of them would have to take charge.

'Go and check the bedrooms.'

Kit ran breathless up the back stairs and around the corridors. He had to drag a virtually comatose woman out of Room Ten and push her down the stairs. In a top-floor room a couple were screwing; the pumping of the man's hairy backside, the woman's heels on the man's back, a crumpled green silk dress on the floor. The man looked over his shoulder at Kit with a mixture of triumph and indignation until Kit yelled at them to get out.

After that he was to have only fleeting recall of the ensuing hours. How he had grabbed his shoes and the photograph of Sophie from Room Seven, not caring about anything else, as the room filled with smoke. How Marianne fixed a hosepipe to the taps in the cloakroom. How, even with the tumult and the shouting around him, he felt a stab of satisfaction when she screamed at Tony, fumblingly trying to help her, 'Get out of my way!' How calm, apart from that one moment, she was, how efficient and dispassionate. How for a wild, hopeful moment it had seemed as if the hose might be having some effect, until they realised that the hissing was the sound of wood burning. How they had stood in a shivering group on the lawn, waiting for the fire engines as windows shimmered, then popped and shattered. How the fire engines couldn't get close to the house because of the jumble of cars parked outside. How it was only as the sun came up that the fire was brought under control, by which time the east wing of Erringby Hall had been destroyed, windows blown from the billiard room and the rooms above it, Kit's room and the Uncles' former nursery, and the bedrooms above those, where two people had been celebrating the birth of 1991 with sex; all those rooms had been gutted by fire.

After the fire brigade and the other emergency services had left, and a preliminary investigation had determined that the cause of the fire was someone – no one remembered who – knocking over a candlestick and setting fire to the curtain, Kit and Marianne assessed the damage for themselves, in defiance of the firemen who had declared the entire main house not safe and had boarded up the front door, itself badly damaged. The house reeked of smoke and ash and of something foul, as if the charred and sodden woodwork had already set to rotting.

They were the only ones remaining; the acolytes had all melted away. Kit had been selfishly glad to overhear Marianne's dismissal of Tony, her refusal of his help, the cavalier way in which she silenced his entreaties that she phone him soon. She preferred Kit's company after all.

They made their way gingerly, embers pricking the soles of their shoes despite the hours the firemen had spent with their hoses, dampening down. The fire had destroyed the hall and the billiard room entirely, the oak panelling reduced to charcoal. The lower part of the main staircase had collapsed, making it impossible to reach the upper floors that way. The drawing room and the library were wrecked by smoke damage, the books, the piano, the sofas, the tables ruined by water.

'Can any of it be saved?' Kit asked. She shrugged but did not reply. There was less smoke and soot in the dining room but the two wine goblets were smashed, the silverware badly tarnished, the white tablecloth grey and sodden. Water dripped from its folds onto the Persian rug. Though the fire had not penetrated the gun room it had been soaked in water as a precaution. Kit tried to pull one of Col's LPs from the shelf. The albums were clumped together in twos and threes, fused by soggy cardboard, the sleeves ruined. Kit realised that he missed Col, very much, that he would never hear 'Layla' or 'The Great Gig in the Sky' or 'Kashmir' now without thinking of him. The carpet squelched beneath their feet.

They took the back stairs to the first floor. There was a huge hole on the landing where the floor had collapsed into the hall below, making three of the bedrooms, including Room Seven, entirely unreachable.

It was in her bedroom, relatively unaffected and which might dry out, although the wall coverings were black with smoke and soot, that Kit asked, 'What will you do? Will the insurance pay for you to stay somewhere else? The – what do you call them – loss adjusters?' and she had looked at him and said nothing and he understood immediately, without needing to be told, that she had no insurance, and a wave of misery and guilt washed over him; at his barrelling his way through what must have been a significant part of her fortune, at his not being in a position to pay any of it back, to help out. With a hot surge of embarrassment he remembered the day of Susannah's funeral when he had crassly offered to pay their heating bill. And now a huge part of Erringby Hall needed to be entirely rebuilt. How much would that cost?

'Oh, Marianne,' he said, and still she said nothing as they stood looking at her bed, unscathed but marooned on the soggy rug. *Nightwood* by Djuna Barnes lay on the bedside table, a strip of leather marking her place. 'Oh, Marianne,' he said again, and could have wept, another memory crowding him, of the night when, stupefied with drugs, he had fallen asleep with his head on her breast. Had he been in this room since?

'Kit,' she said now, as if she understood, was gently chiding him even as she read his thoughts. She was utterly calm. In that moment she was like Susannah: the stoicism, the refusal to buckle, even as her world literally crumbled around her. She was of another era, Marianne, one of chilly politesse, of thank-you letters after a party and Dunkirk spirit and make-do-and-mend and lacrosse on the freezing playing fields of dismal English private schools. And of bad food. For her food was a tiresome necessity, fuel merely, as evinced by her refusal to learn to cook properly. And she certainly viewed housework, cleanliness, even, as petit bourgeois. That might be the source of her enmity with Kit's mother, for whom a spotless house was synonymous with respectability.

That and competition over Col, it now occurred to Kit. Col was the adored little brother, ten years younger than Janet. The other uncle, Alan, father of the tiresome cousins Ian and Joanne, played little part in the Greenfield family lore – throwing up on the living-room carpet notwithstanding – but Kit's mother was full of Col anecdotes: the time spent looking after him as their father worked his long days at the Hereford branch of the Westminster Bank – not that he would have done much child rearing, this being the 1950s – and their mother cared for her own elderly parents; how on the day sweet rationing ended all Janet's pocket money went on treating her six-year-old brother. Kit remembered the excitement Col's airmail letters had caused, how his mother would read out the funny bits at the breakfast table, how she kept the letters in a hatbox, minus the stamps that he – Christopher – had cut out for a scrapbook. The scrapbook was long gone; the hatbox still sat on top of his parents' wardrobe. Kit couldn't remember Col meeting Marianne, but it must have been soon after he came back from travelling, that summer's day he went looking for her to ask her out for a bet. He did remember his mother's disgruntlement, disguised as disapproval, at Col moving into Erringby Hall so soon after meeting her – she would have loved having Col to stay with them of course, would have relished looking after him – and that must have been the start of it, the bad feeling. And Marianne, being Marianne, would have made no attempt to win Janet over.

'You seem lost in thought,' Marianne said. They were standing at her bedroom window, looking out over the grounds towards the woods.

'I was wondering how on earth you're going to manage,' he lied.

'Oh, I dare say I shall survive,' she said. 'Worse things happen at sea, and all that.'

'I'm not sure they do,' he said. 'Not since the naval reforms of the seventeenth century at any rate.'

She laughed, linked her arm through his.

'You are better, aren't you?'

'Yes,' he said. 'There is that.'

It was only after they had returned to the ground floor that a chink in her armour appeared. They were standing in front of what had been *Woman in the Bath*, scorched and soggy beyond recognition.

'Oh,' she said. 'We should have saved it. We could have saved it.' Did her voice tremble? Kit reached for her hand and gripped it.

'It's only a thing,' he said. 'Didn't you say that to me once? When I broke your vase or whatever it was, trying to draw it.'

'I don't remember,' she said.

'I remember,' said Kit.

'It was a beautiful thing, though,' she said. 'It was one of my best things.'

'Was it?'

'You know it was.' She kept hold of his hand, squeezed it back. 'So.' She turned to him, as if something had been decided upon and agreed. 'You will paint again. I don't mean replicate this painting. Or even paint me again. But something else. Something as good.'

'Maybe,' said Kit.

PART IV

22

October 1998

The man had been loitering outside the school for some time, the caretaker told Kit.

'There.' Terry nodded towards the man, who was picking fag ends off the pavement. 'I don't like the look of him.' Kit looked across the street, where the man seemed to be positioning himself as if waiting for the children to come out.

'I'm going that way,' Kit said. 'I'll check him out.'

'Right you are.'

The man saw Kit approaching and turned away, suddenly engrossed in rifling through his pockets. His coat was too small for him, buttonless, and filthy. Kit wasn't sure what he would say. The man was much bigger than him, possibly a street dweller, probably drunk, and doubtless handy with his fists. Kit's hope was that, seeing himself under surveillance, the man would follow the line of least resistance and move away from the school gates and become someone else's problem. He looked round to see Terry watching him from the playground.

But the man did not move away, in fact he was staring at him. His eyes, Kit saw as he got closer, were bloodshot but piercing, and the way he looked at him, the intensity of his gaze, chimed somewhere within him.

'Fucking hell,' the man said. 'It *is* you.'

And in that instant Kit recognised him, though he was old now, and weather-beaten, his skin blotched and broken-veined. He had a beard, straggly and unkempt.

'Jesus,' said Kit, and came to a halt. 'Col.'

'Kit!' said Col, and something in his demeanour changed; he was straightening to make himself more presentable even though he stank of stale alcohol and sweat. He ran his hand through his hair, iron grey, lank and dirty, in a familiar gesture. 'Fucking hell.' He stuck out his hand, huge, red and puffy, the fingernails filthy, the wrinkles of the fingers and knuckles ingrained with dirt.

Col stuck his hand out a little further. Kit took it gingerly and Col's fingers closed round his. Kit felt his own hand small and white in comparison, almost girlish. He was relieved that Col didn't want to hug him. From the corner of his eye he saw Terry watching, professional concern replaced by morbid curiosity.

'Well, look at you,' said Col. 'I've not seen you for... must be...'

'Ten years,' said Kit.

'You're looking well.'

'Thanks.'

'You're a teacher?' Col nodded towards the school.

'Art therapist.'

'Ah,' said Col. 'You living in Stepney?'

'Camberwell. Yourself?'

'Oh, I've got a place. Sort of. Near here. Do you... I don't suppose you've got time for a cup of tea? You're busy...'

'No, it's OK.' Kit wanted very much to get Col and himself out of Terry's line of sight and away from the school before the children came out. 'A cup of tea would be nice.'

'I know somewhere,' said Col, and led the way up the street. He had a pronounced limp. There was a café round the corner that Kit had never been into. It was a modest place, no frills and probably cheap, but at the door Kit paused. The café was tiny, Col's bulk would fill it, and – there were no two ways about it – his uncle reeked. It would be unpleasant for the staff and the other customers, excruciating for Kit. Col saw him hesitate and

Kit thought that he guessed the reason why. Though Col had chosen the place. Perhaps he had progressed beyond caring, his sense of others' propriety and disgust eroded over years of serious drinking. Perhaps he was a regular here, the café used to him, tolerating him even, during non-busy periods.

He's an alcoholic, Kit thought. *He doesn't want a cup of tea. What difference would it make? It's mild; we could sit outside.*

'Or perhaps...' he said. 'I haven't seen you in so long... Why don't we go for a proper drink?' Something behind Col's eyes lit up.

'Really?' he said.

Kit did know the nearest pub, the Rose & Crown, but school colleagues sometimes drank there and he decided instead on the Duke of York, a short distance away.

'So... are you married?' Col was asking as they walked.

'Not married, no.'

'Thank fuck for that.' Col's demeanour, now that a drink was in the offing, sanctioned even, had changed; his limp was less pronounced and he seemed taller.

'You got off all the drugs, then?' he asked next.

'Yup. Clean for seven years.'

'Good for you.'

The pub had space to sit out at its front, though the view was of passing traffic and the anonymous block of council offices opposite.

'Why don't you grab a seat,' Kit said, 'while I go to the bar?' The seating was picnic style, its wooden benches part of the same unit as the table. Col's bulk, and his bad leg, whatever was wrong with it, meant he got himself onto the bench and his legs under the table only with difficulty. Kit wondered about helping but decided against drawing attention to Col's awkwardness.

'What'll you have?'

'Oh! Well now...' Col pretended to consider. 'Pint of Guinness, maybe.'

Kit went into the pub and ordered a pint and a half of Guinness. When he came back outside Col was rolling a cigarette. In spite of his shaking hands he rolled it with practised movements.

'You want one?'

'Oh, go on then.' This was turning into such an extraordinary day – the shock of seeing Col, the state he was in, having a beer at four o'clock on a weekday afternoon – that a cigarette seemed neither here nor there, though Kit couldn't remember the last time he had smoked. Col struck a match and lit Kit's roll-up, hand cupped round the match, Kit leaning in with the unlit cigarette in his mouth, and the intimacy of the moment made his heart contract, even as his nostrils filled with the smell emanating from Col's body and that coat.

'It's lovely to see you, Col,' he lied, sitting back and inhaling, feeling the forgotten sensation of smoke in his nose and throat, doing his best not to cough like a neophyte.

'Yeah,' said Col. 'Been a while.'

'Susannah's funeral,' said Kit.

'Yeah?'

Kit sipped at his half-pint. He had a tendency to get drunk quickly on the infrequent occasions when he did drink. His uncle, he was unsurprised to see, drank far more rapidly.

'Got a girlfriend, though?' Col asked him.

'No. But...'

'Playing the field, then.' Col sounded pleased.

'No,' said Kit. 'It's not that either.' He pulled out his wallet to show Col the picture of Robin.

Col took the wallet and brought it near to his face to peer at the photograph. He put the wallet down and looked at Kit.

'Fucking hell.' Kit said nothing.

'Older guy, is it?' Col said finally.

'Yes – he's forty.'

'And you're... don't tell me!' Col, drumming his fingers on the table, was visibly calculating. 'Thirty.' Kit nodded. 'Fucking hell.'

'I know. It's been ten years, Col.' And Col would be fifty-two, though he looked much older. Kit didn't need to be told that the intervening decade had not treated him well. There had been news in the early years via his mother but this had dribbled away. The last concrete information was that the pub in Littlehampton had been a failure and Col had had to leave; an imbroglio with someone else's wife had been admitted to, the factor of his drinking less so. He had drifted for a while before ending up in London; there had been Christmas and birthday cards hinting at projects: he was finding his feet, he was starting a business, he would write properly, come to Hereford for a visit, *when...* 'When' had never arrived, and to Janet's distress, less so to Kit's, they had not heard from him for at least two years.

'So.' Col waved at Kit's wallet on the table. 'What's his name?'

'Robin.'

'Where'd you meet him?'

'At a gallery opening. He's a photographer.'

'You were having an exhibition?'

'No, it wasn't mine. A friend's.'

'But you're painting again?'

'Yes. Bits. Just stuff for me, you know. It's difficult because we've only got a small flat and Robin uses the spare bedroom as his darkroom.' Kit's forays into painting were so timorous, so provisional, that he didn't mind one bit Robin's appropriation of the spare room. It was his living, after all. And his flat.

'You've bought somewhere?' Col asked.

'No. It's a housing association flat.'

'I'm getting a housing association flat,' Col said. 'Well, bedsit. Well, probably...' He tailed off. Kit nodded encouragingly.

'Where are you living now?'

'Oh... with some people. It's temporary.' Kit guessed he meant a hostel of some kind.

'What are you up to these days?'

'Oh, you know,' said Col. 'Bits and bats. You know me. There's a pub I've got my eye on not far from here. Bethnal Green way. Free house.'

'That sounds good,' Kit said. Col must have forgotten telling Janet that he had lost his licence, irrevocably, following the Littlehampton mishap.

Col was two thirds of the way through his pint. Kit had barely sipped at his half. Col's hands were trembling badly. He rolled another cigarette.

'Want one?'

'No – this was enough. I don't really smoke.'

'I can tell. Lightweight.' Kit half laughed.

'You've got me bang to rights.'

'Ha,' said Col, and drained his glass. He sat back and inhaled deeply on his roll-up, his eyes closed. He looked terrible, lined and jowly, his blotchy and open-pored skin a livid colour, as if heart attack or stroke were only moments away. He opened his eyes to exhale smoke and looked pointedly at his empty beer glass.

'Would you like another?' asked Kit.

'Yeah,' said Col.

'So,' he went on, when Kit had returned with a second pint of Guinness. 'A gay art therapist.'

'Well, I think I'm probably bisexual but... yes.'

'What do your mum and dad make of it?'

Christ. He doesn't know.

'Dad died, Col. About two years ago.'

Col dropped his cigarette. He scrabbled on the ground for it, picking it up only with difficulty.

'You're fucking kidding me.'

'He had a heart attack. When he was at work. We… we didn't know how to get hold of you. To let you know. I'm sorry, Col.' For Col's face had assumed an expression of hurt, even of offence. Annoyance rose in Kit. 'Mum wrote to the last address she had for you.'

'Must've got lost in the post,' Col said defensively. Kit decided to let it drop. 'Bob…' Col went on, as if to himself. 'Poor bugger.'

'Oh, I don't know,' said Kit. 'He was happy when he died. He had a pretty good life.' This was the narrative that he and Janet had constructed between them. Although it had been a huge shock, and obviously a happy and healthy old age would have been vastly preferable to being felled at the age of sixty-two, at least they had been spared an alternative of a slow decline and failing, they'd told themselves. Col clearly wasn't buying this.

'Good life? After all you put him through?' He took a long swig from his glass.

Anger flared up in Kit. For a moment he was nineteen, twenty, again, feeling the old dismissal of, even contempt for, his uncle. Col had missed entirely Kit's rebuilding of his relationship with his parents, so that by the time Bob died he and Kit had almost reverted to the easy dealings they'd had with each other in Kit's early childhood. He took a deep breath, as he had taught himself to do when riled. But still he felt Col should not be allowed to get away with this.

'Well, what about you and Mum?' He tried to keep his voice level but was aware of sounding indignant. 'She's worried sick about you.' Col looked at him mutinously.

'Well, I guess that makes us equal, doesn't it?' he said.

No, it doesn't, Kit thought, but said nothing.

'Tell her I'll come for a visit,' Col said. 'As soon as I'm sorted. How is she doing, anyway?'

Paradoxically Janet was doing better than she had in years. She had, in the months after Bob's death, finally been put on a combination of medication that seemed to work for her. After years of agoraphobia she now volunteered several mornings a week for a couple of charities.

'Oh, good,' said Col, when Kit told him this. 'I'm glad things have worked out for her.'

'No thanks to either of us, I guess,' Kit said, before Col could start accusing him again.

'I said I'd go and visit her!' Col said hotly. 'Jesus, you sanctimonious little...' The sentence died away. He was getting drunk. Or drunker, since he presumably was more or less constantly inebriated, needing just a pint or two to push him over the edge. He drained his second pint of Guinness and looked meaningfully at Kit.

The nerve of him, Kit thought, even as he recognised a little of himself, from his drug days, in Col's self-centredness. Buying his uncle booze was probably not the best thing he could be doing for him, but what difference would it make?

'I'll go to the bar, shall I?' he said.

'Oh, thanks, Kit!' said Col, all smiles now, managing in his disingenuousness and his current state to summon some of the old charm, the charm that had led Janet to spoil him like she did, forgive him for so much – *You're tipsy again, Col!* – the charm that had won so many women over to him.

Kit came back from the bar with a third pint for Col and another half for himself.

'So,' Col said, with the air of getting down to business, of having needed two pints to say what he was about to say. His speech was a little slurred. 'We have to talk about her sometime. So? You ever see her?'

'Marianne,' said Kit. Col closed his eyes.

'Yeah. Marianne.' He made what was probably an involuntary grimace, as if he hadn't spoken the name in years. He opened his eyes and looked directly at Kit. Those eyes, that had once been so arresting, so blue, were bloodshot and yellow.

'I don't see her very often,' Kit said. He told Col about the fire, since it was unlikely he had heard about it from Janet. He didn't tell Col about the New Year's Eve party, since that would have involved explaining how *Strassburg Pie* had become a cult, which would have opened up the whole can of the financial dealings, best left unspoken. Col's ham-fisted deal with the film company had meant he was entitled only to a percentage of box office takings, which had been poor; neither he nor Marianne had seen a penny of video sales, still buoyant even now. Col didn't seem very interested in the fire.

'The last time I saw her she was living in the staff flat,' Kit said. 'It's hand to mouth, but I think she's OK. She has this chap John to help her.'

'Fucking him, is she?'

'No, she's not.'

'Wouldn't blame her. She's free to do what she wants. I have.' Kit did not mention Tony. 'I've had my share of women,' Col said smugly. 'I can still...' He smirked. Kit tried not to picture Col's current sexual liaisons.

'Fucking bitch,' Col went on. 'Her sort... they always get their own way. They think they're better than us. Her mother was the same.'

'You liked Susannah,' said Kit, remembering the funeral, the seventy-year-old port that Col had saved.

'Yeah, well,' Col said grudgingly. 'Her fucking daughter destroyed me and she nearly destroyed you. I wish I'd never met her.'

Kit wondered if he should tell Col about the dining-room shrine and Marianne's enduring conviction that he would return. Best not, he thought. Wanting to lighten the mood, he said, 'I heard you went after her for a bet.' Col looked sidelong at him and inhaled on his cigarette.

'Who told you that?'

'The landlord at the Three Hares. Years ago.'

'Yeah, well,' Col said again. 'That day, the day I walked along the Meaburn looking for her... I wish to God I'd kept walking. Everything would have been different. I'd've had a family. That was all I ever wanted. You know what she did? You heard what she did to me?'

'Yes,' Kit said. 'She told me.'

'That was all I ever wanted... You know I could have been a father?' Col stubbed out his cigarette and picked up his tobacco to roll another. Kit shook his head. 'You remember Lois? From the film?'

'Oh yes,' said Kit.

'I got her pregnant.'

'Oh! But...'

'She went and did away with it, didn't she, without consulting me, like I had no rights. She's another. Fucking hard-faced bitch.'

'I didn't know,' Kit said.

'No. Of course Marianne didn't tell you *that*. But you!' said Col, suddenly remembering, and Kit's heart plummeted. 'How the hell is your kid? Little girl, isn't it?'

'Sophie.' Kit's heart trickled into his boots. There was no scope for lying here.

'How is she?'

'She's very well,' Kit said. 'I believe.'

'Huh?' said Col. He looked as if he were having difficulty focusing. He would soon finish his third pint of Guinness. *I'm not buying you another*, thought Kit.

He had tried to keep up contact with Sophie; had, after getting clean, made real efforts to see her, but Georgina and Giles's lifestyle – they had a place in Umbria they were forever going off to – plus Giles's obvious reluctance to have even a drug-free Kit near his adopted daughter had made things problematic. Sophie was now nine years old and had a half-brother, William, aged five, and Kit had decided not to push things for the time being. He had seen his daughter so infrequently that she was not very comfortable with him when they did meet each other, and although the arrival of Robin in his life should have reduced Giles's suspicions that Kit was really after getting back with Georgina, Kit suspected homophobia as well.

'I don't see her very often,' he admitted. Col looked incredulous.

'Christ, if I had a daughter, a beautiful little girl, I would have moved heaven and earth.'

Easy for you to say, thought Kit.

'Did you fight for her?'

'Yes – yes I did,' said Kit. 'When she's older, hopefully I can...'

'You should've fought harder!' Col declared. Kit said nothing. 'I'm going for a slash,' Col said. He got up from the bench, with considerable difficulty, and lurched into the pub, pausing to lean heavily against the door frame.

A sudden memory came to Kit, decades old; his uncle in his underpants in the kitchen at Erringby, stretching and yawning, revelling in his own physicality, his vitality. Something caught in Kit's throat at the thought of it.

He closed his eyes. He was tempted, very tempted, to grab his wallet and bag and just leave, leave Col here at the pub, but something stopped him, vestiges of loyalty to his uncle, genuine loyalty to his mother. Janet would want him to stay and hear Col out to the grisly end. He would phone her as soon as he got home. And already he was imagining telling Robin – *You'll never guess who I ran into...* Robin knew about Col, and Marianne, though he had never met her. And Robin would be sympathetic, even though he would have had a stressful day himself – he was working on a shoot for a City bank, which was not going well – and would want to hear about it, and share in Kit's discomfort at having to talk about Sophie and the rest. After dinner he would come up behind Kit and rub the back of his neck and say, 'Sure you're OK about it all?' and put his arms round him and nuzzle at the place where Kit's neck met his shoulder in that way he had and which Kit found infinitely comforting and made him feel loved and looked after and safe.

Col returned with a pint of lager for himself. He didn't bother trying to get his legs under the table again but sat on the edge of the bench, twisting to lean on the table.

'Col, you shouldn't—' Kit began. Col interrupted him.

'Did you fuck my wife?' he demanded loudly.

'Col, for God's sake!' A couple who had just sat at another table were looking at them.

'Oh, well,' said Col. 'Let me put it another way, then. Did my *wife*. Fuck *you*. Her darling nephew?' Kit didn't reply. 'Christ, it was warped, what went on with you. She chewed you up and shat you out. Just like she did me. Ruined you. With her money, with her... fucking hell. The cunt.'

'I can take responsibility for my own life, Col.'

'Meaning I can't?' Kit said nothing. 'Fucking bitch. I've never got over her. I can't. She ruined me. All I ever wanted was kids. She knew that. She pretended she did too, the cunt. Pretended to be trying for years. And God knows, we did try.' A lascivious expression came over him. 'We tried a lot.'

'I know,' said Kit. Col smirked. 'I heard you once. When I was eleven.'

'Did you? *Sorry* about that. I remember one time,' Col mused, 'before we were married. I was looking for her to ask her about something and I followed her into the greenhouse, and she pretended she hadn't heard me and walked on ahead of me, and she lifted up her dress – it was the summer – and walked on with her back to me, and she wasn't wearing any underwear, and she...'

'Col!' The couple at the neighbouring table were agog.

'Huh!' said Col, and to Kit's enormous relief, stopped his reminiscence. Kit changed the subject.

'You shouldn't hang around outside primary schools, Col.'

'I'm not a pervert. *She's* the fucking pervert.'

'I know you're not, but...'.

'I like watching kids play. Remember the parties we used to have for you at Erringby? When you were little?'

Kit did remember: anarchic treasure hunts and games of hide-and-seek that went on for hours because at least one of his friends would get properly lost in the woods or in the outbuildings, leading to a mad scramble of Col and Marianne and Kit and the other children scouring the house and grounds, dogs enlisted in support, a chaotic and hilarious manoeuvre led by Col. Kit – Christopher – had found it all immense fun.

Col started crying, tears running down his face unchecked. The couple at the other table looked over at them.

Oh Jesus, Kit thought. He was reminded, and it was not pleasant, of how he himself had been at his lowest point. That Christmas Eve when he tried to deliver presents for Sophie and ended up sprawled on Georgina's doorstep, crying. How she must have felt as discomfited as he felt now. How kind she had been to him, a kindness he was struggling to find in himself now.

'Maybe I'll get a job working with kids,' Col said chokingly. 'Like you.' His nose was running and tears were creating rivulets of cleaner skin in the dirt on his face.

'M'mm,' said Kit.

'Look at me!' said Col. 'I'm a fucking alcoholic. I'm all washed up. It's all I can do to get up in the morning, Kit.'

'I know, Col,' said Kit.

'Tell your mum... tell her you saw me, I'm fine, and I'll write to her. Tell her that.'

'OK,' said Kit. 'I will.'

Col gave a tremendous sniff, stopped crying and wiped his face on the sleeve of his coat. He drained his glass.

'I don't suppose you could lend me a few bob?'

'I can't... sorry.' Buying the drinks had emptied Kit's wallet, and he was supposed to be stopping off at the supermarket on the way home to get something for dinner for him and Robin. He would have to go by way of a cashpoint.

'I should be getting going,' he said. 'Here.' He ripped a page out of his notebook and wrote down his address and telephone number.

'I'll walk with you,' said Col, looking down at the piece of paper.

At Stepney Green Tube station they said goodbye. Kit pretended to be about to go through the ticket barrier but lingered instead, turning to watch Col limp away from the station. At a pelican crossing he stopped to go through a litter bin.

*

Though the dog, Balzac, was rather deaf, he heard them before she did. He sat up and stiffened, and growled. She put a hand to his head to shush him, got up and padded to the door and turned the key. Really, she should remember to keep herself locked in all the time. She turned off the radio and turned out the lights in the apartment.

Looters had become a fairly common occurrence. The condition of Erringby, its blackened and ruined east wing, was partly visible from the road, more apparent if you made your way on foot round the back of the estate. John had been on at her about getting the perimeter fence properly fixed, making it harder to get in that way, through the woods. She agreed it was a good idea but had never done anything about it. Let them come, she thought, sometimes; sometimes it seemed as if Erringby's contents, burned, smoke damaged, water damaged, rotten, gnawed away by the mice that had colonised the house – the cats could not keep up – were shackles weighing her down, and each looting spree relieved her of a little of it. Still, she knew herself to be vulnerable, a lone woman in a huge, decaying house with just an elderly dog for protection, and the sensible thing to do was to lie low and let them get on with it.

And when she made her occasional sorties out of the apartment, going gingerly round the house with a flashlight, her progress cautious because each time another piece of floorboard would have rotted away entirely – it would be too easy to fall through the ceiling of the storey below – each time she went into an abandoned room she found she couldn't remember what had been there before, whether she was unable to put her hand on something now because it had been lost, or burned, or stolen.

The other thing John had suggested was to sell up entirely without attempting to make the house more habitable – the land alone would be worth *something* – and move into a house in the village or surrounding area, or otherwise throw herself on the mercy of the authorities. But that would be giving up. And if she moved no one would be able to find her. Col would not be able to find her.

She'd moved the things laid out in the dining room to save them from looters, almost the only things she had made a point of saving. There was no hot water for laundry other than from the ascot in the apartment's tiny bathroom – the one in the kitchenette was broken and needed replacing, but there was no money for that – so she had been unable to wash the tablecloth and napkins. They had been folded, blackened with soot and mould, and stashed in a drawer in what had been the housekeeper's room. But she had washed the hand-painted plates with their pink roses, and the bone-handled cutlery, in the washbasin in the bathroom, and fetched two only slightly less nice wine goblets to replace the ones that had been smashed in the fire, and set out two places on the table in the apartment lounge. She ate her own meals off a tray while sitting on the sofa, listening to the radio. The firemen's hoses in the gun room had ruined the television and she had watched it so rarely she couldn't justify the expense of a replacement.

John, on his infrequent visits to the apartment, never commented on the place settings, never asked who she was expecting to join her. It was one of the things she liked about him. They never delved into each other's histories. There had been a wife who had come to an early, tragic end – suicide? a wasting disease? – but Marianne didn't care to find out.

She sat very still, now, her hand on the dog's head to calm him. Whoever was in the house was clattering around noisily. There were two of them; she heard them calling to each other.

'Fuck!' said one of them, a man. There was a giggle in reply and a woman's voice said, 'I'm rather partial to inspissated juice!'

Oh, for the love of God, thought Marianne. She flicked the lights back on, went to the door and unlocked it.

'In here!' she called. There was a silence.

'Oh fuck!' the man hissed, and the woman said, 'Shit, Geoff.'

Marianne stepped out of the apartment.

'Come on,' she said wearily. 'Reveal yourselves.' The man and the woman came out of the kitchen.

'Oh Christ,' the man said.

'We're *so, so* sorry,' the woman said.

They were getting younger, the pilgrims. These two were barely out of their teens. The man had a geeky look, with thick spectacles and hair that stuck up. Marianne supposed it was the fashion. He was gawky and thin, prominent Adam's apple bobbing up and down with nerves. His accomplice was surer of herself. Unlike her swain she could look Marianne in the eye. She was attractive, with very dark eyes, her blonde hair worn in a thick plait. *You're too pretty for him*, Marianne thought.

'We... we heard the place was empty,' the man said.

'Well, you heard wrong,' said Marianne.

'We only came to...'

'...look around.' Marianne finished the young woman's sentence. 'As you can see, there's not much to look at any more.'

'We know,' the woman said. 'We knew about the fire. We wanted to see anyway. There's some really cool pictures on the internet.'

'The what?'

'The web. You know.'

'I don't know,' said Marianne.

The young woman looked at the man, who raised his eyebrows.

'Well,' he began, with the air of explaining to someone very simple. 'It's...'

Marianne waved him away.

'I don't care to know,' she said. 'Whatever it is.' The young woman laughed. She had a loud, surprising laugh.

'I don't blame you,' she said. Marianne felt a sneaking affinity with her. She was in the mood to be magnanimous. Possibly it was relief that these people were harmless, unlike some of the looters who sounded full of the potential for violence.

'Well,' she said. 'Seeing as you've come all the way from... where *have* you come from?'

'Henley-in-Arden,' the woman said.

'...all that way,' said Marianne. 'Why not have a cup of tea with me?'

'Gosh,' said the woman. 'That's really very kind of you.'

'It is, isn't it?' She led the way into the apartment. 'Excuse the mess.' The couple followed her. 'Off!' said Marianne to two cats who were occupying the sofa, shooing them away. 'Do sit down.'

'Lovely dog,' the young man said. The briard had gone up to him and was licking his hand.

'Is he friendly?' the woman asked.

'Very,' said Marianne.

'What's his name?' the man asked.

'Balzac.'

'Does he drink fifty cups of coffee a day?'

'Ha!' said Marianne. 'Very good.' The young man wasn't so bad, either. She made tea and found biscuits that were just the right side of stale.

'You find me here in my cubbyhole, virtually the only part of the house that's still habitable,' she said. 'They used this flat as the staff office during the shoot of *Strassburg Pie*.'

'Really?' said the man.

'Wow.' The woman looked around her as if Marianne had uncovered the ceiling of the Sistine Chapel.

'Oh yes,' said Marianne. 'The production office was here. And after each day's shooting we sat and watched the rushes in this room.' This was nonsense, but these young people didn't know any better.

'Did you realise at the time,' the man wanted to know, 'what a great film you were making?'

'Oh no,' said Marianne. 'It was just a little picture that needed to get made, you know? And of course neither Darren Fenby nor Henry Melville were at their zeniths, for quite different reasons. And so they were both wonderfully cheap.'

The couple laughed, looked eagerly at her to continue.

She enjoyed herself that afternoon, spinning anecdotes she made up as she went along; the shenanigans on the shoot, the behaviour of the actors, the feuds and intrigues. Afterwards she told the woman and the man that, as a special favour, she had something for them, and retrieved a badly tarnished silver egg cup from the dining-room sideboard.

'This was used in the breakfast scene,' she told them. 'You may have it to keep.'

The young people had gone away satisfied, and Marianne wondered, as she cleared the tea things away, tuned the radio to the World Service and got ready for bed, how many more there would be.

23

June 2000

The letter was waiting for him when he got home. It lay address side down on the doormat and on the back of the envelope was a sweet but pointless note in his mother's neat script, the handwriting perfected at the long-ago-closed village school and never updated; unlike most adults' it had never descended into semi-legibility. *This came for you. Mum x.*

And as Kit picked the envelope up and turned it over his heart skipped several beats, for the cursive hand that had something Dickensian about it and the thick cream envelope with its watermark were instantly recognisable. He still had the original wove envelope in his possession; had managed somehow to hold on to it during that chaotic period when he had lost virtually everything else he possessed.

There couldn't be more money, surely? There *was* no more money. An appalling thought came to him as he stared at the envelope: he had breached some obscure clause of the trust deed, perhaps by spending the money so quickly, was now required to pay some of it back; Marianne, going mad in her Erringby seclusion and her increasingly straitened circumstances, had had a volte-face and come after him, even in the knowledge that he didn't have very much. The envelope was fat; there were several things contained in it. He tore at it and his heart thudded; if he wasn't careful he would rip one of the documents inside and he knew instinctively that he mustn't, that whatever was in the envelope was very, very important.

There were three documents. A letter from the financial services company that had written to him just after his eighteenth birthday, another envelope with *Christopher Antrobus* typed onto it, and a newspaper clipping. He read the letter from the company first.

Dear Mr Antrobus,

In respect of the bare trust established on 31 May 1986, of which you were the sole beneficiary, and in accordance with the wishes of the settlor, please find the enclosed letter. If we can be of further assistance then please etc. etc.

Kit looked at the newspaper clipping, much yellowed. It was from the *Jersey Evening Post* and was dated 12 January 1971. *Le Hocq murder: wife jailed for life.* There were headshots of a man and a woman. Kit could not make sense of this. He opened the envelope. It contained a letter dated 14 August 1986 – his eighteenth birthday – and had been typed on thin paper using a manual typewriter. Tippexed corrections had been overtyped or in some instances amended by hand.

Dear Christopher,

I am writing this on your eighteenth birthday, shortly before the trust which I have set up for you will be made known to you.

You are now an adult, though I have no way of telling how old you will be on reading this. You will be surprised by what I am about to write down as you have, I know, been told that both your parents died in a road accident. I made certain, when I gave you up for adoption, that you were found a family on the mainland, also that no one, including your adoptive parents, was made aware of the true circumstances.

You will by now have realised that I am your birth mother, and I know that this news will be surprising and even shocking to you. I write to you to set out the facts of my life and your earliest years and to offer some explanation for the secrecy that has shrouded them.

I was born Gabrielle Snowdon in 1944 and grew up in Buckinghamshire. My father, a pilot in the second War, died when his plane was brought down over Hamburg in 1943. However, he had left my mother and I well provided for and my childhood was one of considerable financial comfort. I had no siblings. In 1967 my mother died and I inherited a large sum of money. I had by that time married your father, George Lejeune, who was from an established Jersey family. Twenty years older than I was, he worked as a lawyer with chambers in Grays Inn.

You were born at St Thomas' Hospital, London. When you were a few months old we moved to Le Hocq, Jersey, as your father wished to set up in practice in St Helier.

There was another reason for moving to the island – or should I say, an overriding reason – your father had a longstanding mistress, unknown to me at the time, living in the town.

Our marriage was not a happy one, even without the infidelity. There were many, many fights and arguments. Your father was occasionally violent, although never, I should stress, towards you. You were a lively, bright, happy child with an insatiable curiosity about the world. I was a young woman who had given up a career as a fashion designer to marry your father, and I chafed at the lack of freedom and the strictures of Jersey town life, which I found stultifying, and was isolated with a young child and a husband who worked long hours (as I thought; in reality he was spending evenings with his mistress) and was seldom home.

In the spring of 1970 I discovered the fact of the woman when I found a letter from her among your father's papers. An immense showdown followed, in which I threatened to leave for London, taking you with me, and he promised to give her up. In my desperation and my naivety I believed him.

Sixteen years ago today – on your second birthday – your father had promised most particularly to be home early from the office to celebrate with a special tea party and a cake that I had ordered for you. However, he was not. He had, of course, lied about the relationship with the other woman ending. It was after ten o'clock in the evening when he returned, by which time I was in a state of considerable agitation and anger. I confronted him, he did not deny it and another blazing row ensued.

I am trying to set this out as factually, as objectively as I am able to.

Unbeknown to me, you had crept down from your bedroom and into the kitchen and were helping yourself to more birthday cake. You would have heard us arguing in the dining room. Your father kept a gun, which I brandished at him. I believe I planned only to scare him, shock him into contrition. At that moment you came into the room and I was distracted. I was entirely unused to firearms, the safety catch was off, and, without intending to, I shot your father in the forehead and he died instantly.

I cannot recall much of the subsequent hours, but a neighbour, hearing the shot, telephoned the police, I was arrested and you were taken to your paternal grandparents. They were, however, elderly and in poor health and unable to look after you, and you were taken into the care of the Little Sisters of the Poor at St Aubin while I awaited trial for the murder of your father.

The clipping I am forwarding is probably the least lurid of the newspaper accounts but it will give you some indication of the feverish atmosphere around the affair – and the shockwaves it caused in a small Jersey town. Your father's family was well known on the island; I was an outsider, portrayed as unstable, hysterical and blinded by jealousy. My defence of provocation, of it being accidental, was rejected, and I was sentenced to life imprisonment in Newgate Prison, St Helier.

It was at that time that I made the arrangements for you to be adopted on the mainland. I hope I can make you understand that I had no option but to give you up. I knew I could expect to spend at least fifteen years in prison and had no relatives of my own to take you in. I regret that your father's family were not much interested in you and agreed fairly readily to your adoption. I was determined to get you off Jersey, so that you could grow up without the stain of being the child of a murderess – as would surely have come to light had you been adopted on that small island. You had a far better chance of a happy life without your past weighing on you. I know that you were brought up by a Mr & Mrs Antrobus in Hereford and that they kept the name I gave you, Christopher, and I pray that your childhood has been a happy and a secure one.

I was released from prison earlier this year which has made the management of my affairs far more straightforward. I was unable, of course, to inherit your father's estate, which passed back to his family. The assets that I have put in trust for you are a sizeable part of my own fortune and I sincerely hope that they have eased your way into adulthood and have given you a basis for a successful life, whatever you choose or have chosen to do.

I should set something down about your father. Please be assured that he was a good father in his own way, and did love you. As for me, I loved you more than my own life, but my life ended on your second birthday.

I have given instructions that this letter not be forwarded to you until after my death, or you might have been tempted to seek me out for yourself, and it is better for both of us that we leave each other alone.

Yours sincerely
Gabrielle Lejeune

Kit felt as if he had stopped breathing. He could not bring himself to read the newspaper clipping. He looked instead at the yellowing, smudgy photographs of his parents. His father wore a shirt and tie, had slicked-back dark hair and a moustache and a plump face. His mother was young and very glamorous. Her long dark hair, parted in the middle, fell over one shoulder. Yes, she was the woman who had come to Kit fleetingly when the rush of the cocaine was crashing into his vein.

When Robin came home some hours later Kit was sitting on the living-room floor holding his mother's letter and staring at the abstract painting of green and blue rectangles that he had been working on, tears coursing down his face.

*

Kit took a train from Paddington. Robin had offered to come but Kit told him he needn't. It would have meant cancelling an assignment and they could do with the money since Kit's employer, the London Borough of Tower Hamlets, had cut back its budget for things like art therapy. And, lovely though it would have been to have Robin with him, he needed to make this trip alone.

A woman took the seat opposite him, the man she had come with remaining on the platform. When the train was pulling out they each made an identical gesture, kissing their fingertips and waving them at the other. As the train drew into Slough the woman, thinking herself unobserved, opened her purse and slipped a ring onto her wedding finger.

Kit had been in a state of high agitation since receiving Gabrielle's letter. He'd found more newspaper accounts on the internet. She had been right: much of the reporting was sensational. He'd felt his chest contract when he came across references to himself, to his having witnessed his father's shooting. *The child, who cannot be named for legal reasons, is currently in the care of a church charity...* He'd tried to find the Little Sisters of the Poor in St Aubin but learned that the convent had closed its doors in 1990. There had been a brief campaign, it seemed, to have his mother's conviction overturned on the grounds of provocation, or of diminished responsibility, or at least commuted to manslaughter as a crime of passion, but this must have dwindled away. *This was a wicked and premeditated act, born out of spite and revenge,* the judge was reported to have said on sentencing. *Your attempts to blame it on the unexpected appearance of your innocent child are execrable.* Kit had not been able to find a picture of Bailiff Sir Robert de Gruchy. He imagined a pompous, florid-faced man, a crony of his father's respectable old Jersey family.

Much rested on his mother's admission that she had known about the gun for some time, had fetched it from the safe in his father's office before he came home that night, had it resting in her lap as she sat waiting for him in the dining room. He had hoped that more photographs of Gabrielle might come to light but the newspapers had all used the same shot. He thought perhaps he could see something of himself, and of Sophie, around the eyes.

Kit was worn out by the extremes of emotion that had stampeded over him: shock, elation, anguish, rage. Now he felt furious with Gabrielle Lejeune, for not giving him more solid information, more details of his father, for withholding herself from him, for insisting on anonymity, for *dying*.

What had she done, on leaving prison? She would have been only forty-two years old. Surely she would have left the island it seemed she had loathed so much. It was tempting to suppose she had come back to London. Ealing, maybe. Or Clapham. They might have passed each other on the street. He had an image of himself hurrying – he would have been late – towards an engagement, at the Criterion Brasserie perhaps, made up and in his pomp, oblivious to the beautiful, dark-haired woman stepping out of a theatre, with a companion possibly, or alone, hand raised to hail the taxi that would have sprung to the kerb for her.

Why had she married his father, the unpleasant-sounding, 'occasionally violent' George Lejeune, twenty years her elder? Clearly it had not been for money. *I believed I planned only to scare him...* He could not know if this were true, and there was no one to ask. He knew enough to know that there were always two sides to a marriage. And what of his father's family, *not much interested in you*? Was that true, or had she sought to punish them as well? Was it worth trying to find them, only to be rejected all over again?

At Hereford he got off the train and walked the one and a half miles to Flatley Close. Janet had lunch waiting on the table.

'Let's eat first, before I look at any letters,' she said. Lunch was cold ham and salad, followed by tinned peaches with cream.

'How's Robin?' she enquired as they ate. In an unexpected turn of events – or perhaps not, given how amiable Robin was, how skilled at putting people at their ease – she had taken Kit's boyfriend to her heart. They weren't allowed to share a bedroom when they stayed over, but you couldn't have everything. Kit told her about the exhibition Robin was having at a small gallery next summer.

'How exciting!' she said. 'I'll come along to it, if I may.' Kit was surprised. She hadn't been to London in years.

'Are you sure?' he said. 'I mean, the train and everything. Do you want me to come here and travel with you?'

'I'm not that gaga,' she said. 'I'm sure I can manage getting on one train to London.'

After lunch they sat together on the sofa.

'OK.' Kit was unable to put it off any longer. 'Are you ready?' He passed her the envelope.

She took a long time going through everything. Kit went out to the back garden. The lawn that had been there in his father's day was gone, replaced by a patio with shrubs and flowering plants in tubs. He bent to inhale the scent from a pastel display of sweet peas. Janet was going through the last page of Gabrielle's letter when he came back in. When she put the letter down she was crying.

'Oh, Kit. We truly didn't know.'

'I know you didn't.' He sat next to her. 'She did an excellent job of covering her tracks. Of disappearing.'

'You don't remember it – any of it – do you?' Janet was looking at him pleadingly. He was going to tell her about his dream: the cake, the jam on his face, but thought better of it. He shook his head.

'At least now we know why I was so much trouble,' he said, trying to make light of it, but his voice wobbled, and then he was crying with her.

'You weren't,' she said. 'When you first came to live with us... I can't remember if I've ever told you this? You didn't speak or cry for over a week. Then one afternoon you fell down the stairs, and it was like a dam had burst. You screamed and screamed for a whole day and a whole night. After that you were much happier. And naughty! You were into everything. Oh, but Kit, to think of what you saw... your mother...' She dabbed her eyes with her hankie.

'She wasn't my mother,' said Kit. 'You're my mother.'

'Oh...' said Janet, and went on crying.

'I'm sorry I was such a terrible son,' he said. 'For all I put you and Dad through.'

'You're back now, though,' said Janet, 'and that's all that matters.'

He borrowed his father's car, kept on in the garage and driven to the shops by Janet every couple of weeks to keep the engine ticking over. She guessed where he was going, but didn't say anything.

The gate was open. Out of habit he got out of the car to close it, but it hung off one hinge and would probably collapse altogether if he tried. The paddock to his right had always been grazed by cows – first those of Bill Carter, the farmer, then those belonging to the company that had taken over the farm on his retirement – but now it held a group of donkeys, dozing next to the water trough.

He parked next to the ancient Morris Traveller. The back door was unlocked, as it always was. The house stank of must and rot and worse, as if something had died in there. He tapped at the door to the staff apartment.

'Marianne?' When no answer came he turned the handle and went inside. There was the pungent smell of tomcat. In the lounge-cum-kitchen area the stove was thick with grease and dust, the sofa leaning on the floor, one of its legs broken, as if it had gone down on one knee. On her single bed that had been stripped bare, coiled springs jutting through stained mattress ticking, a cat was eating the corpse of a mouse. It looked at Kit disinterestedly and went back to its meal.

Kit closed the apartment door behind him and went up the back stairs. Several treads were missing entirely, others gave ominously under his feet. It wasn't at all likely she would be in her old bedroom, but he looked anyway. The wall coverings were still heavy with soot, the windows thick with grime. The curtain rail was coming away from the wall and hung perilously from one end. On the bed, her bed, her and Col's marital bed, was a jumble of stale-smelling blankets and black bin liners. One blanket lay half in and half out of a bin bag, as though she had tired of the task partway through, or realised its futility.

He went back downstairs and made his way carefully to the front of the house. Many floorboards were missing and where he had to he walked on the joists. The floor of Room Seven had collapsed into the vestibule. The floor of the room above had also collapsed, as had that part of the roof, so that the vestibule was full of rubble and timber and old plaster and Kit was able to look right up to the sky. The sun was disappearing behind a fluffy cumulus cloud. In the hall, also open to the sky, a sapling grew from the ruined floor.

Kit left the house and stood in the walled garden. Maybe she had left Erringby without telling him, though she had his Camberwell address. He was going to drive back to Hereford when he saw the open window on the upper level of the gazebo.

His feet clanged on the spiral staircase.

'Is that you, John?' Her voice came before he had a chance to knock.

'No, it's me.' He opened the door.

She sat on the threadbare sofa that had lived in the gazebo for as long as he could remember, longer. A dog, not Balzac, was at her feet, an open hardback book lying face down next to her. She looked up at him.

'And what wind blows you here, Kit?'

'Can I come in?'

'By all means.'

He took a seat on a swivel desk chair. Against the wall was a camp bed with a pillow and a sleeping bag on it. In one corner of the room stood a Calor gas heater. There was an ancient paraffin lamp on the desk.

'No kiss for your Auntie Marianne?' she said. He stood up, went over and kissed her cheek. She was gaunt and unwell-looking, her face and hair the same ash-grey colour. She wore an old jersey, though it was a warm day. It looked huge on her. Her hands were filthy, dirt now so ingrained it would never wash off. He sat back down on the chair.

'You're living in here now?' he asked.

'For the time being,' she said. 'Until I get back on my feet.' When he didn't reply she said, 'I sold the paddock. You saw the donkeys? They're very comical. He likes them, don't you, Wilkie?' – this was to the dog. 'I'm afraid I'm not very geared up for entertaining. Would you like some squash?' Kit said he would and she took down a glass from the bookshelf and filled it from a thermos.

'What do you do for...?'

'Facilities? Erringby's not quite ruined. There's some running water, and the kitchen still works. I suppose I might sleep there when the winter comes.'

He sipped at his glass of squash.

'That's not a solution, though, is it? Why don't you sell up? Move out?'

'Oh, I've thought about it,' she said. 'But then how would Col know where to find me?'

Christ, thought Kit, *she really still believes he's coming back. She's completely deluded.*

'Uh-huh,' he said.

'How is... how is...?'

'Robin.'

'Yes. Him.'

'He's very well. We're both well. Look, this isn't really a social visit, Marianne.'

'Ah,' she said.

Kit took the letter out of his pocket. He was going to pass it to her but something stopped him.

'You know, I always thought you and Col had the most fucked-up marriage in history,' he began. She arched an eyebrow. 'But it seems I was wrong.'

Instead of giving her Gabrielle's letter he summarised its contents for her. She said nothing until he had finished.

'Ah,' she said again.

'That's all you can say?' She looked at him. The smallest trace of a smile was playing at her lips. Kit tried tamping down his anger but his voice shook.

'I assumed, Marianne, that you gave me the money. I carried on assuming it.'

'Yes,' she said.

'You let me go on assuming it.'

'Yes, I did.'

'Was that kind of you, Marianne?'

The smile vanished and something like anger flashed across her face.

'Who am I, that I should be kind?'

'Why, though? Why did you do it?'

'Do you remember the night of Mother's funeral?' she asked. 'Do you remember how happy you were? When you said it was all down to me? I wanted that.'

But it had been illusory, that happiness, thought Kit, based on quasi-celebrity and money and drugs and the fantasy that Georgina really loved him.

'That is so fucked up, Marianne,' he said. 'If I had known it wasn't you I could have pursued things. Got the finance company to give me more details. Gone to Jersey. Maybe found her before it was too late.'

'It's perfectly apparent, from what you have told me,' said Marianne, 'that she did not wish to be found.'

'You've kept me beholden to you under false pretences,' he said. She shrugged.

Kit, wounded, wanted to hurt back. He had never told her about running into Col in London and was tempted to tell her now, tell her how much Col still loathed her, that there was no way on God's earth he was ever coming back. But he couldn't bring himself to.

She stood up suddenly.

'It's rather a lovely day,' she said. 'Shall we go for a walk?' Kit felt defeated.

'All right.'

She made her way slowly down the spiral staircase, leaning on him at one point.

'Arthritis,' she explained. 'It's gone into my hips. Mother was the same, you may remember.'

They walked only as far as the end of the walled garden where there was a wooden bench. They sat down. The garden was not in a bad state. It had been weeded and its plants were flourishing. On the wall behind them a clematis was in full bloom, its purple-and-white flowers huge and blowsy.

It was tempting, Kit thought, in this unruined corner of Erringby, to pretend that things were as they had been, the two of them sitting together in the sunshine, the dog, a hybrid of a rough collie and something else, settled at their feet; tempting to ignore the existence of the house, rotting away only yards from where they sat. But things were not as they were, and never would be. He tried again.

'Can you be honest with me about one thing?'

'This,' she said. 'Again.'

'Yes, again, Marianne. It never goes away.' She was silent. 'So?'

Against the adjacent wall a ceanothus was in full bloom, its cobalt flowers attracting innumerable bees, buzzing drowsily in the hot sun.

'I may have...' she began. The dog stretched and yawned.

Kit waited.

'I may have... What *would* be the form of words?' She looked at him and her eyes widened disingenuously.

'Fucked me?' he said. 'Wanked me off?'

'The latter,' she said, and closed her eyes.

'*May have*,' he said. 'You don't remember?'

'It was a long time ago.'

'Don't give me that.'

'Don't ask me to say more.'

'So you're not sorry, Marianne? For any of it?'

'For loving you?' she said. 'No.'

He thought of Janet, waiting for him in Flatley Close. Of Robin, waiting for him in their Camberwell flat. Gabrielle's letter was in his shirt pocket, next to his heart.

'Your kind of loving is warped,' he said. 'I don't need it any more.' He stood up. 'I'm going, Marianne.'

She was silent. He forced himself to look into her face. She looked at a loss, for the first time ever. A tear started in her eye. Kit knew he had to leave. Now.

'You'll be back!' she said, as he felt for his car keys. He heard a catch in her voice, even as his own tears blurred his vision. He turned to walk towards the door that led out to where Bob's car was parked. 'They always come back,' he thought he heard her say.

Epilogue

August 2001

Kit was walking along Kingsway towards Holborn station. He had just left his City Lit class, portrait painting, which he had recently taken up again. It had been inspired in part by the photographs of himself in Robin's exhibition.

'You have the perfect face,' Robin had told him when they met. 'It wouldn't be possible to take a bad photograph of you.' Kit had been much photographed by him in the course of their relationship but had not wanted those pictures in the public domain. Being photographed for magazines, papped for the celebrity columns of newspapers, blown up on the side of a bus, these were aspects of himself he wanted to leave behind.

But Robin had insisted, had wanted the pictures as the cornerstone of his exhibition, promising Kit that he would not be identified, and Kit had finally relented and *Man Sleeping #1, #2, #3* and *#4* had been a success, many of the limited-edition prints selling on the preview night alone. The thought of his image hanging in Little Venice duplexes and Brighton apartments was discomfiting, but Kit had been happy for Robin, and very happy about the sales income.

Janet, despite Kit's worrying, had made the train journey from Hereford without incident, even claiming to enjoy it. They had had dinner together near the small Kensington hotel Kit had booked her into.

'I'll come for a visit again,' she said. 'Now I know it's so easy.' She even asked about Robin's parents, who lived in Blackheath, and when she might meet them. Kit said he would organise lunch for them all.

She asked him how he was doing. It had been a tough few months. He'd resigned from his art therapy post after finding he couldn't cope with work. 'You need to sort out your own mental health,' Robin had said, and took on more assignments photographing weddings and corporate events, often out of town, to make ends meet, which Kit hated and which made him feel guilty. He also felt guilty about the expensive therapist Robin had found for him, a woman who specialised in early trauma. Slowly and painstakingly, she was helping him piece together his childhood and early adulthood and start coming to terms with the gaps left by the people who were missing: Sophie, Georgina, Bob, Emile and all of the others. Col. Gabrielle. He'd found it hard telling people about Gabrielle's letter. For over thirty years his parents had been Bob and Janet Antrobus, in spite of his adolescent denial of them. *They are your parents*, Nicola had told him in the attic bedroom at Erringby. *They brought you up.* And she had been right. And now he found himself constantly qualifying, when talking to his therapist or to the small circle of trusted friends. *My mother – my birth mother, I mean. Gabrielle.*

Gabrielle Lejeune. Robin had looked, since Kit hadn't been able to. Found a record of a death from emphysema in Charing Cross Hospital on 20 May 2000. So she had come back to London. He thought of this again and again. He told his therapist that he was both desperate to recall the events of his second birthday and terrified of doing so. His therapist said that this was fine. He had so immediately shut down the one friend who suggested hypnotherapy that she hadn't mentioned it again.

He hadn't told Janet about the therapist but he did tell her now that, after much dithering, he had tracked down relatives on his father's side and was thinking about a trip to the Channel Islands. George's brother was dead but there were two cousins in Jersey and a third on the island of Alderney.

'I'm scared, though,' he said to Janet. 'They didn't want me.'

'You don't know that,' Janet said. 'You only had your mother's word for it. And she had good reason to get you off the island. I see that now. And your cousins were young themselves when it happened. It was your uncle who rejected you, supposedly.'

'And I've found out something else as well.' Kit had uncovered the war record of a Henry Snowdon, missing in action over Hamburg in July 1943, who might be his grandfather. That had been easy. A grandfather who had predeceased the mother he couldn't remember felt remote, and his death had a heroic, historic aspect. It felt like research.

Kit had worried again about Janet at Robin's preview, anxious that she was out of her milieu.

'Don't keep fussing,' she had said. 'I'm fine talking to Claire.' Claire was a friend he had met at Goldsmiths when he was studying to be an art therapist. She'd been the one who had introduced him to Robin at a mutual friend's exhibition preview.

'Yes.' Claire made a go-away gesture with her fingers. 'Go mingle.'

Kit stood in front of a photograph of Wilton's Music Hall with his glass of wine and watched Robin talk to a magazine critic. At the front desk was a queue of what were hopefully sales enquiries. A man Kit did not know came up to him.

'I recognised you from your portraits.' He was around Kit's age, hair cropped close to conceal male pattern baldness. 'You're Kit Dashwood, aren't you?'

'I was Kit Dashwood,' said Kit. 'I've gone back to being Kit Antrobus.' On the other side of the gallery Janet was laughing at something Claire was telling her.

'We've met before,' the man said, 'though you won't remember.'

'I'm sorry,' Kit replied. 'I don't...'

'I'm David – I waited on you once. In Kettner's. It would have been in 1986. Maybe '87. You were there with your mother.'

'Oh… yes.' Kit remembered the evening, if not the waiter. It was the evening with Marianne. After they had held hands in the art gallery and she had claimed that the naked woman in a photograph was her. The evening she told him that Col was the love of her life, poleaxing him. The night he had gone on to kiss her at 62 Crouch Vale. 'I'm very sorry,' Kit said. 'I don't remember you.'

'That's all right,' David said. 'I just wanted to tell you how much I love your portraits. You have a real melancholy about you, but it's rather wonderful.'

'Thank you,' Kit said. Neither of them knew what to say next. 'Well…' said David.

'Thanks,' Kit said again, and a friend of Robin's came up to ask him about something, and David melted away into the crowd.

At the bus stop on Kingsway Kit's mobile phone beeped. There was talk of Robin's exhibition going on to New York; he had been seeing his agent today and had promised to let Kit know as soon as the meeting was over.

But the phone, when he pulled it from his pocket, displayed an unknown number. He brought up the text message.

Hi Kit. Got this phone fro my birthday. Thank u v much 4 yr present. I am playing the flute in a recital at st saviours next sat. Do u want 2 come mum says it is ok. Love Sophiexxxx

Kit, not used to texting, fumbled for a while before replying. *Hi Sophie, I would love to come. Love Kit xxxxx*. He pressed Send as the 171 bus lumbered to a halt at the stop. He showed his Travelcard to the driver and climbed the stairs to the top deck. Kit Dashwood wouldn't have been seen dead travelling by bus but Kit Antrobus liked it, liked the lack of urgency, the views of London – its buildings, its people – spooling out before him. As he sat down his phone rang. ROBIN, said the screen. Kit pressed the button to accept the call.

'Hi sweetie,' he said. The bus set off towards Aldwych.

Acknowledgements

Thank you so much to Laura Shanahan for seeing the potential in *Erringby* and to everyone else at Fairlight Books and beyond for their work in bringing the book to fruition.

I also owe Anna South from The Literary Consultancy an immense debt of gratitude for her input into the earliest drafts. Her encouragement, criticisms and insights were invaluable, as was her constant faith in the project. Thanks also to other early readers: Alison MacLeod and Juliette Mitchell from the Arvon Foundation, and the Manchester Women Writers' Group.

I'm grateful to Mark Whyman for generously sharing his experience of being adopted in the 1960s, to Alice Pickering for the notes on portrait painting, and to Ross Raisin for the sage advice. To Sarah Childs-Carlile, Sue Harvey and Felicity King for letting me borrow their houses to write in. To Louise Kenton for always being there.

And finally, my love and my heartfelt thanks to Paul Gill for sticking by me through it all.

About the Author

Gill Darling grew up in Hinckley, Leicestershire, and graduated from the University of York with a degree in Economics and Statistics. She currently lives in Manchester, where she works as a chartered accountant in the charity sector. In 2015 she was selected as a fiction mentee in the Jerwood-Arvon mentoring scheme and was published in their anthology, *Whisper the Wrong Name*. *Erringby* is her first published novel.